WITHDRAWN

Property of Congregation Beth Shalom
Bloomington Jewish Community, Inc.
3750 East Third Street
Bloomington, IN 47401

The Glitter and Other Stories

Stories and Poems
on Human Relationships

Curt Maury

Selected and edited by Hans Tischler

iUniverse, Inc.
New York Bloomington

The Glitter and Other Stories
Stories and Poems on Human Relationships

Copyright © 2010 by Curt Maury

All rights reserved. No part of this book may be used or reproduced by any means, graphic, electronic, or mechanical, including photocopying, recording, taping or by any information storage retrieval system without the written permission of the publisher except in the case of brief quotations embodied in critical articles and reviews.

iUniverse books may be ordered through booksellers or by contacting:

iUniverse
1663 Liberty Drive
Bloomington, IN 47403
www.iuniverse.com
1-800-Authors (1-800-288-4677)

Because of the dynamic nature of the Internet, any Web addresses or links contained in this book may have changed since publication and may no longer be valid. The views expressed in this work are solely those of the author and do not necessarily reflect the views of the publisher, and the publisher hereby disclaims any responsibility for them.

ISBN: 978-1-4502-1036-2 (pbk)
ISBN: 978-1-4502-1035-5 (ebk)
ISBN: 978-1-4502-1034-8 (hbk)

Printed in the United States of America

iUniverse rev. date: 6/16/10

Curt Maury was Hans Tischler's brother. He changed his name after he fled from Vienna to England in 1938.

Curt was a social worker in New York City, but his love was writing. His many travels to India produced two manuscripts about the folk art in India. One, <u>Folk Origins of Indian Art</u>, was published by Columbia University Press in 1969. The second is in manuscript form in the Smithsonian with 10,000 slides for study.

We found the manuscripts for the stories in this book in Curt's apartment following his death in 1989 when we emptied his apartment. Charmed by the stories, Hans set to editing them for publication. There are also several Jewish stories which Hans planned to edit, but, regrettably his life ended before he could complete this. Perhaps in the future these stories can be readied for publication. Curt also wrote a stunning Don Juan which he titled: <u>Roadside Inns: The Final Years of Don Juan</u>; all 700 pages are in blank verse. This was another project which Hans edited and had intended to carry through for publication. Sometime soon I will try to find a publisher for it. The manuscript is in the Lilly Library and available for reading.

I hope you will enjoy these stories.

Alice Tischler

Contents

The Great Hollow	1
The Blessed	15
A Name of a Canvas	55
Brief Visit	93
Focus	107
Nine Poems	131
1. Untitled	131
2. Untitled	132
3. The Ballad of the Old Shoe	133
4. Untitled	134
5. Dreams	134
6. Across a Telephone	135
7. Drum Song	135
8. Slum	136
9. Little Song	137
Encounter in the Sunset	139
Mission to a Foreign Place	285
Mister Flannery	309
The Glitter	365
Flowers	391

The Great Hollow

It did not take long for her searching glance to find him.

There he sat, in the farthest booth, caught in the half-dark of crumbling lights and further blunted by the tavern air thick with smoke and the vapors of liquor. Sat there, head tilted to one side, a stray ray of light fraying the hair above his temple; a sprinkle of gray kept count of the years gone by more gently, more kindly than time's ravage of his features. From beneath drooping lids, his eyes were lost, watching one index finger draw a drop that had trickled down from the chaser, draw it into a wet figure of planless fancy.

There was not the slightest acknowledgment of her presence, not even when she stepped to his side, close enough to touch him: He was absorbed in the meanderings of that finger, now tracing the spiral aloft from the butt expiring on the brass ash tray—stagnant ringlets of blue-green hovering over the half-emptied glass of bourbon.

Not the first one, either, she could tell: That familiar flush was spreading his cheeks with porous coarseness. But this time its sight did not evoke her angry, damning disgust—only relief that she had managed to find him, so she could tell him …

"Greg," she said, softly.

His finger stiffened, paused in the middle of another liquid curve. He looked up, falteringly, struggling with a recognition he was reluctant to welcome.

"Oh, it's you, Petra."

"Greg!" she said once more, irascible in spite of herself. His eyes could be so nice and clear and expressive, yet there they were looking at her, clouded by a hazy film, lower lids reddened, corners watery. Dull, insipid, vacant eyes. Stupid almost. Telling her she might have come for naught: In his condition, how could he be reached, how could he be expected to respond? Once again he had foreclosed any meaningful communication. As so often, oh how often! Still, maybe she was wrong detesting him: A few drinks, what of it? If it brought him some relief … Yet she could not help it; the tavern smell about him made her sick with contempt, filled with loathing, furious and irrational. And he surely knew it! Then why, why did he have to make life so miserable for her? Though it was not so happy for him either, and had not been for a long time. Perhaps that was why? Her acrimony dissipated. All that would be different now, after she told him … This time she must, this time she would reach him.

"Come to fetch your lush home?" Greg's lips distorted. But the mirthless chuckle never came off. "Hell, what happened to the time? Had no idea it was so late that it would send you hunting for me."

"It isn't late at all." Her voice was throbbing with impatience. "I just had to find you, be with you."

"Be with me," he repeated, and there was an edge to his voice. "You were not in when I came home."

"I'm sorry, Greg. Should've warned you I might be late. But I felt sure I'd be home in time to fix your dinner."

"Dinner …" His glance turned away from her, returning to his finger, which, like some mechanical toy, was stirring to complete the fluid design. "Oh that! Never mind, Petra. There's always the icebox. I had my fill."

"You ought to have had something warm."

"Something warm is right." The finger lifted itself from the drawing, pointed a damp tip at the bourbon. Then his shoulders sagged with a shrug. "Sorry, dear. I know you hate it. But it makes you feel warm inside, it does … And the house was so still. So awfully empty."

Empty. There had been no barb in the word. No complaint. No anger. Almost casually it had dropped, oblivious of any dramatizing innuendo. A quiet statement of fact, yet like an enormous black fist striking at her. The failures, the frustrations, the irritations of their married years were locked in its ferocious punch. The estrangement. The recriminations. The gaping silences. The thirst for bourbon, too; the hours of drunken escape and the blues that would follow, sullen and self-destructive.

Empty.

She tried to shake off the assault of this verbalization, extricate herself from its impact. Unexpressed, the awareness had always been lurking, a relentless shadow inside him, a soundless echo, a muted, perennial counterpoint to the humdrum tune of his daily life. Emptiness—that was what their home meant to him. But if it were resounding with a child's high-pitched, cheery voice …

"Greg," Petra said seriously. "You know what kept me out so late? I was to see Dr. Weston."

His head angled up to her swiftly, "You haven't been feeling well?"

"Oh, quite well, Greg. I just wanted to check up."

He shook his head. "You wouldn't see a doctor unless there was some real trouble. What is it? You never told me about it."

"There was no reason to tell. I should've had this examination a long time ago."

"But you were afraid …?"

"Afraid?"

"Of the doctor's verdict?" His eyes contracted with an effort to pierce the bourbon fog. For one moment they managed to focus on her, and he nodded. "I take it, though, the fear was unfounded."

"What makes you think …?"

"I don't know," he said, vaguely. "The way you look, I guess."

"What way?"

"Sort of …" his lips twisted, struggling for the appropriate term, "Happy."

"Happy!" she repeated, to listen to the echo of her voice fading slowly, a reluctant, mischievous ghost.

"Oh." A shrug, its limp indifference belied by a tinge of listless irony. "Well then, say, relieved. So the doctor found nothing wrong with you."

Nothing wrong? But there was. Perhaps this was why she appeared so … relieved. Dr. Weston had rendered his verdict. At last Greg would know; there would be an end to that mystic nonsense.

"Mind if I sit down?"

"Sure." A gesture cumbrous with surprise. "Thought you'd come to take me home."

"I'd like a drink, Greg."

"You would?" He blinked. "Of course. What shall it be? Bourbon, too? Gin?"

"Same difference."

She saw him waving his hand at the man behind the bar, holding up two fingers. Two? He had not even finished his drink, yet he was arranging to have another on tap. More of what would make him feel warm inside. Warm enough so the house would seem less empty when he returned, staggering through a happy fog, chuckling with a merry monologue or squalling with bloated self-importance.

For God's sake, Petra thought, and that old loathing gushed up in her, a geyser of nauseating slime, choking her. *For God's sake, Greg! When will you stop running away? From me, from yourself, from reality, from life itself? Running to hide in your private world of fuzzy fancies and dizzy dreams, to sustain your illusions, to lie to yourself, to pretend!*

"Two bourbons, coming up." The counterman was setting the glasses down with a faint whir. "See you got company for a change. Now, ain't that nice?"

"Nice, sure." Greg's hand described a vague figure in the air. "This is my wife, Jake," he added thickly, and his lips parted in a grin. As though it all were a joke.

"Oh yeah?" A wave of tepid breath brushed past Petra's ear. "Got yourself a pretty missus. Here for the first time, eh? Why you hide her all these years?"

"It's got to be a special occasion, if she'll touch the stuff," Greg said.

"Celebrating or something?"

She felt Greg's glance piercing the haze again, trying to focus on her. His voice came to her, suddenly changed, strangely sober.

"Could be," he said. "Could be."

"Why didn't ya tell me right off?" The fat man cackled. "Hell, you don't want me around jinxing your celebration." Then he waddled across the floor.

"That's it, celebration," Greg muttered throatily, shaking his head slowly, left, right, left, right.

Petra stared past him. His eyes had blunted again, had retreated behind those bourbon mists—but his voice was eerily precise with cold sobriety, with cynical clarity, with an odd tinge of vengefulness. As though he wanted to hurt her.

Nonsense. Greg never wanted to hurt her. Never. Yet there was that word, like a demon's mockery. It sent a chill up her spine, slowly spreading like an icy centipede feeling its way.

Celebration.

Indeed. Could there be a more glorious occasion for one? The verdict was in, handed down: Finality. Vindication of your ultimate fear. Proof positive that you were not like all the rest. Three cheers, old girl! Chin up, celebrate your congenital inferiority! Drink to the irreversible emptiness of your own days from here on in!

Emptiness.

That centipede stopped at the nape of her neck. Sat there, a glacial canker. Emptiness. Unspoken, that had been Greg's definition all along. The monotonous chorus to the muted stanzas of his ambitions and hopes, of his marriage and his home life. The image that made him sit there, drinking himself full of dreams and fancies and a sensation of aliveness, escaping from an existence without significance. From a reality that was but one Great Hollow in which he moved about like an automaton, breathing, talking, working, without aim or reason.

One Great Hollow: that was what became of life without children.

Greg, she thought, forlornly, *oh, Greg!* Seeking him, her gaze was dimmed by layers of liquid cobwebs. He was just a blur.

A blur of three dimensions. With a glass in his hand, a drink mixed of emptiness, alienation, loneliness. Yet, in a way he was luckier: to her, bourbon offered no relief, not even for a few instants of delusion. Nothing did, not her job, not her books, not her chairwomanship at the Club. Those were just pegs at the edge of the Great Hollow, too fragile to carry the weight when, desperately, she would try to fasten her emotions to them. Of course, there was Greg, but for all his faithfulness, all his concern, all the sincerity of his devotion, he could not be the anchor to sustain her expectations, her needs, her yearnings. Vaguely she had sensed this from the very start of their relationship, had come to realize it ever more clearly throughout the years of their married life. Something more was required to fill the emptiness. But the doctor had been so very definite. There was no longer room for anxious uncertainty, for hopeful self-deception. The verdict was in.

That blur was stirring, a body in shapeless motion. Anger once more sprang up in her, a sizzling fountain. Emptiness. Here he was, boozing himself away from a damnation which was not his, truly, but hers, knowing how those drunken sprees must make her loathe him, must deepen the wall of their perennial quarrels. Yet for all his hundred promises, back he would come to his tavern to drench himself with bourbon. To warm himself with the echoes of children's voices coming to him through hazes of alcoholic dreams, echoes the walls of their home would not throw back at him, echoes lost in the Great Hollow.

Petra's glance softened. That blur gained shape, became human, became Greg again: A man, weak perhaps, too easy a prey to his despondent moods, but still a man who tried his best to carry his load.

A stepchild of fate, she thought—a stepchild of fate, like herself. The boiling of resentment ebbed into a tepid wave of compassion.

Emptiness, she thought. Emptiness was being deprived of those echoes. More than once she had watched his eyes brightening at the sight of children in the park, the furtive glow of fondness when one of the tots would come near him; she had seen the spastic gesture of a hand shy with inhibition, struggling to restrain a caress he had no right to extend; noted the happy smile when a giggly laughter thanked him for a toy fixed, for a ball tossed back; registered the weary tenderness of his greeting when little Genevieve from across the street would come running to him, calling him uncle. Deprivation—yet, all along, there had been hope for him, still.

"What about the doctor?"

His question tore through the stillness like the shrill blast of a trumpet.

"What's the matter?" Greg peered at her. "Cold?"

"Cold?"

"You were shivering. Why don't you have your drink? It might do you some good."

She shook her head, perplexed. Something about her response must have betrayed her when his question made her remember the verdict. She had always been a poor actress. But she did not mind, not this time. She wanted him to know. Had she not come after him to tell him Dr. Weston's diagnosis would put a stop to his old imaginings, at last, to his irrational, destructive conclusion. It would restore peace to his mind, proving that the cause of their childlessness was all physical. An unfortunate fact, even a tragic one—but still, one of physical, not emotional, constellation.

She had been trying to tell him so all along. She had never been able to understand how someone like Greg could entertain any different explanation. A down-to-earth businessman, a rationalist with a brain like an adding machine, educated to accept only the precisely calculable and scientifically provable—yet obsessed with the idea that they had remained childless because she did not want to conceive by him. Impervious to her protestations, he had kept clinging to his weird remnant of magic superstition, of mystical absurdity, believing in it with a conviction so intense that for a time he nearly had her believing in it, too.

That was during those first few years with him, when, indeed, she herself had been less than certain that she would want Greg's child. When, with her emotions still not quite weaned from the absorbing memory of an earlier, traumatic entanglement, her marriage had been an act of resignation, of mere dutiful reconcilement to the company of a good man who had waited for her with self-denying patience. Then Greg's quiet devotion had gone to work on her and she had found herself growing fond of him, however vaguely, however tentatively—still, fond enough to realize that she, too, wanted a child.

But no matter that she kept telling him: As her body refused to yield the proof, his bizarre contention only gained momentum. It was useless for her to argue that procreation was a matter of biology, at times beyond human control, useless even to wrest concurrence from him in an occasional moment of calm and reason, for, inevitably, the rational superstructure would again crumble before the force of his abstruse certainty. Then, like a man possessed, he would turn every word against her, distort it until it would supply new confirmation for his belief, material for another morbid depression drowned in bourbon. For some time now, she had given up even trying. No more discussions. No more explanations. Just that lingering myth. The Great Hollow. The liquor.

"Yes," Petra said, reaching. "Let's have a drink together." Perhaps, she thought, perhaps this was an occasion for a celebration, after all. Now, with the verdict in, childlessness would stand revealed as a spiteful whim of nature only, would cease to be an imaginary symbol of rejection. Now Greg would no longer have to run away. Her hand clutched the glass. *Here goes my toast,* she thought, *here goes ...*

Just one sip, but the unaccustomed acridity of the drink drove tears to her eyes. Through the moist film she saw Greg raising his head, looking at her from lusterless, vapid eyes. "Well, well," she heard him murmur, "seems you are all set for your celebration."

Her celebration. The word burned her more acidly than the bourbon—its oblique indictment, its odd, warped paradox. Her celebration. Yet, maybe, sort of ... when she would tell him about the verdict.

"Sure." The ghost of a gray smile crooked his lips. "Sure, you would not forget an anniversary."

She set her glass down. For an instant all memory of Dr. Weston was lost in a frantic search for an anniversary she might have missed: His birthday? But that was in September. And two months ago, in December, they had observed their wedding anniversary. Perhaps the date on which he had opened his business? He had always cared to remember it as a token of his success. But that would not come until June, almost four months off. The anniversary of their engagement—yes, today was the eighteenth, but ...

"Greg," she said, "but that was the eighteenth of April when we got engaged. And this is February."

"February eighteenth." He nodded. "Right, didn't you tell me that was when you first met Cliff?"

"Cliff!"

Her gasp was feeble, desolate, a pale shivering breath of a name that was sheer terror, like the sudden sight of a revenant climbing from his grave to stalk her. The Great Hollow was yawning inside her now, a dark hell of nothingness, resounding with drab echoes: Cliff, Cliff, Cliff, a thousand times magnified, overpowering, maddening.

"February eighteenth," Greg was saying again. "That's when it all started."

His voice came from afar. Like a low soundtrack reeling off along a sequence of distant visions, a scurrying caravan of ghosts: February eighteenth, so many years ago. Edna Potter's party. The man at the piano, his dark handsomeness overly plastic in the whitish ray from the music lamp. Fervent eyes seeking her, magnetically, inescapably. Tender arms clasped about her in a dance. A giddy sensation, as though her feet were no longer touching the ground, as though she were soaring. The slow way home through soft new snow. The kiss, the caress, the embrace—the first of so many to follow, each a great festival. The days, weeks, months of dreamlike abandonment, of fantasies, hopes, desires ...

"Cliff," Greg said absently, and poured down his drink in one big gulp. "His house wouldn't be empty."

Like a thin blade, carefully honed, his voice cut through the spectral parade of her remembrances. Abruptly that caravan of ghosts scattered to the winds, was lost in the nowhere. The echo of that name died away. The Great Hollow was filled now with the grief of the man facing her across the table. And with her own.

"Greg," said Petra. Her hand crept across the table, faltering, searching for his, finding it, covering it with the now icy roundness of her palm, feeling how it grew limp under her touch. "Listen, Greg. Cliff's house, too, would be empty. Any man's ... Don't you see? I just can't have any children, Dr. Weston told me today. That's why I went to see him. We had to find out, Greg, didn't we?"

She waited for his reply. But there was none.

"I should've found out long ago, but … Anyway, now I have. All the tests were completed. He was quite positive. Said there were lots of women like myself. Some biological deficiency; I just couldn't conceive. I guess, deep down, I've known the truth all along and just been afraid of it. Now, here it is, Greg. Here it is. That's why I came here. Just couldn't wait to tell you."

Still he said nothing. Merely nodded forlornly. His hand slipped from beneath her palm, sought his glass. Found it empty. Reached for her still-nearly-full one.

Petra felt herself growing rigid. Her voice was throaty as her words poured on, stumbling over each other in oddly frightened haste.

"Don't you see, Greg? Things can be different now. If we adopted a child. We wouldn't, while we thought there was still a chance, but now, with the verdict in …"

"Oh yes," he said. "Yes." He raised the glass to his lips, sipped the drink slowly, thoughtfully, down to the last drop.

"Our house would be a real home, Greg! No longer silent and empty."

"Oh yes," he muttered again. "Yes." And set the glass down, careful lest it clink against the table.

"A real home, with an echo, with life in it. You will be happy, Greg, won't you?" And once more, almost whispering, "Won't you?"

He did not stir. Only his hand retreated from that glass, felt for hers. Began to caress it, stroking it slowly, lightly, softly. Stroking it for endless, silent moments. "Petra," he said at last, in a deep, tired voice that was strangely sober. "But you still don't love me, darling."

Deep in the pit of her stomach something hurt cruelly. "Perhaps I do, Greg ..." she murmured wretchedly, listening in vain for an echo which would make the faintness of her words alive and real.

He just shook his head. Still his fingers kept fondling her hand, running up and down the length of her forearm, quietly, tenderly, up and down ...

And then they sat there, staring into the same blind distance. Sat there, truly together for the first time in all those long years. Together, two inanimate points in the center of the Great Hollow that spread around them, expanding and expanding until it enveloped everything but the loneliness that they had found to share.

The Blessed

Just as he was reaching for his cup of coffee, it happened. The blast of the explosion quite nearly threw him off his seat. It sent the cup smashing against the wall, its splintering clay joining that of plates swept from other tables to crash to pieces on the floor.

And then came the screams, the yells of terror and pain, the shouts of people rushing past the coffee shop and on up the street; the shrills of police whistles; the voice of the man behind the counter, hoarse, trembling with fury, "Those bastards! Those damned bastards again … another of their bombs!"

He needed no elaboration. He had long become too familiar with the scenario. Twice before, he had been caught in the vicinity of an identical calamity, once in Tiberias, and then again in Tel Aviv. Still shaky, he was on his hurried way outside.

Ordinarily, he might not have gone to join the crowd, might have preferred to stay put and calm the other two guests in the shop right then—an elderly couple, crouching chalk-faced, frozen in their shock. There was no point in idle attendance of suffering: He was no doctor, knew nothing even of first aid; he would be of no help. He would detect himself being a useless spectator at what he knew would be a spectacle of agony, being a passive witness to death and mutilation. One such experience was quite enough, up in Tiberias, when he was too close to escape the sight. He surely would not bargain for a reprise. But he must see about his companion, make certain that his sudden, anxious premonition was unfounded. Somehow, irrationally, he felt responsible for the young fellow.

Stepping into the June afternoon's glutting heat, his glance immediately caught the totally shattered front of Avidor's small department store on the opposite side of the street, some fifty yards away. The charge of the explosive must have been substantial. He accelerated his pace as much as his heart would permit, but, at sixty-four, its cooperation was severely limited. By the time he reached the crowd, two police vehicles had already pulled up; several soldiers, machine guns at the ready, were standing guard and, from the distance, high-pitched sirens were announcing the approach of ambulances. Converging from the nearby offices, physicians were pushing their way through the steadily mounting throngs toward the center of the tragedy. Through a momentary opening in the wall of horrified humanity, he beheld what he had feared: the blood-covered figure in the tattered uniform sprawled on the pavement amid the debris, one of the five unstirring shapes surrounded by a score of wailing, whimpering, moaning wounded, mostly women and children.

Shouldering his way past some reluctantly yielding onlookers, his heart pounding madly with his realization that, as so often, his premonition had not been unfounded, he bent over the young man's still form, scanned the ashen face, mechanically touched the limp wrist, felt for the pulse. There still was life—weak, irregular, but life.

"You a doctor?" A police lieutenant had stepped to his side.

"No," he replied, his fingers still wrapped around that fluttering pulse. "A friend."

"You know who he is, then?"

The Glitter and Other Stories

"Yes. Corporal Luigi Roselli, U.S. Marines, from the embassy in Tel Aviv."

"Oh?" The officer made a quick note in his report book. A motion of his hand summoned one of the volunteer physicians. "And your name?"

"David Glick, Tel Aviv." He produced his identification.

"A friend of his, you say?"

"I emigrated from the States," David Glick said. It seemed to him a sufficient explanation. And to the doctor who was kneeling beside the fallen man, examining him quickly, cursorily, "What about him?"

The physician exchanged a swift glance with the intern from one of the ambulances, who had just joined him. "Not good," he answered. "Not good at all. There's no time to be lost."

"We will do the best we can," the intern added, while his crew was bedding the marine on a stretcher. "If he can be saved, he will be." It did not sound too reassuring.

"May I come along?" David Glick asked.

The urgency of the question was not lost on the intern. "Why not? Yes, of course."

Checking back, the police lieutenant consulted his notebook. "Corporal Luigi Roselli, correct?" And, satisfied with the silent, confirming nod, he added, "We will notify the embassy immediately," just as the ambulance was starting to pull away.

Another patient was sharing the ride to the hospital, a middle-aged Israeli woman with a broken spine and a half-severed arm. Intermittently, she was softly whimpering what sounded like a delirious prayer. A tourniquet had stopped her bleeding, and now the intern was busying himself trying to stem, as best he could, the flow from the unconscious American's torn abdomen.

David Glick crouched between the two stretchers and stared at the youthful, pallid face. And, he thought, *how much like Dino's, this face ... Dino's ... Oh God, let him live, let him live!*

It was this almost uncanny resemblance to Dino, the Dino of forty years ago, which had promoted his friendship with Luigi Roselli. Sitting in one of the outdoor cafés, he had caught sight of the American marine sauntering past and had been immediately struck, indeed jolted, by the young fellow's looks: the same round face with the high cheekbones, the aquiline nose, the deep-set, clear eyes, the same stocky muscularity, the same quickness of movement, the same firmness of gait. Even the slight tilt of the cap seemed like a copy of the way Dino had worn his, that last time on furlough in New York. Except that this soldier had none of Dino's cheerfulness: his saunter appeared to be aimless, somehow hesitant, even distraught; there was an air of forlornness about his bearing.

Still staring down at the wounded man, David Glick's mind was acute with the memory of that moment three months ago when a casual glance at the passing figure had propelled him from his seat, and he had accosted the marine.

No, Luigi Roselli had told him, there was nowhere in particular he was going, nowhere at all, he was just walking about, taking in sights of the city on his time off from duty. But anyway, it was a lucky treat to meet a fellow countryman, an ex-New Yorker; he himself came from Jersey City, had been to New York a few times and liked it there. He had eagerly accepted the invitation to coffee and cake; it would be good to talk to someone who spoke his language.

Luigi Roselli had not been referring to the English language but the language of internal understanding. Intuitively, he had perceived the older man's willing partnership in some homey conversation, his almost grandfatherly readiness to be entrusted with personal confidences which for too long had remained unshared. The fellows in his present outfit were good soldiers and decent enough comrades, but most of them were a couple of years younger than he; they were bachelors, whose interests had little in common with what was the center of his concerns—his wife, Pietra, and his infant daughter, Carlotta, now two years old. Now, at last, he could talk about them, for there was someone listening: listening not only with patient indulgence but with warm, personal involvement.

After that random encounter, they had been meeting regularly, nearly every time the marine was off duty. They would sit over coffee in one of the small cafés along Dizengoff or take long strolls along the beach toward, and sometimes into, the old Arab quarters of Jaffa; sometimes they kept company in increasingly concordant silences, but were more often engrossed in vivid conversations about anything and everything—though mostly about Luigi Roselli's preoccupying subject, his utter devotion to his Pietra and his little Carlotta. These conversations never failed in their undertone of passionate longing, in their quality of feelings, which would even further reinforce the recall of Dino and thus forge their bond of friendship even more firmly—a bond between two Americans who took the diversity of their backgrounds for granted and equally regarded it as an irrelevant detail. In fact, Luigi Roselli seemed to become conscious of it only when one of his fellow marines remarked about how strange it was for such a devout Catholic to form so strong a connection with a Jew. On that occasion he had looked at his born-again Christian buddy with an air of pensive surprise. "A Jew is he?" he had replied, untouched by the other's thinly veiled mockery. "Only goes to show that decent people come in any shape; when you find one of those, you'd better hold on to him."

When casually and with an accent of disgust, he mentioned this exchange, David Glick had stared at him for a long time. "That's precisely, word for word, what Dino said," he remarked at last, slowly, wonderingly.

"Dino?"

The older man's eyes clouded as he nodded. And then he told Luigi Roselli about Dino and Angela and the long-past days in far-off Brooklyn.

*

It was not only the powerful muscularity of his stocky frame, not just his at once admired and feared physical superiority, but a manifest gift of self-assured leadership that had placed Dino di Santo in acknowledged and uncontested command of a gang of Irish and Italian neighborhood youths who contributed to the liveliness of the Brighton Beach sector by their sometimes funny, sometimes malicious, though strictly noncriminal pranks. It seemed natural that one of their favorite activities would be the harassment of the Jewish boys, who, on their way home from Hebrew school, had to traverse what the gang claimed as its turf. It was Dino's distaste of taking advantage of his companions' always numerical as well as physical superiority and his personal influence that prevented those assaults from assuming more serious dimensions than an occasional bit of cuffing around or a couple of stones thrown, but deliberately missing their mark. But, true to the traditions of his background, he was in no way averse to leading his mates in the no less wounding verbal assaults, the foul epithets, the viciously degrading expletives and demeaning insinuations, which for generations on end had so nobly enriched the Catholic vocabulary.

Two years younger than Dino and but half his size, David Glick had never run from those attacks. Silently he would endure the verbal abuses and fight back as best he could, hopelessly overmatched, when the pushing and shoving started. He would not afford to those *goyim* the satisfaction of showing his fear. But this very refusal to cringe and thus acknowledge the obvious and intrinsic inferiority of the Jew only further antagonized the young leader and challenged him to make this recalcitrant Jew his prime target. In time, there was hardly an encounter that would not end in a direct personal confrontation, which added new stimulation to the attacks and escalated their vituperative violence.

When therefore, rounding a corner on another trip home from Hebrew school, he and two fellow students discovered their way blocked by what seemed the full gang, assembled less than a hundred feet up the street, they expected a particularly poignant installment of the usual unpleasantness—the more so when they saw the leader step out in front of the bully band and, his hands stuffed in his trouser pockets, slowly move toward them, the scowling tightness of his features heralding his apparent belligerence.

Just a few feet short of the three Jewish boys Dino di Santo stopped. His frown seemed to intensify as he stared at his favorite whipping boy for a long, silent moment.

"Your name is David?" he asked at last.

"Yes." The reply came wondering at this uncommon and uncalled-for formality as a prelude to the inevitable hostilities. "Yes. David Glick."

"Then that's right." A thoughtful nod. "David Glick. They tell me you are the one."

"The one …?"

"On the beach," Dino said quietly, "the day before yesterday. You pulled my sister out of the water."

"Oh that. Yes. That was your sister?"

"You didn't know, did you? My little sister, Angie. She's dear to me, very dear." His words came falteringly as his deep-set eyes sat on the smaller boy, studying him intently. "You ain't too strong, are you? A bit frail, they tell me; not much of a swimmer, either."

A shrug answered him. "She was out there, thrashing about, calling for help. I was afraid she might be drowning …"

"Yes," Dino said, slowly, "bringing her in, you nearly drowned yourself."

"Just swallowed a bit of water. Nothing much. They sent me home half an hour later. How's your sister?"

"Angie, she's all right. Back home. Because of you." There was a tremor in the big boy's voice. "Otherwise she wouldn't be back home. They told me, she would've drowned for sure. Except for you … You jumped in after her, not thinking of yourself."

"So?" The reply was uncomfortable with embarrassment. "She needed help, didn't she? At such a moment one doesn't think, does one?"

The frown had abandoned Dino's brow. A strange light had come into those deep-set eyes, and an unexpected softness, an oddly measured lilt to his voice. "Yes," that voice was speaking now. "But one ought to think, each of us, all the time. One ought to think, David Glick. I'm ashamed. Very much ashamed." Then, hesitatingly, almost pleadingly, he took his hand out of his trouser pocket, extended it. "Would you …?" And then he clasped the smaller hand for a long moment, firmly, strongly, warmly. "I haven't been thinking, David. That's why … I haven't been thinking right. But …" An oddly timid smile completed the phrase.

One of the gang up the street—tall, gangling Larry McPhee—came walking over. "I, too," he said quietly, offering his hand. "I, too, am ashamed, Jew boy."

Dino whirled, his eyes fierce, his fists clenched.

"I didn't mean it that way, Dino," Larry said. "I meant it with respect." And, turning, he walked away, back to the group.

"With respect," Dino di Santo repeated. "Yes, that's how." He pointed up the street. "None of them will ever touch you or your friends again, or insult you, either. They'd better not. But they wouldn't anyway. They've learned to think a little, too." For some moments he kept standing there, rather forlornly, searching for words. "There's something I'd like to ask. Though, I wouldn't be surprised, if you said no. My little sister wants so much to thank you. And my folks, too. If you'd come over to my house …?"

"Now?"

"Now. Any time. It would be very important. To me. To Angie. To all of us. Would you?"

The reply was immediate. "Of course I would, if you will have me." Then, after an instant's pause. "But not now. My mother would be worried if I weren't home on time. I'll be late, as it is. But any other time …"

"Tomorrow?"

"Tomorrow would be fine."

"Tomorrow, then." Dino fumbled through his pocket, extracted from it a piece of paper. "Here, the address. Already wrote it down for you, hoping …" But there was an accent of uneasiness about his awkward gesture, as he held out the crumpled note paper. "I'd like to ask you for dinner. But Mama would not know how to cook Jewish."

"Kosher, you mean?"

"Yes, that's it. Kosher."

A quiet little smile answered him. "We ain't that religious. My mother's a bit old-fashioned, maybe. The way she was brought up. But my father always says that surely God's got a lot more important matters to take care of than to worry about what people will eat."

Dino's eyes brightened. "I guess I'd like your dad, too," he said, thoughtfully. "Yeah, I think I would. Tomorrow for dinner, then? Meatballs and pasta."

"Meatballs and pasta," David Glick confirmed gravely. And then they both laughed.

"*Shalom*," Dino said. "They tell me it means 'peace.' *Shalom*."

"*Arrivederci*," he countered, watching the other's stocky figure move back toward the waiting gang.

Then, halfway up the street, Dino turned once more to call back, "Till tomorrow, David!"

'Tomorrow!' Dino's voice seemed somehow, enigmatically, to ring with a promise. 'Tomorrow.' The word proved to be the herald of a new beginning.

'Tomorrow.'

*

But would there be a tomorrow for Luigi Roselli? David Glick wondered, staring down, shuddering, at the still unmoving, unconscious figure, at the ashen face, that even in its mask-like rigor seemed so much a copy of Dino's. *Would there be a tomorrow for this marine, who had become his friend?*

"Not good at all," the doctor had diagnosed. "If he can be saved …"

If … face, that even in its mask-like rigor seemed so much a copy of Dino's. Would there be a tomorrow?

That 'if' had carried an insinuation, an anticipated verdict. Still, it need not be true, that verdict; it must not be true! If a skeptic's prayers were heard, it would not be true. If there was a God, He could not be so cruel; He could not take this young life. And yet … had He not taken Dino's? But not his one, again! Not this one, now … no, not now!

This had been Luigi Roselli's final full day of liberty before his tour of duty in Israel would terminate and he would return to America—to his Pietra, his little Carlotta. It was to get presents for them and once more to see the Holy City, whose religious past carried so much significance for him and whose aura of antiquity so intrigued him, that he had insisted on this jaunt to Jerusalem. Once more, he wanted to wander through the narrow passages of the bazaar, visit the citadel of David, watch the faithful praying at the Wailing Wall, admire the elaborate beauty of the Omar and Al Aksa Mosques, and pay his devotions in the churches that remembered the presence and passion of his Savior.

He might have bought vials of 'holy water from the Jordan' and 'blessed soil from Bethlehem,' together with more useful items—available in Tel Aviv just as well, and more cheaply, too. But, somehow, he felt their purchase in Jerusalem would invest them with a more profound meaning. He might have found a more knowledgeable guide through the ancient quarters but none as patient and understanding, as intimately responsive, as the retired Jew from Brooklyn who only too willingly had, from gate to gate, touched all the points to which Luigi Roselli wished to bid his farewell. He had, on the marine's insistence, taken their route past the monument of the Holocaust for a few moments of reverence paid to his friend's victimized kindred before emerging into the new city. Then, at last, in the café along the avenue they had taken their long overdue rest and indulged in some modest refreshments before Luigi Roselli had taken off again to find some extra little gift for his adored infant girl at Avidor's, up the street. Aware that the older man no longer enjoyed, indeed had never possessed, equal stamina and by then must be rather tired, he urged him to stay put and, over another cup of coffee, wait for his return.

His return …

Unable to stir from his crouch, David Glick had watched the medics as they carefully removed the stretcher from the ambulance; watched vacant-eyed, still holding on, idly, to the bag containing Luigi Roselli's earlier purchases.

Noting his shocked distress, the intern gently touched his shoulder. "Close friend of yours, is he?" His voice was soft and sad. "Be sure we'll do for him all we can. He's being taken directly to the operating table. From the looks of it, though, it's going to be quite a while. Maybe many hours."

"I will wait," David Glick said. "I want to be there when he comes out of surgery."

"Of course." The intern's affirmation was compassionate. And responding to the other's mute question, he added, "No telling now. We'll know tomorrow."

Tomorrow, David Glick had repeated to himself, alighting from the vehicle, every step a heavy, crushing burden. It had not sounded like Dino's 'tomorrow,' some forty-eight years ago, not like the promise of a new beginning, of a future.

Yet one must hope … perhaps, yes, perhaps …

The Glitter and Other Stories

David Glick paused. His heart was acting up again. The stretcher with the marine's still shape had disappeared into the hospital.

"Tomorrow," he repeated once more in a whisper. There must be a tomorrow for Luigi Roselli. A future. A new beginning. As it had been for him, nearly half a century ago. In him, there was the echo of Dino di Santo's voice. "Tomorrow," it said, "tomorrow …"

*

"Tomorrow" had proved to be just the first of countless meatballs and pastas with the di Santos; and the next Thursday, only the initial one of equally countless matzo-ball soups and gefilte fish dinners at the Glicks' table. Yet it was not just the ready warmth and unqualified acceptance that each family extended to the other's offspring, nor even the two boys' deepening friendship and, soon, inseparable camaraderie, which mutually provided both youngsters with virtual second homes. Progressively, the initially shy and subtly tentative, then ever more emotionally certain and openly assertive relationship between Dino's little sister and himself became the center of the social rapprochement. Two years younger than he, Angela made no secret of her fascination and fondness; and had she endeavored to keep her sentiments concealed, she would have utterly failed. Her tender passion was written all over her countenance, her smile, her glances, the moment she caught sight of him. But then, his own expression and manner seemed no more capable of denying his adoring devotion to the gentle, graceful girl with the raven hair and glowing ebony eyes, the delicately sensitive features and timidly sensuous lips.

Even in its early stages, this escalating mutuality did not escape the two families' notice. But given Dino's role as the silently encouraging, always protective and assuaging intermediary, it was meeting with tolerant acquiescence, even benign connivance, aided by the older generation's misjudgment of the adolescents' involvement as mere puppy love, which they surely would outgrow. Thus, while from the very outset Dino had taken that involvement's eventual denouement for granted, it was not until after a considerable time that, for all the ever-more conspicuous indications, the two parental couples awakened to a full realization of the implicit course of events; which, as they reluctantly had to admit, by then had become an inevitability, leaving them with no choice but to get used to the idea of its certain impending consummation. In consequence, when Dino's best friend and his beloved little sister jointly announced that they would be married, the confrontation with the actuality of an interfaith union evoked but minor commotion and no more than token objection.

The fathers in particular were rather swiftly reconciled to what to them seemed an obvious conclusion. Liberal and free-thinking, Samuel Glick would merely remind his son that, statistically, the prognosis for such marriages was not too encouraging, but he would quickly accept the counterargument that statistics were inapplicable to any given individual case. On his part, Giovanni di Santo, staunchly socialist and anti-clerical but fiercely proud of his national heritage, would offer only the grumbled comment that it surely was awkward for a daughter of his to have a husband who could not speak a word of Italian. But when Dino countered that, after all, Angela did not speak a word of Yiddish, he just responded with a little sly wink, "Fair enough. Bene. I guess they will just have to speak English with each other then." The truth was that his fondness as well as respect for the quiet and serious young Jew had steadily grown, and he secretly admitted that Angela could hardly find a better, more dedicated and caring husband, even among her fellow Italians.

On the part of the mothers, though, resistance was more pronounced. Of more conservative background than her husband, Erna Glick found it beyond herself to accept her son's choice. Neither often expressed personal liking nor frequently admitted appreciation of the qualities that would make for a fine, loving wife could overcome her parochial mind's ingrained prejudice. To her, Angela, the Italian, the Catholic, would always remain a stranger, an intruding outsider, whom she could never welcome into her strictly and unalterably confined world, never regard as an integral part of her own family. No argument could prevail. Certainly she did wish for her son's eventual marital happiness, but quite as certainly, from the inexhaustible pool of eligible Jewish girls he could find one to supply it. She would nag and whine, implore, and finally threaten: Her son's explicitly and adamantly announced prospective defiance of his mother's wishes would call forth irremediable injury and irreparable estrangement. Yet, only too well aware of her David's internal strength and determination, she entertained no doubt that her 'never' was going to prove a losing proposition. In the end, she would have to acquiesce or lose her son.

It was Angela, the Italian stranger and interloper, who rescued her from the dilemma by the sudden, equally unexpected and unequivocal, declaration that, certainly, she intended to convert to Judaism—a decision she announced without her future mate's prior knowledge nor even any consultation about the matter, astounding him as thoroughly as everyone else except Dino, who was too close to his little sister to fail divining her sentiments. But, caught unaware, unlike his friend, David felt quite uneasy about Angela's decision. He had never touched on this subject, much less exerted any influence whatever. He had not considered their diverse creedal backgrounds a problem—not for people who loved each other the way they did. There would be a union, not of Christian and Jew but of two human beings whose devotion to each other would encompass the totality of their common faith and render the diversity of their accidental affiliations extraneous and irrelevant. But Angela refuted his contentions: What about their children? By Jewish law, did they not follow their mother's religion?

Even if, as he averred, he did not care about this one way or another, she most definitely did. A Jew had saved her life; she would bear Jewish life for him.

Above all, it was this decision that fueled her mother's most strenuous and vociferous objections. In lifelong opposition to her husband's aberrant and 'ungodly' attitudes, Anna di Santo had persevered in her captivity to the doctrinal ways of her Church. The idea of her own bambina's defection from this 'only true faith' outraged her; and she endlessly agonized over the prospect of grandchildren, who, unbaptized, would be damned to eternal perdition. For a long time, even Dino's intervention proved unavailing. Still, his persistent persuasiveness slowly wore down her bitter resistance, until one day, at last, it won out, though only after another heated controversy. That time, reminding her once again that it was his closest friend to whom her bambina owed her life, he added this challenge: was not his sister's life the paramount issue? A living Jew was a whole lot better off than a dead Catholic. Anna di Santo's repudiation was scathing: the way she had raised him, Dino ought to know better. If David had not pulled her from the sea, Angie would have gone to heaven; now, if she was going to die as a Jewess, there would be no salvation for her soul.

Somehow, in a flash, Dino perceived an opening. "Then, what about the Holy Virgin?" he countered. "Before the advent of the Lord Jesus there had been no salvation for anybody's soul, since before the coming of Christ there had been no Christians. The Madonna had been a Jewish girl; yet when God decided to send his son to save the world, he selected her to bear his son—a Jewish son. Thus, if God was so pleased with a Jewish Maria that he would choose her as the mother of his only begotten son, would he not likewise be pleased with a Jewish Angela as the mother of Jewish children? Surely the Madonna would understand and plead for God's blessing to be conferred upon Angie and her offspring."

Anna di Santo pondered this for a long while, digesting the rationalization that would resolve her quandary. "Si, Dino," she decided at last, "the Holy Virgin will understand. I'll pray to her every day. For Angie, and for her bambini."

Then Dino knew he had well earned the place of honor as his friend's best man at his little sister's wedding—a brief ceremony conducted by a justice of the peace and witnessed only by the immediate families. Intended only to legalize an internally long-validated bond, the perfunctory ritual had been arranged hastily, well ahead of the couple's original plans. For America had gone to war, and both Dino and David had been drafted into the armed forces. But Angela insisted on being a bride before the boys left for camp—her brother eventually to join an airborne battalion, her husband to serve, because of his frailty and heart murmur, this side of the ocean, in the section of ordinance and supplies.

Consideration for her parents', especially her mother's, sensibilities had determined the wedding's nonreligious character, even though Angela's completed conversion had made the union eligible for a rabbi's consecration. But although she never regretted the step that would make her life with David even more perfect, her conversion's initial motive proved sadly irrelevant: the Jewish child that she had aimed to bear never materialized. Supported by other expert medical opinion, the obstetrician attending her first pregnancy strongly advised its immediate termination. Due to a latent but severe functional disorder, parturition would cause permanent infirmity and might even place her life in jeopardy. Buried in perpetual silence, this deprivation occasioned one of the only two clouds to ever darken an otherwise as tenderly harmonious relationship as two people might be favored to experience—a relationship spanning twenty-four years of mutual devotion, terminated only after some years of progressive invalidism and suffering, by Angela's succumbing to the very ailment that had prohibited her from giving to her beloved David what above all she had wished to give him.

The other cloud, no less bleakly persistent, had been the loss of Dino. Having survived the horrors of the landing at Anzio and having remained unscathed throughout the battles in southern Italy, he was killed by a grenade somewhere in Umbria, not far from the place from which the di Santos had immigrated to America. It had been a loss far more incisive in its impact on both of them than the demise of either's parents, which punctuated the even flow of their time together—a loss, which, by the subtle corrosion of unreconciled grief, had aggravated Angela's disease and accelerated her passing. Although rankling for two decades, this loss had revealed to David Glick its true dimension only after Angela's death. Perhaps with Dino around, he might not have been quite so utterly prey to bouts of desolation, to forlornness, to all-encompassing loneliness. Perhaps, sharing his pain with his friend, he might have been able to endure the memories attached to every street of the neighborhood, every landmark, every store in which Angela and he had done their shopping, every pebble of the beach on which they had spent their holidays. Perhaps, had Dino lived, his friendship might have filled some of the ever-expanding, ever-deepening void, might have mitigated that engulfing sense of uselessness, of internal decay. Dino might have provided the link to a past, which, left to be visited alone, day by day was becoming an ever-more-unbearable burden, and possibly, by his steadying influence, he might have provided the link to a new start.

But the war had robbed him of Dino, as the unfathomable cruelty of destiny had robbed him of his Angela. There was no more link, no more incentive for a new start, not where he had lived with her, where she lay buried, where the very air was full of the reminders of an irretrievable past. Every passing month reinforced his conviction that he must get away. When loneliness became unendurable after several agonized years, he sold the haberdashery store he had taken over from his father. The proceeds and other accumulated assets would allow him a retirement of modest comfort in Israel; and that was all he was seeking. He would not venture a new beginning; there was no desire left in him. All he aimed for was living out his days in an environment unencumbered by constant reminders, by sights whose familiarity had come to be hostile—an environment offering only superficial, friendly connections unassociated with the forlorn past. There were two married cousins, who decades ago had gone as pioneers to help build the Jewish homeland; there was an old classmate who had settled there many years ago; there would be a few new acquaintances, picked up in one of the cafés, older, retired men like himself, with whom to play a game of chess or argue politics. And there always were books and leisurely walks along the beach.

"Mr. Glick." The intern's voice made him start from his rumination. "Mr. Glick, they are wheeling him to his bed now."

"Then he is …?"

"Alive?" The reply was flat. "Yes, but barely. I'm afraid it may be a matter of a few hours only."

"A few hours only." David Glick repeated, his voice a faint tremor.

"Too many vital organs injured," the intern said, "beyond repair. There was just no chance at all, except to keep him as free of pain as possible."

"Until …" The word fell into the momentary silence like a pebble dropped into a dry well.

The intern nodded, then said softly, "I'm sorry, Mr. Glick, but your friend won't see the morning. If you wish to stay with him, I'll take you to his room."

"Thank you." David Glick rose from his seat. "Of course I'll stay with him. Be there, in case he regains consciousness."

"He well may. Briefly. In fact, once for an instant he did, while being taken into surgery. He was mumbling something that sounded like pet … and otti …"

"Pietra, Carlotta—his wife, his baby." David Glick took a deep breath. "If you don't mind, let's go. He must not feel alone, when he comes to."

"Surely." Then there was silence between them. Only when they were stepping from the elevator, the intern said, "Poor fellow. But he's lucky to have a friend like you in a foreign country."

David Glick shook his head. "I was lucky to have a friend like Dino …" And suddenly there were tears trickling down his cheeks.

Then he was sitting there, oblivious to time ticking away, hunched as though in pain, sitting at Luigi Roselli's bedside, staring at the motionless figure—the wan, haggard face with the half-open ashen lips. Sitting there, praying, not to God, in whom he had not believed since his days in Hebrew school, but for nature to perform a miracle that medicine was incapable of delivering. Sitting there, oblivious to the nurse who noiselessly entered to inject another dosage of morphine; oblivious to the surgeon, who dropped by to take a look at the patient and left again; oblivious to the sting in his eyes, which had run dry of tears. Sitting there, motionless, until a tap on his shoulder startled him from the rigor of his vigil.

"Someone from the embassy in Tel Aviv is on the way up," the intern was saying. He shrugged. "He insisted, even though he was told that the patient was in no shape for an interview." There was more than just an inflection of anger in his tone.

The Glitter and Other Stories

"An interview?" David Glick repeated, rising swiftly, to step from the room and pull the door shut behind himself.

"I thought you might want to talk to him first," the intern said, unsmiling, his glance pointing to the tall man who was just emerging from the elevator and now, finding himself intercepted, was stopping short.

"I am George Winthrop, counselor, U.S. Embassy." His introduction was a clipped announcement whose snap of self-importance somehow seemed to come naturally with his crew cut. "I'm here to see about Corporal Roselli."

"You may be sure, sir," the intern said, quietly, "the corporal is receiving the best of care."

"No doubt." The reply was irritable, betraying both a lack of confidence in the assurance and annoyance at the bothersome business of duty, which had interrupted a pleasant round of bridge. "But that is not the point. I'm instructed to talk to your patient."

"I'm afraid, counselor," the intern responded, frowning, "at present, of that there can be no question. The corporal remains unconscious."

"So I was informed." George Winthrop did not care to hide his antagonism. "I'm prepared to wait until he regains consciousness."

"If he does." The intern's voice had an edge to it.

"Yes." The other's ill-humored impatience sharpened. "I understand Corporal Roselli's condition is critical. Which is precisely why I must talk to him. Maybe with some help on your part, we might get him to come to."

"Medically undesirable." The rebuttal was definitive.

The tall man's stare reflected his growing antagonism. "Well," he countered, his words grating, "if you say so—you are the doctor."

"Yes, I am." The rejoinder was unyielding.

"In that case, then," George Winthrop declared, thin-lipped, "I'll just have to bide my time, won't I? Until your patient comes out of it, as he might, might he not?"

"He might."

"Well, then," the counselor said curtly, brushing past him. But, advancing toward the room, he found himself blocked by the frail elderly man, who had, as deftly as unobtrusively interposed himself between him and the door.

"Because he might come out of it," David Glick spoke softly, "perhaps you will allow me one moment before you enter, sir?"

"Another doctor?" The question was blatant in its peevish scorn.

"No, sir," David Glick replied, evenly. "Just a friend. A friend of Corporal Roselli's, just a good friend."

"A good friend," the tall man repeated, his stony tone a sonant translation of his antipathy. "We weren't aware that the corporal had any friends in Israel."

"He was aware of it," David Glick retorted, placidly. "I'm a U.S. citizen, residing in Israel. That's made for some personal closeness—you might even say, intimacy. The common background, you know."

George Winthrop let his glance take stock of the small, balding figure in front of him, confirming his suspicion that it belonged to a Jew. "The common background …" He took up the phrase, barely suppressing an accent of mockery. "All right, so you were his friend."

"Luigi Roselli is still alive," David Glick reminded him, "and I am still his friend."

"So?"

"So I'm trying to act as one, sir."

"By getting in my way?"

"By making certain that, if and when he regains consciousness, your presence would not upset him. "

The other man was startled. "Upset him?"

"It well might."

"Upset him? What in hell are you talking about, Mr. ...?"

"My name is David Glick," the quiet voice filled in the pause.

"So it is." George Winthrop had been quite convinced by now that this man's name would not turn out to be Francis Xavier Mulrooney. "Now look here, Mr. Glick. We're talking here about a soldier *in extremis.* He would expect a representative of his country to look after him, someone to give him official assurance that his family was going to be properly looked after as well."

"That," David Glick said, "is precisely the issue, sir. No," he went on quickly, holding up his hand to thwart the tall man as he was moving to step past him. "Please, listen to me, Counselor. I'm sure you'll see for yourself. There's only one thing in this world that matters to Corporal Roselli: his wife and his infant daughter. He was to be with them in just two weeks, when he would be shipped back home. He was living only for that reunion …"

"He was, was he?" The counselor's rejoinder betrayed a whiff of uneasiness. The strange passion of the other's tone had had its effect on the harshness of his own. "We appreciate such sentiments. Good, old-fashioned, truly American sentiments. Nor are we insensitive to them, Mr. Glick. We intended to provide for that reunion in a fashion appropriate to … to the altered circumstance. The Defense Department made immediate arrangements to fly Mrs. Roselli and the child to the corporal's bedside. Unfortunately …" His glance ran past the older man, uncomfortably. "Unfortunately, given our later information, those arrangements had to be canceled. There would have been no sense to pursuing them, when we were advised that there was no chance whatever that his people could make it here in time."

"Yes." David Glick faltered, struggling to repress the tremor in his speech. "No chance whatever. But … Corporal Roselli does not know that."

A stare was seeking him. "You mean, he's not aware …?"

"No," the frail man said, his voice steady again and more forceful. "He isn't. Nor ought he be made aware. It would be too devastating, the realization that he would be dying without seeing his loved ones again. It would mean final despair. Don't you see, counselor? This would be exactly what your kind assurance that his family was going to be well cared for would produce. It would imply to him the truth, would make him aware. And whatever span of consciousness may be left to him would be sheer agony. Don't we owe to this soldier his chance to die in peace, die with hope?"

"With hope?" George Winthrop repeated, almost softly, ruefully. "But there is no hope."

"There will be, if you'll grant it to him," David Glick said carefully. "If you were to tell him that the wife and child are on their way to join him, to be with him, stay with him, until he's well again."

Beneath a frown-deepened brow, those steely blue eyes sat on him for a long moment, coldly, blankly. "You propose I should lie to him?"

"Isn't this the least we owe him?"

"The least?" George Winthrop repeated, his tone mirroring his antagonism. "It may seem so to you, I suppose."

"It does." The affirmation was unblinking.

"No doubt." The retort was grating with its repudiation. "But as for myself, I won't judge whether or what we owe. I just won't lie. I couldn't. It wouldn't be in keeping with my beliefs."

"Do these not comprise compassion and charity, counselor?"

The pointed suggestion was trailed by what seemed an endless silence. At last the tall man spoke again, each word brittle with subdued hostility. "Compassion and charity ... Perhaps. Still, I would not offend my conscience."

"There may be no need ..."

"Maybe so." The steel in those blue eyes clouded over with thoughtfulness. "True, there may be no need. No telling if and when Corporal Roselli might come to, is there? I do have my instructions; but I also have a time frame. It's a rather limited one—too limited for waiting around to talk to someone I may never be able to talk to, in any case. There wouldn't be any profit in that, it seems. For, regardless, I could not, would not lie. I shall leave that to you, Mr. Glick. I'm sure it won't bother your conscience; and besides, you'll be a lot better at it than I."

"I hope so," the older man said, softly. "And thank you for your understanding ..." But the last phrase remained unheard. Already George Winthrop had stepped to the elevator without even so much as a glance back.

Only now did David Glick realize that all along he had been facing the government's emissary alone. Unnoticed, the intern had slipped away. Returning to the room, he found the intern bent over the marine's still form.

"Glad to have you back." The young physician's smile was warm. "Seems our soldier may come to sometime soon. Not for long, I'm afraid. In any event, it'll be good to have him find a friend at his bedside."

David Glick did not miss the accent of antipathy. "It's not the American in him," he said. "Insensitivity. It's an occupational attribute of officialdom."

"True enough." The intern's shrug conveyed a weary apology. "Some here, in this country, too. The George Winthrops are international … Just as are the David Glicks," he added, his mien brightening again. He was moving toward the door. "I've given him another injection. In case he does come to, it'll keep his discomfort to the possible minimum. Sadly, that's all we can do for him."

"I know." The older man pulled up a chair next to the bed. "And thank you for your efforts, Doctor. And your caring."

"It's the caring that controls the effort, isn't it?" The intern closed the door behind himself.

In his wake, the echo of his phrase lingered on. *Caring—that is the clue to everything,* David Glick thought, wishing to be certain that this kind of caring and this kind of doctor had been there to attend Dino in Umbria. Or had he been killed on the spot? They had never learned how he died. "It is our sad duty to inform you …" That had been all. A later few lines from some buddy had mentioned only a grenade as the medium of his death, no details that would have put their minds at rest. Perhaps not knowing the details was the most charitable option? Yet it had left scope for their aching imaginings—a silent specter of undefined horror, it had kept haunting them. As much as the fact of

Dino's demise, the not-knowing had undermined Angela's will to live; insidiously, it had aggravated her fragile health.

David stared at the still form of the young marine. *Dino, he had been even younger, when ... Had he been lying like this on a hospital bed? Or just on the naked ground where medics had carried him back out of the line of fire? Or was he left, his torn body bleeding to death, where he had fallen? When he breathed his last, had there been someone, anyone with him, giving him comfort, a sense of caring? Dino ...*

A faint twitch enlivened Luigi Roselli's pallid face; his lips curled with a muted moan. Above the covering sheet fingers were stirring, feebly, fitfully. Then, barely audible, a sigh, and a flutter of eyelids struggling to lift themselves.

"Luigi," David Glick said softly, bending close.

It was not the sound of his whisper but the quiver of his breath that flowed from it, which seemed to touch his stricken friend's perception. Laboriously pried open, fogged eyes turned in the direction of this impact, straining to focus.

"It's me, David."

"David?" A murmur, mere mechanical repetition of the auditory impulse; and again: "David?" now searching for its meaning. For slow, gradual moments those eyes were unclouding, at last to be brushed by a spark of recognition: "David."

"Yes, Luigi. It's David." The man at the bedside was feeling his insides tighten and cramp as, anticipating the soldier's effort to raise himself, he warned, "You must not move, Luigi."

"Not move ..." A toneless echo, bare of comprehension. "Not move ..."

The marine's eyes were clearing, wandering. "What ... where?"

"You are in a hospital," David Glick said, fighting down the turmoil within, the memory of Dino, determined to sound calm and untroubled.

"Hospital …?"

"You are hurt, Luigi."

"Hurt …?" A stare, wakeful now with the shock of a sudden realization.

"An explosion. You got hit." The older man forced an assuaging smile. "But don't you worry: they'll fix you up all right. Right now," he added quickly, thwarting another attempted movement, "right now you must lie still. It'll help them to get you well again fast."

"No!" That stare was a mirror of the frenzied, fractured stammering now. " … go home. … furlough … Pietra, Lotty." The jerk of a shoulder was far too feeble to shake off the restraining hand. " … must go home, David. Go home!" Calling on some last residuum of strength, he tried to pull himself up. His face contorted with the shoot of pain that punished his effort, and a groan writhed from his lips.

"You see, Luigi?" The older man's hand was gently passing across that agonized brow. "No way you can go home just now. Your condition won't allow it. But …"

" … Must go!" The frenzy was rising to a feverish pitch. "Pietra, Lotty … must see …!"

"You will," David Glick said, somehow contriving to hide the choking burden of his assurance behind a masking smile. "You will see them, Luigi. The people in Washington, they understand. They're flying in Pietra and the little one. They're on a plane now. Will be here before we know it. To stay right here with you, all the time, until you're well again."

Through some moments of silence those haunted eyes sat on him. "You mean it, David?"

"I do," the man at the bedside affirmed, wondering what empowered his reply with its accent of conviction, then knowing that it was the thought of Dino, who had died, alone and friendless and hopeless somewhere in Umbria. "I do, Luigi."

Those bloodless lips moved fretfully: "You ... friend, David ... not just saying it ... lying to me?"

"Friends don't lie to each other, do they?"

"Pietra, Lotty ... coming?"

"They're on their way."

"You promise?"

"I promise," David Glick said firmly, solemnly. "Yes, Luigi, I promise." And watching those waxen features slowly smooth, he added, "But you'd better rest now, so you'll be in good shape, when they get here."

"... Get here," Luigi Roselli mumbled after him, letting his lids droop. The ghost of a smile passed across his face, endowing it with a touch of fragile happiness.

Noiselessly, the door opened. David Glick did not notice the nurse's entry until her light, swift tread had carried her almost to his side. His eyes pointing to the now still figure on the bed, he put his finger to his lips. She nodded and bent, rather hurriedly, to whisper into his ear. His features tightening with a responding frown, he rose immediately.

"I'll stay with him meanwhile," the nurse said softly, reassuringly, countering the split instant of hesitancy, before his steps, quick and resolute, moved past her.

He was just barely in time to head off the visitor. Pulling the door shut and, interposing himself to block access, he brought the new arrival's progress to an abrupt, and evidently reluctant, stop.

"Yes?" His voice was a noncommittal courtesy as he confronted the short, black-frocked man. He surveyed the haggard, chiseled face between the Roman collar and the flat, broad-rimmed hat which completed the canonical vestments, and the crucifix, dangling from a scrawny neck, conspicuous to the point of obtrusion upon the hallway's dim quietude by the glitter of its studding gems.

"This is the American's room, isn't it?" The priest's tone was frosty, with an undercurrent of antagonism. Responding to the confirming nod, "I am Father Feruccio Valenti."

"Yes?" The rejoinder came with the same polite aloofness.

"My presence should be self-explanatory, shouldn't it? I have come to see the patient."

David Glick ignored the hard-bitten impatience of the rebuke. "I'm afraid Corporal Roselli's condition does not favor visitors," he said evenly.

A stony stare answered him. "It is precisely his condition which favors a visit of this kind—indeed, demands it. His very condition, which, I understand, is most critical."

"So it is," the man in front of the door agreed impassively, not giving one inch of way to the other's intended forward motion. "This is why, as a friend, I'm trying to protect it from any further aggravation."

"As a friend," the priest repeated, in a snarl that made no attempt to hide his resentment. "A friend, you say?"

"Friends come in all shapes and colors, Father Valenti," David Glick said quietly, disregarding the discrediting inflection. "My best friend was a man by the name of Dino di Santo, an Italian and a Roman Catholic like Corporal Roselli."

"Is that so?" The cleric's tone changed to caustic urbanity. "In that case, that friend of yours should have taught you some better appreciation of a visit like this one—a visit designed, far from aggravating the patient's plight, to alleviate it—a priest's visit. But," he added, accenting each slow, grating word, "of course you wouldn't be prone to understand. Corporal Roselli is a most loyal son of his Church, a very devout man ..."

"I know," David Glick said.

"Hardly as well as I. Only this morning he came into my church to pray ..."

" ... for his wife and child." For all its softness, the interruption was pointed. "I know; I was waiting outside that church."

Father Valenti dismissed this with a wave of his hand. "I happened to spot him, talk to him," he went on, grimly, chafing with his escalating frustration. "Just briefly, yet not too briefly, to recognize how deep his commitment was, how profound his dedication. So, naturally, as soon as I learned of the ... unfortunate accident and the very gravity of his predicament, I rushed to offer him the consolation of his faith."

"Consolation," David Glick murmured, his glance straying past the cleric to the young, insipid-faced boy, who, robed and white-aproned, was trailing, carrying the ritual paraphernalia.

"The consolation of his faith!" the priest repeated emphatically. "However well meant your protective concern for your friend, he is in dire need of such consolation. Well then ..." he added sharply, taking one step forward.

But the frail man in front of the door did not yield. "No," he said quietly, but the evenness of the rebuff was unmistakable in its adamant determination. "Not when that consolation consists in administering the extreme unction."

"The proper and necessary sacrament!"

"Necessary?" A shrug. "But surely not proper. For what it would offer would not be consolation. It would be utter devastation." And, forestalling the other's outraged rebuttal, he continued, his speech now crisped by an edge of emotion, "Exactly because he is so devout a Christian and a son of his Church, it would be so devastating. For the exercise of those rites would imply to Luigi ... tell Corporal Roselli ... that he is about to die—die, without having seen his loved ones, even for a last time. It would despoil him of every last hope, rob him of the prospect of whatever happiness is still left in him; it would shatter his trust in mankind, seeing that even his friend deceived him with his promise that his wife and child were on their way to be with him."

"A promise which was a lie!" the cleric broke in, his voice rising with its choleric indictment. "A God-forsaken lie to a dying man!"

"A *mitzvah*, Father Valenti," David Glick amended, placidly. "A *mitzvah*, a sacrifice, a sacrifice of truth to ensure that the last moments of life not be lived in despair, that departure not be in final agony. Such a *mitzvah*, isn't it the least we owe to the dying?"

The priest's haggard, chiseled face reddened with the effort to suppress a burst of rage, which made those rasping lips tremble with the acrimony of the repudiation. "I do not expect the likes of you to comprehend what is owed to a Christian. The hope of salvation, the prospect of heaven, the knowledge of being blessed by our Lord, that's what we owe to the faithful. This hope, this prospect, this knowledge, the rite I have come to perform will ensure these to this poor soul. That is all that matters—that he die attended by the comforts of his faith!"

"That may be all that matters to you, Father Valenti." The steely resolve of the repudiation carried an inflection of contempt. "To me, all that matters is, that my friend die in a state of peace and dignity; and I shall insist that he does."

White-knuckled, the priest's fist clenched about the glittering crucifix. "You will insist?" he repeated, cold fury turning every word into a dagger, stabbing at the other. "Insist on barring a servant of God from doing his sacred duty by him? Who are you to 'insist'? No Jew, no friend, no one can presume the right …"

"I can!" a voice came to them, level and sonorous. Absorbed in the acrimony of their argument, neither had noticed the gray-haired man in the white coat who was advancing along the corridor. "I do have the right. If not as a Jew or even a friend, then surely as a physician. I'm Yakov Avrom, chief surgeon in charge. And with all due respect for your clerical obligation, Father Valenti, it is my medical judgment that the purpose of your visit will not benefit this patient's condition; indeed it will critically exacerbate it. Even your very presence would. I therefore shall not allow it."

"Not allow it!" The shout was a shocking struggle for breath. "You, you will not allow it?"

"That's what I said." In its even soberness, the finality of the reply was unchallengeable. "As this gentleman has been trying to enlighten you, your visit would run counter to the best interest of our patient. Which, naturally, is our paramount concern."

"The best interest of your patient!" Father Valenti repeated in a voice shaking with outrage and with venom. "What would Dr. Yakov Avrom know about a Christian's best interest?"

"A human being's best interest," the surgeon corrected him. "Even Dr. Avrom recognizes that Christians, too, are human beings."

"Human beings, baptized into the true faith!"

"I don't suppose that this circumstance makes them human beings with a lesser claim to consideration," the man in the white coat returned. "Consequently …"

"Consequently!" The priest spewed out the word as though it were an oath. "Consequently you presume to defy the will of God!"

"I do not so perceive my action." That resonant voice never abandoned its equanimity. "If you do, that opinion is your own business."

"It certainly is my business!" The response carried an accent of threat. "And you had better accord me the respect a servant of God commands!"

"Aren't we all his servants?" Yakov Avrom countered. "Each in his own way. You are serving him by serving your Church, I am doing so by serving men. And, I'm afraid, here it is my way that will prevail."

"No, it will not!" The decibel of the snarl escalated. "You will not deny this Christian man his chance of salvation, will not deprive his immortal soul of its eternal bliss! You will not frustrate his call for the benefactions and comforts of his faith!"

The surgeon had already turned to leave. Now he reversed his movement, again stood facing the cleric, mustering him from eyes almost pitying in their very disdain. "Father Valenti," he said. "I'm not prepared to be drawn into theological arguments. I shall leave that to those whose preoccupation is with such matters rather than with helping the sick and stricken. But I might remind you that it was not you nor the benefactions of his faith that the dying man in that room has called for, but for his wife and his child. They were his concern, his sole concern, which, accordingly, we are attending to as best we can."

"By lying to him?!"

"By offering him an illusion which will fill his last hours with hope rather than final despair." A curt gesture of a hand cut down the frenzied rebuff. "This is how we here perceive our obligation, our human obligation as well as our medical one, as servants of God," Yakov Avrom added dryly, "which we all are. Your vocation only grants you the privilege of such service, but surely no monopoly. But …" once more a hand's sharp wave stymied the rebuttal. "But we do respect your own obligation, as you see it. We intend to accord to it its proper due. It is my understanding that, had Corporal Roselli died on the spot, certain rites would have been performed to ensure his post-mortal bliss. Well then, after we have done all within our province to facilitate his passage from life, you may immediately claim his mortal remains, so you can facilitate his passage to afterlife."

"You would not expect this proposition to be acceptable, or even taken seriously, would you?" The repudiation was blistering. "Or maybe, again, you would. Your creed may permit such evasion, such circumvention of its decrees, such … bargains. Not mine, doctor. Nor the man's inside that room. Such subterfuge would satisfy neither the requirements of our doctrines nor the needs of a Christian soul; it may even place it in jeopardy."

"In that case," Yakov returned, unblinkingly, "there should be but little to worry about for Corporal Roselli. If something should prove amiss with the proposed procedure, and he should have trouble upstairs on account of it, he can always blame his failure on the Jews. History has shown this to be a most effective argument. Anyway, in the event, it will have to make do."

"It will not!" Forgetting his Savior's injunction of moderation and meekness, Father Valenti stamped his foot. "I demand …!"

"Demand?" the man in the white coat repeated. "But this is not your church, Father Valenti. This is a hospital; here I command."

"God's authority is supreme!" The snarl died, annihilated by the imperviousness of a small smile.

"So it is," the surgeon said. "But God's authority is not the issue. Yours is. And my interpretation of that authority is at variance with yours. It so happens that within these walls my interpretation prevails. However, let's not waste any more time; mine is too limited to allow any further exercise in futility. The church is your domain, Father Valenti, the hospital mine. I don't presume to intervene in your precinct, so I won't bear your presuming to intervene in mine. There will be no admission to the American's room. That's final."

The priest's features contorted into a mask of blatant scorn. "Think again, Doctor! Or should I remind you that the charter of the State of Israel guarantees freedom of performance to all religions?"

"So it does." The rejoinder was cold with repugnance. "But that charter does not guarantee freedom for the performance of inhumanity."

"Inhumanity!" The cleric's voice rose to a pitch of gasping shrillness. "Inhumanity, that's what you are calling godliness? Blasphemy! This is why there was Auschwitz!"

"There was Auschwitz because of men like you," Yakov Avrom said, stonily, with one quick, interposing step thwarting the other's sudden jerking motion toward the sickroom door. The quiet inwardness of his eyes was abruptly shattered by a dangerous light. "And now I recommend that you remove yourself forthwith from these premises. I do not wish to inflict on you the embarrassment of having you escorted out by an orderly."

For one moment Father Valenti remained motionless. Blanching to its last pore, his face looked more pinched than ever. "You may be sure you will hear about this," he said, each word grating. "Hear about it, all the way from Rome!"

A shrug. A thin smile. "I have no doubt, I will. I shall be privileged by Rome's attention and take proper note of the inevitable official censure. Which, however, will not keep me in any similar case from following the dictates of my medical judgment and my human conscience."

Then Yakov Avrom stood watching the receding figures of the cassocked man and the robed boy with the tray until they had disappeared into the elevator.

Luigi Roselli lay still, his eyes closed, when David Glick returned to the room. It could not have been the utter noiselessness of his friend's entry that caused him to stir ever so slightly. Perhaps it was the hardly perceptible whiff of draft from the opened door, perhaps a restless sense of anticipation, alerting him to a presence, for which he had been waiting.

"David?" A mere trickle of sound, faint to the point of near inaudibility.

"Yes, Luigi," David Glick answered softly, nodding to the nurse, responding to the silently expressive movement of her head, which told him it would not be long now. "Yes, I am here, Luigi."

Gradually, with a laborious effort fueled by sheer willpower, the man on the bed forced his eyes open, struggled to focus them. Then a hectic gleam broke the dullness of those pupils, as they wandered, searching, groping. "Lotty ... Pietra ... not come?" Dripping from his pallid lips, even the fractured feebleness of his stammer seemed deafeningly shrill with despair.

"Not yet, Luigi," David Glick said, stepping to his side.

"You were gone … I thought … but you didn't bring them … you promised!"

David Glick winced, burning with the acridity of the indictment. He strained to coerce himself into investing his reply with calm and reassurance. "Yes, Luigi, I promised."

"Pietra, Lotty … where …?"

"Soon, Luigi," the man at the bedside said quietly. "They will be here soon. It's just such a long flight. But they're on their way to you."

"On their way …" The fevering eyes turned to him, seeking him, frenzied with torment. "You are not … not lying … to me, David?"

"No, Luigi." Defying the shivering ache that froze his body, David Glick spoke carefully. "No, Luigi," he repeated. "I told you about Dino, didn't I? I wouldn't be lying to you any more than I would be lying to Dino." He watched the agony of doubt slowly relax its hold, the fever in those eyes dim. "No, I wouldn't lie to you," he said once more, firmly. "Pietra and Lotty, they'll be with you soon. Their flight's already left Frankfurt. Just another three hours more, four at most, and they'll be here."

"Four hours?"

"At the most."

"You promise?"

"I promise."

A strange, almost unnatural smoothness spread over the glassy hollowness of that young face. "I'm tired," Luigo Roselli muttered. "… don't want … be tired when they come."

The Glitter and Other Stories

"You won't be, not then," David Glick said, somehow managing to choke back the tremor in his voice. "All you need now is some more sleep. A few more hours will do it. You'll be rested and ready for them."

"Not sleep …" Luigi Roselli was struggling to keep his eyelids from drooping. "Must be awake when … when …"

"You need not worry, Luigi. I'll be here to wake you, just as soon as they get here."

"… you stay here?" The momentary flurry of agitation was ebbing, and the lids let themselves close over the eyes.

"Of course I'll be staying with you, Luigi. Right here."

"Staying with me … friend …" A murmur, faint, and fading with every word. "Wake me … Pietra, Lotty …" Eerily, the ghost of a smile crept across the chalky brittleness of wasting features. "…you here … meet them … see why I love them so much … love them so much."

David Glick sat rigid, anxious lest some slightest motion disturb that limp hand still resting on his own, dim that spectral smile still hovering over the now tranquil face. Suddenly he felt very old and very alone. He did not perceive the nurse's bending to him, nor the tear in her dark, pained eyes; he barely discerned her whisper. "The button, there … the doctor … when needed," and then her faltering steps, which, even in their tiptoeing soundlessness seemed like beats on a giant drum. A waft of fluttering air from the door and the quietude in its wake told him that she was gone.

He remained still, all sense of time lost to him, of space, of his very being; not stirring even when Luigi Roselli's hand jerked, cramped about his in a squeezing, clenching grip. There was no hurry about pressing that button. There was no more the doctor could do.

He had felt that same jerk before, that same squeeze, that same final grip, when he had held Angela's hand. From the depth of an unforgotten past, the echo of her words came to him, words spoken just before that ultimate moment, the echo of a waning, sonant breath that knew it would be the last and knew about his grief. "I have been blessed, David," that echo said, "blessed, for I have known love …"

Slowly, carefully, David Glick at last extracted his hand from the dying clasp to let it drift, tenderly, across the lifeless brow: Luigi Roselli, too, had passed in a state of bliss.

A Name of a Canvas

She spied him the moment she entered and crossed over to him, her light steps noiseless on the carpet.

"Hi, stranger," she said softly.

He looked up, frowning. Alone with his thoughts, he had been glued to one of the red velvet-upholstered benches, too absorbed to notice her arrival any more than the earlier one of the pale girl, who now was hunching on another bench, her head buried in her palms and her dark hair half covered by an iridescent scarf. Nor had he noticed the youngish-looking man with the rimmed glasses and the suggestion of a blond mustache, who seemed to entertain a hope of getting to know the pale girl.

"Hello, Harriet," Charlie Duncan said, smiling vaguely. "What are you doing here?"

Her laugh was brittle, with just the faintest trace of irritation. "An art gallery is not the most unlikely place for an artist, is it? I am one, too, remember?"

"And a good one. A very good one."

She shook her head. "We both know that's just a reference to a potential future. For the present time, it is a matter of trying, working, striving. But thanks, anyway." She sat down beside him. "Haven't seen you for ages."

"Ages? Last Friday, at the Club."

"Oh, that!" She dragged out the chill of her rebuttal. "The Club, true. We did say hello there, didn't we?" Then a shrug glossed over her resentment. Her glance pointed to the adjoining gallery. "I just had another look at your *Wanderer in the Night*. The more I see of it, the more I like it."

He nodded absently, silently.

Her eyes followed the direction of his own, and her brow puckered. "That painting again?" she asked testily.

"There's genius for you." His gaze kept clinging to the canvas.

"It's great stuff," she admitted. "Yet, somehow I can't like it, Charlie. There's something about it, something ..." She was searching for the precise expression. "Something alien. Something unwholesome. Something sick."

He declined her challenge, merely saying, "It fascinates me. Now even more so, perhaps, than when I first saw it. It grows on you."

"Not on me," she said, a bit too sharply. "Rather the opposite. Anyway, I'll take your *Wanderer in the Night* any time."

He ignored her praise. "It fascinates me," he repeated, still engrossed. "It's been on exhibit for almost three years now. I must've seen it dozens of times, but every time, I find something new in it, one more puzzling, exciting, stirring facet, that tells another chapter of the story, yet will not tell the whole of it."

"And, being Charlie Duncan, you want the whole of whatever your mind's set on."

He seemed impervious to her impatient irony. "If a problem has been intriguing you for so long ... Besides, now it's not just wanting, but needing the answer. You know, I got the job with Hanson Brothers."

"Doing the Cranshaw book?" Her surprise sounded hurt. "Congratulations. Why didn't you let me know?"

"When could I have? The contract wasn't signed until the day before yesterday."

"There are telephones," she muttered. Then added, "But it's great, Charlie. You've wanted it so much. It's a big job."

"Not an easy one, either." His hand ran across his brow. She knew this gesture so well; it would recur when he was fretting over an idea whose grasp kept eluding him. "Not an easy one," he said again. "A complete edition of Madeleine Cranshaw's productions, plus critical and interpretive texts. This is, why ..." his glance pointed. "The one there, no doubt, is her most important painting. And her most baffling one. I've got to understand it. You see ..." he turned to her, as though soliciting her help. "I need to find a title for it. The present one is just a description of the obvious. *Nude Without Head.* Typical of Fisher. He knows art well enough to run a gallery, but imagination?" His lips curled. "*Nude Without Head.* It doesn't mean a thing. Offers no suggestion to the artist's intent. Above all, it doesn't do justice to this work. Not to the internal experience that created it. That's been bothering me all along. I've had a few ideas, but none seemed quite to the point. What I'm after is not just a fancy name but its true title."

"Can you make out what's wrong with the one it's got?"

The voice made them start around. Neither had noticed the approach of the couple now standing in back of their bench: a tall young man with athletic shoulders and a girl snuggling to his arm, a slim thing with a bit too prominent a bosom, a bit too blonde hair, and a bit too definite a look of honeymooning for financial security.

"*Nude Without Head.* As far as I'm concerned, that about describes it, don't you think so, Janie?"

"Natch," his companion agreed. "Though, I could think of some other title, one a lady wouldn't care to mention. The filth they dare exhibit these days!"

Charlie Duncan gave her a swift, rather unkind glance, before turning back to Harriet. "I'm looking for an inspiration—the name Madeleine Cranshaw herself might have given to it, a name conveying a clue to its significance."

Although it was evident to whom this remark was addressed, the athletic young man presumed to take it as a reply to his own comment. "Excuse me," he protested, "a clue to what significance? There's a nude woman and her head is cut off right at the neck, as though guillotined. A study in morbidity, I'd say. Of course, I'm no expert; still, art classes at Harvard do something for you, too. What name would've been more appropriate?"

"One which tells the story behind the image," Charlie Duncan said curtly.

"It's shocking. What do you say, Alan, hon?" the blonde pouted. "I sure wouldn't hang it in our parlor."

"Because," Charlie Duncan rebuffed her wearily, just wishing those two would go away. "Because pleasantness is not a measure of genius."

"If psychopathy were a measure of genius, the Cranshaw woman would sure be tops," a guttural voice interrupted him. The bald man had been standing a few steps to one side of them for some time now, listening in with the smiling condescension of would-be connoisseur.

"Our inability to understand a work is hardly any proof of its author's psychopathy," a vivacious, carefree voice interposed; somehow, the girl had appeared out of nowhere, a pretty, redheaded sight.

"Proof?" The pale, dark-haired girl was talking now. She had risen from her bench and was pointing a rigid hand at the canvas. "Isn't that sufficient evidence of her psychopathy?" The bald man approved boisterously. "Right. There you have the evidence. No need to look for any, though. Not, when you know the story of that Cranshaw woman."

"I know it," Charlie Duncan said tersely, coldly.

"Then you couldn't help appreciate, what sort she was. Crazy. A real nut." The bald man chuckled harshly.

"What story, hon?" the blonde asked petulantly. Her companion bent to her, started to talk to her in a low voice.

Harriet did not hear his explanation. Nor was there any need; the story had come back to her—the queer tale of Madeleine Cranshaw, who, a penniless and unknown art student of obscure background, had been the bride of socialite Gerard Cranshaw, young and handsome heir to a large Eastern lumber fortune; only two years later, she had won public acclaim as a leading artist, when, at the International Art Festival, her paintings had carried off all the prizes. Her career had ascended through a succession of brilliant triumphs, the more gratifying as they were achieved within a setting of ostensible domestic happiness. Then, without any warning, without any explanation, and without any trace, she had one day vanished from the Cranshaws' Oregon estate. That had been nearly three years ago, and nothing had been heard of her since. After an extensive but futile search, police had officially assumed her dead and abandoned their efforts. Theories of abduction and murder had been proposed, considered, and discarded for lack of evidence or even credible clues. And, with her marital life so obviously cloudless and happy and her artistic aspirations so splendidly fulfilled, neither voluntary desertion nor suicide had entered the realm of speculation; not at least until a consultant psychiatrist had examined this last picture of hers, found in her studio after her disappearance."

Harriet heard Charlie Duncan replying to another of the bald man's comments. "Insanity? But not even that psychiatrist was ready for such a diagnosis. He thought this painting projected a state of deep depression and proposed that she might have wandered off in a condition of mental alienation. But again, there was no proof. Madeleine Cranshaw was not seen alive again. Other experts maintained that they perceived ample evidence of aggressive and destructive tendencies, suggesting that she might have committed suicide. But neither was her body ever found. One or two supposed experts claimed that this final canvas of hers reflected fear of violence, of death. But she had no known enemies, no perilous involvements of any kind. To this day, no one knows what happened to her. This painting? Alienation, fear, self-destruction? Just suppositions. The borderlines of artistic expression are too delicate for a positive clinical evaluation. Yet this canvas is all the clue she left."

"Well, all we've got to do is look at it," the bald man growled stubbornly, his index finger stretching toward *Nude Without Head*, "and compare it with her earlier works. This painting's deviation from them—there's the answer."

"Indeed, there it is," Charlie Duncan said quietly, thoughtfully, after biting back an initial flurry of irritation at the inflection of opinionated certainty. "The answer. But it is a coded one as always. Every work of art is a cryptogram, conveying a piece of autobiography. For complete comprehension one would have to solve the cipher."

"No doubt you're going to solve it," the bald man remarked peevishly.

"I'm trying to."

"And knowing you, I'd bet you are going to." Harriet's assertion was soft, with an accent of subtle jealousy.

"Wish I could share your confidence," he demurred. "This is no simple cipher. That painting there shows a total reversal of all of Cranshaw's previous patterns: her style, her usual subject choice, her tested technique. It's like an absolute break with her past. Yet there's so much clarity, so much logic and congruity in this work, so much consciously creative genius … I feel the actual story of Madeleine Cranshaw is told by those very contrasts. But what that story is …" He shook his head. "All I'm sure of is that that *Nude Without Head* is its symbol. And the essence of what it seeks to convey, I think, would be the real title, the one I'm trying to find."

He looked at Harriet expectantly, challenging her comment. But instead, it was the redhead who exclaimed gaily, "A picture in search of a title! I like this game. How do you play it? Draw lots, who has the first guess?" Her vivid greenish eyes darted impishly around the small circle, now swelled by a few new arrivals who had stopped by while Charlie Duncan had been speaking.

"Just count me out of this!" the bald man declared gruffly, turning as though to leave. But he merely retreated to another bench, the one on which the man from Harvard was still whispering to his blonde, and sat down with bored aplomb.

"I th-think it's obvious wh-what the title sh-should be." The stammer belonged to the blond-mustached man. He had followed the pale, dark-haired girl as soon as she had abandoned her seat on their shared bench, and now stood directly behind her, wiping his glasses with nervous care.

"Hurrah!" the redhead sang out. "The first bid. One, two, three, sold! Tell the name and win the game!"

A blush and a twitch came to the boyish face. "I-I'd call it *L-Lust*," he blurted out at last, half choking at the word.

There were snickers of mockery from somewhere. Charlie Duncan lied charitably. "I had a similar idea myself, but then I saw the contradictions. There's desire, to be sure. There's prurient surrender. But it's warped. By shame, perhaps. Or loathing. Look at that torso's rigidity, at that right hand, raised as though in defense. It doesn't seem to me that lust would know of resistance and repulsion."

"With s-some w-women it w-would." The young man's voice was taut with a zealous conviction. "Wh-when a girl's pure in mind, untouched by passion …"

"Poor wench!" a woman's voice piped up, but lost itself before its source could be identified.

Charlie Duncan was quick to head off the jeers: puerile revelries about womanly purity were too vulnerable. "In any case," he said kindly, "how would your title account for the absence of the head?"

"That's s-symbolic, too, l-lust being of the b-body's ex-c-clusively."

"And the money? The bills she is crumpling in her left hand?"

The young man jerked the glasses to his eyes and gave the painting a brief, almost hostile stare. "Also symbolic," he then pronounced. "Sh-showing how the exp-perience of ecs-stasy will d-defy and d-defeat the c-corruptions of mat-terialism."

"Nonsense!" the female voice cut in, oddly grating. The one to whom it belonged was small and frail. Sharp lines framed her mouth, heralds of frustration and disillusionment. Her restless hands were busy smoothing imaginary creases in her black outmoded jacket. "Symbolic, nonsense! It's always the same—what's wrong with modern art is the public. The artist does some simple, ordinary stuff; but the self-appointed experts won't be happy unless they can have their two bits worth of mystery, of hidden meanings, obscure significance, 'transcendental design,' or whatnot. Why not examine that Cranshaw picture without such pretensions? All you will find is an everyday scene."

"Oh, no!" the pale, dark-haired girl's voice rose above a counterpoint of assenting and dissenting murmur. "Oh, no! It would be too awful if this were an everyday scene!"

"Sure. As awful as today's world!" the bitter little woman in the black jacket retorted. The lines around her mouth deepened with the somber triumph of self-torment. "A world in which this scene's happening every day, every hour, around the clock, and no symbolic fiddle-faddle will diminish the cruelty of its humiliation. If you want a name for the episode portrayed on that canvas, just call it *The Adulteress*."

Charlie Duncan studied her, wondering. "That's one title that wouldn't have occurred to me. Adulteress. Why?"

It was a long moment before the reply came, its harshness now oddly aching. "Suppose a woman's totally in love with her husband and believes to be loved the same way. And suppose one day she finds a baggage like that in her husband's bedroom ..."

"All by herself? What a waste!" the redhead cracked.

The older woman merely glared at her; relentless in their fidgety play, her fingers intertwined and separated again. "Wouldn't the adulteress appear to the wife just like that female in the painting?" she snapped. "Wouldn't her nudity become an exhibit of shameless vulgarity? Wouldn't her beauty be repulsive, her allure hateful? Wouldn't her posture of obvious readiness carry exactly that blatancy of the obscene, of filth, of scurrility?"

"No one would expect a wife to be objective in that sort of a confrontation," an elderly man remarked in a quiet voice ever so lightly tainted with benevolent irony—a voice which, even in the largest crowd, Harriet would never have failed to identify as that of George Gould, the art dealer. "But was Madeleine Cranshaw likely to have faced such a situation? Hardly. All reports confirmed that her marriage had been very happy."

"What would outsiders know?" the woman in the black jacket rebutted, somewhat shrilly. "Besides, if she was really happy, only the more terrible would be the shock of such a discovery."

"The assumption being that, just as boys will be boys, husbands will be cads," the redhead commented with a glittering laugh.

"Easy to make light of it when you haven't had the experience," the older woman said tonelessly.

"True," George Gould intervened, his voice assuaging with compassionate comprehension. "The experience would be devastating all right. Still, the question remains, was Madeleine Cranshaw exposed to it? What's more to the point, does this canvas reflect such an exposure?" He had stepped over to Harriet and now sat down next to her. "Now, does it, if we examine this painting objectively? Does not everything about this nude suggest disgust and resistance? Surely, we would expect an adulteress to be ready for love rather than repudiate it. Also, what about the money she is so furiously destroying? There are not just these bills in her left hand, but all the rest, crumpled, torn, obliterated, surrounding her like some weird rosary."

"Oh that …" the woman in the black jacket faltered but would not concede. "I suppose that's meant to symbolize how she's wasting what should've been rightfully her husband's."

"Ah, Gerard Cranshaw could afford to squander," someone quipped. "Financially and physically. Give the man credit."

"And why," disregarding the interjection, George Gould continued, quickly glossing over it to rescue that frail, fading woman with the haunted eyes from this implicit mockery, "why would the adulteress be depicted without a head?"

She responded with a grateful glance. "Perhaps her face was hidden or otherwise unrecognizable," she said uncertainly.

"Too simple!" somebody commented—a very tall man, with clear eyes of a brilliant blue and an unlit pipe pushed into one corner of his mouth.

"Or perhaps," the woman in the black jacket went on, helpless like a trapped animal, "the face was irrelevant. If her man betrayed her love and trust, what difference to the wife with whom? Or again, discretion might've prohibited identification?"

"Or fear," Charlie Duncan found himself muttering.

"Why fear?"

He hesitated. Only one moment ago the notion had made perfect sense to him. But now, torn from the context of flitting thoughts by the pale dark-haired girl's drab question, it was foundering, a tinsel of illogic severed from the broken chain of intuitions.

"Because," he heard Harriet replying in his place, "we only so expressly omit what we are afraid of."

"Exactly," the gaunt man with the pipe agreed. "This omission, then, would be purely symbolic. But symbols are employed to convey fundamental verities rather than individual peculiarities. That's why I can't see this painting portraying an adulteress. Nor any specific person, but depicting a type."

"A precious type, to be sure!"

The tall man's glance grazed the thin, bony figure of the one who had interrupted him. His eyes lost none of their blue brilliance, only his lips curved wryly with the long-ago memory of a shriveled spinster in the classroom of a red-brick schoolhouse. "No type's precious," he returned unruffled, deaf to the acid scorn of the present spinster's censorious interjection. "But art may make it so. Creative perfection will make any type precious. Even that of a prostitute. That's what I see in that painting. That's how I would title it."

"N-now, now!" Acute with embarrassment, the blond-mustached young man nervously rubbed his hands.

Charlie Duncan's glance strayed to him, but on its way caught at the dark-haired girl with the iridescent scarf, pulled toward her as by some intangible magnet. Her lips were pressed into two thin, bloodless lines, and she seemed even more pallid than before.

"*The Prostitute!*" Abandoning his retreat into bored silence, the bald man seemed acutely animated by the suggestion. "Of course, that's it! There you have the lurid beauty, the sultry challenge, the habitual indecency—the frigid readiness for another night's routine. The hand clutching the reward, not destroying it, but playing with it carelessly, for it's easy money, which another debauch will earn for her again any old time. Of course, she would have no head—because all that counts, all she is, all she lives by, is her body, which ..."

"I'm sure," the bony spinster cut in, her domineering voice pungent, "by now everybody appreciates your explanation as well as your expertise."

"I still say they shouldn't show filthy pictures like this one," the honeymooning blonde complained. "Don't you think so, hon?" Her nostrils were vibrant; her eyes, no longer dull, had acquired a sharp glint of excitement.

"Pictures of prostitutes?" Charlie Duncan's eyes were still resting on the girl with the iridescent scarf. The alabaster opaqueness of her profile created an illusion of utter inanimateness, as of a death mask, cast in accents of uncanny loveliness—a death mask whose unsmiling lips now were stirring with colorless words, each austere in its clipped precision.

"There is nothing filthy about prostitutes. Pay your money and get your merchandise. The pretense, that's the real filth. Prostitutes—there is no pretense. They're honest in what they're doing."

"Honest!" the spinster rasped out. "That's the new generation for you! Praising tramps for their sinfulness. Handing out medals for immorality, shamelessness, brazenness!"

"Who knows?" The woman in the black jacket broke into the tirade, a pained chuckle wilting on her lips. "Maybe one ought to be brazen, vile, vulgar ... Doxies, that's what all men want, anyhow!"

"If that were true, wouldn't we women love to accommodate them?" Harriet spoke up suddenly, pleasantly. "If the ladies will excuse this generalization—but the truth will out." She grinned wryly at Charlie Duncan, but immediately her smile faded and a little furrow was digging itself across her brow. Not even her quip had succeeded in gaining his attention. Perhaps that's really the truth, she thought, sadly ironical with her awareness that, given her miserable inhibitions, she had no alternative but stick to her 'intellectual' approach and patiently deploy every new evidence of their 'mental affinity,' playing for a chance that Charlie might yet discover her.

"How about you, Harriet?" she heard a voice, as though from far away, breaking into her reflections, but it was just George Gould's. "What name would you suggest for this canvas? You've always been strong on imagination as well as on analysis."

"Have I?" she responded, but her voice had lost its usual buoyancy. "Well, when I look at that background of gray curtains, floating as if in some magic breeze; at those lights of reddish purple and sulfurous yellow, running into the same nowhere from which they're coming, simultaneously somber and glaring; at those uncanny shadows; most of all at that female torso—the technique, the style, the character of work seems too abstract to be a mere reproduction of anything so specific as *The Adulteress* or *The Prostitute*. Rather it's the expression of an idea, the projection of a concept …"

"Right!" the gaunt man with the pipe assented with an air of intrinsic superiority. "As I've tried to clarify before, this painting presents the essential content of a human experience made visible. You know what I'd call it? *Degradation*. How's that for a title, young lady?"

She shook her head. "I don't think so. Don't you see? There is something about that female, something more shattering than her objective awareness of being degraded—her subjective response to the act of degradation. It is all over her contorted, cramped, tormented form. She's rebelling, but not just against some lecherous assault …"

She paused, for Charlie Duncan had raised his head, and his glance was seeking her, reaching for her with a spark of admiring recognition—of her intellectual acumen, her mental affinity. This time perhaps she had made it happen? But the thought was void of elation, void even of passing satisfaction: acknowledgment seemed so meaningless, unless it was of her as a woman. She returned a saddened, subdued smile. Yes, as George Gould had said, she was strong on imagination and analysis, but …

"Rebelling against an abuse of her self," she went on, every word a weary burden, struggling from her in spite of herself, "rebelling as, captive to a compelling urge, to a passionate yearning to give—and give all—she is crushed by the realization that the one who is to receive this all will never appreciate more than a trifling fraction, at best, of what she wants to give, needs to give …"

A little chuckle, like the rattling of pebbles in a tin can, tore into her phrase—a chuckle, paradoxical, grotesque, almost scurrilous. Then, once again, those ashen lips lay rigid, reinforcing the lines of that pallid death mask in their chilling contrast to the vividness of the framing iridescent scarf.

"Well, what's your name for that canvas, then?" Like a thin blade, the question shattered the effect of that weird chuckle. Reacting to it, the blue of the gaunt man's eyes was piercing with an edge of sudden anger.

"The name, yes," Harriet muttered, shaken unaccountably. That sordid giggle had struck a chord in her, a chord which was still reverberating, powerfully mournful in the wastes of her own loneliness.

"The name," Charlie Duncan prompted, tense with some odd, incongruous excitement. "It's obvious you've found it now. So tell us."

Harriet's mien hardened. She was aching with the recognition that he was deaf to the vibration of that chord deep within her. And the ineluctable awareness that he was acknowledging her only as someone who might help him solve the riddle of the Cranshaw picture made her voice sharp and brittle. "*Humiliation,* that's my name for it."

"*Humiliation?*" Charlie repeated. An inflection of demurring disappointment framed the word, as, engrossed in the canvas, he shook his head. "*Humiliation?*"

"Yes," she affirmed bitterly. "For a woman there's none greater than to be ready to give all that is hers and finding her gift deemed worthless."

She broke off abruptly, wretchedly aware that her comment had been lost in a wasteland of disregard, lost without resonance. For one moment more she waited in a forlorn hope for some echo from somewhere. Then she rose abruptly.

"Leaving?"

"I'd better be," she whispered back to George Gould. "Almost forgot an appointment."

"You mind?" He, too, was getting up from the bench.

Her glance strayed to Charlie Duncan, but he was still absorbed in his contemplation. "It's just around the corner," she said woodenly. "Thanks, George. Don't trouble."

Dimly he sensed that she wanted to be alone. He nodded, watched her passing through the crowd toward the exit.

"Ready to give, yet finding her gift deemed worthless," the bald man quoted with a disgruntled sniff. "Petticoat sentimentalities."

George Gould swung around to him. "I think there's a lot to recommend her contention. *Humiliation* sounds like an excellent title to me." His voice was temperate as always, but the rebuke had a finely tuned edge to it.

"Same here," the redhead concurred vigorously.

George Gould smiled at her and inconspicuously started on his way to the door.

"I still prefer *The Prostitute*," the athletic young man volunteered peevishly. "But of course, I'm no expert."

Charlie Duncan looked up suddenly, sharply, stirred into unwelcome confrontation with a world beyond that of his own roaming thoughts, with a confining world of objects and people, into which that voice had recalled him.

"It's not a question of anyone's preference," he said irritably. "This is not a guessing game. It's not up to us—or anyone—to pick a title, for this painting already has got one: the authentic one. Don't you see?"

"Do you?"

He turned to the pale, dark-haired girl. This time her drab voice had been colored by a touch of irony. He nodded. "It's written all over this canvas. It's been there all the time, staring at me. But it took someone to spell it out for me." Straying, his glance searched for Harriet; only now he apprehended that she had left, without even telling him good-bye. Uncomfortably, he wondered why. It was not like her at all.

"So you are going to call it *Humiliation*?" the girl in the iridescent scarf asked, her irony again gray with melancholy.

He shook his head.

"But that was her suggestion."

Charlie Duncan considered. "It was, wasn't it? Strange. She told the story without knowing it. The yearning to give, she said. That's what I had missed. But it's there, all over the painting. Everything about that torso is alive with it, telling the tale as from an open book …"

"Aw, Alan, hon, let's go," the blonde sulked.

Her companion patted her hand and pleaded, "Be good, angel, now comes the real stuff," with the complacent sarcasm of Harvardian superiority.

Charlie Duncan ignored him. "Imagine," he continued, preoccupied, groping for a fuller grasp of his discovery, "a young woman, passionate with the desire to bestow herself, all of herself, on the subject of her love—a desire which seeks its fulfillment through marriage. The union she enters seems most auspicious. It promises untroubled harmony; her husband is considerate, devoted to her, good-natured, generous—in fact, everything a woman may hope for. Nevertheless, somehow she is not happy and can't see why. An absurdly paradoxical feeling of antagonism becomes irrefutable and is constantly growing more acute, more pervasive. Until, one day …"

From somewhere there came a sigh like a faint little sob. But it was gone before it could be traced.

"Gradually, this unfathomable antagonism turns into ever more violent revolt against her husband's touch, his caress, even his very presence. But, at length, this revolt is shedding its irrationality, for she has become aware that all she is giving is her body; that by giving this, and this alone, she is not fulfilling her yearning, but a contract; merely acquiescing in what she has neither the right nor an excuse to deny to her husband; haunted by her recognition that he isn't the one to receive what she's longing to bestow, has never been the one; that, in truth, she has never loved him …"

"Aw nuts!" the blonde griped. "Making a tragedy out of an everyday thing! Most girls find out too late they didn't pick the right guy. So, either they put up with him, figuring they might be doing even worse with the next—or they simply get themselves divorced."

"Simply?" Charlie Duncan's face showed none of his distaste. "It may be simple for some. But that woman had integrity. Moral courage. She faced up to the truth that she had willingly deceived herself into believing her own pretense of love so she could—without dismay or scruples—pick the right guy, through whom to fulfill her ambition. For social prominence perhaps, or for security, or for the lazy convenience of untroubled pleasure, or just for the glamour of wealth. But even if her motives for driving her bargain should've been less materialistic, less shallow, her conscience proved incorruptible. Once aroused, it wouldn't countenance any alibi for having sold herself."

"Sold herself—to a husband?" The spinster gave a cackling laugh.

"Not all streetwalkers walk the street," the pale girl with the iridescent scarf said, and again that mirthless chuckle was trickling from her lips.

A flicker of irritation crossed the features of the gaunt man, and the blue of his eyes hardened. "So the twain shall meet," he remarked, sucking at his cold pipe. "The sordid rottenness you perceive in this picture seems to lead up, inescapably, to my own conclusion, after all. You see in that nude a woman selling herself, and I called her portrayal *The Prostitute*. Not much difference, is there?"

"Not in our perception," Charlie Duncan muttered absently, "but in our choice of a fitting title."

"What's your choice then?" Impatience was roughening the countering query.

"Aw, who cares?" the blonde whined. "If you ask me, Alan, hon, this is a lot of hooey. Let's get out of here!"

"Look, angel," the man from Harvard tried to appease her, "I just want to find out …"

"So do I," the bald man spoke up again, and his sardonic undertone invested his voice with a queer twist of joviality. "That authentic name, didn't you claim you discovered it?"

"I won't assume the credit for it, though," Charlie Duncan's eyes strayed again to the seat on the bench. Harriet had left it vacant, without so much as a good-bye. He shrugged, oddly depressed. "I still might never have realized, except for a remark from … a remark thrown my way. It opened a different perspective. All of a sudden, that design seemed so clear, so simple, so logical."

"The cut-off head especially, I suppose." The spinster's voice was grating like a saw on marble.

Charlie Duncan turned to her, untouched by the interjection's sneering taunt. "Yes," he said, "that missing head. It makes the point. For it isn't cut off at all. Observe those shadows, their distribution. Those patches waiting to stalk their prey, phantoms to stalk her shame—and fear, and guilt, and hopelessness—greedily lurking all about the woman's torso, creeping from her feet along the legs and thighs and hips, tightening about her bust, touching her shoulders, veiling the base of her neck with their ghastly grays, condensing into the total blackness that hides the head. It isn't severed—the phantoms have finally caught up with it, have swallowed it, concealing its identity, not from us alone but from the nude woman herself. The merciless candor of self-confrontation has obliterated the countenance which used to belong to that torso, while the new one, for which she is struggling, she as yet cannot recognize. That's why there is no head. Because you couldn't portray what you can't visualize."

The gaunt man was shaking his head, faintly derisive. "Don't you think Madeleine Cranshaw was too much of an artist to miss such a fascinating and rewarding challenge? Contrasting what that nude had become, to what she'd used to be? No artist of her caliber would forgo that effect. Surely, as the one who conceived this canvas, she must also have conceived her subject's new countenance. Naturally she must have visualized it."

"But she didn't," Charlie Duncan retorted, captive to an image which, shapelessly, undefinably, touched his mind, and was lost again.

Uncertainly his hand ran across his brow to wipe it clear of an invisible cobweb, spun of longing and loneliness, shrouding its memory as with an imponderable mourning veil. "She couldn't have. That's what that remark made me see. The young lady who was sitting here, remember? 'There's something about this female,' she said, 'something more shattering than her objective awareness of being degraded: her subjective response to the act of degradation.' That's when I understood what's so profoundly stirring and at once so weirdly appealing about this painting: not its subject, nor the manner of its presentation, but the extraordinary subjectivity of its treatment—the impassioned agony of its expression, which no one could've rendered except one who had lived through the hell of which it tells."

"I see." The gaunt man dragged his words, pondering. "Yes, I see. Perhaps Madeleine Cranshaw couldn't conceive this nude's countenance …"

"She couldn't," Charlie interrupted him, "because there was no concept, no intellectual process. Just the experience—her experience. She screamed it out of her tortured self, screamed it out in color and form. She could not have projected it because she did not know what would come to be her future self."

"Her future self?" the gaunt man repeated, slowly, with a wondering question.

"Yes," Charlie said, "for the name of this canvas is *Self-portrait*."

"Oh, no!" the woman in the black jacket broke a spell of sudden silence. "You can't seriously believe there's a female in this world who would portray herself in such a fashion!"

"If she's mentally unhinged, she might," the redhead observed. "Anyway, it's an interesting guess."

"But worthless as a title," the man from Harvard gloated.

"I know," Charlie Duncan muttered, oppressed with an inscrutable sense of guilt.

"Why worthless, hon?" the blonde drawled apathetically.

"Because using it may get him into a mess of troubles."

"Troubles?" Charlie Duncan seemed surprised. "I wasn't thinking of that."

"You'd better, though, if I know my law. You could never prove this was a self-portrait. The way it reflects upon its model, Gerard Cranshaw might pin a beautiful libel suit on you. After all, the original used to be his wife and is still linked to him by name. Not to speak of the Cranshaw woman herself taking exception. I for one wouldn't blame her for raising sweet hell."

"I thought she was dead," the pale girl said.

"Well, I forgot about that. Still, one never knows. As long as her body hasn't been recovered, there's always a chance. Why, hundreds of people have managed to hide and reappear later, sometimes under assumed names, and have gotten away with it."

"Not sh-she!" the blond-mustached man objected eagerly. "Sh-she used to be a c-celebrity, s-someone would be b-bound to r-recognize her."

"Once publicity stops, there is no more celebrity," the blond man snarled.

"In any event, she wouldn't be likely to kick up a fuss." The woman in the black jacket ventured a bleak chuckle. "In her place, I at least would crawl still deeper into my hole, if that painting there would be suggested to be my self-portrait. I wouldn't want to be around, hearing what people would think about me."

"I don't think she would care," the pale girl's voice was utterly drab.

"If she had an ounce of shame left …"

"I'm not going to use this title anyhow," Charlie Duncan cut in abruptly, almost brusque with a sense of disgust, honed by a nagging, undefined culpability. Suddenly he could not bear those people around him, a bunch of snoopers and gossips satisfying their curiosity without empathy. He swung around sharply and walked to the door with quick, angry strides.

At the door, an attendant stopped him. Would he be good enough to see Mr. Fisher in his office?

The art dealer came straightaway to the point. "A Mr. Freese was here to see me. Some big shot from Nevada. He's enthusiastic about your *Wanderer in the Night*. When I told him it was not for private sale, he made me promise to find out whether you would do another like it for him."

"I don't think I could," Charlie Duncan answered.

Fisher nodded. "I assumed as much. That sort of work one couldn't do on commission. Have a cigarette?"

"Thanks. I knew you'd understand."

"Sure," Fisher said. "I shall tell Freese, no go." Then they had their smokes, silently. When Charlie Duncan stepped into the street, the sun was preparing to retreat behind the tall roofs. He turned left, to saunter his way north, still chafing with a vague sense of discontent, the more aggravating as it grew fussier the harder he tried to trace it. Harriet came to his mind—a nice girl, very nice and pretty and talented. But she would act oddly at times, like this afternoon, leaving without a good-bye. He'd call her up, find out why; besides, he liked talking with her. She had lots of brains and imagination and intuition. Would be good to have her around now, someone who'd understand, someone with whom to discuss his perception of the Cranshaw canvas.

He nearly bumped into a body that was suddenly swinging away from a store window toward him. With a mumbled, "I'm sorry!" he just managed to dodge the collision.

"Oh, hello," the gracile figure in the iridescent scarf said in a colorless voice. As, surprised, he stopped, she added, "You don't recall, do you?"

His gaze beheld the pale mask of the dark-haired girl. "But I do. Fisher's gallery—you were up there, too."

"Listening to you. It was quite … fascinating."

"Thanks." His tone was brittle. Somehow her praise disconcerted him.

"You left so suddenly."

A question mark hung in the air, uncomfortably, compellingly. He suppressed a frown. "It was about time I stopped making a nuisance of myself, haranguing innocent bystanders at an exhibit."

"Haranguing?" There was repudiation in her rejoinder. "I don't think you were." And after a short lapse of silence. "I was pondering that title you came up with, *Self-portrait*. Why won't you use it? As you said, it isn't because the Cranshaws might object, so why …?"

"Because …" He broke off sharply, for all of a sudden he knew what had been bothering him. "Because," he went on firmly, "I have no right to use it."

"No right, how? You reasoned it out. You found it."

"But I had no right to find it; or even to look for it. That painting was a confession; its name was another person's most intimate secret."

"Which you managed to share."

"About which I should've kept my mouth shut," Charlie Duncan retorted tartly. "This is the very least I owed to a great artist and to a rather singular woman. Yet, there I went and made a public exhibition of her private life. Using this title, I would commit the same indecency on an infinitely larger scale."

"I see," the girl muttered, her voice as drab as ever. "Going this way?"

Only now he realized that they had started walking side by side. "Why, yes. It's such a gorgeous day. I love walking along the park. And you?"

"Oh, I …" She dragged out the word. A curious smile lent to her features an odd translucency—or perhaps it was just a ray from the parting sun, which flooded her face. "I was just window-shopping. But that's done with."

"For me it's just some twenty blocks home," he said, irrelevantly, combating a flurry of discomfort. "It seems like a crime, riding the bus on a day like this."

Emerging from beneath that scarf, her hair sparkled with tiny reflexes of light as she nodded. "Yes. I always prefer walking also."

"You are living uptown, too?"

"In the eighties, just off the expressway."

"We share the same direction then." His tone was tentative, noncommittal.

She kept looking past him. Only while they were crossing over to the park, she added, "My name's Mary, Mary MacLean."

"Nice to know you. I am Charlie Duncan."

For the first time she turned fully to him. "The artist?"

"You have no prejudice against artists, I hope?"

She ignored the whimsical remark. "So you are Charlie Duncan," she repeated.

Then, again, they were walking side by side, silently. Somehow they seemed to have run out of conversation. Mary MacLean kept gazing straight ahead, curiously absorbed, as though unaware of her companion, who was furtively busy studying her profile—which again had become the mask which had so strangely perplexed him at the gallery, a mask of perfect loveliness, of ageless evenness. Only when, momentarily, he bent more closely, he noticed that fine vertical line running down her forehead, deep and sharp like an irreparable crack in a statue's alabaster.

Her voice came very suddenly. "I saw your *Wanderer in the Night*. I like it a lot."

"Thanks." He smiled at her wryly. "I sort of do myself. So we have something in common there."

"It's an excellent work, Mr. Duncan," she went on, ignoring both his flippancy and the malaise coloring his remark. "You conveyed its complex mood perfectly. I know how hard it is to produce those precise shades of gray, at the same time luminous and murky …" She noticed the surprise in his inquiring glance and responded listlessly, "Oh yes, I've been doing some painting myself."

He stopped short. "Mary McLean? That Mary McLean?" Hastily, he caught up with her. "How dense of me, not making the connection right off!"

"It's not an uncommon name." Her voice never lost its languid evenness. "No apology needed."

He shook his head and said carefully, "Some of the most common names belong to some of the most uncommon people."

"Uncommon?" she murmured after him. Imperceptibly, her steps quickened. "Everybody is uncommon. Individuality knows no duplication."

"Yours certainly doesn't." He had stopped again, this time slightly in front of her, forcing her to stop also. "I have often admired your work, quite an extensive exhibit of it, as a matter of fact. At Fisher's, and elsewhere. Some of your paintings are truly magnificent. Most of them really. They would quite hold their own even with the best of Madeleine Cranshaw's."

"You flatter me." Fleetingly the drabness of her reply was enlivened by the faintest timbre of mockery, as, sidestepping him, she continued on her way. Then, before he could protest the sincerity of his praise, she turned to him abruptly. "What about your *Wanderer in the Night?* Not too common a creation either, is it?"

When he finally replied, his nonchalance was none too convincing: "One tries, one endeavors. It's just a study of one of the millions of alienated people."

"Just one of millions, true." Once again, that trace of irony relieved the monotony of her voice. "Precisely. Just one; the uncommon one— the balance of those millions would be 'Wanderers into a Bar' or 'Into a Fix.' If people were more honest about themselves, there wouldn't be many self-portraits that could rightfully carry your painting's title."

"Whatever the title, every piece of art is in some measure a self-portrait, isn't it?" he returned tersely, a snap in his tone betraying his disinclination to pursue this subject. He felt too ill at ease about his public interpretation of the Cranshaw picture to cherish this drift of their conversation.

She nodded absently. Her eyes, which had with her last words been seeking him, slowly turned away again. Like a cloud of white, her slender hand passed over her hair in a distraught essay of straightening the iridescent scarf.

He was angry with himself. Now he had sent her creeping back into her shell; he had rebuffed her when she had ventured at last to feel her way out of it. "I've only seen your oils." He spoke hastily, searching for a way to re-establish contact. "Have you done other work? In chalk perhaps? Charcoal, pencil?" But left without resonance, his attempt was fading into an empty monotone, oddly like the rattling rhythm of a passing bus's motor, at last to fizzle into a spell of muteness.

Only a recalcitrant strand of her hair stirring with the breeze lent a touch of aliveness to Mary McLean's impassive countenance. Yet, the mask seemed so austere no longer but almost mellow with a hazy dream.

They were walking on, side by side with silence spreading between them, silence so encompassing that he gave a sharp start when she said, "I think I'll rest for a little while … that bench there."

"Would you mind …?"

"Why, no." A smile lit her features with unexpected charm. "It's nice to have company."

He let her lead the way toward the yellowing hedges, aglow with a last ray of wine-red light. The sidewalk was deserted except for a huddled couple of youthful lovers and an old man who, with his cane, was absently drawing evanescent figures on the asphalted ground.

Mary MacLean paused for an instant, as though lost in some reflection. Then she stepped to the bench, wordlessly, and waited for him to join her. Behind them sloped the wilted meadows of the park, waiting for the approach of the autumnal evening. Around them hung stillness, oddly unbroken by the hums and screeches of passing cars. The reality of Fifth Avenue seemed worlds distant.

"You're still troubling over it," Charlie Duncan heard Mary MacLean say. "Still haven't come to terms with it, have you?" His stare was a puzzled question. "With your intrusion into Madeleine Cranshaw's world. With thus throwing the door open for others to intrude as well, because you would not want any such intrusion into your own world."

It was not the very suddenness of her directness which left him at a loss for a reply; it was the implicit revelation that she had understood him all along, her quiet assuredness, which needed no confirmation.

Nor did she appear to expect any. Already carried by another whiff of the breeze, her voice came to him. "Certainly, Mr. Duncan, anybody as scrupulous about other people's private worlds has every right to demand of others a similar regard for his own."

"That was not how my remark about self-portraits was meant ..."

She cut his disclaimer short, gently. "But it might as well have been. I was intruding. I'm sorry. It was wrong. And inappropriate. *Wanderer in the Night* is just a fine title for a fine painting, that's all."

There was a subtle cadence of disappointment about her comment that touched him, a tinge of desolation, which, for all its faintness and repression, was too acute in its appeal for some resonance. This time he would not let her down, would not rebuff her again. "But you were right," he told her. "I might just as well have called it *Self-portrait*."

She said nothing, kept gazing into the twilight of a distance that knew no horizon. Only her shoulders slumped slightly, at last relenting. Then she rose, began to walk away from the bench to continue along the park without a word, not even glancing back to see if he was following her.

But she knew he would be, was aware of his presence by her side. For, traversing a patch of darkness where overhanging branches roofed off what light had remained of the parting day, she was speaking again, abruptly, as though impelled by an erratic flash from the depth of some fathomless intuition. "Not all my paintings are on exhibit. Some I keep for myself. One day, perhaps, I may have you see them."

"I'd love to," he responded, unable to restrain an inflection of urgency.

"Yes, one day perhaps," she repeated, and there was that chuckle again, pebbles rattling in a tin can, but its echo no longer seemed scurrilous now, just forlorn like a small child's helpless whimpering.

Charlie Duncan stopped dead in his tracks. "Why," he demanded, his voice husky with an emotion which defied his reason as well as his control.

"Why what?"

"You were laughing?"

"Just something that occurred to me." Her voice was even again, and bleak. "Something that made no sense."

"Things will make as much sense as we will invest in them."

"Exactly," she agreed. "There is your answer." And there was that toneless laugh again.

He started around to face her. But his impassioned rebuttal remained unspoken. For now, as they were stepping out from under the dome of trees, the parting ray caught her in its flaming radiance, turning her hair into a glittering maze of black gold and her face into a mask of limpid glass. It was not just the loveliness of its brittle contour which startled him, but, shining through its transparent pallor, the starkness of features, fervent with dreams and hopes and at once carved by disillusionment and suffering—a countenance alive alike with the scars of a devastating experience and the glimmering of indomitable yearning.

Charlie Duncan felt his lips stirring with words he did not want to utter yet could not dam up. "Perhaps if I had met you sooner, I might not have painted the *Wanderer in the Night*."

Her shoulders contracted in a shiver. "You are better off for painting it," she muttered and swung away brusquely. The rhythm of her steps became ever so slightly more hurried, but their beat ever so slightly less resolute.

Near the museum, the park side of the avenue became more populated. A girl's soft giggle would rise and ebb; a man's raucous shout; the anonymous chatter of passersby, like surf splashing against rocks, would punctuate and puncture their silence—sounds void of actuality. Real alone was the play of the waning light in the trees and their own dim shadows on the pavement.

"Then, have you decided how you're going to title that painting?" at last Mary MacLean's query broke through the cocoon, spun from the fragile threads of a timid mutuality.

He looked at her uncertainly. "I'll stick to *Wanderer in the Night*, I guess."

"Oh that; of course," she returned edgily. "I meant Madeleine Cranshaw's canvas."

His eyes fastened upon her. "Odd that you should be asking this now."

"Odd, why?"

"I was just reconsidering a title that occurred to me a short while ago." He paused, giving the stridor of an impatient car's horn leisure to lose itself in the distance. "*Prey of Shadows*. Perhaps I shall use this one; it seems like a good name for it. Or maybe I'll yet come up with one more expressive, more adequate still. I'm not sure."

"Except that *Self-Portrait* is out?"

The subtle inflection of irony irritated him. "I explained why," he said curtly.

"I remember." Stopping, she plucked a handful of leaves from a bush, only to release them one by one and watch them flutter slowly away in the breeze. "The explanation made no sense to me."

He shrugged, ill at ease. Fumbling for a cigarette, he told himself that it was absurd to give in to a growing dejection, that he had no reason for presuming, and surely no right to expect, any such concurrence. Nonetheless, somehow this exercise of logic made his disappointment no less intense, no less obstinate.

"It didn't make any sense," Mary MacLean spoke once more. "Your reverence for the privacy of Madeleine Cranshaw's experience. Of course one may respect her accomplishment as an artist, but otherwise."

A match, flaring toward the cigarette, lit his face briefly. "One might respect her for the kind of woman she was," he countered, heedless about hiding an accent of resentment.

"For the woman you choose to perceive her, rather." For all the softness, her riposte was pungent with repudiation. "That woman of integrity and moral courage may never have had any actuality. She may be a figment only of your imagination, an illusion through which you're trying to deny the truth, which you so clearly perceived. Still, for all your self-deceiving effort at ennoblement you couldn't shut your eyes, nor your mind, to the evidence that told of her rottenness, her corruption; told of the fact she sold herself. We have a name for the sort of woman she was, Mr. Duncan. That fellow with the pipe, he spelled it out all right."

He deeply drew in the smoke. For a long moment he seemed engrossed, watching the ringlets rise from his cigarette and dissipate in the air. "He spelled out what he perceived," he said at last. "But will that tell the whole, the real story? Perhaps Gerard Cranshaw appeared to promise fulfillment of her one great yearning, of her self, completely, unqualifiedly. Perhaps he appeared to be the perfect mate, the perfect subject to be in love with. So she expected to love and be loved, to give and be given. But Gerard Cranshaw never was what he appeared to be. There was no love, only possession. There was no mutual giving, only his own orgiastic fulfillment. All she was left with was the man's wealth. She had sold herself, not knowing."

"Not knowing, because she may not have wanted to know." Mary MacLean's voice was no longer colorless now, but glowing with a fierce contempt. "Has it really not occurred to you that she may quite simply have run from a difficult and unpleasant existence; that she may have determined to make her deal for an easy life and a well financed career and then contrived to enjoy the profit of that transaction, unencumbered by the ever-present reminder of her prostitution, by pretending to herself that she had married for love, thus hoping to eat the cake and have it, too?"

"Perhaps so." Charlie Duncan's shoulders stirred with a weary shrug. "Perhaps your version of the story is the correct one. But even so, it would be an all-too-human story. People make mistakes, and they will always pay for them, and pay dearly, often too dearly. That's why I would pity rather than condemn her."

Mary MacLean turned to him. He felt her eyes reaching for him, felt their surprise, their strange shimmer of humility. But it seemed like an eternity, before he heard her voice, deep and constrained. "You are a nice man, Charlie. Real nice."

She broke off very suddenly, as though she had already said too much. But she did not shrink, as he moved toward her. "If I seem so, it's you who's bringing it out," he spoke gently, and he could feel the warm throb of his breath. "You are a lovely person, Mary, so lovely. If only you could relent a little. Have just a bit more mercy. A bit more compassion."

"Compassion?" Her echo was soft and sad, a distant whisper in the wind. "How easy for you. All you know about Madeleine Cranshaw is the romantic image of your own making. Your own creature; why shouldn't her idealized tragedy command your compassion? But when you know the reality of her sort …" Her eyes roamed the distance, blindly. "I know it, Charlie. And in my book they, not the sorry lot that hang about the bars and wait around the street corners for a pick-up, are the real scum. They're a thousand times more corrupt, those wholesalers of sexual merchandise, who were clever enough to get themselves equipped with a trade license called a wedding band and a permanent customer called husband—some poor sucker for their counterfeit affection. Who, even if, in a rare moment of unwelcome self-confrontation they should perceive what they truly are, will shut their minds to their insight rather than give up their bargain, unwilling to pay for a decent and clean life with their labor and hardship, perhaps even want—but instead pay with routine embraces and sham endearments for life on easy street. Who ply their trade from behind their respectable façades, never exposed to the disrepute of their dealings. They're a thousand times as dishonest, I tell you, a thousand times more despicable, pocketing the profits of their profession without risking its hazards, without facing the penalties of social rejection—and laughing at you because they manage to eat the cake and have it, too."

Stopped by his at once dissenting and assuaging gesture, she let this last phrase fade, listened to its harshness lose itself in the twilight. Her voice had run hot with a consuming passion, which tinged its cadence with violent bitterness.

"But it's a cake for which they pay the price," Charlie Duncan was speaking quietly, soothingly. "Sooner or later they do, every one of them. That is the chapter of your version of Madeleine Cranshaw's story—the chapter in which she found out that the cake was poisoned and the poison was destroying her; found out that she had been every bit of what you maintained she was. That's in her painting, too—the pain, the suffering."

"Yes," Mary MacLean muttered absently. "Perhaps."

He went on evenly. "For that she deserves our compassion, Mary. For her courage, and honesty, and agony. She has paid the price. She may still be paying it. Perhaps a bit of compassion might help her forget, help restore some happiness to her life."

"If she is alive …" The vehemence had gone from Mary MacLean's voice, to leave only a dim trail of desolation.

"Yes, if. Let's hope she is, somewhere ."

She said tersely, "If you were right and she did face herself, she may be better off dead."

"Still unmerciful, Mary!"

"On the contrary," she answered slowly. "For what could life hold for her? Disgust. Self-contempt. Loneliness without relief." She checked herself, plucked another handful of leaves, but kept them clenched tight. "The past would never let go of her. It would stand between her and whatever new life she might have found—a wall, against which every new relationship must smash itself. She would know she was too dirty, too debauched, to repulsive to expect from any worthwhile, sensitive, decent man anything but loathing and rejection …"

His shadowy gesture silenced her, but he did not reply. Deliberately, with a rigid motion, he raised his cigarette to his lips, inhaled deeply. Then, in the rapidly descending dimness she could see the smoke rising like a spiral of blue dust, when he blew it out. "You are wrong, Mary," Charlie Duncan said at last. "So wrong! A woman like that would have a man's trust, and respect, and love. For not they are most precious who have always been impeccable and remain so, but those who fall, yet refuse to stay down; who have the honesty to admit their failure, the courage to struggle and suffer, and the strength to make themselves over again. A woman like that is clean and wholesome because she's made herself so. That's why she would earn a man's admiration, why she would be even more worthy of his love."

Mary MacLean was staring past him into some fathomless nowhere. But on her lips stood a smile. "I think you might really fall in love with Madeleine Cranshaw," she said softly.

He considered, and shook his head. "About her, I don't know. But true, I well might with a woman who would possess the personality, the character I ascribed to Madeleine Cranshaw." The butt of his cigarette was trailing through the air like a comet, to die with a sighing whir as it struck the trunk of a tree. "Ascribed," he repeated, and there was a lump in his voice. "For you were right about that, Mary. What do I know about Madeleine Cranshaw? My interpretation of the painting? A guess as good as anybody else's. More ambitious perhaps, more pretentious; but still just guesswork." Charlie Duncan nodded to himself as though he had at last resolved a quandary which had been troubling him. "You see, Mary, this is another reason why the name I devised for that canvas is no better, no more valid than any other proposed this afternoon, and for the same reason. Because the story behind that name is just a creation of my own fancies. Like any interpretation of a work of art, it is framed by the complex of the interpreter's personal experience. Of his own longings, his own needs, his own aspirations. I shall use some other title. *Prey of Shadows,* perhaps."

"It's a good title, Charlie," Mary MacLean said placidly. "But it's not the right one. You see … I did call my painting *Self-Portrait*."

Her hand, pale and transparent, rested on his, lightly, but firmly.

Brief Visit

Bob was worming his way through a desk full of work when Betty called. Hearing her voice, he was surprised—she was not given to calling his office.

"How are you doing today, dear?"

"Oh, well enough," he lied. The day had not gone all too well, but why burden her?

"Very busy, dear?"

"No more than usual, I guess. Just routine."

"Just routine. That's what I was afraid of. Even so, maybe you could manage to be home on time this once?"

"I could try. Why?"

"We have a dinner guest."

"We do?"

"Henry Johnson."

Bob sucked at his pipe; it had gone out and tasted stale and faintly bitter. "Henry Johnson. Didn't know he was in town."

"Just passing through. I was so flabbergasted, when he called, so. I felt I had to ask him over. You don't mind, do you?"

Bob struck a match and watched it flicker before he sank it into the bowl. "Of course I don't, darling."

"I'm so glad, Bob. It was a surprise. I asked him on the spur of the moment. On second thought, though, I wasn't so sure. You never seemed to think much of him."

"Didn't I? Well I suppose Henry is all right."

"All right? Oh Bob. If only you knew him a little better, you'd realize what an extraordinary person he really is."

"Quite possibly."

"This evening you may have your chance. There aren't many around like Henry. So gentle, warm, understanding. You've met him but once or twice, casually, at large gatherings. That's not the setting in which you come to truly appreciate him. It's in more intimate constellations that the real Henry emerges. When he can be himself—he will lose himself in his dreams and take you along with him. You don't know how fascinating he can be then—how he can charm beauty even from the ugly, uniqueness even from the humdrum; how he can give you such courage, such hope, make you feel you're no longer lonely, that there's someone concerned about you. Wasn't it tremendously nice of him to call up, first thing when he got off his plane from San Francisco? Call, to make you feel remembered after all those years. But then, that's just like Henry. That's how he's always been. Maybe we'll see him more often now, and you'll get to know him better."

There was a pause, a total and infinite vacuum.

"Yes," Bob said at last, flatly. "I'll come home as soon as possible. 'Bye now, darling."

He rose, stepped to the window, and let his glance stray to the sky, hazy beyond the vapors from a million flues and exhausts. Betty's voice was still ringing in his ears, ringing with a fervor that had been missing for so long. For five years and two months exactly. It did not take much figuring. Five years and two months was how long they had been married.

It was this fervor of hers with which he had fallen in love, this capacity for enthusiasm that was so much part of her person. He had adored her for the passionate urgency of her emotions, for the youthful ebullience of her commitments, for her unqualified abandon to joy and suffering alike, for the very force and integrity of her feelings. It was that quality of ardent aliveness for which he had envied and admired, loved and desired her; that intensity of happiness and despair, that spark of boundless vitality, that he had wanted around him at all times—that spark, which had been rekindled only now that Henry Johnson had returned.

Henry Johnson, who was coming to dinner tonight.

Bob shrugged to himself. It was all right with him. He had nothing against the man. Sort of strange, this Henry Johnson, but you could find no fault with his conduct. Probably a nice enough fellow, if you could take to his type. Quite gifted as a musician. A rather brilliant mind, too, though a bit phony, it seemed: too idly speculative and forever roaming. The kind that never managed to keep his feet on the ground. Too little concern about the practical exigencies of life. Just dreams. Fancies. Sentiments with which to impress people, with which to fascinate them …

Fascinate.

Somehow the word hurt Bob. There was Betty's voice, the fervor of its intonation. "You don't know, how fascinating he can be …" It was not her susceptibility to someone else's mentality that hurt him. Why should other men stop impressing you, just because you were married? Nor, even if he himself could not share her admiration, would he deny that Henry Johnson's personality was forceful and uncommon enough to exert its spell? What ached was that her enthusiasm, lost for so long, had been recovered only this afternoon.

Recovered because Henry Johnson had called. Because he had remembered her, first thing, when he arrived.

Bob drew on his pipe, but the remains of the black, charred tobacco were no longer smoldering. Absently, he fingered his pouch. His glance, restless, caught at a window across the street, at the ash-blonde secretary behind it, who, in front of her typewriter, was painting her lips with a devotion worthy of some world-redeeming cause.

Naturally Henry Johnson would remember Betty. After all, at one time it seemed, he might have been in love with her—in his own way. One never quite knew with a fellow of his type. In any event, would any man's vanity permit him to forget a girl who had so zealously admired him as an artist, so devoutly worshipped him as a man? To be wanted, desired, preferred to wealthier, more successful, socially more accomplished and prominent rivals would surely be an experience boosting a man's conceit, a memory he would always treasure. Even if that girl had eventually accepted someone else's ring. Still, Henry Johnson's knowledge that she would have been his any time, his without a moment's hesitation, without any qualification, without even considering the difficulties and hardships such a union was bound to entail—this certain knowledge would remain paramount in the catalogue of his experiences.

A lucky guy, Bob thought wearily, *who can draw on such an experience.*

His eyes lost themselves in the blue distance, dull with dust and soot. He had had a rather dismal, harassing day. Why did he have to be made to face squarely now what always had been a dimly admitted awareness of his failure? He had courted Betty, had deluged her with presents, tried to anticipate her every wish, had done his best to adjust temperamentally, to adapt his own sober outlook on life to her exuberant romanticism. Yet all the evidences of his love, all the testimonies of his devotion, all his demonstrations of self-sacrifice, when they meant to win her affection, had never sufficed to make him her first choice. It had always been Henry Johnson. It was him she would have married, if only he had been available.

But whatever one might say about him, however one might be critical of his rather unconventional ways and far-out opinions, one had to grant that Henry Johnson was a decent, honorable sort. Even though he might have been in love with Betty, he had never spoken of marriage, never even intimated its possibility. As a musician with no public acclaim to substantiate his faith in his talent, with no certain prospects but struggle and privation, with no predictable future, with no means of reasonable hope to ensure some measure of security, he had not felt ready for a permanent commitment. If he had been less scrupulous, less responsible, or perhaps just a little less diffident and self-doubting, less skeptical of his chances, he might have asked her to wait for him. And she would have been happy to waste her life doing just that. This she herself had told him in a last, desperate attempt to solicit just such an appeal from him. But he had ignored her challenge, had in fact gently but firmly discouraged her. Surely, had he then been able to foresee how soon his art was to find recognition, how rapidly and brightly his star would rise, matters might have taken a different turn. As it was, by that time she had become Mrs. Bob Willis. But naturally he would remember Betty as he had known her, so ebullient in her devotion, so lavish in her admiration, so soaring in her happiness—a Betty who no longer existed, had not existed for a long time. For five years and two months, to be exact.

This, though, Henry Johnson would not discover. That consuming vivaciousness of old, that spark of vitality had returned to her; he would find the Betty he remembered, the one he had called up, first thing as he arrived.

Perhaps from now on there might be more such moments of aliveness, Bob reflected. Something indefinable hurt him, as though the emptiness within had a sharp edge. Yes, there might be more such moments for …

"Maybe we'll see Henry more often now …"

He let his mind drift, aware that he was merely repeating an echo which had kept reverberating in the silence of the office like a sound wave arrested in its linear flight and forced to proceed in a circular path. An echo chiming with happiness and reborn vitality, beautifully pure with joy and hope; suddenly Bob found himself wishing that Henry Johnson might come more often to see them, to kindle the spark which had so long been missing.

Abruptly, he turned back from the window and sat down at his desk again. There was a stack of documents, letters, and records in which to bury his rising sense of irreversible defeat. But this pretense did not work. Against a background of futility, the compelling reality of his failure stood out, bleak and irrefutable, a milestone along the road into nowhere. Mechanically, he fingered through the papers, in the idle hope that their rustling might somehow briefly grant him an escape from his desolation. And all the while he felt how, oddly, the palpable, almost corporeal sensation of his shame and self-contempt was pervaded by a vague, shapeless consciousness of guilt, an obscure, incomprehensible perception as of some wrong he had committed. And at the same time, mingling with it, there was a yearning for that fervor in Betty's voice, for a rebirth of that wonderful aliveness that he had so loved—a humbling wish that perhaps it might become a more frequent experience now.

A dim recollection, preserved in a remote corner of his mind, grew more distinct in its refutation of that wish—a story in the afternoon paper, caught by a perfunctory glance, was gaining new relevancy: the story about the renowned pianist Henry Johnson, due in town ahead of the next morning's departure to start an extended concert tour to South America, Europe, and the Near East.

Bob sat very still: it would be a long time before Henry Johnson would come to see them again.

A strange calm took possession of him. That aimless skimming through the pile of work gave way to determined concentration. One by one, he examined those papers, thorough as always; piece by piece he laid them aside, satisfied that they were properly worded. Some of the pages did rustle, but it no longer mattered.

When he looked up, the clock showed close to six. Only now he felt his eyes straining, as the descending dusk had settled over the room. He switched the desk lamp on and, blinking, reached for the phone.

There was a buoyancy and clarity about Betty's answer, as though a sunray's glitter had been put to music.

"Look, darling," Bob said. "Just this minute Jim called. Jim Owens. Asked me to attend an emergency meeting with those people from France, tonight. God knows what's up. Must be damned important, though. Jim sounded quite agitated, which isn't like him at all. You know Jim. If he rouses himself from his apathy that way, something must be badly awry. I'm awfully sorry about dinner with Henry Johnson, but I guess I just will have no choice."

"Maybe you could join them after dinner?"

"They're meeting at six-thirty. Cocktails and dinner. I'll just have time enough for a quick shave. Tried to get out of it, but no dice. Hope you'll not be too angry with me."

"Angry," Betty repeated. "Angry, why? Of course not. It's just, because …" Her voice trailed off before she added, "But I suppose you couldn't very well refuse Jim. You don't do that to the boss, do you?"

"I knew you'd understand," he replied warmly. "You're a darling. Tell Henry how awfully sorry I am, will you?"

"Oh, you'll probably be back in time to meet him."

A tired smile stood on Bob's lips. He was glad she could not see him. "Probably," he responded carefully, gently. "Probably I will. But you never know. Such conferences, they have a habit of dragging on. Talk and more talk, most of it sheer waste of time, but you just can't get up in the middle of it … Where's that music coming from?"

"The phonograph. You can hear it? It's nice listening while getting dinner ready."

His smile grew thin and wry. He could not recall when she had last put on some music. But the gay tune, coming faintly over the wire, seemed like a perfect counterpoint to the melody of her speech.

"It sure is," Bob said deliberately. "Try to have a nice time, sweetheart. 'Bye meanwhile. And in case I should be late and you feel tired, don't stay up waiting for me."

"Take care of yourself, Bob."

He slowly set the receiver back on the fork, tasting the timbre of her voice to its last fading vibration, until it was swallowed by the silence. For one brief, aching moment, he had the feeling of being utterly deserted, but he shook it off at once and stepped to the door.

The outer office was empty except for Rex, who tried to hide his impatience behind a burst of jerky activity.

"There are some letters to mail," Bob told him sympathetically. He liked the awkward boy, who tried so hard to make good. "They're ready

The Glitter and Other Stories

on my desk. Get them, and then beat it, or your girl will think you're standing her up." He grinned at Rex and added, "No, don't wait to lock after me. I'm going to work for a while yet."

He did not stay behind for long, though. The mute loneliness of the office acted like an amplifier to the heartbeat of his restlessness. The clock kept ticking away reminders, sixty to the minute, that Henry Johnson was due any moment now. He soon decided he was not going to get anywhere this evening, working—least of all here, with Betty's picture facing him on the desk, with the phone still alive with the memory of her happy voice.

Bob got his hat and coat from the closet, turned out the lights, and locked the office. Aimlessly, he remained standing in front of the building looking down the street, crowded with homeward-bound humanity, and wondering where to go.

"Hi, Bob." About to pass, a car stopped.

"Hi, Gene."

"Is she pretty?"

"Pretty? Who?"

"The one you're waiting for."

"Very pretty," Bob said. "But it looks like she's dropped me, doesn't it?"

"A shame. But what can you do? Except ruefully go the way of all husbands: Home. Want a lift?"

"Thanks. I got my own car parked around the corner."

"Okay, then. How's the wife?"

"Fine. How's yours?"

"I'm on my way to find out," Gene said, surly. "And pronto. I'm late tonight, and she doesn't care for that. You'd better get going, too. Or the soup will be getting cold and your missus's face long. See you, Bob."

"So long, Gene."

Bob had his soup, but it was not cold. This was the best that could be said about the but slightly colored water he was served. Tired from an hour's driving through the clogged streets, he had pulled up right where he happened to pass at the time and stumbled upon this drab little restaurant. But it did not matter. The meal was just a pretense; he was paying for a place to watch time creep by. It was well past eight when he determined that he had consummated his six dollars and twenty-five cents worth of loneliness. He decided to turn a few more dollars into an even more economical investment and bought himself a license for three hours' refuge in a movie theater.

It was past midnight when he came home. The apartment lay in dark quietude, broken only by the distant crooning of a neighboring insomniac's radio and the swish of the curtains bulging with the draft. Perhaps it was the chill of the night air streaming in through windows wide ajar, perhaps the dim echo of his own creaking steps, perhaps the play of shadows on the wall: suddenly he was gripped by a sensation, as if he were moving in an alien, barren world, along a path he did not know. But when he turned on the light, he found the living room precisely as he had left it in the morning, as sober and orderly, as clean and familiar as he had found it every night for the last five years and two months. The coffee table had been cleared, the easy chairs pushed in to their proper places, the slipcovers straightened over the couch. Only the phonograph, its lid closed on hundreds of previous nights, had been left open, a record still resting on its disk, and from the vase on the mantle piece, a nosegay of roses and daffodils spread its gentle fragrance.

It was some moments before Bob proceeded. Tiptoeing across the floor, he lowered the lid over the phonograph, closed the windows, and put out the light. He felt spent and empty as he undressed, slowly, laboriously, as though buckling to some hard toil.

She was asleep when he entered the bedroom. Her head, slightly tilted, rested on one arm. Her features were smooth with a peaceful dream, her form rose and fell with her even breath. Her lips were soft with a smile, which made her face translucent with the unaware loveliness of the happy. The sudden glare of light did not seem to disturb her slumber, nor did the intensity of Bob's gaze as he stood there, greeting a Betty whom he had not seen for a long time.

Only when, under the weight of his body, the bed springs let out a groan, did she stir. Her head half veered toward him, her hand tugged the cover into place. But her eyes remained closed, as if determined not to relinquish the visions of a cloud-borne world from which she was being recalled.

"Bob?"

"Sleep, darling," he said, "I'm sorry to wake you."

"That's all right," she mumbled drowsily. "That's all right, Bob."

"Shshsh." He turned off the light. "Sleep now. Good night, sweet. Pleasant dreams."

Her whispering came through the darkness. "I was so tired, you know. Wanted to wait up for you, but … Must be well past midnight now. You stayed out so long."

"You know how time flies." His casualness was worn and phony, but it managed to drape the bareness of his self-irony.

"Henry couldn't stay long," she said. "His flight's leaving early, and he still had to see his agent. It'll be a year, maybe two, before he'll be back." But her tone was untouched by any sadness, any bitterness, as of someone unaware of any separation.

Bob made no reply. He lay flat on his back, immobile, his eyes lost in the darkness.

Her murmur was a mere suggestion of sound. "I had a lovely time, Bob."

He said evenly, "Hoped you would. Now, sleep well."

Seconds of silence dragged past him, a mournful procession of macabre thoughts.

From her bed came the rustle of pillows.

"Bob?"

"Darling?"

"I forgot to tell you. Jim Owens called. Wanted to know about the Roscoe deal. Said just to call him back in the morning."

Bob did not hold his breath; it simply seemed to cease, leaving a vastness of stillness into which he heard her whispered words fall like gentle drops of coolly soothing rain.

"Thanks, Bob. Thanks so much."

Her hand felt its way toward him and rested tenderly on his hair before it drifted down over his forehead, eyes, mouth, in a slow, delicate caress. An arm-length of dark nothingness gaped between their fatigued forms, yet there was a closeness as Bob had never known between them before.

"Good night, Bob."

Her hand receded. But the quietude of imponderable black carried her voice, made it last as a deep, sweet resonance. Muffled though it was by a new siege of drowsiness, a distant glow of fervor animated it with a strange aliveness.

"Good night, darling."

Bob listened to the melody of his own words oozing away, a few tiny, irrelevant drops of foam to be lost in the boundless waste of an ocean whose waves washed the shores of the dream islands. It was as though he were standing on an observation deck, left behind to wave after a plane that just was taxiing out, to wave farewell to someone dear, who, come for a brief visit, now was returning to that distant, inaccessible world of yearning dreams which was her permanent residence.

Noiselessly he rose. Groped his way to the window.

He still was standing there, staring out, when the first faint luminosity of dawn brightened the gray horizon. There, beyond the park, beyond the rooftops and chimneys of a dormant city rested the jet, ready to take off. In just a few hours a man would look out of the plane's window, taking leave from a fading skyline, winging toward horizons bright with the unfading memory of that last evening—a lucky man, for his journey would not be lonely.

Focus

Beyond the wall, the floor was creaking with the burden of restless steps. Forth and back, forth and back. Then, again, there was silence.

She waited for a few moments: There might be another burst of those disquieting treads, another of the intermittent spells that had been puncturing the stillness ever since she had returned, hours ago. The unpredictable inconsistency of these drumbeat sounds from the neighboring room was grating on her nerves, making it increasingly hard to bear many more such disturbances, such interruptions. Composing this note required every last effort of concentration. No merest suggestion of self-pity must creep into it, no languid sentimentalities, no maudlin bitterness, no recriminations, no *pater peccavi*—nothing that might taint the honesty and rationality of its terse, explanatory statement. It must leave no one able to attribute her action to an assault of hysteria or to doubt her mental competence in taking it.

Not that she was much concerned with the prospect of how people might come to talk about her—those few, who might trouble to talk about her at all: Perhaps her older, married sister in Seattle, correspondence with whom had been sporadic over the years and during the past several months had dwindled to naught; but then they had never been close. Possibly her two cousins, Lilian in Montreal and Charles in Augusta, with whom she had not been in contact for, she could hardly remember, how long. Even less likely—any of the meager handful of casual acquaintances she had picked up locally, a scatter of friendly irrelevance, of emotional nonentities. No, she was not concerned with their opinions; she would not be around to learn of them, anyway. Nonetheless, somehow the thought of those near strangers engaging in postmortems, advancing their diagnostic speculations and fanciful theories, pleasantly secure from disproof or contradiction, stirred her with a sense of revulsion, which was only inadequately lessened by a nuance of somber amusement: Even though they would have her own explanation, set forth in clear, sober writing, they would not credit it. They would not accept her claim, that she had determined to call it quits because she had lost her job. They would judge it far too trifling a reverse, especially since she had been fired from so many jobs before—jobs more pleasant and interesting, more highly salaried, and more promising than this last one, which, in fact, she had disliked and, but for inertia, would have quit on her own long ago. Surely, they would never be persuaded, that now, all of a sudden, a routine incident like that …

A routine incident, she repeated to herself, as she bent over the sheet of paper again. Indeed. But this was exactly the point. Failure had come to be a routine, a pattern of her existence. Dismissal from that last employment had symptomatic significance only: Once again she had flopped. No matter that she had despised its grinding boredom; she had tried so hard, she had wanted so much to hold on to that job, yet she had not managed to last on it any more than on the previous ones. Nor could she offer Mr. Davies as an alibi. True enough, he had been a mean, inconsiderate, uncouth boss, but Mr. Whiteman and Mr. Prince had been kindly, sympathetic employers, and they, too, had let her go. Even a genuinely soft-hearted man like Sam Levine would not keep paying out wages, when she could not get her work done.

Slowly, deliberately, the pen moved across the sheet: *I simply cannot see any hope of ever accomplishing anything in this life, whether in the personal or the professional sphere. My erratic flights will not allow it. Whatever the given situation and its demands, my thoughts keep straying, diffuse, disoriented, aimless, irrelevant, lost in a thousand vague problems, none of them of any importance, none even remotely justifying or excusing such wanderings. In fact, the less substantial and substantive those thoughts, the more harassing they seem, the more they are shattering my concentration on whatever the issue at hand, and thus they foreclose the achievement of whatever purpose I might have set out to pursue. And with every new instance of nonachievement, those fancies only grow hazier, more indefinite and inconsequential, yet more inescapable. It is a vicious circle in which I am trapped and from which there is, finally, no other way out.*

The vicious circle, she repeated to herself, as the pen momentarily rested on that last phrase. For as long as she could remember, she had gone round and round it; she could bear no more of it, not even for another day.

Jumping with a violent jerk of her hand, the pen was sketching a thin blue line across the sheet, a meandering, broken line, as scattered as her mind's peregrinations: Her neighbor was pacing again, forth and back, forth and back. There were no rugs in Mrs. Summers's rooming house. Every step was a resounding thump that sent her head hurting, as though it were being sawed open from inside. Exasperated, she wished that Mr. Wyatt go to hell; then, ruefully, she retracted that wish. It was not his fault, of course, that these walls were entirely too thin; through them one might hear a needle drop. Actually, she had to admit, he was the quietest sort of fellow roomer, rarely seen or heard. In fact, throughout the five months since he moved in, their acquaintance had been limited to a half-dozen exchanges of hello-how-are-you smiles when they had happened to bump into each other in the hallway. It was just as well; she did not particularly care to know him. For no specific reason—in a somewhat shy way, he seemed courteous enough. She just had no use for his stoop-shouldered, pale-faced, sad-eyed type. God knows, she was depressed enough as it was, she needed no one seconding her mood.

Abruptly, the restless tattoo of those steps died. But perversely, she found the sudden quietude as enervating as their distracting beat before. The chain of her thoughts torn, she was at a loss for a link to mend it. Her neighbor's doings were raising havoc with her concentration. But berating herself, she perceived that shifting the blame onto Mr. Wyatt was but so much self-deception. It seemed like destiny's ultimate comical joke on her, that now she could not even discipline her mind to complete this final note; for she knew that if she had been able to truly absorb herself in this project, no activities whatever on the other side of the wall could have interfered. Once again she was being thwarted by the very failure against which she had been fighting her perennial losing battle—even now, when she was affirming that the battle was irretrievably lost.

It had been a many-faceted battle. For it was not only on her jobs that her mind had been roaming afar, unbridled—her aversion to routines of drawing cheesecake advertisements and painting saccharine greeting cards would have furnished a legitimate reason. Nor was it just her inability to concentrate on her artwork, attested by scores of unfinished paintings which bespoke both her significant natural talent and its sheer waste. Though she often envied those who possessed an uncompromising drive toward achievement, recognition, public applause, fame, she would tell herself that not everyone was endowed with it, that she had to make do with not being so endowed, as best she could. It was discouraging; still, maybe one day … But it was in her personal relationships as well, and above all, that she had been failing with devastating consistency. However captivating, however genuinely engrossing her several passionate encounters had been, she had proved incapable of sustaining any of them. Her dreams and fancies would always reach beyond the actuality of her love's given object for something indispensable that was missing and still eluded her definition. She was forever groping, yet never grasping; forever searching, never finding. Again and again, trying to find an answer, she had pinpointed this lack of emotional fulfillment as the key to her professional failures. In nights of sleepless quandaries, it had seemed to her that it was those very failures that framed the debacles of her personal life. For the past desperately haunting months, she had, without comprehending the internal dynamics, come to the conclusion that the two fiascos were interrelated and somehow interdependent, and that therefore there was no hope of ever breaking the vicious circle.

From the street, remote and desolate, the long-drawn wail of a car horn rent the stillness. But she did not hear. She was gazing down on the words she just had written: *Without focus, life just has no significance.* Over and over she read it, wondering how she had come to set it down. She could not recall formulating this phrase; it did not fit into the context of the preceding paragraph. Yet there it was, in her own hand, staring at her boldly, forcefully, convincingly—and around it all the rest of her final communication seemed like mere idle embroidery, as though those few words contained the totality of her self-explanation.

They do not engrave epitaphs to suicides on stones, a morbid thought flitted through her mind; but if, by chance, they did engrave one on hers, this ought to be the text: *Without focus, life just has no significance.* For here, dragged from her subconscious to gain formulation, was the essence of all her deliberations during the past forty-eight hours. It had not been on the spur of some intolerably agonizing moment that she had come to her decision. Carefully, in a curiously pervasive mood of detachment, she had considered all the aspects of her existence, past, present, and future. The aggregate of her contemplations had rendered the verdict: there was not, never had been, never would be any focus to her life. That was why she would finish this note—the only thing she would ever pursue to its completion, she thought with sardonic satisfaction. She would sign it, swallow those sleeping pills she had cunningly conned from her physician, go to bed, and turn out the light. The vicious circle would no longer enchain her.

Still, that phrase which might be her epitaph was staring at her. *How true,* she thought. There never had been a center of transcending import around which she might have crystallized her dreams, her desires, her aspirations, her goals. Early on, many years ago, she had tried to find this within her family, but she had discovered herself being loved only as a child, as part of a tradition she was expected to uphold and perpetuate. She had never been accepted as the one she was, as an individual in her own right, as an individual who was at odds with those traditions, who would not and could not be a mere extension of her parents' aspirations. Her sister, of insipid temperament and conformist outlook, had always remained a remotely disliked stranger, an alien to her own world. At any rate, Amy had long been married in Seattle, and her parents had died in an accident eight years ago, thus once and for all eliminating even this only hypothetical and in actuality effectively unavailable center.

Again and again, her overweening need for some stabilizing polestar had led her to fancy a love that might serve as a focalizing lens for her nebulously random yearnings and impalpably hazy hopes. Pitting her wish-born illusions against the hard contingencies of a spiteful reality, she would only too readily accept whoever seemed to promise himself as the vehicle of her dreams, only to find the promise unredeemed. This persistently recurrent experience was, as she at length had come to realize, due not necessarily to her haphazard partners but necessarily to

The Glitter and Other Stories

her own unfailing lack of commitment. But somewhere, at some point, there had to be a limit to such hurtful waste, an end to self-deception and self-abuse. She must not permit any more of those foredoomed involvements. Already there had been far too many of them. And she clearly foresaw that inevitably, as long as she was around, her loneliness would drive her to repeat this sordid pattern.

The man next door was becoming active once more. Indistinct noises penetrated the wall: a chair moved about; a drawer opened and shut again; a few steps, bed springs groaning with a restless burden; then steps again, shuffling and irresolute.

Compelled by her escalating irritation at this source of constant disturbance, her thoughts scattered in that direction—that troublesome Mr. Wyatt. And suddenly it came to her, what she disliked about him: he reminded her of Frank Hogston. Not that, except for his lanky figure, he bore the slightest similarity in either looks or demeanor to that urban cowboy with his ten-gallon hat and his guitar, that third-rate imitation of Elvis Presley, who, equally obnoxious, performed around the cafés of Greenwich Village; in fact, Mr. Wyatt seemed quite the opposite of that peddler of macho conceit. Yet, irrationally, at their latest casual encounter in the hallway he had conjured up the memory of crooner Frank and his stable of adoring females, in which she had briefly included herself—conjured up also that final confrontation when she had demurred at being treated as just another face in the crowd and Frank had, with true Texan delicacy, let an eloquent glance wander up her legs to the crotch and drawled, "Well, girlie, you haven't been, precisely, a face in the crowd." When she had spit at him, he had beaten her half senseless, which exercise, she suspected too late, appeared to be the grand finale to many of his romances. Why, of all things, would she be thinking of Frank Hogston now? He was just a rotten pebble in a rotten mosaic. Because, she decided, even though her neighbor in no way seemed like that fake minstrel at all, by his intermittent activity he imposed upon, and interfered with, her fragile concentration. Gratefully she noted that the adjoining room was quiet again. She must use this respite. She bent over the sheet in front of her, poised the pen. Only a couple of lines were left now to complete her farewell.

Just as she was ready to affix her signature, she was startled by a knock at her door—a single soft knock, as though pleading for, rather than demanding, a response. She turned, stared in disbelief. Surely, she must be mistaken. Who on this Sunday evening? Nonsense! It was just her tangled nerves playing a trick on her; some random noise, which she had misjudged. No one had knocked on her door, not since Georgie Howard, her latest abortive center of interest, had walked out of it six weeks ago. Certainly he would not be back, not after the way she had shown him out; no fellow would return for more of the same, even as dedicated a glutton for punishment as he. Her nerves were getting the better of her, that was all, and if, by chance, that knock were real, she would not answer the door. These final hours were to be hers alone, just hers …

But another muffled rap made her reconsider. Mrs. Summers, no doubt. Always alert on her perch by the ground-floor window, the landlady had seen her return from her forlorn early-morning walk, which had followed an endless, sleepless night; if now her knock were left without response, the old thing, partly from nosiness, partly from genuine concern, might trouble, start wondering whether something was amiss, perhaps even suspecting …

"Come in." The invitation floated on a timbre of huskiness that seemed bizarrely foreign to its source.

The man was standing there, mute, framed by the open door, his shoulders slightly drooping, his hands fidgeting with his collar, a figure awkward with faltering embarrassment.

"Yes, Mr. Wyatt?" Her prompting cut through the curiously disconcerting silence a little more sharply than she had intended, impatiently questioning his presence, which seemed as though calculated to crown the continuous disturbances inflicted on her all afternoon; at once she wondered how that one there, on her threshold, that study in diffident dejection, could ever have reminded her of Frank Hogston.

"Hope I'm not disturbing you too much." Clearly he was struggling for words. "I ... I knew you were in, have been all the while since early in the day, when I heard you unlock the door ... So I thought, hoped, perhaps I might ask you for a favor?"

"By all means," she said edgily, unable to suppress a sardonic inflection. A favor he was asking, a favor from her, now! What exquisite timing, when all she wanted was to be left to herself and her purpose!

His courage seemed to wither in the frost of her manifest resentment. His voice fell to an even lower pitch, slightly stammering, "Just a notion, rather out of place, I guess ... but you being alone, too ... if, perhaps, you'd join me, just for a friendly drink somewhere ... maybe McBride's across the street ... anywhere you prefer—would you?"

As though pulled by a spiteful magnet, her glance ran to the paper on the table in front of her, the note she had just completed. "I surely wouldn't!" she replied, harsh with her sensation of this encounter's utter absurdity.

"Oh!" His form seemed to sag, as though in fatalistic surrender to a preordained rejection, expected as but part of an inevitable routine. "Of course, why should you? Silly of me, really. I'm sorry, Miss Reed."

As she watched him turning away, the helpless despondency of his movements awakened her to the intemperate rudeness of her rebuff and to a flitting parade of remembered occasions when her own cry for help had remained unanswered.

"Sorry, why, no reason at all!" she found herself retorting, surprised at the sudden gentleness of her words, which went out to him, strangely autonomous, live with empathy beyond her control. "No harm in asking me, inviting me out, Mr. Wyatt. In fact, quite nice of you. Only right now, I'm in no mood to make the effort of getting dressed and venture … It's too late …" Her lips twitched with the acrid awareness of the implicit irony. "Besides, I don't care much for drinks."

The man from the room next door had retreated into the hallway. He looked at her from deep, dark eyes. "It wasn't the drinks," he said absently. "Not really." And noting the flaring hostility of her frown, he shook his head unsmilingly. "No. Miss Reed. That neither. Just a human voice, that's all."

Dimly she felt ashamed of her obtuse misunderstanding, her automatic imputation. This was not another fellow making a pass at her. There was too much aching sincerity about him. "I wouldn't want to go out now," she repeated softly. "But if you feel like staying for a while …?" She faltered, as her glance caught at the sheet of paper in front of her. It was all ready, except for her signature. But there was ample time for adding it. What matter, if she swallowed those pills an hour later or two?

"That's very nice of you. Real nice," he muttered. But he did not move.

"Why don't you come in?"

He nodded uncertainly. "Very nice of you," he said once more, thoughtfully, as though he had to ponder a difficult decision, before accepting her invitation.

"Have a seat then." Her hand pointed to the pink easy chair, Mrs. Summers's pride.

"Thanks a lot." Then he sat there, awkwardly, stiffly, fidgeting with his hand. It was a while, before he spoke again. "I'm imposing on you. I ... It's quite selfish of me, but ... I only can hope you're not misreading my motive."

"You made yourself quite clear." A ghostlike smile crept across her lips and crumbled away. She rose and closed the door, deliberately, pointedly. "You were alone; and so, you noticed, was I. Just as you said. So you figured, why not try, if together we might spend the evening more pleasantly."

Her visitor was staring down at his restless finger tips. "Spend the evening more pleasantly," he repeated. "But will you? I'm afraid I was thinking of myself only, how nice it would be to have someone around, someone to talk to, someone who might listen, maybe. So ..." He shrugged, his listlessness fraught with an accent of guilt.

"So," she took up his word. "Naturally, and why not, Mr. Wyatt?"

He shook his head, slowly. "It wasn't very fair to you, was it? Trying to use you, exploit you, just because you happen to live next door. It's not really how I'd act normally. But somehow I could think of nothing but of being alone. It's silly, childish—but it seems, on your birthday it's even harder to take."

"I can see nothing silly or childish in that at all," she responded bitterly. From the hazes of the past, memories were rising up of birthdays spent all by herself or in the company of some illusion-bloated somebody, who, not caring, had been as deaf to her silences as to her monologues. "On one's anniversaries, isn't it then that one would take stock of one's life? Of the assets and liabilities ... when you need someone to go over the accounts with you, the human voice?"

"Yes." His reply was tense with muted passion. "That's when you need it most." His glance strayed, groped past her, blank and unseeing, roamed on aimlessly, and stopped. "Oh!" he mumbled, hesitantly rising from his seat. "Perhaps I'd better leave. I shouldn't have butted in here like this. You were busy writing, weren't you? Something important perhaps; I'm keeping you from finishing it."

The swift sweep of an unsteady hand turned the sheet upside down. "Just a letter," she remarked perfunctorily, fighting down a surging tide of morbid, self-baiting sarcasm. "Don't worry, Mr. Wyatt. You're not keeping me from anything. I'll just finish it later, that's all."

"Are you sure?" He looked at her dubiously, puzzled by her tone.

A moment of silence was glutted with taunting wraiths of failure. "Quite sure," she then said very firmly, very determinedly. Her fingers, intertwined by a passing spasm, relented, separated, before she added drearily. "I think I'd care for a drink now, after all. Won't take too long, putting on something more presentable."

"No need," he said quickly, stopping her incipient motion. "If some scotch will do …? I have half a bottle stowed away in my medicine cabinet." His smile was mirthless. "I'll fetch it, if you'll excuse me for a moment."

Her eyes lost in the blank white of the reversed sheet, she remained seated at the table, not stirring, captive to a sense of utter incongruity, until he returned with the bottle and a couple of glasses already bottomed with ice cubes. Silently, she watched him pour, then settle back again in the pink easy chair, holding his drink in front of him, staring at it. Still motionless, she was silent, somehow waiting for something, she knew not what—a word from him perhaps, some motion to unravel the tangled threads of mutual distress, which seemed to be grating on him no less than on her. But the word, the motion never came. At last, jerkily, she raised the glass.

"Happy birthday, Mr. Wyatt," she said throatily. "Here's happy birthday to you!"

His lanky fingers seemed to grow rigid, and the corners of his mouth warped with asperity, almost cruelty. "Thanks," he returned, his voice hoarse with acrimony. "Thanks, Miss Reed," draining his scotch in one big gulp. Then he sat there, frowning, gazing at the empty glass.

Minutes ticked away, a caravan of eternities on their spectral way through a desert of muteness. Only once that uncanny procession stopped, when abruptly he murmured, "You're very nice to me, Miss Reed, very …" without easing his rigid posture, without even glancing at her. After which that shadowy parade of silences resumed its traceless path, chilling her with a sensation of infinity, as though, amid the vastness of their uncommunicative mutuality, existence had been stripped of all reality.

In incoherent flashes, her thoughts lost themselves in a yawning vacuum of irrelevance before they could define themselves, leaving her with a growing awareness of the very absurdity of this twosomeness, of this stranger, who on his flight from loneliness had wound up escaping to the company of a corpse. To all intents and purposes, she considered death had come with her decision to put an end to her life. She was merely on leave from the army of the defunct into which she had conscripted herself.

"Care to have another drink?"

The suddenness of his question startled, almost frightened her. It took a few moments, before she shook her head. "My glass is still practically full."

"So it is." His voice was drab. "Sorry. Didn't pay any attention. But you won't mind if I have one more?" he went on, reaching for the bottle. A wry smile arched his lips. "Don't worry, even a lot more wouldn't affect me. Never does, unfortunately. Lucky guys, who can drink themselves off their senses."

"That's no way out, either," she remarked vapidly.

"Some people, most people it'll help for a few hours at least." His voice was even against the counterpoint of the scotch gurgling into his glass.

"Still, it wouldn't be your way of coping, would it?"

"I tried to make it my way, a long time ago. It didn't work. Not even for a few hours. So I figured I was better off without … Anyway, I've hardly touched any hard drink for the past couple of years. It's just today."

"Your birthday," she observed, trying to sound upbeat. "Reason enough. A birthday would call for something special, wouldn't it?"

"A birthday," he repeated, slurring the words with a weird, toneless chuckle. But his posture seemed to relax ever so slightly as he sat pondering, his eyes lost in a distance unblocked by the room's walls. "You're very sweet," he said at last, but his tone was utterly aloof, remote, impersonal, as though he were announcing some abstract, clinical finding. "Very sweet, Miss Reed."

"Nell."

"Nell?"

"Short for Cornelia. Always disliked the name. Too long, too pompous, somehow, don't you think?"

He disregarded her comment, merely raised his glass. "Martin, here. Hi, Nell," he said in the accent of a casual routine, and poured down his drink.

"Hi, Martin."

Perhaps it was the faint, melancholy whir of her glass as it touched his. Suddenly his eyes sought her, as though just now, for the first time, he had actually discovered her presence. "You're not too happy, either," he spoke slowly, carefully, "are you?"

Her head moved to elude his quiet, searching gaze. Unsteady, her hand crumpled the edge of the sheet, whose blank reverse was staring at her. Her lips were brittle with an acrid rejoinder. "I guess I'm not very good company tonight …"

The inflection of aching resentment was not lost on him. "I'm sorry," he said slowly, "I really am. I didn't mean to pry."

"But it's true!" she insisted, breathless with an overweening fear lest they come to talk about herself. "I should've known better than let you stay here with me and spoil the evening for you. Instead, you might have gone out someplace, anyplace, to celebrate with a drink, the way you had planned—might've met people who'd make a lot better company, maybe provide a bit of cheer …"

"Cheer," Martin echoed, and there again was that mirthless chuckle. "Going out, that was just a silly whim. Where to? Some bar, jukebox music, clanking glasses, half-drunk babbles, bull-session jokes? Could that have done any good? It would've kept me thinking just the same."

"Still," she protested, "it would be preferable to this. I'm making a dismally poor partner for a celebration."

"A celebration?" he repeated forlornly.

"Which seems to be the right agenda on one's birthday."

"Oh yes," he muttered in that same flat, far-away voice, "my birthday, isn't it? My birthday … She didn't even write to me."

Nell's shoulders slumped. A frosty shudder was creeping down her spine. The figure in the pink easy chair seemed to dissolve into a hazy, oddly formless blur, as though she were looking at him though a flimsy shroud woven of unwept tears. Vaguely she perceived his stiff, automaton-like gestures, as he pulled closer the small silver plate which served as an ashtray, fumbled through his pockets for a mangled pack of cigarettes, absently picked one of the king-size, then fumbled again aimlessly, vainly. Mechanically, self-unaware, she struck a match, but he did not seem to notice as she extended the light to him. He kept turning the cigarette around and around between his fingers, absorbed in its contemplation, until the flame nearly singed her and she had to blow it out. And then, with sudden vehemence, he crushed the cold, unsmoked butt against the ashtray.

"Didn't even write to me," he said once more. "I thought, on my birthday at least. But of course she wouldn't. She didn't." Another drab chuckle warped his lips, and died. "Here's celebrating for you. Some birthday! What in hell are you born for, if you can't live for somebody?" Oblivious of their activity, his fingers were still busy crumbling the tobacco in the silver tray. "Not a line from Birdie. But then, I should've expected that, after Lydia wouldn't let me send any more presents, not even on the kid's birthdays. So Birdie wouldn't feel like having to remember mine. So that, in time she'd altogether forget that her father was born at all. Maybe that would be for the best, anyway, if she did forget. No divided loyalties, no emotional dilemmas. Still …" He shrugged wearily. His palm slid across his brow furtively, as though to wipe it clear of the memories that had furrowed it. "Who knows, Lydia may be right, though. The dead don't celebrate birthdays anymore, do they?"

As though responding to some magical command, Nell groped for the bottle, poured another drink for him wordlessly, with a hand that suddenly had found strange, sure steadiness. Moving with a mechanical reflex, he reached for the glass, took a sip from it. "This December it will be four years we've been separated," he muttered, staring down at the brownish liquid. "Four years ..."

And then he talked. Not to Nell, not even to himself. Just talked, talked ... Of Lydia. Their meeting at the bank, for which they both used to work. The days of their hectic, hungry love. The beautiful two years they had lived as husband and wife. The birth of little Katie, fondly called Birdie by them.

Of the war. The farewell from Lydia and the baby. Vietnam. His life in the army. The heat, the jungles, the pestilences. The bamboo-hut villages, burned and ransacked. The massacres of innocents. The misery, the devastation. Pete Golden, his best buddy, whom he watched dying, with his face blown off. The two natives he killed with his grenade, never comprehending why he had been told that those people were his enemies. The weeks in the field hospital after a bullet had had his name on it.

Of his discharge, with a citation for honorable service to a dishonorable cause. His homecoming. Homecoming? The shock of discovering that there was no home, that after all those interminable months of dreaming and longing for her, he had become a stranger to Lydia and, worst of all, of knowing that she was right, that indeed he was a stranger, that the man who had returned was not the man who had left but someone harsh with bitterness, someone with a scarred, brutalized mind, someone who drowned himself in liquor to anesthetize his memories but could not drown them, someone she could not love, someone whose touch repelled her, someone she came to hate ...

Abruptly Martin Wyatt fell silent. He bent forward, tensely, as though he were trying to capture the echo of his own words, which, from faltering, stammering beginnings, had steadied themselves into an unrestrained flow of quiet coherence. His features wore an expression of incredulous astonishment as his eyes, roaming, paused to fix themselves upon the girl by the table, clung to her, alive with sudden wondering awareness.

His gaze sent a shiver through her: That stranger in the pink easy chair was a blur no longer, indeterminate and remote. He was real now and close, as though he had stepped from behind an obfuscating cloud into the sudden glare of floodlights to face her, confront her. That shiver spread, took increasingly hold of her, made her wish she could escape from the silent, intense scrutiny of those dark, pained eyes and the ceaseless refrain they sent pulsing through her mind, a compelling rhythm of words he had spoken. "What in hell are you born for, if you can't live for somebody? What in hell are you …" Incongruously, fear was haunting her, fear that somehow he might find out about her, about that note on the table, about the pills. Hastily she turned away, trying to elude his searching glance.

"Some more?" she asked, pointing a fidgeting finger at the bottle.

He shook his head, his features still taut with that mien of wondering incredulity. "Things don't seem half as bad if you can talk about them," he said very softly.

"I'm glad, Martin," she murmured.

"And if someone's listening," he added in an even lower tone, half to himself, dropping back in the easy chair, limp with deep, placid relief, as if, for the first time in a long, insufferably long spell, he was able to relax at last. And then, quietly, soberly, as though such a revelation were the natural response, the only one appropriate to this evening's companionship, he went on telling her.

About those harrowing months of a daily ineluctably widening estrangement, that climactic hour, when Lydia had told him that it was all over, that she despised the one he had become. About his own slowly dawning realization that the total of the war's casualties equaled the total of troops deployed; that the men who came back were all invalids; that given the traumas of his experiences, he could not be, except the one he had become, the one to whom Lydia could never find the way back, though, for Birdie's sake, she proposed to have him stay to keep up the appearance of a common home, provided.

About the torment of sharing the household with Lydia without living with her. The futile, self-destructive drinking sprees in which he sought relief from his loneliness and deprivation. About the growing contempt and hostility greeting his returns from those abortive escapes. The ever more frequent quarrels and bursts of violence.

About Billie, who happened to cross his path when solitude had become unendurable. The illusion of affection he bought from her with gifts and more gifts, all the while aware of his folly yet incapable of dispensing with the erotic dope, which for brief hours would bestow a pittance of oblivion. The final blow-up when Lydia found out about Billie. The separation. The divorce. The court's verdict, awarding the child's custody to the mother and, because of his immoral conduct and demonstrated proneness to violence, restraining him from any further physical contact with either.

"And now Birdie won't even write to me on a birthday," Martin said, and his mouth hardened. "Not even Birdie. It's Lydia's doing. For three years I kept trying for a reconciliation or at least some viable compromise. But Lydia refused, insisted on strict adherence to the court's decree. Perhaps, who knows, there's another man in her life now, a better father for Katie … She'll be eight next spring, growing up without me, not needing me. But of what significance, of what value is one's existence, when one isn't needed? Seems, the way things have gone, as far as Birdie is concerned, I might as well be dead. As far as anybody's concerned, for that matter." His shoulders moved with a slow, painful shrug. "By now, usually it's not bothering me all that much any more. That's just the way the cookie crumbles. My cookie. You get used to anything. Working, too, working hard does something for you: It keeps you from thinking too much. Just some days it seems too much to take, that there's no one."

"No one?" As though from a foggy distance, an echo came to Nell, the echo of a phrase, compellingly recurrent, yet too remote to be articulate. "No one?" she repeated searchingly, straining for that phrase to formulate itself, disclose its meaning.

"Oh that!" Martin replied, irritably defiant with disdain. "Sure, there's always someone—people; fellow workers; guys you say hello to, join at lunch. Some of them decent enough, but still a bunch of ciphers, aliens. What significance can people have for you when they don't speak your language?"

"But it's almost four years, you said, that you have been separated?" She broke off sharply, terrified by her sudden awareness of a suggestion she had not intended, but

which had insidiously crept into her question—a challenge that was so utterly inane, because only the living had a right to venture it, not the dead. There, on the table in front of her was the certificate of this inanity, the last pronouncement of a corpse on furlough. But Martin Wyatt appeared not to have apprehended that treacherous quaver in her voice. He never even looked at her. And she was glad, gratefully glad.

"Plenty of time to find myself a girl, you mean?" A dreary smile faded across his lips. "Sure, there's no dearth of ready supply. For kidding around, a date on Saturday night, a movie, an occasional one-night stand. That's all … all that could be another Billie only. A girl that does not mean a thing to me really, what good could she do me?

And one who might get to mean something to me, that's just the kind to keep away from. The way I am, have come to be, I'd make her only unhappy, miserable. Lonely, wasting herself, she'd be hopelessly confined to the periphery of my life. For that's the only spot she could occupy. There's just no room in the center." He nodded absently, the corners of his mouth twisted with melancholy irony. "Lydia. I guess I'm still stuck on her."

Nell stared at him, sightlessly. That echo had now broken through the fog, mocking her with the phrase she had committed to that upside-down sheet: *Without focus, life just has no significance,* this restless echo was whispering, *without focus ...*

"You're lucky," she murmured, in spite of herself.

He did not hear her. He seemed absorbed in listening to a distant church clock striking the hour. When the last sound had died away, he checked his watch. "I'm sorry," he said guiltily, "I really had no idea I had kept you up so late."

"Oh, that's quite all right." But her gesture was too slow to stop him from rising.

"No, it isn't," he insisted. "You'll be short of sleep, and tomorrow's another workday,"

"Tomorrow ..." she said, and her shoulders contracted. "Never mind tomorrow."

"Today, rather," he amended, with that same inflection of culpable concern. "Today already, for a couple of hours now. High time you get some sleep at last."

"Don't worry, Martin," Nell said. "I'm going to get all the sleep I want."

She saw his lips move with some reply, but its sound and meaning were lost, drowned out by that relentless echo. *Without focus, life has no significance ... without focus ...* now rising above a haunting counterpoint. *Of what significance, of what value is one's existence, if one isn't needed ... what significance, what value?*

"Good night," Martin Wyatt had moved to the door. His voice now came to her full and clear again. "Good night, Nell."

She did not rise. She watched him fuss with the doorknob, which, oddly, did not seem to work. "Good-bye, Martin," she answered listlessly.

He turned around once more, hesitatingly. "And thanks a lot," he added uncertainly, his glance seeking her. "An awful lot, really. I think you can't even guess what you've done for me."

"Sure, I've drunk some of your scotch." She was shamefully aware of how lame, how bedraggled her joke was. But no matter, if only it would tune out the sudden fervor of his tone and dispel the vibrant suspense, which, incongruous yet compelling, was gripping her.

He generously passed over her beggarly quip. "I haven't felt this quiet in years," he went on slowly, deliberately. "Not this relaxed, at peace with myself. There's never been anyone I could talk to the way I've been talking these past hours. That's why."

"Anybody might have done as much for you."

Martin Wyatt shook his head. "But you were listening, Nell," he said in accents of a strange solemnity. "You were listening. That made the difference. Only now I realize, how desperately I needed ... someone listening, someone speaking my language. I wish ..."

She knew he was talking on, talking to her. But his words had become mere sound, distant and unintelligible, submerged by the echo that was closing in on her, engulfing her with its ceaseless repetitions of that same phrase, which she herself had unwittingly composed—the phrase, which, strangely mild and soothing now, was rising above a counterpoint, which no longer was haunting but tranquil and sweet. *Without focus,* sang the echo, *without focus life just has no significance.* And merging with it into one wholesome harmony, the counter-voice answered. *But if someone needed you, wouldn't there be significance? If someone needed you ...* "What do you say, Nell?"

Perhaps it was the sound of her name, that startled her into responding to him; perhaps that accent of anxiety, which imparted to his question a tense, high-pitched edge.

"What do I say?" she repeated, bewildered.

His reply was a hesitant plea. "I know I keep imposing, asking you. But it would mean so much to me, if we could spend time together again ..." His voice lost itself. Leaving only its diffident, humble echo. His hand still clenched around the doorknob, he stood there, slightly stooping, waiting for her verdict.

She never pronounced it, but faintly, a soft smile curved her lips.

He sensed it more than he saw it. His form seemed to straighten, and his speech came more evenly, confidently, almost boldly. "We could have dinner somewhere. You name it. Tonight I'll be off at five. Your job keeps you until six, doesn't it? So I could pick you up there, right after you're through."

"No," she said quietly. "I lost that job. You'd better wait for me here. I may be late, it's hard to be on time, being on the go, looking for a new position."

"Right," Martin Wyatt agreed. "I'll be waiting. And thanks, again."

"Thanks, for what?"

"For existing," he said softly, vibrantly. His hand was no longer fussing with the door knob. It seemed to have suddenly discovered the mechanism. "Good night for now, Nell."

"Good night, Martin."

The door opened. A current of draft swept through the room, took hold of a square white sheet on the table, carried it on its fluttering, rustling flight, until it dropped it to a rest on the floor, its unsigned legend face-up.

Nell did not notice. She was watching a lanky figure, erect now and vigorous, stepping beyond the radius of the light into the dimness of the corridor.

Nine Poems

1.

And there we sat, confounded by the past,
the flow of time since we consorted last,
ensnared by thoughts of what occurred and when,
by the chimera of the word 'again,'
deluded by the fraud of the 'before'—
as though the past were that which is no more,
and not the bottomless, internal store
of myriads living, haunted 'nows,'
that, even as we breathe, still grows;
that will not let us spurn one single now.
Dim though we might, we could not douse its glow;
once lit by life, it will forever burn:
That which has never left cannot return.

2.

And as you look at me, your eyes uncover
that which you are beyond that which you seem:
The little mother and impassioned lover,
and the eternal journeyer for a dream.

And as you smile at me, you come to reach me,
for in that smile you lay your yearning bare.
It is this bareness which contrives to teach me:
There is a child in you; the child needs care.

3.
The Ballad of the Old Shoe

There was an old shoe that sat on a shelf
in the midst of discarded clutter,
resolved to the prospect that soon itself
would follow the rest to the gutter.

It had been so long that last it was worn,
and always in filthiest weather:
so it got wrinkled and slightly torn,
and the color had gone from its leather.

Its style, and that was its destiny's root,
was too old to be gladly admitted;
so it would pass on from foot to foot,
yet to none ever properly fitted.

Whoever had tried it would put it away,
for its oddness proved disconcerting;
it seemed it could serve for no more than a day,
for somehow it would be hurting.

There was an old shoe, desolately bemused
with its uselessness's idle awareness,
until a girl thought it might be used
to shield her foot's shivering bareness.

She put it on, and lo and behold,
it felt as though made to her measure
and suddenly neither odd nor old.
And to her foot, now no longer cold,
its comfort became a treasure.

The moral of this: No shoe on a shelf
is ever so odd to be tragic:
There may be a foot, perhaps odd itself,
that will disclose its magic.

4.

There is the hour, stunned by disbelief,
when one whose breath was part of our own
has gone, returnless, and left us alone.
There is the weeping hour, deep with grief,
racked with the pain of unredeemed despair,
of unwalked valleys, mountain peaks unscaled,
of dusky roads we, fearful, did not share—
a grief that can bewail but not repair,
that is atonement for the lives we failed.

5.

Dreams

Dreams are the stuff of which your eyes are made:
dreams darkened by a pain that would not fade,
but luminous with the purples of desire;
dreams haunted by the ghouls of past despairs,
of wasted years and unrequited cares,
yet left aglow with passion's undimmed fire.

Dreams are the stuff of which your eyes are made:
dreams daring still with hopes, and yet afraid
to trust yourself to their enchanting power;
dreams once thought dead, when they were but asleep,
and now, aroused, are rising from the deep,
to find, if you but will, their ultimate flower.

Dreams are the stuff of which your eyes are made:
dreams of a morrow, when all ghosts are laid.

6. Across a Telephone

There was your voice, a-dancing on a wire,
gossamer like a fairy's silhouette
abandoned to the rhythms of desire,
gyrating with subtle seduction, yet
masking the glimmer of a wondrous fire.

There was your voice, in tones of everyday,
yet vibrant with a festival's breathless strains,
its song of hope and happiness still prey
to counterpoints of unforgotten pains,
of dreams unanswered, longings gone astray.

7. Drum Song

The recruiters came to the town one day—-ratataplam, ratataplam,
and they took with them my love away—-ratataplam, ratataplam.
On the banners there was vict'ry written—-ratataplam, ratataplam,
yet my loved one, he with death was smitten—-ratataplam, ratataplam.
Heard the drums roll well from far so muffled—-ratataplam, ratataplam,
our emp'ror, he returned unruffled—-ratataplam, ratataplam.

Curt Maury

8. Slum

And the evening hangs over the town,
and the stores are all silent and closed now,
and the windows are blind and dull,
and the walls are quite cold and bedraggled.

And the backyards are sticky and damp,
and everything around is inferior.
And the people are tired and worn
and are all o'er a thousand years old.

9. Little Song

A house and a garden, a forest and field,
and cupboards of jewels and bags full of gold,
if Heaven granted all that I could wish—
yet were there no love on earth, 't would leave me cold!

A gold-adorned throne and a powerful state,
and emperor, king, any honor I sought,
if God would give me all power and might—
yet were there no love on earth, all would be naught!

The mountains, the valleys, the rivers, the lakes,
yes, if Heaven granted the whole earth to me,
I'd languish in sadness and mourning away,
for were there no love on earth, I'd not agree!

And were I to fly up to Heaven one day
and came there to kneel in front of God's own throne,
enjoyed fully all the ineffable bliss—
yet were there no love up there, I'd fly right home!

Encounter in the Sunset

Unhurriedly moving past, the scenery was greeting her with a vague familiarity, which, insistent with its appeal to carefully nurtured and increasingly treasured memories, was fraught with new emotional significance and pulsing excitement. Somehow, the invariable alternations of vast fields and sleepy villages, of clusters of dilapidated huts and tiny colonies of simple but well-kept cottages, of quiescent palm groves and small, busy countryside bazaars—islands of contrasting vitality and an expanse of crushing, foul-smelling wretchedness—no longer evoked that sensation of utter, bewildering and distinctly repelling alien-ness that had weighed on her four years ago when she had first glimpsed this landscape through the window of the tour bus. The sights along the trunk road had not changed—yet now they seemed pregnant with a suggestion of some arcane intimacy, of some oddly homey belonging.

The taxi had moved out of the narrow, tangled streets and the noisy, crowded marketplace of Khurda. Appointed by the Government Tourist Office to fetch her from the airport, it was proceeding at the cautiously leisurely pace, dictated by bustling traffic, interspersed with idly wandering cattle and, here and there, the blocking hulk of a lethargic water buffalo by the fissures in the road surface. The driver, a short, stocky man with a jolly face who had introduced himself in broken English as Kamesh, was piloting the vehicle expertly past the recurring obstacles, undisturbed by the pendulant swings of the idol Ganesha, his elephant-headed divine protector, suspended above the windshield. He was humming a strangely unmelodious tune, interrupting it only occasionally to wave at a passing trucker, and leaving her to herself.

She was grateful for his ready perception of her wish and need for privacy. Ever since the morning, when, after a restless night in the airport hotel at Calcutta, she had boarded the plane for the one-hour-and-twenty-minute flight, she had been preoccupied with fantasies about the prospective return-encounter, one so different, so wondrously different from their meeting four years ago. Her reveries had projected a seemingly endless diversity of possible dreamy scenarios, each glowing with the halo of fulfillment. It must be that expectation, she thought, that was endowing the passing scenery with its new, comforting aspect and its new, exhilarating meaning; the mystical promise of the beckoning experience that was transforming India's countenance for her.

The car was slowing down, inching its way into a larger township, alive with the hubbub of trucks and bullock-drawn two-wheeled carts and bicycles, finally coming to a stop next to the gutter separating the road from one of the small tea stalls—a hole in a two-story dwelling's wall, fronted by a couple of rickety wooden benches.

"Balugaon," the driver said, turning to his passenger. "Short rest. Chai. Lady, chai, too?"

"Chai?"

"Ah … Tea," Kamesh interpreted with a demure smile.

"Oh yes." She remembered: the sweet tea and milk, brewed in a pouch, the standard native refreshment. Brought to a boil, it was quite a safe drink, she had been reliably told, even when served in a setting of a ramshackle, not-too-clean-looking place like this one; and, as experience had taught her, it was an excellent antidote to heat and thirst. Still, although her throat felt rather dry, she would not venture. "No, thank you, not now," she replied, leaning back in her seat.

"Five minutes," Kamesh said, "me come back."

She hoped so. Experience had made her aware that Indian minutes, like estimated distances, had a way of extending exceedingly. She tried to suppress a flutter of impatience as she watched him cross over to the stall and immediately involve himself in an animated, though apparently friendly, argument. Leaning back, she closed her eyes in a futile attempt to recapture the last chapter of her interrupted, fugitive fantasy. When she opened them again, a goat was sticking his head through the open window, inspecting the steering wheel and, judging it inedible, departing. Only then did she notice the children, half a dozen of them, pressing toward the car—small, bedraggled figures with their hands outstretched. Her wandering glance caught at a girl among them, a frail thing in a tattered green sari; she might be nine years old or twelve, there was no telling about this hollow-cheeked face with the sad, knowing eyes, which wrenched her with a memory of Jenny ... Jenny. Searching her pocket, she found no coins, just a few crumpled single rupee notes. She distributed them and harvested a bounty of shining smiles.

The little girl shyly touched her hand. "Lady good," she whispered, clutching her rupee bill.

Jenny, Barbara Easterly thought, and the pain inside her was sheer acid. *Jenny ...*

There were more children now, crowding close, attracted by the rapidly spreading news of unexpected largesse. But Kamesh chased them away, gently but firmly. "Not all poor," he explained, climbing behind the wheel. "Foreign lady. Take advantage. Rupee too much."

He shook his head thoughtfully and started the car. "Lady American?" he asked.

"Yes, American." She wished he would not talk.

"New York?"

"No," she replied curtly. "Reading."

"Read ... ing?"

"Near Philadelphia."

"Ah, big city, too."

Philadelphia ... Jenny ... That little dark-brown girl in the torn green sari, looking at her from those bitter, knowing eyes ... 'Lady good,' a touch of a feeble hand ... Jenny ...

Jenny.

*

She had always felt very close to her niece, had loved her with the hungering passion of a woman constitutionally deprived of motherhood, loved her as the unconceived child's surrogate. From the moment of Jenny's birth, her emotional life, left so largely untapped, had revolved around her younger sister's infant. Only with difficulty had she restrained herself, curtailed her visits to Gloria's home in Philadelphia, from fear lest her possessive affection hurt her sister, wake in her a jealousy that might turn against the intruder into her own sphere of happiness. And even on her sparsely spaced visits she would achingly compel herself to keep a safely tended distance from the growing child.

Sometimes restraining herself with an almost unbearable effort, she had managed to perpetuate this self-imposed aloofness, when, after

Kenneth Easterly's lethal accident left her so prematurely widowed, Gloria had prevailed on her to dispose of her house in Reading and move in with them. She had managed, but at the price of ever-increasing stress. With every phase of her development, Jenny revealed more of the traits akin to her own—a gentle dreaminess reminding her of her own childhood and growing years, a bent of mind so like her own inwardness. Still, she had managed, despite the increasingly irrefutable evidence that intuitively Jenny, too, sensed the cogency of this affinity and was responding to her aunt with an uncommon adoration, the extent of whose intensity she instinctively concealed from her mother. Unspoken and divulged only in secretive glances and small, subdued gestures of tenderness, the bond between the two of them had deepened to an intimacy, which, at times threatened to undo the precariously preserved distance and seemed to leave no option but the escape of temporary separations.

She watched unseeingly the alternations of the scenery flit by. The panorama of India's eastern coastal flatlands was but one of the many that had previously served to mitigate the loneliness of those escapes. Her mind was occupied by the vast variety of sights and impressions that she had always craved, but that throughout her married life she had had no chance of indulging. Kenneth Easterly had shared little of her own interest in foreign peoples and lands, in alien cultures and lifestyles—an interest that had broadened since her college days. Left with his substantial legacy, she had been free to gratify her long-stunted inclinations. She had visited most of Europe, Egypt, Japan, and, once before, of course India; everywhere, for all the plethora of novel and fascinating discoveries, for all the at times overwhelming impact of the beautiful and the bizarre, there always had been the presence of Jenny, of an affectionate smile, of deep dark eyes veiled by a strange searching sadness, a faintness of some somber anticipation—like the hungering eyes in the hollow-cheeked face of that child in the tattered green sari.

*

The abrupt stop of the car jolted her from her ruminations. She bent forward, scanning the climbing road ahead for the herds of cattle on their treks to the market, the stubbornly uncooperative water buffalo, the overturned truck—for any of the common obstacles which might be responsible for the sudden halt. But as far as her eyes could reach, the passage seemed entirely unimpeded.

Kamesh had already stepped from the vehicle. "Lady excuse," he said humbly, "here puja."

She frowned with puzzled impatience, but as her glance followed his pointing hand, she recalled that puja meant homage, devotion. Apparently the small rotting and half-crumbling structure by the road's edge figured as the object of her driver's piety. She watched his measured walk toward it; watched as, on his way across, he bent down to pick a few of the white flowers from the curbside greenery, place them carefully inside the shrine, and, from a cup, pour some of the water he kept in a jar for cooling the motor, then stand there, hands folded in front of his lowered brow. Intrigued and captive to an unburied memory, she alighted and trailed after him.

He had heard her footfall and turned.

"May I?" she asked softly.

He nodded, his face lit with an inviting smile. "Lady come," he said simply.

She peered into the interior of the wooden shelter at the idol: a rather shapeless,. vermilion-tinted stone with superimposed painted tokens of eyes and nose that produced an oddly surrealistic suggestion of a grotesquely uncanny countenance, hiding some weird, ghostly mystery. But she was no longer chilled, appalled, perturbed, as she had been that time so long ago when a similar image of a godhead had confronted her for the first time. Curiously, now it instilled her with an indefinable but undeniable sense of comfort, an unfathomable sensation of irrational comprehension and internal security. Noting the iron-wrought, red-glittering three-pronged symbol at the image's side and recalling the countless similar indicants of divine presence and the attendant explanations, she asked. "Shiva?"

Kamesh shook his head. "This, no. This Ban-Durga, goddess of woods, jungle." And, expanding his reply, "This Khallikota Ghat—mountain road; danger sometimes. Ban-Durga protect; make good trip, Lady be safe."

She smiled at him. He had offered his puja for her sake as much as for his own. For all his contrasting physique, he reminded her of Ramlu. Would he be there, too, when she arrived? When she arrived …

It would not be long now, an hour and a half, two at the most, depending on the traffic, the impediments, and on Ban-Durga's favor. Impulsively, she cast a glance back at the time-worn, moldering sanctuary of the goddess. Halfway up the hill the road crossed. Strangely enough, it occurred to her, four years ago the guide had not pointed it out to the tour group, even though the bus had stopped almost precisely at this very spot to allow its passengers a vista of Chilka Lake, which, an immense, stagnant surface of greenish-blue, stretched below into the horizon. That guide, a plump, pompous man who had introduced himself as Mr. Pradeep Appaya and had taken pains to identify himself as a Kshatriya, a member of the princely warrior caste, had interminably, indeed sometimes redundantly, held forth about the temples of Bhubaneshwar and Puri and the one of Konark, too, although in that case his references to the incredible profusion of the figures had been somewhat studiously perfunctory and constrained—quite appropriately so, as she then had thought. Mr. Appaya had never tired, though frequently he had been tiresome, delivering his detailed recitals about the lords of the Hindu pantheon and the myths associated with them. Yet, whether from inexplicable ignorance or considered judgment that an idol of such primitive, unrefined aspect was not worthy of attention, he had utterly disregarded this modest focus of her driver's reverence; just as he had stopped not even once to point out, much less to discuss, any of the ever-present objects of the local population's devotion, any of those flimsily sheltered images, which, sometimes hidden behind bushes but just as often readily accessible right at the edge of the road, had lined the tour's route. What a curious omission, she pondered, settling back again in her seat. Or was it really so curious? Vaguely she suspected the reason for Mr. Appaya's default; dimly, in some recess of her mind, the answer was nestling. But there was no need to pursue it now; surely Leonard would clarify it for her, explain it fully in his quiet, knowing way. She must not fail to mention it to him.

To Leonard Jordan, whom now but an hour and a half, or two hours at most, were separating from her ... Leonard Jordan, to whom she was coming all the way from America ... to whom she was coming, never to leave again.

Echoing through her mind, the phrase suddenly struck her with the full, merciless force of its utter absurdity—struck her yet more overpoweringly, more irrefutably than that time before, when, just airborne out of Cairo, the realization of her venture's incredible incongruity had assaulted her with paralyzing anxiety, at last to crystallize itself into the decision to cancel her onward flight as soon as she arrived at Delhi and return home on the next available plane. There had seemed then, as it seemed even now, no viable alternative to undoing the preposterous illusion governing her heedless, inane impulse, which had taken possession of her a few days earlier: to come to Leonard Jordan and never to leave again.

To come to a man, whom she had known for exactly four days, and with whom there had been no contact whatever for four years—none, not even one letter, one token of remembrance, one sign of life. True, Leonard Jordan had had no way of writing to her. In the rush of events, she had failed to give him her address. It had been up to her, knowing that every winter he would be returning to Gopalpur, she might have reached him. But for the first year or so after their encounter, she had been incapable of transcending the bitterness of her disappointment, incapable of even contemplating a possible bridge across the abyss that had sprung up between them; when at last the acid of her antagonism had slowly, gradually worn off and a distant, tentative glimpse of such a bridge had offered itself on the far horizon, she had judged it as yet too fragile, too precarious for a commitment, which, she knew, a resumption of contact would, indeed must, imply. And when, in the aftermath of her Jenny's demise, impelled by the twin onslaughts of devastating grief and desperate alienation, that bridge had assumed full, clear, indubitable distinction, a bridge strong and firm, solid and sure to sustain such a commitment, there neither had been time nor could she have brought herself to essaying a communication, which, by the very nature of a four years' interval of silence, would have had to be detached and noncommittal. She could not write such a letter, not to Leonard Jordan …

Then, just a few frenzied days ago, she had glimpsed the way to traverse that bridge, the only way. Two days later, she had been on the plane to India. On that flight out of Cairo the awareness of her impulse's frantic ineptitude, now redoubled in its intensity, gripped her anew, petrified her. Yet on her arrival at Delhi she could not, would not turn back. More powerful, more persuasive than her logical assessment of this journey's implausible quest, there was her irrational certainty of its impulse's intrinsic validity, her absolute expectation of ultimate fulfillment—an expectation shaped by those wondrous and traumatic days that had begun on the twelfth of January in that seaside hotel at Gopalpur, which now, on another twelfth of January four years later was her destination; an expectation sustained by her intuitively unequivocal knowledge of the man Leonard Jordan was, of the person which had revealed itself through his every word and gesture and action, the memories of whose minute details time's passage had not dimmed but, on the contrary, contoured still more starkly for her, still more tangibly, more yearningly compelling, the memories she was now once again hauntingly resurrecting.

*

At high noon, the bus halted in front of the sprawling one-story complex chosen as the group's home for a spell of rest and ocean bathing which was to conclude the tour of northern India. The appreciation of the elaborate welcoming lunch had been minimized by weariness from the long ride in the heat—in spite of the midwinter season well up in the eighties—and by the impatient eagerness for an extended swim and an even more extended respite on the beckoning beach. But that eagerness had been severely dampened by the guide's stern warning of the punishing sunburn and some possible graver discomforts which exposure to the powerful dosage of ultraviolet in the midday sun's rays would make a virtual certainty. The warning had induced a fretful retreat to the fan-cooled quietude of the room she shared with Ann Glyn, a companionable enough if rather loquacious divorcee from Cleveland a few years her junior. Indifferent, idle hours had passed in waiting for tea time and the subsequent, comparatively safe, enjoyment of the clear waters and fine, powdery sands, replete with a view of the fishermen in their characteristic, oddly shaped high hats, who, some hundred yards distant along the beach, spread their nets in preparation for the next morning's catch.

Half dozing, she had lost track of the time. Only when a couple of beggarly children stopped by to offer necklaces of seashells strung up on a thin thread, smiling in the hope of their pittance of reward, she became aware that most of her tour partners had already left the beach. Shaking herself free of the sand, she slipped into her robe and started up the gentle incline toward the terrace and the oddly beguiling interplay of contrasts: while one half of the framing lime-washed arcade was already wrapped in the first shadows of the lowering dusk, the other half was resplendent with a deep, carmine glow. By the low fence, which separated the beach from the hotel grounds, she stopped to discover the source of that unearthly brilliance; she stood there, overwhelmed by the unbelievable beauty of an iridescent sunset, a display of ever-changing luminosity, such as she had never seen. It was perhaps only for seconds that she gazed at those gradually altering, purpling tints, but they seemed timeless.

"This sunset," a voice in back of her remarked, "magnificent, isn't it?"

She only nodded, still too enraptured to even turn.

"I must've watched it a thousand times," the voice continued, "and still the thousand-and-first time is as singular, as enthralling, as incredibly lovely as the very first one. Oh, there are beautiful sunsets in many places, but none quite like this—no, none quite like this."

Now at last she broke herself, rather unwillingly, from her captivation, to turn to the speaker. "Watched it a thousand times," she took up his phrase. "You live here?"

"Only temporarily," the man replied. "New York is my permanent... residence. But these last ten years I've spent my winters in this part of India. Hence those thousand times," he added, pointing toward the horizon, where the sunset was already dimming, paling, merging with the evening's semidarkness. "I can see the experience of this spectacle has done to you what it did to me the first time and keeps on doing to me. As often as I've stayed in this place, I've never missed observing the sunset. Somehow it gives me strength and faith to store up against the rest of the year back … at my New York residence."

She had not missed the slight, now repeated hesitation. There was some strangely vibrant significance filling that brief hiatus, and it compelled her question. "You do not call it home?"

"No," he said softly, "for home is where we love."

She stared at him. Only now she fully beheld his chiseled face with its high forehead, its calm, deep-set eyes, its firm mouth; beheld his spare and bony, well-proportioned, medium-height figure, and long-fingered, finely shaped hands. But it was not his quiet, unobtrusive handsomeness nor even the deliberate earnest of his reply, it was the compound of serenity and sadness, of unrealized yearning and internal contentment, which invested the cadence of his phrase with a passionate verity, which touched off an echoing resonance within her, a sudden pervasive, overpowering counterpoint. Of all the oppressive sultriness that had descended with the onset of dusk, she felt a chill gripping her, freezing her into a spellbound incapacity to turn her gaze away from him.

Something was happening to her, something she instinctively acknowledged yet found beyond her intellectual grasp, an experience heretofore unencountered which left her unprotected and helpless; a sensation at once enchanting and frightening, thrilling and anguishing; a perception of some novel dimension opening up before her, a vista of a world utterly foreign—yet, she suspected in a flash of awestruck bewilderment, always latent within herself—a world conjured into her consciousness by that stranger's reference to love, carrying the suggestion of an emotion unrelated, she had instantaneously, irrefutably apprehended, to either her impassioned affection for Jenny

The Glitter and Other Stories

or the tranquil fondness tendered to her husband or indeed her feelings toward anyone in her past—unrelated, because qualitatively different, substantively incomparable. It was a world exploding with a consuming, aching desire for that stranger, who suddenly seemed a stranger no longer, for intimate closeness, total belonging, physical possession, and surrender, a world of ardent potentialities, left untapped and now demanding to be discovered: the terra incognita of her self.

In seventeen years of matrimonial coexistence, her husband had never let her discover this world. Nor, a confounding realization struck her, had she offered him any inducement to abet such exploration. She had liked and respected Kenneth Easterly, had been truly content to marry him. The son of one of her father's business friends, he was good-looking and bright, hardworking and ambitious. He had rapidly climbed the corporate ladder, yet his preoccupation with success and status had never curtailed his attention to her. He had always been a decent, completely faithful, invariably considerate mate, to whose physical endearments she had responded with ready compliance though with inherently subdued cooperation, occasionally pleased, accepting them as an implicit and sanctioned but fundamentally not too desirable part of the conjugal relationship. She had apprehended Kenneth Easterly's efforts to make her happy; above all, his tolerant awareness of their diverse endowments and proclivities and tacit consent to letting her pursue her unshared interests in art and alien cultures. Placid and practically unperturbed, their days and months and years had passed harmoniously, side by side rather than together. And thus, when he perished in a hotel fire, suffering the fate of so many of the convention guests, she had mourned the departure of a dear person, but the void, with which she was so unexpectedly confronted, had been defined by the loss of a long-accustomed presence, not of an irreplaceable focus of existence.

But then, such a passionate focus had never been part of her life, not before, not during her marriage, not after she had been widowed. Not that there had ever been any lack of applicants to just such a role. From early on she had attracted a substantial crop of admirers, and throughout the days of her widowhood, particularly in the course of her extensive travels, the frequent and vivid evidence of male interest had sharpened her awareness that her more mature years had enhanced rather than diminished her attractiveness, that, in fact, now at forty-six, she might be at the peak of her female charms. She had always accepted the proffered gallantries with amiable reserve and rejected the insinuations of a more intimate relationship with gracious but unequivocal firmness. Her upbringing in the puritanical setting of a Dutch Baptist home had interdicted any expression, indulgence, or even admission of her own sexuality. It had left her with a subliminal but ineluctable repugnance of male carnality as vulgar and shameless or at best always faintly obscene, coarse expressions of animal lust, to which no decent woman could or should respond.

Yet now, within moments of a fortuitous encounter, just such a response was happening with an implausible impact of flaming fancies and passionate urges. And pulsing terror mingling with soaring elation, she knew it was happening to him, this stranger no more. She read it from the light in his eyes, the slight tremor of lips, touched by a quickened breath, that minute, barely perceptible quiver in his voice, as it came to her, breaking into the spell of silence between them, forcibly calm, constrained in soberness.

"Hope my comment didn't distract you from your experience of that sunset."

"Not at all," she replied, careful to emulate his reserve. "Quite the contrary. Such enthusiasm could only add to the experience."

"I'm glad." There still was that accent of willed aloofness. "It was an impulse, you know, Somehow I felt your reaction was duplicating mine, when I for the first time beheld this incredible display."

"And those thousand times thereafter," she reminded him, smiling.

"Yes, those thousand times," he agreed, and the tightness of his tone seemed to be easing. "One never tires of the truly beautiful, does one? It remains ever new in its capacity to astound, to entrance—as you will find out for yourself."

"Hardly." There was an involuntary and unwanted touch of regret tinting her retort. "I won't have the opportunity of a thousand times. Four days is all I'll be spending here."

"Even four sunsets' magic will be enough to stay with you."

"Even four days," she repeated softly, captive to an irresistibly sprouting wish. Observing his silent nod, she sensed that he shared that wish.

"Experience," he said after an instant's pause. "Experience is not measured in units of time but in degrees of intensity." He appeared to be waiting for some answering comment, but faced with her reticence, he continued evenly, "Four days in this hotel will ensure our bumping into each other again. So I might as well satisfy the rules of sociability. I'm Leonard Jordan."

"How do you do, Mr. Jordan," she returned, and suddenly, inexplicably, the formality of her response struck her as embarrassingly inept, inane. "I am Barbara Easterly."

"I know," Leonard Jordan said.

"You do?"

His glance seemed to avoid her. "You are with that tour group. Sharing room sixteen with another lady, Ann Glyn, I believe." And noting her startled mien, he smiled a little guiltily. "Mr. Ghose told me. The assistant manager. He's an old friend of mine."

So this Leonard Jordan had inquired about her. This encounter then had not been quite so fortuitous. Anxiety was pulsing more hauntingly in her, elation soaring more wildly.

His words were flowing on, with a taint of mocking amusement enlivening their cadence. "Mr. Ghose is a loyal and ever-ready informant. He's known me for all these ten years I've been his guest in room twenty-one, that one over there, occupying the corner. He holds it for me from season to season, from early November to the middle of March."

"Escaping from the New York winter, Mr. Jordan?"

"Leonard, just Leonard, please. Formality doesn't wear well in Gopalpur. Yes, getting away from that abominable New York weather is a wholesome and most welcome bonus. But actually this reprieve is incidental to my primary purpose."

"Yes?" She could not quite suppress the prompting eagerness of her monosyllabic question. A perfect stranger, this Leonard Jordan—just Leonard, please—but she wanted, she needed to know all about him, his life, his thoughts, his aims, his dreams …

"The purpose?" he returned, immediately sensitive to the urgency of her inquiry. "Studying the customs and lore, the beliefs and imageries of this region's tribal people.

Exploring the roots of their religious prepossessions, their rituals, their institutions—the fundamentals of their existence."

"A hobby?"

"A hobby?" he repeated thoughtfully. Yes, perhaps in a way you might call it that. For unless your vocation is also your hobby, unless work is also enjoyment and what you do is also what you desire to do, your efforts will fall short of real accomplishment. I'm lucky this way. The paramount hobby of my youth has become the endeavor of my adult life."

"Anthropology?"

He nodded. "That's the academic discipline under which my studies would be categorized. But," he added reflectively, "anthropology is only a subsuming label for a broad range of scientific explorations, covering so many aspects, so many facets. Perhaps the way I perceive my own subject, the way I approach it, I would rather term my work an essay in uncovering the psychological roots of human evolution."

"Sounds fascinating. But I'm not sure …" There again was that inflection of prompting eagerness, of the urge to probe, to search , to understand, to penetrate.

"Sounds like a bunch of big words, doesn't it?" His lips curled with a hint of self-deprecating irony. "This is how it is with scholar-ese. The phrases sound impressive, tremendously important, but one doesn't quite know what they really mean. In fact, shorn of their academic verbiage, the thoughts behind them are far less esoteric, indeed quite simple, quite elementary most of the time. Regarding my own work, all it means is an attempt to explain the roots of our intellectual heritage— our beliefs and prejudices, our irrationalities and rationalizations, so as to learn to better understand ourselves. But I see, I'm again falling into that irksome habit of lecturing. You must forgive me, Mrs. Easterly."

"Barbara," she amended. "Just Barbara, please. Here formalities don't wear well, do they?" She bit her lips; she had not meant to parody him.He winked at her good-naturedly. "Yes, informality wears decidedly better."

Then, more earnestly again, "Simply, my purpose boils ultimately down to a discovery of why we are what we are, of the roots."

"Through exploring the tribal people?"

He did not miss the accent of dubiousness. "Precisely," he replied, quietly firm with conviction. "There is no more certain, no more eloquent, no richer source. What man has come to be finds its reason in what he was. Everyone of us carries, within the total bequest of mankind's millennial past, back fro, the very dawn of homo sapiens … now lecturing again," he added with a little rueful chuckle. "Old habits die hard."

She disregarded the remark, just wished he would go on speaking. The cadence of his voice encompassed her with a singular, unaccountable captivation from whose encroachment she did not want to be freed. "A most interesting hypothesis, that concept of the past's all-important bequest, though, I'm not certain …" She broke off abruptly. A memory flashed through her mind of her father, the Baptist Dutchman Jacob Van Dine, of Bible readings, of an absolute presumption that what she was had been preordained by the Lord and finally defined by her faith in the Gospel of Christ. But this was not the time for such arguments; they would spell the end of this wondrous encounter. "Then," she continued rapidly, "through the study of these tribes you aim to trace that heritage to its very beginnings?"

"Trace to the beginnings?" He shook his head. "That's beyond the range of the possible. The dawn of homo sapiens is far too remote. the discernible trail extends at best through only a measly few thousands of years. All one can hope for is some clues which may emerge from the residue of tribalism."

"I see," she said, searching for a rebuttal, a comment, a question, something, anything that would keep him speaking, keep the sound of his voice perpetuating this moment of never-known enchantment.

"But isn't this primeval residue spread all across the globe? There are so many tribal societies."

"You are wondering, aren't you," he responded to her unfinished query, "why, among all those opportunities, I would choose the tribes of India and this region in particular? Because there's been very little, and in approach inadequate, previous exploration. Because of a singular wealth of potential information. Because of several other academic reasons. But perhaps," he added, and his smile seemed lost in a distant dream, "perhaps the ultimate determining reason is that I love this country, its people, its atmosphere."

She could nor turn her gaze from him. For one timeless moment she beheld not the scholar but the man. There was personal revelation, intimacy, inner attunement—and that chill was groping her again, pervasive in its ambivalence of anxiety and elation. For one timeless moment ...

It was abruptly punctured. Pointing across the flower-framed courtyard toward the center of the building and the tourists congregating in front of it, Leonard Jordan said, "Seems dinner time's upon us."

"Already?"

"Time's been flying, hasn't it?" His glance, quietly probing, was resting on her. "In some instances more swiftly than in others. They always serve at this hour."

"I'd better get myself ready then." Her tone betrayed the displeasure at the interruption.

"You are ready, as far as I can make out. This robe will do famously." His eyes blinked with gentle mockery. "As we agreed, this is no place for formalities."

"Even so," she said lightly, "I'll change into something differently informal. It won't take a minute." She moved away two, three steps; stopped. "If you'd care just to wait a few moments, I'd be glad to introduce you to your compatriots, so you might join us all at dinner."

"Very thoughtful of you." His reply was markedly, disappointingly aloof. "But I guess, not. I usually have my meals in my room, and particularly tonight. I'd be no asset to a social get-together. I'm afraid I've never been a great one for chitchat."

"Just for … lecturing?" But her teasing rebuttal had an edge of acerbity.

He seemed deaf to the inflection. "I fear you've got my number," he retorted cheerily. "But lecturing aside, I'm tired. It's only a couple of hours ago that I returned from a three-week stretch in the interior. It does take something out of you. Also, there are some notes I need to jot down before calling it a night."

"I see," she muttered, emptily. That chill was still there, but now bare of anxiety or elation—a chill just of sudden loneliness. You'll excuse me then, won't you? I'd better go change for dinner."

He nodded. "No doubt, we shall meet again tomorrow. For now then, good night Mrs. … Barbara," he corrected himself, and a vibrancy of sudden warmth, of distant yearning endowed the lilt of her name with renewed enchantment. But already his slender figure was moving through the deepening darkness toward room twenty-one, the one occupying the arcaded corner, the one that had been held in readiness for him for the past ten winters.

For endless moments she kept standing there, abandoned to a bottomless void of loneliness, increasingly filling with sparks of consuming expectancy: of the incomprehensible wonder of what had happened to her, had happened within herself; of the novel dimension of a self-discovery fraught with trepidation and exultation alike; of a world haunted by aching, throbbing desire—a world whose shapeless promise was made endurable by the persevering echo of Leonard Jordan's assurance. "No doubt, we shall meet again tomorrow."

However, for all her straining search, the next morning offered no sight of him, no intimation whatever of his presence. Listlessly she sat through a dutifully consumed breakfast. Listlessly she took her dip in the ocean before the sun would grow too punishing. Listlessly though restlessly she wandered about the terrace and the adjacent grounds, the small flower garden, the beach, the trees and underbrush atop the dune which stretched to one side of the hotel's territory. She was weary, exhausted, drained by the fitful night which had followed the nearly interminable tedium of a long drawn-out dinner and the attendant bantering sociality of the group—a night that had bestowed no respite from her mind's turbulence; a night, which, to avoid disturbing her roommate's sleep, she had sought to pass on one of the lounging chairs outside, futilely, as the swarms of mosquitoes had soon driven her back inside, to seek shelter behind the protecting screens.

"No doubt, we shall meet tomorrow." Like a vicious taunt, that echo was still reverberating within her in accents of mounting apprehension. This phrase held a promise, a wealth of tender assurance. She could not credit such a breach of faith, not on Leonard Jordan's part. Yet even at lunchtime there was no trace of him. Might he be ill? She rejected the fleeting suggestion; he had seemed only a few years older than she, perhaps in his early fifties, and he had left her with an impression of ageless vigor, of sinewy resilience. Ill? Moreover, there had been no sign of activity about his quarters, such as some untoward development would have caused. In fact, unless it somehow had eluded her anxious watchfulness, no lunch had been served to his room. Or should it be that, aware of what had happened between them and intent on preventing any escalating sequel, he had decided to hide from her? Appalled and ashamed of this thought, she instantly drowned it. He was not that sort of a man, not he, whose presence the evening before had taken such total possession of her.

It was just after tea time that a car drew up at the entrance and discharged him. Caught on her way to her room to dress for the swim, she paused, watched him bend to the driver for a brief, inaudible exchange, the straighten, turn, eye her, and come toward her.

"Hello, Barbara!" His greeting was vibrant with an inflection of warmth and gladness, "Had a nice day, I hope?"

She could not tell him the truth, yet neither could she lie. "It's good to see you back," she returned at last vapidly.

"Oh!" His exclamation bespoke immediate, rueful understanding. "Of course," he added after a brief pause, which to her seemed a passage of successive eternities, "you must've puzzled, not seeing me around."

"Just wondering." She tried to sound noncommittal.

He nodded. There again was that regretful little smile of his. "Yes, a longstanding appointment, an obligation. I forgot to mention it when we parted last night."

"Why should you have mentioned it?" She forced herself to invest the reply with a lighthearted note. "After all, as you predicted, we are meeting again today."

"Yes, aren't we?" His eyes rested on her with a knowing tenderness, in whose glow the last evening's enchantment found its resurrection, "Still, it might've been appropriate … Would you join me for tea?"

She had had hers. But she nodded.

He made a quiet sign to the waiting servant before turning to her again. "Selfishness!" he said, an edge to his voice. "Just not considering. Here I'm robbing you of your dunk in the sea."

"That's all right!" she said quickly, a bit too quickly, she felt. "I had a long one this morning. While you were away."

Then for a while they were sitting silent, sipping their tea.

"While I was away." Leonard Jordan at last took up her phrase, bridging the mute interval, as though there had never been one. Had to get an early start. Long before breakfast; it was still dark. Ramlu got me to Berhampur for the train's arrival, though. Professor Senapati coming up from Vijayawada. Art historian. Specializing in religious imagery. Had promised to take him to Kavithi. The temple of Nilamma. It's just five, six miles off the trunk roads, but it might as well be on another continent. Except for the natives of the immediate environs hardly anyone knows of its existence. Senapati surely didn't, even though for his field of study that shrine presents a veritable treasure chest. Material enough to produce a whole big tome on hagiography. So Ramlu drove us down to Kavithi. However," a wry chuckle and a shrug filled a momentary pause, "I doubt the venerable professor gained much from all that wealth of figurations. Indeed, he seemed rather disappointed when we took him on his way back to Vijayawada. Owing to a different inspiration and tradition, folk art is of no value to him." A small sigh accompanied his shrug. "A profoundly learned man, and a just as profoundly bigoted one, that's Senapati. As with all orthodoxies, so, too, with his own: it limits his horizon, his objective perception, his unbiased response, his freedom of inquiry. In India, as elsewhere, exploration and doctrine just don't mix too well. There simply is no way for scholarship and religious fidelity to coexist. But," Leonard Jordan interrupted himself, noting the sudden tightening of her mouth and the frown crinkling her brow, and misinterpreting it, "I must be boring you with all this. Somehow I got lost in verbiage once again. I'm a glutton for monologues, am I not?"

She could not suppress a smile in response to the undertone of contrition. "No more than other men; just par for the course," she countered, consigning her irritation at his remark about scholarship and religious fidelity to a forgiving oblivion. "Monologues are not all that bad, really, when they happen to hold the listener's interest." Fleetingly she recalled Kenneth Easterly's monologues about the stock market and interest rates, prospective mergers and projected profits. "Never mind your monologues. They could never bore me. I've always been fascinated by foreign lands, cultures, and ideas—in a perfunctory, amateurish way only, of course. There's been little scope for me to acquire any expertise, any real knowledge."

"But scope for longing and receptivity," he interjected softly. His glance was embracing her with a strangely luminous intensity. "Yes, that's what I sensed when I found you standing there, absorbed in the sunset."

"Longing, receptivity …?" she repeated uncertainly, wondering.

"Not for any expertise, not for any knowledge as such," he answered, "but for meaningful experience, new horizons."

She could not escape the enthralling force of those eyes, their penetration of her self, their compulsion. "Must not everyone go seeking?" she murmured tremulously.

"Yes," Leonard Jordan assented emphatically. "Everyone!"

*

"Rambha," Kamesh announced, pointing ahead in explanation of the car's markedly slowing pace. "Much traffic. Much people. Market day."

"Mela?"

"Lady know about mela?" The driver's broad face brightened with a pleased grin, as he half turned his head to her. "No, this no mela, no festival for temple, for go. Just market day. Every week market day. Cannot go fast. But after Rambha, Gopalpur no more far. Less than one hour."

"Yes," she said, "I know." And noting the road which branched off to the right, "This one to Nirmal Jhar?"

"Nirmal Jhar?" he repeated, surprise in his tone. Then his grin expanded to evidence his appreciation of her familiarity with his own country: "Achcha. Nirmal Jhar. Small place, big temple of Lord Krishna."

"Jagannatha," she added mechanically, prodded by reviving memories.

"Jagannatha. Achcha." Kamesh swung the vehicle around a sluggish bullock cart. "God of Puri. Lady see Puri?"

*

She did not respond. Her mind was traveling back across four years, to that the last morning prior to the group's scheduled departure home, to Leonard Jordan, who had arranged with Ramlu that drive to Nirmal Jhar so he might show her the shrines surrounding the spacious courtyard and the plethora of exquisitely sculptured figures crowding their walls—back to that moment of appalled, perturbed, irrationally anguished confrontation with the ghostly idol, which, in its spectrally uncanny repulsiveness, looked like a grotesque parody of all that was sacred, a blasphemous disparagement not only of the Lord Krishna Jagannatha, Lord of the World, but of all divinity.

"Nilamma," Leonard Jordan had explained, noting her shocked reaction with a surprised frown. "The black mistress of primal India, worshipped here as Gudi Mata, Mistress of the Sacred Precinct. For here, as everywhere throughout the country, she is the real, the truly presiding godhead, regardless of any given shrine's specific, nominal dedication."

"This?" she had remonstrated shrilly, aroused by an overwhelming sense of repugnance. "Look at her! A godhead? This compound of terror and violence and grimacing odiousness, an image of godhead?"

"It loses its terror and odiousness once you come to understand," he returned with a placid smile.

"Come to understand what?" Rather than calm her, that smile of his had antagonized her. Try as she might, she had not been able to fight down a rising tide of resentment, even hostility sweeping at him, whom she loved, yet who would not share her abhorrence of that sacrilegious outrage, which struck her as a burlesque of her image of divine transcendence, this monstrous abomination, which, staring at her, seemed to mock her very faith. "In Christ's name, come to understand what?"

"The truth behind the image."

His reply had been even, soft, but its gentle timbre of sadness, of weary regret at her incomprehension, had only enraged her the more thoroughly with its sting of what seemed to her an ever-so-subtle nuance of condescending disdain for her own truth, her own vision of godhead as the essence of transcendence, of ineffable beauty and ultimate perfection—disdain, indeed, for her very faith.

But before she could formulate it, her impassioned repudiation had been forestalled by his even, though oddly somber, voice. "Let us not pursue it here, though. On our way back, there will be more material for further consideration. More opportunity perhaps for comprehension." His speech had carried an inflection of rigid decisiveness, which, like a blast of breath-stifling, icy wind, not only crushed all further argument and discussion but any manner of communication on their way back to Rambha and onward.

Even now, across the arid expanse of those last, lost, four years, she still could feel the impact of that repudiation's wrenching, rending hurt, as though she were just now standing in the courtyard of Jagannatha's temple at Nirmal Jhar—the hurt that had pierced her with a sudden irrefutable sense of estrangement and had marked the beginning of those four lost years; the hurt that had remained as unyieldingly acute as every word, every gesture, every instant of harmony and controversy, of emotional concordance and mental disparity, of exultant mutuality and desperate alien-ness, that had integrated the experience of her encounter with Leonard Jordan. The experience that had had its inception in an evening's sunset and its flowering in the course of that prolonged late afternoon tea on the terraced court overlooking the sea on the following day.

A poignant silence had settled between them, a profound, magic silence pregnant with a thousand unasked questions and yet unquestioningly accepting of each other. Both of them alike had been striving to perpetuate those moments of mutually enchanted involvement, but at once seeking a way to escape their ever more engulfing enthrallment. It was Leonard Jordan who at last had broken the spell, speaking slowly, carefully, following up on their last exchange.

"Yes, all of us must keep searching, for that is the impulse that keeps us alive. The ways and means of this search are diverse; incidental to each personality, they matter little. The ultimate aim must forever remain the same: new horizons, new experience, new scope for self-discovery, self-unfolding, self-achievement. It's this search now, which has brought you to India, isn't it, Barbara?"

"The search," she repeated wonderingly, "my search?" And then she told him about her life, told him impersonally, as though referring to someone else whom circumstance had allowed her to observe and the events of whose past she now was relating in brief, barely connected bits of data, delivered without any judgmental commentary, detached from any sentimental elaboration:

An untroubled and privileged, though strictly guided childhood within an affluent and religiously devout setting. Her preference for college overruled in favor of an elegant finishing school. The course of this marginal education cut short by early marriage to Kenneth Easterly. The trauma of nature-imposed childlessness, which had proved so instrumental a factor in making her married life an undisturbed, virtually frictionless passage through days of ever-sameness as well as in reinforcing the fundamental and unbridgeable distance between the worlds of that union's partners. The substitutive love for Jenny, escalating after her husband's sudden, catastrophic demise. The initial months of lonely, wasting widowhood and retreat. The move to Philadelphia. The flight from the ineluctably deepening attachment to her sister's child. The refuge of her trips abroad, at last satisfying her long-frustrated curiosity about alien ways and cultural diversities. Her visits to the monuments of human genius and artistry, to the castles and cathedrals of England and Germany, of France, Italy, and Spain, the ruins of Greece and Crete, the pyramids and the Valley of the Kings, the Shinto shrines of Japan, and now the temples of India—yet another flight, which in the end had brought her to Gopalpur.

Leonard Jordan had smiled, repeating thoughtfully, pointedly, "In the end … yes, perhaps in the end …" And then, perceiving her barely suppressed pallid gasp at that insinuation, he had calmed her flaring apprehension by quickly telling her about his own life. Not about its early phases, perfunctorily touching some of the signal data, concentrating on its course over the last ten years, when, after the death of his wife, he had resigned his professorship and, aided by the financial independence conferred by a substantial inheritance, had devoted himself to his present research. Describing to her his excursions into interior Orissa, his sojourns, two or three weeks at a time, in the tribal settlements; his alternating returns to Gopalpur for short intervals dedicated to the organization and elaboration of his notes and to some sorely needed rest from the strain and deprivations of the preceding periods. Telling her about Ramlu, who would drive him as far into the hinterland as the wilderness would permit and fetch him back again at the appointed time; who had parlayed the modest profits from his diligently attended coconut and banana plantation into the ownership of a car, which, put to serve the transport of the hotel guests, provided an additional income; who, founded on a deepening relationship of mutual respect and fondness, had become his trusted and dedicated friend. And he spiced his account with references to some aspects of life among the tribal residents with little anecdotes, some funny, some tragic.

She had been listening, absorbed in the adventures of his chosen pursuit in the vista of an alien world which he conjured up before her mind, endowing its facets with sparkles of vitality; she was completely absorbed in her unfolding discovery of the man behind those accounts, the man Leonard Jordan—a discovery even more fascinating than the experiences he was discussing. "I wish I could be along on those forays of yours, to see for myself, be part of those adventures!" she had exclaimed when he paused, carried away by a tidal rush of emotion, totally unaware of her suggestion's implication.

Immediately alert to the oblivious innocence of her impulsive challenge and awake to the force of her need and yearning that had prompted it, his reply had come slowly, carefully, gently, "It would be lovely to have you become part of it, Barbara. But the hardships would be too taxing, the hazards too unacceptable. The circumstances prevailing in the interior are just too prohibitive. I'm afraid your acquaintance with tribal India will have to remain vicarious, its romance as well as its jeopardy experienced by proxy only—my proxy, as far as you may see fit to make use of it." And spontaneously, his own emotion overriding his better judgment and restraint, he had added: "No, Barbara, no matter how I may wish to have you a part of it, I could never allow it to happen."

His speech had gripped her mind, only to be lost in a throbbing void, its unqualified rebuff of her impassioned appeal drowned by the incessantly reverberating echo of that last phrase, "However I may wish to have you a part of it …" The phrase, whose tenderness was all that mattered, whose promise encompassed all that needed to be said: "However I may wish …"

Perceiving the deepening flush of her cheeks, he had suddenly been beset by the anxious, vaguely guilty realization of what his declaration had conveyed to her. Not that he regretted the impetuous revelation of his own feelings, but he rued what he judged to be the premature nature of their expression and the evident turmoil it hat precipitated in her. Searching for some way to assuage the almost unendurable tension, he had spoken quickly, evenly. "Still, I might arrange for you to enjoy some taste, at least, of direct experience. Yes, I shall ask Ramlu to drive us some distance into the back country, just to give you an inkling. Would this please you, Barbara?"

She had nodded absently, automatically, still engrossed in her discovery of a Barbara she had never known and of a dimension of existence beyond all imagination. This was a dream, a utopia, a fantasy of the impossible, which mysteriously had become possible!

"Look, Barbara!"

She had felt his light, fleeting touch on her shoulder, heard his voice wafting toward her, soft with affection. Almost unwillingly, reluctant to be returned to reality, her glance had followed his pointing hand.

There again was that incredible sunset, if anything, even more glorious than on the evening before. And then, for time on end, they had sat in captivated, concordant silence.

They would meet again after dinner. There had been no need for a scheduled appointment, when, equally dismayed at the forcible interruption, they had separated, he to take his meal served in his quarters, she to endure her group's unwelcome, boisterous, and trite sociability, distractedly, impatiently, unresponsively. Her preference for different company had not gone unnoticed. Ann Glyn's miffed coldness, not untainted by jealousy, was no less pointed than the others' more covert, inquisitive references. The questions left unanswered, her presence soon was treated to resentful, ostracizing aloofness. She could not have cared less. Three more days, and she would be seeing none of them ever again. Three more days—and they belonged to Leonard Jordan.

He was waiting for her in the arcade in front of his room, absently contemplating the ringlets of smoke rising from a bundle of incense sticks placed between his seat and the one he had prepared for her at his side.

"To keep the mosquitoes away—and the flies and gnats," he explained. "They don't like the scent."

"Neither do I," she admitted cheerily. "Too sweet. But anyway much preferable to mosquitoes."

"Just as long as it will not keep you away."

The light in her eyes spelled her answer.

"I arranged with Ramlu," Leonard Jordan announced when she had seated herself. "Tomorrow, right after lunch, he will take us into the countryside. He was all regrets and apologies for not being available in the morning. Some previous engagement. But that's just as well. Will allow you to enjoy the sea and the beach, and myself to attend to my work. Lunch is being served early here." He let his warm smile respond to her undisguised disappointment. "Which will allow for a long afternoon, won't it?" Bridging an uneasy moment's pause, he went on quietly, "Sitting here, it occurs to me that somehow I never got around to asking you about your impressions of India."

"Before Gopalpur, you mean?" There was a tender insinuation coloring her bantering tone, and she was acutely aware of both the insinuation and the tenderness. Astounded, she could not recognize herself in either. But then, everything seemed so magically altered. How different the world looked with Leonard Jordan close—the world about her and the world within her.

"Before Gopalpur," he confirmed with mock earnest. "It's your grand tour of India I'm referring to. Has it lived up to your expectations?"

"Oh, it's been fabulous, magnificent! Every place, every sight unique in its own way, in its own right. At times truly overwhelming, the beauty, the grandeur, the poetry in stone!"

"That's a lovely description, 'poetry in stone,'" he said. "Yes, that's just about the way I felt on my first visit. As a young fellow just out of college. That's when I fell in love with this country."

"Love at first sight?"

He nodded. "Perhaps that is the only real love," he returned softly, "if…"

"If?"

"If it will pass the test of that first sight's validity," he completed pensively. But her expression of perplexity immediately dissipated the faraway smile with which some fond memory had painted his lips, and he continued, "For me, India passed this test, absolutely, conclusively. And so this initial affinity laid the foundation to my lifelong occupation and current endeavor."

"I can understand," she muttered, not quite certain she did, yet again carried away by the intensity of his commitment.

"I'm glad." His glance sought her, rested on her. "I felt there might be an affinity of our spontaneous responses to the experience that is India."

"You felt?"

"When I found you spellbound by that sunset," he answered. "Yes, right then …" His voice trailed into a long instant of silent reliving, by both simultaneously, the strange immediacy of that encounter. There was only the murmur of the surf as the tide came rolling in, providing counterpoint for their mutual enchantment.

"That tour of yours," Leonard Jordan remarked, in an effort to feel his way back to the present reality, "is covering the usual route, I presume? Delhi, Agra?"

"Jaipur, too," she seconded vividly, grateful for being rescued from an assault of emotionality which threatened to surge beyond control.

"Yes, Jaipur, of course," he agreed. "Quaint place, isn't it? Those arrow-straight streets of pink and blue and green and yellow dwellings. I don't suppose, though they took you to Amber? They usually don't on these tours."

"They did this time," she contradicted him. "What a palace! And that deserted capital city! So dead, uncanny—a graveyard of the past. And they took us to Gulta Pass, too."

"Gulta Pass," he repeated, abandoning himself to the memory. "Glorious scenery, and those frescoed temples …"

"And those big, ferocious monkeys …"

"A rather rambunctious bunch, and aggressive, aren't they?" he returned, "but really harmless, if you don't come too close."

"I wouldn't be that curious or that brave," she conceded with a small laugh. "We visited Benares also—Varanasi, as they call it now—the Ganges, the shrines and hospices along the banks, the pilgrims …"

"And Khajuraho?" he intervened. "No doubt they must have shown you Khajuraho. Nowadays all tours do, routinely."

"Khajuraho—yes, we went there."

The marked curtness of her reply startled him. The sudden tightening of her mouth and the frown clouding her brow did not elude his observation. "You … You didn't like the place?" A breath of surprise animated his question.

"Well …" Her reply was slow with its accent of dismay. "Certainly the place is most impressive. All those many temples. Quite exquisite; structurally. And that plethora, one might even say, surfeit of sculptures and carvings. Artistically, I suppose, of the highest order …"

"Quite extraordinary," he concurred, increasingly wondering at the odd undertone of resentment vibrating through her every word.

"Extraordinary," she repeated, and the tightness around her mouth became still more pronounced. "Extraordinary, no doubt, in many ways—in the extravagance of some of the designs, an unhealthy, unsavory, offensive extravagance. At least, that's the way it struck me," she added quickly, anxiously. But to her amazed relief, Leonard Jordan did not repudiate her disparaging critique. Even more astounded, she noted his smiling, assenting nod.

"Your instincts are preciously acute," he said, and his profound contentment was unmistakable. "Your reaction was precise and to the point, Barbara. However intellectually unaware of the underlying motive you may be, your intuition told you the truth."

"The truth?"

"You were referring to those portrayals of sultry eroticism, weren't you? To those depictions of carnal acrobatics, orgiastic exercises?"

Her mute stare mirrored her utter repugnance, the flagrant odium of revolted sensibilities.

Again he nodded. "You perceived the actuality behind the artistic skill and glistening polish of those configurations: their very decadence. The degeneration of ideational substance into the fraudulent refinement of trivial externality; the degradation of transcendental experience into the frivolous exercises of a mechanical, frigid, wholly meaningless sexuality; the reduction of a precious gem to the glittering worthlessness of tinted glass. That's what you sensed, what you spotted. For this I admire you, Barbara. Not many people possess such keenness of immediate discrimination and response."

She sat very still, as though afraid lest some slightest movement dispel the vision of a miracle. Once more there was only the susurrous song of the surf between them and the scented fumes of the incense sticks rising into the vast silence of the evening.

"I'm so happy." Her voice was low and vibrant when at last it reached for him. "So very happy that you feel this way, too, Leonard."

"That's how I've always felt about Khajuraho. From the first. And each of my several visits only fortified my original reactions to art turned into artifice, essence turned into elegance, sanctity turned into scurrility—to the cultural antithesis to Konark."

"Konark?"

"Why, yes." He looked at her, wondering what had become of that vibrancy, which but a few instants before had endowed her speech with an almost lyrical mellowness. "Surely you must have been to Konark? Your tour couldn't have missed taking you there from Bhubaneswar?"

"It didn't miss."

The bony ring of her reply, its strange snap was not lost on him. Baffled, he could find no reason for her so abrupt change of mood. In his mind he rapidly reviewed his last remarks, but they offered no answer. He could discern nothing in them that might possibly have displeased, much less offended her. All they had endeavored was to convey the contrasting mentality and aspirations, which had prompted the builders and artisans of Khajuraho and Konark. "Then you must know what I meant, he said slowly, still searching for an explanation.

"I'm not sure I'm following you."

"But you saw the Durya Temple?"

"The Sun Temple? Yes, we surveyed it quite thoroughly."

"But then …" He broke off, beset by his growing awareness of the chilling rigidity, the throaty harshness, which seemed to be deepening with her every utterance.

"Quite thoroughly," she repeated. "Perhaps that's why I can't follow you. You somehow seem to differentiate between Khajuraho and Konark. You reject the degenerate style of the former's shrines, yet you seem to admire that Sun Temple!"

"I seem?" An inflection of impatience tainted his retort. "I don't just 'seem.' Indeed I do admire it. How could anyone not be overawed by its grandeur, overwhelmed by its beauty, elevated by its inspiration? Of course I admire it. To me it's always been the most glorious, the supreme one of India's monuments."

"You are not serious!" For all its dullness, there was a curious grating shrillness to her voice. Ever so slightly, she was moving, shifting, as though intent on putting some more distance between them.

However hardly perceptible, the gesture caught his attention. His lips tightened, and his hand passed across his brow, as though to smooth away a frown that had creased it. "But I am serious, Barbara," he said quietly. "And I can't comprehend, how, given your sensitivity, intuition, acuity of grasp, you could not, as it would seem, share my response to the ultimate product of India's creative genius."

"You can't comprehend," she muttered after him in a voice which had surrendered its edge of harshness to a cadence of dirge-like desolation. "You can't comprehend … But neither can I, Leonard. Not this enthusiasm of yours. Not your fervent praise of that temple. Not your evident fascination with what is so much worse, so much more flagrant in its filth and odiousness than even Khajuraho."

"Odiousness?" He pronounced the word, syllable for incredulous syllable. "How can physical beauty and metaphysical truth ever be odious?"

"Beauty, truth …" That mournful echo was carrying an accent of bitterness now. "Where is beauty, where is truth at Konark? Oh, I won't deny that that temple complex is striking, imposing, grandiose, magnificent. Until you get close enough for a more careful examination of its imagery; until you discover that each sculpture, each carved panel is yet another outrage of obscenity. That there is no lechery, no lewdness, no perversion, that wouldn't find its brazen portrayal, no carnal debauch that would not boast its nauseating glorification, that, in fact, the walls of what you praise as the 'supreme product of India's creative genius' present a veritable encyclopedia of pornography!"

"I see," Leonard Jordan said evenly when she paused, breathless from the escalating passion of her indictment. Then, curiously stilted in its motion, his hand reached to the table in back of them, plucked from it another pack of incense sticks to replace those that had long since burned down. Unhurriedly, he put a light to the tapering ends and watched the fumes tapering upward. When he at last spoke, after what had seemed to her an oppressive, dragging infinity, a nuance of weary disenchantment lingered in his dispassionate repudiation. "Sometimes, Barbara, first-sight impressions may deceive. On second sight, perhaps, you might find occasion for reconsidering your opinion and a different interpretation might suggest itself to you. It might then occur to you that pornography is a description of sexual activity detached from the context of mutual belonging, divorced from a relationship's emotional validity and thus inherently alien to any experience of two beings' total integration. It is an exercise designed to serve self-gratification of the sensually impoverished, the erotically impotent. But is this the essence, the purpose, the meaning of Konark? To be sure, some of the representations, an irrelevant minority, may well justify the label of pornography. Quite naturally so: the temple's figurations are the work of scores, more likely hundreds, of artisans, people of widely diverse skills and backgrounds. Inevitably, some of them would indulge their own vulgar and idiosyncratic, prurient fancies. But you could hardly have surveyed only those products of inferior, shoddy, frivolous motivation. And the rest of those depictions, the great bulk of them, did they not speak to you of a different inspiration? Was there no message they conveyed to you, no suggestion of a richer perspective, no sense of some profound significance?"

For all its calm, his voice had a subtle sting to it that made her shiver. She was staring straight ahead into the darkness over the beach and the waters beyond, seeking to escape from the intensity of his eyes, from the unspoken reproach she felt mirrored in them, a reproach that was not only discrediting the caliber of her intellectual discernment but striking at her presumptions of propriety and decency, at her very concept of morality; a reproach that compelled an irrepressible antagonism that had to vent itself in a sardonic rebuttal. "Maybe you overestimated my perceptive and intuitive faculties, after all? Perhaps their apparently praiseworthy display at Khajuraho was just a fortuitous exception, a fluke? But at Konark they again proved too inadequate to live up to your standards of fine-tuned discrimination?"

"No, Barbara." He seemed to be untouched by the acid of her counterattack. His rejoinder was placidly level, oddly gentle. "But I may have underestimated the extent and power of rooted presuppositions and prejudices which have blocked your natural capabilities and thus prevented you from observing not only their bodies engaged in sexual interplay but also the faces of those lover couples of Konark." His gesture stymied her attempted objection. "Their faces," he repeated. "Otherwise you might have discerned their luminous, blissful smiles, mirrors of the all-encompassing, all-pervasive ecstasy attending the experience of perfect mutuality and oneness; the experience of not merely a union but a total communion—of a transcendent love, of which the physical expression is intrinsically a part, yet part as but the mundane aspect of the universal principle of universal regeneration: the very aspect, which, within the human dimension, decrees the physical expression of mutuality as the enabling factor of procreation, which in turn constitutes the precondition of perpetual renewal."

For all her instinctive reluctance to pursue the subject, for all her escalating aversion to his notions, for all her vexation at their lecturing presentation, her attention had been riveted by the intensity of his delivery, by the oddly compelling passion of the conviction which had engendered it. Still, she had not been quite able to absorb the thrust of his arguments, not only because of their inherent complexity but because of their frame of reference—one utterly foreign and contrary to her own, thus precluding her immediate comprehension. Yet his last phrase had struck a chord in her, waking a haunting, painful resonance.

"Renewal through procreation," she murmured, aching with the memory of her own denial of motherhood, of her emotional substitution of Jenny—a memory fraught with a guilty suggestion that, possibly, the absence of what Leonard Jordan was calling 'perfect mutuality,' the lacking experience of total communion, might have caused her failure.

"My reference was to renewal in its all-inclusive sense." His tone was compassionate assuagement. Recalling her terse but revealing allusions to her marital relationship, he instantaneously grasped the meaning of the bleakness echoing through her phrase. "Physical procreation will not always be the result even of perfect oneness, absence of such a result should not be taken as the test of a total communion's transcending experience."

"Transcending experience," she took up his phrase emptily, but even in its drabness her repudiation betrayed a harsh nuance of disparaging distaste. "What a lofty term for carnal indulgence that may be ennobled only, in fact can be excused alone by its offering the potential for procreation, which is God's sole intended purpose in what you are trying to varnish by exalting it as 'total communion.'"

"I do not pretend being privy to God's intention." His rebuttal was crisp with an accent of irritable impatience. "But He seems to have arranged for offspring to be the consequence of, rather than the antecedent to, the act of what you label 'carnal indulgence.' Evidently, before the agents of God's purpose become parents, they must be lovers. Possessing the wisdom and the power to arrange matters according to His will, presumably then this was God's intention. Which implicitly indicates the priority, not just chronologically but qualitatively as well, of that oneness framed by the perfect harmony of physical desire and metaphysical compulsion—precisely that ecstasy of total commitment so joyfully, entrancingly exemplified and attested by those imageries at Konark." Again the motion of his hand, quiet and decisive, thwarted her protest. "If, in the conceit of our ignorance, we are to credit God's intention, the priority He so obviously accorded to carnal consummation cannot but indicate its validity in its own right, cannot but affirm its intrinsic design as an instrument of eternal regeneration, of life's perpetuity, not alone by means of material renewal through progeny but by the transmaterial renewal through total integration with another of nature's particles, a human particle. It is this experience, which will, by way of extended self-realization, reintegrate the individual with the universal whole and thus contribute to the perpetual chain reaction of its vital energy."

She was staring at him, caught in a quandary of fascination and antagonism, at once ineluctably spellbound by his eloquence, whose obscure meaning she sensed yet could not fathom, and keenly stung by what seemed to her an accent of casual irreverence, perhaps even deliberate mockery, which had invested his references to God. But granting that the absolutism of her own faith might have made her oversensitive to others' lesser fidelity, she decided to restrain her resentment and let his remarks pass unchallenged. Seeing that he was waiting for some comment, some response from her, she said, dully: "I'm afraid your explanation left me somewhat at a loss."

He nodded and sighed. "That academic jargon of mine again. I wish I could break that irksome habit of speaking in abstractions which obfuscate rather than clarify. Of course, they must throw you for a loss. But more simply presented, the concepts will come across to you—I hope."

The tenor of this self-faulting apology grated on her, made her bristly. There, once more, was that nuance of condescension; it brought a new, keener edge to her animosity. "Some of these concepts, at least, did come across to me," she countered tightly, "even though wrapped in that academic lingo. In sum, stripped of their turgid verbiage, your contentions boil down to a panegyric glorification of man's carnal instincts."

"Do they?" he retorted. And after a pondering pause, "Yes, perhaps they do, in their particular way, within the context of a transcending experience."

"Indeed?" Her rejoinder was caustic. She would not be placated by his indulgently humoring, pointedly qualified concurrence. "But the context should be of concern, not with the body's instinctual urges but with the mind's spiritual aspirations; not with the gratification of our sensuality but with the justification of our eventual concession to it—a justification which can be attained only if the sexual act is sanctified by an incomparably, indeed incompatibly, superior inspiration."

His glance was groping for her from beneath a puckering brow. "It seems the penchant for abstraction is infectious," he added dryly.

The remark did not amuse her. Provoked by its needling irony, she countered it with an acrid parody of his own phrase. "Perhaps more simply rendered, the concept may come across to you—I hope."

"So do I, hope." There was a melancholy ring to the softness of his rejoinder.

She well perceived the progressively widening distance between them, the deepening contrariety, which appallingly, terrifyingly threatened her with the imminence of foreclosing the new wondrous horizons that their encounter in the sunset had opened to her glimpse. Yet she could not help herself. Defying rational scrutiny, she had an obsessing sense of being subjected to an attack, an abuse of some quality of her self which was paramount and must be defended at all costs.

"Maybe I can clarify our shared hope," she said. Aching with her phrase's facetiousness, she said it in spite of herself, incapable of repressing her self-wounding acrimony. "Clarify it by putting my views and sentiments more simply. There are those representations of sexual dalliance, crowding the walls of that temple. But have you not yourself referred to such carnal indulgence as but the mundane aspect of universal regeneration, as an activity belonging, and strictly incidental, to the human dimension? Now, I couldn't agree any more positively with this definition of yours and with the elementary distinction it implies, namely between the dimensions of the sacred and the profane, of the worldly and the otherworldly—dimensions essentially and eternally antithetic, whose dividing boundaries must not be violated."

She paused, and the momentary stillness gripped her with anxiety. There he was, Leonard Jordan, next to her, yet she was chilling with a sensation of utter, bleak loneliness. She scanned his face for some reaction but his features betrayed none. Unsmiling but not frowning, neither accepting nor forbidding, they were as bare of any expression as his figure, now propped against the back of his seat in a sprawl of languid repose which stung her like a deliberate taunt. She felt a challenge lurking in his unresponsiveness, a challenge to prove the courage of her convictions by continuing her discourse, a challenge she knew she must meet.

"There are the dimensions of the sacred and the profane, whose dividing delimitations must remain inviolate," she repeated, still more acute in her emphasis. "But there, at Konark, they have been violated.

It is this wanton, unpardonable transgression, which, assaulting my natural disgust at those shameless exhibitions of vulgar prurience and orgiastic profligacy, insulting my personal sense of decency and wholesomeness, has defined my repugnance and odium. For there, at Konark, the obscenity has not remained confined to the precinct of the profane. However devoted to the worship of false gods and however aberrant and unenlightened that worship's underlying beliefs, nonetheless that temple does constitute a precinct of the sacred, the otherworldly, the transcendent. Yet there those figurations of the lowest, most unspiritual earthiness are invading the dimension of the divine. Whichever the identity of that shrine's presiding deity, this invasion is an ultimate offense against the very essence of godhead."

"It appears that there has been no sign of the godhead's awareness of any offense." The evenness of Leonard Jordan's comment was stark in its contrast to her waxing fervor. Its very tranquility accented its irony, its undisguised mockery.

"Maybe it's just this, exactly, that strikes me as the supreme outrage!" she countered bitterly. "The very idea of a godhead that would tolerate such debasement, that would sanction such defilement of all spirituality! Can you imagine even one single such abomination disgracing a cathedral?"

"No," he admitted in the same placid voice, but one now fraught with a strain of steely scorn. "No, in truth I could not imagine. But then, the Konark temple has been happily exempt from the psychopathy of Paul of Tarsus."

She drew back fitfully as though he were assaulting her bodily. "St. Paul," she muttered, choking at her lumping breath, "you are reviling St. Paul!"

"Paul of Tarsus," he amended emphatically. "He had his own private model of godhead, of spirituality, of the sacred. A demented, obsessively idiosyncratic model. It is the one, which, not necessarily to their own artistic enhancement and hardly to their worshippers' benefit, the cathedrals reflect."

"It's Christ's teaching."

"No!" Her incipient rebuttal was cut down, as if by a guillotine. "Let us not fault Jesus for his disciple's aberrations. In his attitudes closely related to the ascetic mystics at Qumran, by his personal preference he may, or may not, have been a celibate. But in regard to others he did not disparage their exercise of physical love. On the contrary, he showed the highest respect for it—that is why he was so profound a believer in, and ardent advocate of, that perfect oneness, that total communion in which men and women were to find their ultimate fulfillment. Hence, on the presumption of wedlock as the given foundation of that ideal communion, his proclamation of marriage's holiness and indissolubility. But never did he pronounce himself on the subject of sexual activity as such. Neither praising nor condemning, he seems to have taken love's physical expression for granted as an intrinsic part of human existence and destiny. It was for the twisted minds of Paul of Tarsus and his followers to vent their phobia of sex by promoting the preposterous proposition of carnal sin and crowning this dehumanizing notion with the unconscionable doctrine of original sin. No, Barbara, it is not the spirit of Jesus, but the spirit of Paul that has determined and shaped the countenance of the cathedrals. Please!" he thwarted her attempted interjection, now more gently, almost pleadingly, "let me finish. It seems important to me that I should say what needs to be said. Not, though, with the object of converting you to my views. For one, I do not fancy I could succeed; for another, even if I could, I would never endeavor it. Any true and valid conversion must come from within the person, not from without. No, each of us, we must find our own way, our own truth. What I wish for, Barbara, is not your agreement with, but just some understanding, some appreciation, of my perspective."

He paused, moving a hand to chase a mosquito that had defied the incense fumes. But she did not seize the opportunity for a repudiating argument. Somehow the ardor of his plea, the sincerity of his urgency overwhelmed even the mounting force of her antagonism to defy her ever-more-certain awareness that with every explanation he might essay, with every modicum of comprehension she might gain, the distance between them was bound to expand into an abyss of irreversible alienation.

And then Leonard Jordan was speaking again. "You see, Barbara? To you the Konark imageries presented themselves as a sacrilege. You saw in them extreme profanity invading the dimension of the sacred and defiling it. But sacredness is not an inherent property. Sacred is what an individual will hold to be sacred. But, what if the sectaries from whose midst the architects and artists of that shrine were recruited considered those lover couples as symbolizing their own ideas of the sacred? Would then those figurations' presence within the precincts of the sacred not be legitimate, indeed imperative? Would they not be relevant, in fact essential, to the processes of worship observed at Konark? To those tantric artists, who deemed the sexual act as integral to the total communion, their ultimate sacrament—would to them those designs of erotic intimacy and fusion not offer themselves as vehicles of inspiration and exaltation, of otherworldly dedication? Given their own vision of the divine and of universal existence, would those representations of lovers embracing, joyful in their experience of sexual fulfillment, prove not only as provocatively functional but as substantively valid as the depictions of the nativity, the Christ's entry into Jerusalem, or the crucifixion that grace the walls and interiors of the cathedrals?"

"As substantively valid …" she muttered after him, staring incredulously, staggered by his equation of beliefs essentially disparate and intrinsically incomparable. "As substantially valid," she said once

The Glitter and Other Stories

more, trembling with a loathing that was agony. "That then is your perspective which you would have me understand and appreciate? But then," she added coldly, "such would be your perspective, wouldn't it? Of course, if I had only realized it before, I should have expected as much."

"If you had only realized …?" He returned her stare, baffled.

"I might've guessed," she said bleakly, her eyes on the tiny pendant affixed to his watch-band, a golden, six-pointed star glittering in the beam from the lamp overhead.

"Oh that." A half-smile framed his perfunctory nod. "I see. But you would've guessed wrong, Barbara. My grandfather was a Methodist minister. My mother wouldn't miss a Sunday service. When I was a kid, she made me go to church with her. Yes, very Christian," he repeated, as another wry smile was crumbling on his lips. "But this happenstance need not, ought not, prevent one's objective observation and unbiased judgment. One doesn't remain a kid all one's life, does one?"

Momentarily he seemed lost in thought. Then, aware that her glance was still resting on that dainty ornament, he nodded again. But now his smile had altogether faded. "This star of David? It was my wife's. Miriam, she was Jewish. No," he repudiated an unspoken comment, "that does not explain my viewpoint, my 'unChristian' objectivity." A nuance of irony crisped his phrase, but his mien persisted in its unsmiling rigidity. "Miriam's Jewishness was devoid of any religious presumptions. She, too, believed in intellectual independence and objectivity. Her commitment was strictly to Israel, to the political necessity of a Jewish State, which I had fully recognized long before I'd ever met her. But it was not this shared conviction which caused her to give her pendant to me just before she died, knowing she had but hours to live and knowing that I knew, too …" Only for the briefest instant his voice trailed off, like a soft, tender melody. "The star of David—

she gave it to me, not as a token of Jewishness, not as the emblem of Israel, but for me to wear as the symbol of the life we had had together. You could not understand," he answered her glance of unvoiced perplexity, evenly, gravely, "unless you understand the symbolism of this six-pointed star, the significance of a design, which has somehow become associated with David, but which existed long before his day, long before Moses, long before the first pharaohs, tracing back to an antiquity inaccessible to complete assessment. Look at it, Barbara," he went on, detaching the ornament from the watchband to display it in his open palm. "The so-called David, adopted by the Jews as their national emblem. Yet, even though it may well prove appropriate as an indicant of Jewish thought, it seems to have been chosen without any consideration, indeed any awareness of such relevance. Jungians may deem it a manifestation of the racial unconscious—and who knows, it may be just that?" he added, momentarily pondering. "Anyway. There, the six-pointed star. Its symbolism has elicited many interpretations by mystical philosophers and religious crackpots, generally far off the target. Though soberly examined, the fundamental concept is as simple as the figuration itself: two intersecting triangles, one upward-, one downward-pointing. Those same two triangles, which, though separated, appear in Hindu metaphysics and symbolism."

He paused to carefully reattach the golden pendant, passingly fascinated by its gleam in the light, absorbed by the memory it carried. "In Hinduism called 'vani' and 'shakti,'" he continued, "these triangles, bestowed to posterity by an immemorial past, represent the graphic ciphers for male and female essence, respectively. Although the presumption remains unprovable, speculation points to the strong possibility that their original choice as the symbols for the sexual polarities may well have been suggested by the triangular designs of the human genital zones. However that may be, those upward- and downward-pointing triangles, conjoined and intersecting precisely as in the star of David, reappear in a complex of countless multiplications to form the 'yantra,' the magic figuration of Indian metaphysics, which serves as the focus of meditation on universal existence and perpetual cosmic regeneration, indeed on all the aspects of transcendental reality. It is the contemplation of this graphic conjunction, of the sexual polarities' fusion in a total communion, which evokes the comprehending vision of cosmic design and purpose, of human life's significance within a scheme of perpetual, infinite renewals … The fusion of the sexual polarities in a total communion," he repeated, and now the soft, tender melody returned to his voice. "That is the true meaning of the six-pointed star, and that is why Miriam wanted me to have it, as I wanted to have it—as a token of our life together, the very experience symbolized by the ecstatic mutuality of those Konark imageries whose message I came to grasp fully only because there had been Miriam, because she taught me …" His voice trailed off forlornly. In the void of stillness left behind the murmur of the surf seemed like thunder.

And then he spoke again, gently. "Forgive this long discourse, Barbara. I didn't mean to … the old lecturer's habit again. But perhaps it may have gained you a better understanding of my admiration for the Sun Temple. Perhaps …?"

But she was too utterly shaken, too overwhelmed by a shaming sense of inadequacy and aching regret to attempt any response to the question that kept lingering, almost imploringly, in the silence between them. Only after what seemed an interminable spell she stirred, to rise from her seat in a slow succession of awkward movements, each automatic like a doll's on a puppeteer's string. "I guess I've failed the test," she said woodenly, gazing past him into a boundless nowhere.

"The test?"

"The test of that first sight's validity, remember?"

"Yes," he replied quietly, rising to face her. "Yes, I remember. But that was just a generalizing remark. Why apply it to yourself, Barbara? Why jump to conclusions? There was a divergence of attitudes, of viewpoints, that's all. There was no question whatever of a test, of passing or failing."

"Still, the divergence …" she muttered desolately.

"Barbara," Leonard Jordan said earnestly, "people do not meet each other as finished, perfectly matched products. If they are lucky, they grow toward one another. The first sight does not behold a final entity; it perceives only a potential. It takes time and effort, sometimes even pain, to develop this potential, to make it attain its full scope. The perception of a first sight will test out only when one has invested the time, the effort, the pain. It's the potential I discerned in yesterday's sunset, that potential is still there."

"But," she started to protest, in a voice which was a shiver at once of unpersuaded anguish and incredulous hope.

He cut her short, gently. "Perhaps we should leave it there for tonight? It's been a long evening; we haven't been watching the hour. Everybody has long retired. Your roommate will not be thanking you for an even later disturbance. And there will be a tomorrow, won't there?"

She nodded numbly.

"Our little excursion into the hinterland, remember? Ramlu will be here right after lunch."

"Yes," she said, for the first time looking at him again. "Tomorrow. Good night, Leonard."

"Pleasant dreams!" he called after her, watching as she crossed the terrace, watching until the door had closed behind her.

*

An exclamation from the driver's seat jolted her from the revisited past. Unintelligible, its harshness suggested an oath. Only now she realized that the car had come to a halt. A construction crew was repaving a stretch of road. A single narrow lane had been left to traffic, and this passage was currently occupied by a huge water buffalo, stubbornly refusing to yield to either persuasion or whip, which were being used to try to make him keep pulling an overloaded wagon. There was no alternative to waiting out the animal's caprice, as Kamesh's alternative to waiting eloquently proved.

"Nothing you can do about it," she assuaged his apologetic fretfulness, trying without much success to subdue her own impatience. Idly, her glance strayed to the workers along the road: men, naked except for their loincloths, spreading tar and operating an ancient steamroller; women, skin and bones beneath saris that left one breast uncovered, carrying on their heads tin buckets filled with crushing loads of stones which they were transporting from heaps at the roadside to sites of present repair—local natives, young and old, drained alike by the swelter of a merciless sun and the privations of poverty. One of them, a girl, perhaps twelve or thirteen years old, stopped for a moment by the car, scrutinizing her with eyes that were deep hollows in an emaciated, wizened face, staring, until a casual gesture from the man at the wheel sent her on her way.

"Harijans," Kamesh said, in a voice that held neither regret nor compassion, but just bored indifference spiced with disgust. Harijans, she recalled, "children of God," was what Mahatma Gandhi had called those tribal outcasts, those wraiths of starved hopelessness, of utter and permanent misery. *Children of God, what blasphemy,* she thought. *No God could will children like these, could countenance their sight, could tolerate their distress and still be God. But were there not replicas of these wretches back in her own country? A countless contingent of them, to be sure; they, too, were supposed to be creatures of God. Then, did not their very existence repudiate, indeed negate, the existence of God—make any belief in a divine presence a scurrilous mockery?* But then, it was not the first time this realization had struck her.

She leaned back as far as she could, closed her eyes to shut out the sight of those outside, the children of the no-god whose fraudulent image had been imposed on men to enthrall their rational apprehension of mundane reality. Her lips were pressed tightly with the onslaught of this notion and with the memory of a time when it would have appalled and terrified her; yet now it had come to be part of her perspective, part of her self … the no-god. Though it might well have been Leonard Jordan's, the term was not his but her own, born of the catastrophe barely two weeks ago, born in a flash of overpowering agony. Yet she knew it might never have been born save for that encounter in the sunset and a man's unforgotten words and the struggling but irrefutable awakening to new horizons that followed— the awakening that, however rudimentary and unrecognized by her, had had its inception on that evening four years ago, when, crossing the terrace, his voice had accompanied her way to her quarters. "Pleasant dreams!" it had said.

*

But it had not been a night of pleasant dreams. The long stretches of semiwakefulness and the brief interspersing of half-slumber were almost indistinguishable in their captivity to flights of bizarrely alarming, at times grotesquely lurid, fancies. The stillness was alive with the echoes of Leonard Jordan's voice, echoes of contentions at once irreconcilably dissonant and mysteriously harmonious, insistently pleading for her understanding and frightening her with the possibility of such an understanding. The darkness maddeningly swarmed about her with haunting images unfolding in shredded sequences, mercilessly recurrent, overlapping, merging into one another—two figures purpled by a sunset; two figures separated only by the intangibility of incense fumes; triangles, upward-pointing and downward, confronting each other, disjoined; triangles fusing into the golden glitter of a hexagonal star; innumerable human contours glutting the temple wall; contours, their stone turned into flesh, fondling, caressing, embracing, copulating; contours, their faces illuminated by the ecstasy of carnal fusion; faces, their features ever more plastic, molding themselves into the likenesses of Leonard Jordan and herself; a shadowy presence, her father's, with a head that might have been St. Paul's, bending over a Bible, discoursing over the wages of sin; a star of David upon the scriptures, blurring them from sight; shapes on the temple wall, Leonard Jordan's and her own, bright with smiles that knew of no sin …

She had tried to shut her mind to the echoes of that voice, to the tumble of those images, but they would not cease their tormenting evocations, their haunting, taunting dispensations of defilement and guilt. If the room had been hers alone, she might have turned on the light and escaped to the safety of sober reality. But Ann Glyn, already peeved and hostile, would not have taken kindly to such an inconsiderate disturbance. She knew that this concern was pretense: it was not her roommate who condemned her to the interminable endurance of those visitations; even if she had these quarters all to herself, she might not reach for the light switch, might not want to free herself from her captivity to those visions. Frightening, deranging though they were, fraught with repugnance and shame and culpability, they held a promise, still tenuous but steadily solidifying—a promise she would not, could not forgo, a promise that demanded to be pursued. Perhaps there were possibilities of fulfillment left disregarded by her father's creedal absolutism? Perhaps St. Paul's strictures had been too extreme in their prejudice? Perhaps a perfect mutuality, that total communion symbolized by the six-pointed star, might mitigate the sin of lustfulness, might even countermand it, might indeed transfigure the profane into an aspect of the sacred?

Perhaps somehow there might be some truth in Leonard Jordan's interpretation of those designs at Konark? An interpretation born of his cognitive acumen and sustained by his own life's actual experience … Miriam … Miriam, who had given him the star of David as a token; Miriam, who taught him the meaning of total communion; Miriam, a name nagging with relentless anguish, helpless jealousy, conjuring up an image of perfect mutuality, of a unique oneness no one could ever presume to equal, even approach; Miriam, a memory deathlessly possessing, precluding any rivaling experience; Miriam, a past which yet, oddly inversely, carried hope for the future.

For there had been yearning in Leonard Jordan. Yearning passionate and powerful. And a man whose feeling had been so intense, whose commitment so absorbing, would his yearning not urge him to seek a like experience, a union of like intensity, like concordance, like totality of mutual commitment? And had he not spoken of a potential—a potential persisting beyond all divergences, beyond all contrarieties of background and past proclivities, waiting but for time and effort and pain to make it attain its full unfolding; a potential that he had discerned in her on that first sight in the sunset? To be sure, there could never be another Miriam—and yet … "There will be a tomorrow, won't there?" he had said. A tomorrow, yes, there would be, oh, there would be a tomorrow!

Its tardiness in making its appearance, proportionately increasing her sleep-starved impatience, the tomorrow came at last. Yet when it did, its arrival merely proved a matter of meaningless chronometry, a mocking wrinkle in the course of eternity, heralding only interminable hours of irrelevant idling and aimless waste. Not until after lunch would she meet Leonard Jordan again, not until then would tomorrow really begin. The dawn was merely a prelude to the gaping void of the morning ahead, a void which somehow must be filled. No matter how the exhaustion from the night's turbulent fantasies might demand some compensating rest, the brightening day would not rescue her from the echoes, the images, the quandaries. Only by moving, however randomly, by acting, however purposeless, she might hope to blunt their assault. She rose, showered, and dressed, disregarding Ann Glyn's angry glances and vexed mumbling that this was supposed to be a vacation and it was still one whole hour until breakfast.

When she stepped from her room, her straying glance found Leonard Jordan bent over a stack of papers on the table of his quarters. Whether instantaneously sensing her presence or instinctively responding to a contingency for which he had been waiting, he looked up, waved at her, then crossed the terrace toward her with quick strides. Inquiring how she was feeling and whether she had had a restful night, his tone was unmistakable in its warmth, in its barely subdued affection, which drowned the memory of those endlessly besetting hours in a tide of implicit encouragement. He himself, he explained, had awakened early and so had started on his notes well before his usual time. Two more hours or so and this phase of his work would be completed. Then he would be free, and if she cared and thought she could brave the fierceness of the midmorning sun, he might show her around the village that had come to be his second home. Meanwhile, his preoccupation with his endeavor would grant her ample time for an unhurried breakfast and a long, refreshing swim.

There was no more void. It was filled to overflow with happy hope and vibrant anticipation. When she returned from the beach, he was ready, waiting. Rueful that precious minutes of his company might have been lost, she changed quickly. Re-emerging, she found him engrossed in conversation with Mr. Ghose, the bright-eyed assistant manager, who interrupted himself in midsentence, smiled at her, and, bowing, withdrew.

"A fine, decent man, Mr. Ghose," Leonard Jordan commented. "He was telling me about his daughter, Deepti, an extraordinarily pretty child, nine years old. Too bad you can't meet her, she's a joy. Unfortunately he had to take her to the hospital in Berhampur; nothing serious, a bothersome appendix … Shall we get on with our jaunt?"

He led her across the stretch of burning, barren soil, past the well and the women gathered to scoop up their supply of clean water, onto the main road that ran straight into the beach and the sea beyond. Proceeding leisurely to minimize the impact of the pitiless heat pouring from the cloudless sky, he pointed out the crumbling building that contained the generator that provided the village's electricity; the beggarly cubicle that housed the local outlet of the State Bank; the tea stall and the barber shop; the dispensary and the post office; and the tiny market further down the road. Wherever they passed, men stopped to greet them, and the sincerity of their immediate acceptance endowed her with a sense of hominess, of peace, of security. Or perhaps, she thought, it was just the tranquil, undemanding company of the man at her side, the assurance of his unobtrusive but subtly caring presence, the comfort of his calm, unpretentious comments about the people in the street, whom he had made his friends. He showed her the Hindu temple, and the mosque, and the church, which, although equally plain, dwarfed either in size and assertive ostentation and seemed oddly out of place in its marked disproportion to the meager contingent of local Christians, many of whom were only nominal devotees. Serving all denominations, its door was locked all week, allowing access only on Sunday mornings to the few who would wish to attend. But then, he explained, that church had not been built to satisfy the worshipping needs of the native converts; erected in the last decades of the dying imperial glory, it had been intended principally for the British officials and merchants who had chosen Gopalpur for their resort during winter holidays.

Suddenly he paused. "Tired, Barbara?" he asked in a flash of concern. They had been walking for a considerable while.

"No," she replied. "Exhilarated."

He just nodded, but she basked in her awareness of the fondness reaching out to her from his placid smile.

They returned just in time for lunch. There was hardly sufficient time left for a cooling shower. They paused at the entrance to the terrace, looked at each other. He only shook his head in response to her inquiring glance. As usual, he would be served in his own quarters.

"Yes," she agreed, thinking of Ann Glyn and the other fellow tourists, "you will be better off." She wished she, too, need not be exposed to the medleys of chatter and cackling banter, the clank of dishes and din of silver ripping into the priceless fabric of feelings, shredding the fragile web of intimate thoughts, shattering the continuity of moments relived.

"I know," he assented. "You are at a disadvantage. But it won't be for long."

They separated to an accord of understanding smiles.

The car was in front of the hotel well ahead of the appointed hour.

"Which is just like Ramlu," Leonard Jordan commented. "Uncharacteristically Indian: always punctual."

Then he introduced his friend. Ramlu Kumar was a lean, well-proportioned man with an ageless face whose bronze-tinted, chiseled features were accentuated by deep-set, ever probing eyes. She noted the virile gracefulness of his movements as he bowed to her and the accepting warmth of his respect, like that displayed by the people they had met on their morning walk only more direct, more definite, more unreserved. Ramlu turned to Leonard Jordan. "Sorada Road?" he asked with a pretense at casualness and a knowing smile; without even waiting for a confirmation, he climbed behind the wheel.

They drove past a string of small villages and hamlets and across the railroad track into Berhampur, cutting through the crowded center and the large, busy bazaar, proceeding at a crawling pace, but accelerating as soon as they left the city behind. Beyond its confines, the character of the landscape began to change. More and more stretches of woodland replaced the fields of the coastal plain, woodlands broken by grassy expanses and modest settlements along a straight road, lined by old trees that guarded against the most violent assaults of the midday sun. Here and there they provided the shade for some men and women at rest or a stray vendor of coconut milk.

"We're making good time," Leonard Jordan's voice broke into the silent, abstractedly perfunctory survey of the scenery. "Traffic's not as brisk as usual."

Still, it seemed brisk enough. A constant stream of men and bicycles was moving past them; several cattle herds were tramping to some market, each attended by an adult and a number of children with bamboo rods; bullock carts carried the area's produce; an occasional jeep passed, manned by police or some minor officials; there was a negligible trickle of private cars, vastly outnumbered by trucks carrying supplies to the settlements. And now the road was growing progressively busier as they approached what, judging from the distant outline, appeared to be a more substantial locality.

"Aska," Ramlu spoke from behind the wheel. "District center."

"We won't stop," Leonard Jordan advised him. And turning to her, he added, "A colorful enough place. Too close to the main artery of commerce, though. Not sufficiently backwoodsy for a glimpse of native India."

Nevertheless, stop they did, forcibly: a bullock cart had overturned and spilled its overload of timbers across the road. A half-dozen cursing men were sweating to clear the passage. "Just a few minutes," Leonard Jordan remarked, helping her from the car, "and they'll be done with it. Fortunately so, for there's no shade anywhere to offer refuge. Still, with this torrid sun, you're better off in the open than inside a standing car." He shrugged. "The experience of traveling in these parts would not be complete without some such accident."

"At least," she countered cheerily, trying to ease his apologetic discomfort, "this one was considerate enough to happen where there's something to look at."

"Ah yes." His glance had followed hers to the stately edifice, which, flanked by one of the oddly shaped, regionally characteristic towers, was hugging the road. "The Krishna temple." But the rather conspicuously deliberate aloofness of his reply did not discourage her from a closer inspection, which, it seemed, he would have preferred to avoid. Only too precisely had he anticipated her reaction, which her face mirrored in accents of dismay and disgust, as after only the most cursory exploration she turned away. "A countryside replica of the basic model," he embarked on a reluctant explanation of the figurations that adorned both temple walls and tower. Glistening in vivid tints, couples of lovers engaged in flagrantly erotic activities, displayed in square niches. "The pictorial pattern, which, projected by master artists, attains at Konark and Bhubaneshwar to artistic excellence, here finds its primitive and unrefined imitation at the hands of local craftsmen. The garishness of the colors reinforces the crudeness of the designs and thus, indeed, invests them with a touch of apparent obscenity."

"Apparent?" she repeated tensely.

"Apparent," he affirmed quietly, emphatically. "Only apparent; for however sexually demonstrative, these imageries are as untainted by any prurient intent as those at Konark. Their motivation and inspiration parallel those of their artistically so infinitely superior prototypes. However coarsely expressed by untutored, unsophisticated folk, the fundamental concept still remains the total communion, whose intrinsic sacredness is here as worshipfully celebrated as at Konark and elsewhere."

She met his comment with silence. But by its gradual, subtle change, its slowly waning expression of repugnance, her countenance reflected her response. Still these explicit portrayals of ultimate intimacies disturbed, even repelled her; she had no wish for any further, closer scrutiny. Yet their actuating idea no longer evoked her antagonism, no longer frightened her, as she recalled the half-waking visions of the past night, the fantasies, the images—the lovers of Konark wearing the faces of Leonard Jordan and herself. Recalling the outlines of new horizons, still remote and implausible but no longer foreclosed to exploration— there was the potential, had he not assured her thus?

"I think we're ready to get going again," his voice came to her, breaking into her memories-laden contemplation, a voice whose inflection told her, as much as his quiet nod, that her mute response had not gone unappreciated.

Ramlu was already behind the wheel. "This bad," he said, turning to them, his taut, almost ascetic face puckered with misgiving. "Sun too much for lady."

"I really feel fine." She smiled at him, grateful for the sincerity of his concern. "Thank you, Mr. Kumar."

"No Mr. Kumar," he earnestly contradicted her, shaking his head. "Ramlu. Ramlu only. Friend of Mr. Jordan, friend of Ramlu also." It seemed to her that his deep-set eyes were reaching for her with a glow of fondness. "Going Sorada Road now," he added, pointing ahead and starting the motor.

Almost immediately after Aska the landscape assumed a new aspect, not so much one of a radical change and novelty but one of intensification of the scenery's pattern. The woodlands became more prominent and extended, darker and denser, more luxurious and jungle-like. Settlements became ever less frequent, the space between them ever wider, and, with every mile, the traffic became noticeably thinner. Occasionally, hemmed in by the now narrower road, a truck would squeeze past them or a couple of women with heavy head loads might stop to gaze at them. But as they moved on, they would, sometimes for considerable stretches between forest-engirded hamlets, encounter no sign of human life. All around them, an immense quiet was spreading like a gossamer web of entrancing, almost mystical serenity—a quietude which somehow precluded any conversation, as though an interruption of the stillness would be an act of desecration, a despoilment of a wondrously mysterious otherworldliness.

"Ramlu." Leonard Jordan's sudden voice shattered the spell of tranquility.

"I know," the Indian responded, never turning to inquire. He had already slowed the vehicle and now within seconds brought it to a stop.

"Let's pause here for a while, shall we?" Leonard Jordan stepped from the car and held the door open for her.

She followed him uncertainly, puzzled by his suggestion. Her quick survey of the surroundings revealed no reason for this choice of recess. There was no settlement, no temple, no hint of human presence; just another spot along their way, seemingly indistinguishable from miles upon miles of similar ones they had passed: a plot of mossy ground, shielded from the sun by a maze of overhanging branches from trees whose crowns merged into a continuous canopy.

Ramlu nodded, reading her baffled expression. "This place," he answered her unvoiced question, "when going Sorada road, Mr. Jordan, he always stop."

"Let me show you, Barbara." Leonard Jordan's hand lightly touched hers. "If you will join me …?" And over his shoulders, "Coming along, Ramlu?"

The slow movement of a bronze hand conveyed a denial. "Me watch car," Ramlu said. His quiet, knowing smile remained half hidden behind the smoke of a cigarette he just had lit.

Leonard Jordan led the way along a footpath, a narrow strip, at times hardly visible beneath the growth of underbrush. At its end, right by the enormous trunk of an ageless tree, he stepped aside to let her pass. Before her lay a pond, a mirror of the sky's sunlit blue, a surface of perfect smoothness broken only by the white dots of countless lotuses. About it spread an infinitude of charmed quietude, profound with an unsubstantial yet pervasive sensuousness. For a long moment she stood breathless, overwhelmed, spellbound. It was not the magic of the vista alone; quite as powerfully, as engrossingly, it was the concomitant magic of a presence—the presence of a man, no more than three strides in back of her, a motionless presence, leaning against that ancient tree's mighty, protruding roots. A presence, which she had never felt as immediate, as physically possessing of her—and by which, she apprehended in a flash of fright and elation, she wished to be possessed, to be taught the experience of total communion, an experience, for which, beyond the threshold of consciousness, she had always been waiting, for which she was waiting now.

"You ought not to stay out there any longer, Barbara," his voice came to her as from afar, yet in its soberness, its even rationality utterly incongruous, utterly incredible. Amid this enchantment, how could there be soberness, rationality? "The sun's still too strong," that voice kept coming, "and you're not used to it. You'd better move back here, into the shade."

Soberness, rationality, were they just a decoy? When, actually, he was calling her, asking her to his side, to the experience she was waiting for, the experience now, now! But as, irresistibly compelled, she turned to retrace the distance between them, she found him leaning against that gnarled root, still. Only the faintness of a smile greeted her return, and the shadows from the tree seemed to paint his features with a strange somberness.

"I can tell how you feel," he spoke softly. "For it's the way I responded when I first discovered this place."

She did not know why she was saying it, "You were not alone?"

"No," he replied forlornly, "I was not alone."

She never doubted the truth of her intuition. "Miriam?" she muttered.

"Yes." Both his smile and his somberness seemed to deepen. "It was the year after she died. She would have loved this piece of nature, if she had been granted to know it. She would have been in total harmony with it. Its mood was so perfect a mirror of her own. Here, remembrance would be so total, so vital."

"That's why you returned here."

"Again and again."

"And every time?"

He nodded. "Never alone, never." His eyes groped past her, roamed the quietude. "This is not a place to visit alone."

She forced her glance to turn away from him. She feared its eloquence. The spell of silence was too vibrant with unendurable, excruciating yearning and exuberant, overweening happiness. This was the site he had been sharing with the memory of her, who had taught him the experience of perfect oneness—the place he now was visiting to share with another, with …

"Wait!" Leonard Jordan said. He was already walking past her toward the pond; he paused, rolled up his pants legs, waded into the shallow waters, bent down … It was a single pure-white lotus, which, returning, he held out to her.

She tried to hide the tremor of her hand as she accepted it from him. "It's lovely," she said under her breath, instinctively discerning the preciousness of the gift and the message it carried. "Oh, so lovely!"

"As lovely as its eternal significance." An absent smile was riding on his lips, intensifying as he responded to the unspoken question. "Immemorially, the lotus has been India's sacred symbol: the floral equivalent of the womb, the cipher for woman, for the female principle. Since the days of the primal past, this principle has been celebrated, worshipped in the divine embodiment of the Lotus Goddess, the transcendental vehicle of the essentially feminine, physically as well as metaphysically."

"As lovely as its eternal significance," she repeated after him, letting her finger glide over the silken petals and turning away swiftly, abruptly. There was the message, explicit now; she would not want him to see the moisture about her eyes and the longing in them.

Only after a protracted pause his voice at last fell into the brittle silence between them, gently, tentatively. "Shall we go on to Sorada?"

She did not turn. "Must we?" she muttered.

"No," he said tenderly, "we may stay here a while longer."

The Glitter and Other Stories

"Yes, please ... for a while longer."

Then they sat side by side on the moss, in the shade of the huge tree, looking out over the lotus-clad pond into the quiescent distance, wordlessly, as though afraid lest the merest sound despoil the mystique of those moments of intangible oneness.

Time passed, never touching their consciousness. Only when a sudden ray, stabbing through a fissure between the branches, hit his eyes with blinding force, did Leonard Jordan awaken to the realization, that the sun had already begun its slanting descent toward the horizon. But spared the assault of the glare, she stared at him in alarmed disbelief; even the careful softness of his voice came to her as a shocking intrusion, ripping the cocoon of a dream world. "Perhaps we should be starting back, Barbara," he was saying. "We wouldn't want to miss the sunset across the sea, would we?"

She nodded slowly, only with difficulty returning to reality, and rose. No, she wouldn't want to miss that sunset, their sunset ...

They found Ramlu alongside the car, stretched on a parcel of grassy ground beneath a tree. Gazing straight up at the foliage that blanked the sky's radiance, he seemed lost in a dream world of his own. Only the gauzy ringlets from a cigarette betrayed his wakefulness. "Sorada now?" he asked, getting to his feet, more than a nuance of doubt tainting his question. He only nodded, as, confirming his anticipation, he was advised that it was too late and they would drive back to Gopalpur. "Sorada, no matter," he remarked, taking his seat at the wheel. "Lady see little lake?"

"Yes," she replied. "It's so beautiful, so unbelievably beautiful."

"Achcha, beautiful," Ramlu affirmed. "No noise. No people ... Time to think, time to feel." Momentarily a smile suffused the bronze of his face with a strangely translucent glow, as he added, his eyes resting upon her, "Yes, me happy for Mr. Jordan." Then the motor broke into a creaking chatter and they were on their way.

Leonard noted the inquiry in her glance and responded to it. "He means, before. All those times I have come here alone."

"Miriam," she muttered.

He nodded. "Yes, Miriam. Ramlu knows. That's how he understands … appreciates. That's why he is happy for me."

"Then he should be happy for me, too."

"Ramlu is a cautious man," he retorted, and the wink in his eyes lent to his face a sheen of boyish impishness. "He may not be all that sure about your good fortune. Could be, he knows me too well."

"If he did …" She broke off abruptly to let the passion of her unfinished eloquence linger through a silence which persisted until they were in sight of Gopalpur.

Slowing down, Ramlu turned to them. Tomorrow morning he had business in Khallikota; perhaps Mr. Jordan and the lady would like to come along?

"Yes, why not?" Leonard Jordan agreed reading from her mien, that she would leave the decision to him. That excursion might make up for their aborted visit to Sorada and it would offer an opportunity to show her one of the more prominent, if generally lesser known, shrines of the region, the temple at Nirmal Jhar. Yes, they would be ready tomorrow morning after breakfast.

They reached the hotel terrace in time for their appointment with the sunset. For just the third time, but observing that unworldly iridescence fade below the gentle swell of the waters had somehow assumed the character of a ritual, in which the happening of that first sunset would find its almost sacramental renewal. It was the fit conclusion to a wondrous day and the fit prelude to a wondrous evening, the perfect link in a continuance of mutuality, enduring across the dinnertime's compulsory, wrenching caesura.

Afterward, when she searched the rapidly quickening nightfall for him, she found the corner of the arcade in front of his room garbed in darkness. But the cloying scent of smoldering incense sticks betrayed his presence, well before she could discern his shadowy figure standing, oddly tense, in wait for her arrival. He had dispensed with the light from the overhead lamp, he explained. The sultry air would be swarming with insects, attracted by the beam. But if she preferred …

No, she did not prefer. This way, the starry sky seemed even lovelier, more magical. True, he concurred—subtropical nights had a unique aura of their own.

Then they sat side by side, listening to the lilting whisper of the surf. But the quiet was fraught with a curiously besetting heaviness, persisting against all their efforts to find the key that might unlock the troubling muteness that hovered between them. Each fledgling initiative toward some liberating conversation died of its own frailty, of its own keenly felt irrelevance—died in the strangling grip of an escalating oppressiveness, to be entombed in another expanse of silence, pregnant with unrequited longing, repressed passion, unconsummated desire, that no longer could hide from their awareness.

Floating across the terrace, guffaws and giggles from socializing members of the tour group jolted her back to a pitiless reality that she had all evening been laboring to exile from her mind. "Just one more day," she mumbled emptily.

"Yes." His voice was as flat as her own. "One more day. One more excursion. One more afternoon, perhaps a swim together and one more afternoon tea; one more sunset." He seemed to have difficulty with the word. But swiftly, although a bit unsteadily, he glossed over it. "Then tomorrow evening, your tour's farewell party."

"Without me," she interjected harshly, appalled at the very suggestion of her possible participation, the sheer, inane implausibility of it.

"Yes," he repeated, "without you. Then one more evening like this, just one more … I wish there were no phrase like 'one more.' I wish …"

She perceived his shadow move impulsively, tend toward her, felt his breath touching her face. "Yes!" Half a cry, the word fell from her lips achingly, in spite of herself. And she knew, inevitably, profoundly, irrefutably: if he now were to kiss her, take her in his arms, lead her to his room, there would be no question, no doubt, no hesitation, no denial of any intimacy, no restraint, no flight from total oneness, from ecstasy—the ecstasy mirrored by the lovers of Konark, who last night had worn Leonard Jordan's face and her own; the ecstasy she had never known and now would be taught at last, at last!

But there was no kiss, no embrace. There was no more of his breath flowing across her face. Although she had closed her eyes, she realized he had retreated, had cheated his impulse, had cheated her of the experience, had cheated their encounter in the sunset.

"Barbara," his voice came to her.

"I wish," he had said. But when she had been so unconditionally, so nakedly ready to his wish, he had spurned her gift of herself, abused her passionate surrender, had mocked the promise of the total communion, of whose transcendent spirituality his devious persuasions had, finally triumphing over all the beliefs and reservations of her past, succeeded in convincing her …

"Barbara." From across the fumes of incense sticks, across a sudden, incomprehensible distance, that sadly, softly pleading vibrancy was reaching for her again. "This is not the way it should be between us. Please try to understand."

"I'm trying." In the guttural huskiness she could not recognize her voice as her own.

"Then you will see that this is not the way. Not with us."

"If you say so; though, somehow I never figured you to be addicted to celibacy." She had not meant this paltry gibe, wished she could rescind it, dismally realizing how utterly it must reveal what her religious tradition would condemn as concupiscent self-abandonment in its most blatant, shameless nakedness; must expose her implicit, downright renunciation of all her upbringing had taught her, not merely about her own claim to pride and dignity and self-respect but about general female decorum. Yet the rebuff to her passionate readiness was too devastating; fraught with a corrosive sense of violation and humiliation, it would not allow her to heed the internal warning and repress the caustic assault.

"Celibacy?" Leonard Jordan repeated. Even through the darkness she could perceive the weary faintness of his smile pass into oblivion, before he added simply, "It's ten years since Miriam left me. There's a natural need for companionship, isn't there?"

"Yes, isn't there?" she muttered bleakly.

"There is," he said evenly. "But those associations offered no more than what was theirs to offer. For the most part they were pleasant and pleasurable, occasionally fond; yet always, barring none, from the very outset delimited by a tacit but mutual consensus, that, in recognition of the parties' essential incompatibility, they would admit no commitment other than to reciprocal honesty and decency.

For longer or briefer periods, in their narrowly defined competence, these essays in companionship might serve, and serve adequately, the demands of the present. But it was always understood and implicitly acknowledged, that there was no potential for a shared future. Yes, there have been associations, but never once the experience of an encounter in the sunset. This is why, Barbara."

She sat utterly still, staring blindly into a black nowhere, enlivened only by the whispers of the surf, shattered by the desolate awareness of her self-destructive folly. *Why, oh why had she not understood? Why had she let her petty female vanity, her trivial disappointment of a moment's desire, damn her to proving the inadequacy of her own potential, which would, indeed must forfeit her future ...*

"This is why, Barbara," Leonard Jordan said once more. But even when she felt his hand touching hers, gliding over its iciness as in a caress and coming to rest upon it, she persevered in her rigid motionlessness, too terrified that, turning to him, she might read the lethal verdict in his eyes. "This is why, Barbara. Because there was an encounter in the sunset; because there is the potential—not yours, not mine, but ours, together—one to be yet fully, unqualifiedly realized. We've known each other for barely three days. So much has been left unsaid, so much has remained unconsidered, even unthought of. So much more is left to be explored, discovered, understood, adjusted. Diverse preconceptions, attitudes, aspirations, beliefs, they must be given their due, requiring time to find their way to each other, to grow toward each other, so that, at last truly interacting, they would define and justify the total communion, that very oneness, whose promise would have remained beyond this night's experience and, by failing to bestow such experience, might have prejudiced the potential of future consummation. This is why, Barbara."

He paused. His hand now was covering hers in a tighter, firmer grip. Feeling its warmth and reassurance, her body slowly relaxed its rigidity. Turning to him, she scanned his features for added proof. So much of his contention had been lost in the turbulence of her anxiety. Was she apprehending his apparent drift correctly? Had he indeed been speaking of a potential of total communion, of eventual consummation? Could it be that, after all, he had not written off the promise of the sunset? That this smile of his now, a smile quiet and tender, was truly spelling the verdict—not one of damnation but of reprieve and hope?

"Don't you see, Barbara?" his voice was coming to her again, deep and vibrant—coming to her, no longer across an immeasurable distance but from a closeness of tangible immediacy. "Between us it never could be the way it's been with the affiliations of those past ten years. Between us there would have to be a commitment for a shared future. This prospect does not admit compromise, will not countenance our bargaining for anything less, accepting anything less. But such, precisely, would have been the result, had the moment's impulse, however powerful in its longing and genuine in its passion, been allowed to prevail. We might have been close, and this closeness might have been uniquely beautiful, singularly precious. But the fulfillment might not only have proved evanescent; far worse, its aftermath might have been disappointing, disillusioning. For there would have been the awareness that our intimacy had involved only part of our selves. It would have fallen short of that total oneness which for us is the solely possible valid and viable road to fulfillment. Yes, we might have been close, but however captivating in the moments of consummation, in retrospect the experience would have proved disappointing. For it would not have been founded on true interaction, but would have been generated and framed by the fortuity of circumstances: the romance of a new and alien environment; the emotional high, triggered by an encounter amid such a setting; a beguiling confrontation, in which years of loneliness and stinted longings would naturally find their fervid but fragile escape. The sunset, the surf, the lotus-dotted pond, and yes, the however intellectually repudiated but sensorially inescapable evocation, compelled by those imageries at Konark—it's to these circumstances that this night's experience would have owed, not to the person we would wish to find in each other in a future of real mutuality. But if what as yet is but a wondrous potentiality is to attain its full unfolding, it must not be indebted to any collective of favoring circumstances but to our selves' unconditional readiness to be one, founded on our considered and conscious realization of our minds' true concomitance, which alone will justify our union's becoming our destiny. This for us is the only way, Barbara. Must be the only way. This is why, for the sake of an infinitely more precious eventuality, I would not accept the consummation of a passionately impulsive but only partial closeness. The intimacy of our bodies would not have been vindicated by the intimacy of our minds. Not yet, Barbara. But some day …" He let the phrase linger through a spell of silence.

"Some day," she repeated after him at last, uncertainly, comprehending yet uncomprehending, at once buoyed by the promise his words held out and distressed by the remoteness of its fulfillment. "Some day …"

"We still have a long way to go." A strange, irrefutable finality accented his quiet reply. "A long way to grow toward each other."

"There's just one more day left," she muttered.

"Yes," he said, a nuance of sadness deepening his voice, "just one more day of a prelude, a lovely, an unforgettable prelude. One more excursion. One more afternoon, perhaps a swim together, tea together. One more sunset. One more evening, maybe a stroll along the beach—all part of the prelude. Next morning you will be on your way home, and I'll be staying here to complete my work. A phase will have come to an end, another will begin—a period, both necessary and wholesome, of probing ourselves, removed from the fickle impact of fortuitous circumstances; of evaluating the potential of a final commitment, free from the pressures exerted by the suggestive force of direct contact; of discovering our ways toward each other, growing toward each other. Seven weeks more or eight, and I'll be on my way home, too," he gently concluded. "There are sunsets in America, too, if one is ready to experience them."

Only a gray, listless nod answered him. She could find no reply that would seem relevant. She perceived the internal logic of his reasoning, but this perception was countermanded by the prospect of an unendurably lonely wait, extending over the wastes of seven or eight interminable weeks; wastes which no argument could charm into bloom. But the finality of his verdict foreclosed any less desolate option.

Presently it seemed to foreclose any further communication as well. Thus they kept facing each other across a mute void, untouched by any awareness of time's passage—a void, slowly and irresistibly filling with her conviction of that verdict's unacceptability and her hardening determination to repudiate it.

The decision sent a shiver down her spine. "There's a chill on the air," she murmured.

"Is there?" His response was brittle with his keen awareness of the message implied by the incongruousness of her shiver amid the night's sultriness. "Yes, perhaps we'd better call it a night."

She rose. "Till tomorrow then."

"Till tomorrow," he concurred.

"And the last bars of the prelude," she added, in accents of a drab parody, pointed in its mockery. Already moving swiftly, though not quite steadily, toward the terrace and then across it.

But there would be no last bars. The tomorrow would not rise as an end to a prelude, but just as the fourth bar of a continuous melody, to which she shrilled throughout the sleepless hours that followed as her project gained an ever more distinct shape. Examining and re-examining them, she had come to see the validity of Leonard Jordan's contentions. However intense with their wondrous promise of self-discovery, of new horizons opening, of a new vision of her life's purpose and fulfillment, these mere three days of their encounter had indeed left too much unsaid, unconsidered, unshared; too much still to be explored, apprehended, attuned, so the potential might reach its full actualization. "Not your potential or mine," he had said, "but ours …" Ours. It was their joint potential, its attainment their joint venture and their joint responsibility. Its goal would not, should not be, accomplished in weeks upon weeks of dismal separation and brooding loneliness. Their way toward each other must be, and would be, found together, their growth toward each other experienced together, step for step …

The tomorrow would be just a fourth stanza of a perpetual poem. There would be no flight back home now. Home? She had found it here in Gopalpur, with Leonard Jordan. Leaving it seemed inconceivable, absurd. She would stay on. She could well afford to part company with the tour and be on her own, as long as she wished. A telegram to her sister to forestall any undue anxiety about the delay of her scheduled return, and a letter to Jenny, to assure the child of her undiminished affection, would cover the extent of her obligations. The reason for her change of plans would be self-evident, when seven weeks hence, or eight, she would be returning home. For then what had been no more than a permanent domicile would be home; she would not be returning alone.

She would never be alone again. Total communion would have become reality during those seven, eight weeks, even if the periods actually spent together were to be curtailed by the limitations of his intermittent sojourns at Gopalpur, if he still would insist that the incidental hardships must preclude her sharing his trips into the tribal interior. She would cheerfully wait for him back at the hotel, yearningly but happily counting the days and hours, yet never lonely; she would know herself no longer alone, would know he would be with her again, and then theirs would be the perfect oneness.

It was dawn when she at last abandoned herself to a brief interlude of slumber, buoyed by her exultant certitude and enhanced by her fantasy about his surprise when she would not board the bus. No, she would not tell him, would not deprive herself of watching his startled response when she caught him unsuspecting. She would let him go on believing in a tomorrow playing out the last bar of a prelude, a tomorrow spent precisely as planned—a morning excursion; a basket lunch at, what was that place's name? ah yes, Khallikota; a stopover at some temple; an afternoon swim and tea together; an evening in front of his room, side by side, separated by the ringlets of fume from the incense sticks, heavy with a supposedly final eternity of intimate silence; or, perhaps, a stroll along the deserted beach after a hurried, impatient dinner, when she would inform the tour director of her decision.

But then, she had never informed him …

*

"Train come," Kamesh said, pointing at the gate guarding the railway crossing, which was lowered, barring their passage. She hadn't realized that the car had come to a standstill, joining a mass of vehicles and pedestrians already lining both sides of the closed-off track. She bent her head out of the window, wondering. There was no sign of a train in either direction. Kamesh noted her questioning frown. "Train now in Ganjam," he explained. "When leave Ganjam station, gate come down. Must wait."

"Will it be long?"

"Ten minutes. Fifteen minutes." His shrug bespoke the patient acceptance that life has taught the Indian. Alighting, he joined a couple of drivers who likewise had stepped from their trucks. But in another moment he was back. "Lady come out," he pleaded solicitously. "Inside no good. Too hot." He pointed at the sun, which, straight overhead, was burning upon the car's roof.

"No, thank you," she replied. "I'll be all right here." Just now she did not cherish the prospect of exposing herself to the curious stares and unintelligibly whispered comments of the gathering crowd. Besides, she decided, unmitigated by any shading tree, the sun's fierceness would hardly prove more merciful out in the open.

"Achcha," another shrug, with a faint nuance of irritation at her rejection of his well meant advice. Those foreigners, they always thought they knew better, it said; Americans especially. He strode away to exchange bits of chit-chat with the truck drivers.

She leaned back. How oddly circumstances repeated themselves, she thought. Haphazard incidents, of themselves insignificant, but returning as though designed to goad her memories: the enforced halt at this railway crossing outside of Berhampur, where the road to Gopalpur was branching off; the lowered gate, barring their progress. "Train come from Ganjam." It had been Ramlu's voice then. It seemed like a replay of that day four years ago when they had returned from Khallikota, from Nirmal Jhar.

*

The trip had yielded an hour and a half of desolate eternity, of desperate silence deepening with every mile of their way back, a silence that impregnated the stifling air inside the car as with a spreading malignancy. No matter how she tried to block them out, those last words of his, back at the temple, kept reverberating through her mind; their impervious echo carried an acid message of rebuff, which, stoking her resentment and antagonism, choked off any attempt at communication. Yet it was not only this sharpening animosity that struck her with a sense of overwhelming loneliness and an anticipation of an indefinable yet imminent and ineluctable disaster. Even more acutely, it was her irrational and unfathomable yet irrefutable expanding perception of Leonard Jordan as an alien, someone she did not know, someone she had never met—a perception becoming more acute with every surreptitious glance she might steal at him, with every glimpse that beheld his oddly rigid figure, pressed into the furthest corner, as though to accentuate the distance which had sprung agape between them, a figure that seemed wrapped in a cocoon of inaccessible remoteness and suffused by a profound, forlorn sadness.

Although he had not witnessed their conflict at Nirmal Jhar, the increasing oppressiveness of their dissonant muteness appeared to have imparted itself to Ramlu also. At first, in an obvious endeavor to alleviate its aggravating burden, he had offered some casual, irrelevant remarks. But met by Leonard Jordan's laconic, almost brusque responses, these essays had soon been abandoned. Now, bringing the car to a stop in front of the lowered gate that barred their progress across the tracks, "train come from Ganjam," were the first words he had ventured in an hour. Their sober, offhand delivery, though, could not quite belie an undertone of apprehension, of a subtle, mournful disenchantment; still, somehow, they succeeded in breaking the spell.

Leonard Jordan stirred from his corner now and turned to her. "As usual," he commented vacantly. "Hardly ever fails, being held up here by a passing train. But after this it'll be just another fifteen minutes' ride to the hotel, and you'll get some overdue rest."

"I'm not tired," she mumbled.

"Good." A perfunctory nod. "Then, perhaps, we might spare a few moments to let me show you some items of local importance?"

She remembered. "Opportunities for my better comprehension?"

"I hope so!" A sudden accent of fervor enlivened the woodenness of his voice. "Yes, I shall show you, further along the road."

Fleetingly, this accent of fervor merely produced her acknowledgment of his intention, mutely, prey to renewed dejection. It evoked memories of the past three days' passionate closeness; instead of assuagement and encouragement, it promoted a new onslaught of anxiety. His profession of hope had been too perceptibly laced with ambiguity and doubt. Nebulously, inexplicably dreading she knew not what, she felt the prospect of better comprehension looming as a threat. And, while praying she might be spared its denouement, she knew that she could not, must not, be spared—that only such comprehension, explicit and encompassing, might restore the implausible alien at her side to the identity of the Leonard Jordan she loved; that, indeed, it held the key to any future of shared experience, of total communion.

They were moving again, accelerating their pace in the progressively thinning traffic. Villages and hamlets emerged alongside the road, only to be left behind. Already they were passing through Korapalli, which she recognized, recalling the side road leading to the campus of Berhampur University. Just some three more miles and they would be back at the hotel. Wondering, her glance sought Leonard Jordan, who again was leaning in that far corner, apparently absorbed in some troubling contemplation which painted his brow with a frown. Had he forgotten about his project; would there be no guide to better comprehension after all?

But he had not forgotten. It was near the outskirts of Gopalpur, within sight of the church, that he bade Ramlu to stop. Wordlessly, he held the door open for her then took her by the hand to lead her through a short stretch of brambly underbrush, littered with bits of refuse, toward what looked like an irregular cluster of severely undersized cabins, some constructed of clay, some chalk-whitened, others plain in their state of neglect and dilapidation. Of square design, the largest of them were no more than four or five feet high and in width and depth of similar dimension. Their fronts were broken by square openings, which only in one or two instances were covered by flimsy wooden doors. In passing, during their morning walk the day before, she had noted these structures and similar groups scattered about, but they had not paused to examine any of them.

"The homes of Gopalpur's godhead," he answered the unspoken inquiry in her unsure glance. But for all its dry matter-of-factness, there was a strange note of strain about the explanation, a tension compounded of expectation and apprehension.

"These?" She stared at him incredulously.

"Shrines," he said. "Shrines, as sacred to the people here as any of the great temples are to the orthodox believers." And pointing to the nearest one, he added, "You might take a look inside."

"Inside?" she repeated. "Seems they are hardly roomy enough …"

He interrupted, "Just from the outside, looking through the opening. You'll have to bend low."

"Looking, how? It's all dark in there," she remonstrated. Somehow listening to reason beyond reason, she judged she might be better off not venturing this exploration. A vague awareness of premonitory trepidation hardened itself into an unaccountable, but for that no less violent, aversion and an ardent wish to return to the car and drive back to the hotel—a boon, she knew, she would not be granted.

Already Leonard Jordan's voice came to her, made her captive to its compulsion. "Not dark, though. The sun's in back of you; it'll illuminate the altar well enough."

"The altar?"

"There's one in each of these shelters. When you've looked at a few of them, I'll explain."

"A few of them?"

"Their imageries are most diverse, as you will see."

She discerned the demand in his oddly flat voice, a demand that carried the force of a command. But it was not this unyielding firmness that overruled both her trepidation and aversion; it was her own realization, gaining new convincing definition, that in some obscurely complex way her destiny depended on her survey of these—how had he described them?—these homes of Gopalpur's godhead; that there was an internal imperative, she must obey.

She felt his eyes upon her, as, leaning against a tree, he watched her progress from one of these beggarly structures to the next; her brief, cursory inspection of the altar inside each of them; her perfunctory survey of the single or multiple imageries and the ritual articles scattered about; watching her responses keenly, searchingly, undeceived, she knew, by her grimly valiant efforts to suppress any display of her appalled, shuddering repugnance—efforts defeated and finally betrayed, she realized, by the unsteadiness of her gait and the pallid tremor of her lips, when, after the fifth shocking confrontation with Gopalpur's godhead, she rejoined him.

He received her silently, to lead her back through the underbrush. She was grateful to him for refraining from any comment, any question, any reference, grateful for a restraint, which allowed her to collect herself.

Ramlu was waiting by the car. By their return apparently deflected from some engrossing speculation, he looked up, but his welcoming smile faded into a troubled frown. "Lady not feeling well?" his inquiry greeted them.

She forced a perfunctory note of cheer. "Oh, it's nothing. The heat, I suppose. Too much exposure … A nice, cool shower, and I'll be all right."

"And a leisurely cup of tea, too," Leonard Jordan remarked woodenly. "That always helps. We'll be just in time for the afternoon serving, anyway. Will you be joining me?"

For a split second she stared at him wide-eyed, stunned. For three days past, their sharing the tea had been an implicit assumption which obviated any question, but now …

He read her bewilderment from her troubled glance, and read, too, its sudden animosity. "I just thought," he explained laboriously, "you might be too tired from our excursion … the long drive in the heat …"

"The exposure?" she completed slowly, pointedly.

His grasp was immediate and acute. "Yes, and the exposure," he replied, quite as slowly, quite as pointedly.

"Even so, I'm not too tired," she said rigidly, just as the car pulled up at the hotel. "Yes, I will be joining you for tea." And then, moving swiftly past him, she walked toward her room.

It was only a few minutes later that she traversed the terrace, just as the servant was setting down the tray on the table in front of room twenty-one and Leonard Jordan was emerging from inside.

"That was a fast shower," he remarked, beckoning to her.

"Was it?" Responding to his invitation, she sat down, watched him pour the steaming brew. "Well, yes. I suppose so. I rather hurried it." She paused, waiting for some comment, which never came. Her lips tightened, when at last she continued, "I was eager for the tea. Felt I somehow needed it … after the exposure."

"Quite." His smile was unsmiling, and there was a curious creak in his voice. "Too much of the sun will make you crave for a cup."

"You know what exposure I meant!" Her repudiation came rather more sharply than she had intended it. Then, taking hold of herself, she went on more quietly though no less bitterly, "Why did you have to inflict that on me, Leonard?"

"Inflict?" Repeating it, he accentuated the word, investing it with a timbre of mournful disbelief. "Inflict? I did not consider acquainting you with these imageries an infliction. Didn't intend it to be. Didn't expect it to be."

She had expected a challenge, was set to meet it. "Given the nature of those imageries, might you not have anticipated just such a reaction?"

"Might I?" A somber glance sought her, rested on her.

"Yes," she retorted firmly. "You ought to have. Why didn't you?"

A long instant passed, before he answered, "Because you are Barbara." There was none of the former flatness about his voice now, only softness vibrant with an aching plea. "And because of the very nature of these imageries. How could I foresee, that, what to me had been a fascinating, incomparably precious experience, a source of new perceptions, to you would be an infliction as though of some horrible evil? How could I conceive of that? Were you not Barbara?"

"Yes," she returned icily, staring at him. "I was Barbara. I am Barbara. It seems you did not figure on that."

"No," he said gently, disregarding the antagonism grinding in her self-assertion. "Because I did figure on it, I hoped—no, indeed, I felt certain—that those shrines, those idols, were going to suggest to you a new perspective, a new vision. That they were going to open to you a new perspective; were going to open to you new dimensions of thought and thus provide a frame of reference for your more profound, more discriminating comprehension of that icon at Nirmal Jhar, its meaning and message, its essential inspiration, its underlying concept of godhead."

He paused abruptly, struck into silence by the brief, gasping laugh with its naked hostility, which now reverberated in her every word as she spoke again. "You are really quite incredible, Leonard. Quite amazing in your single-minded insistence, on what you call 'my more profound comprehension' of that ghastly image in that temple; my more profound comprehension, I suppose, particularly of the concept of godhead, which, as you assert, it conveys. Quite extraordinary, this insistence of yours in the light of my reaction to that awful idol. Surely, my mortification, my utter disgust and detestation could not have eluded your notice? And neither did it, as your response to my unrestrained horror confirmed. Yet you persisted."

"It seemed important to me," he interposed wearily, "in fact imperative that you understand."

"The concept of godhead?" A cadence of gibing stridor coarsened the rebuff. "But if the image that conveyed it seemed so repugnant to me, would the concept itself not seem equally repugnant?"

"Not, if you learned to recognize …"

"And so, to make me learn," she interrupted him, and her scorn was flagrant in its escalating blatancy, "you subjected me to a survey of imageries far worse yet, far more outrageous, still far more abominable and loathsome than even the one that originally evoked my distress and rejection!"

"Abominable and loathsome," he repeated after her, in a voice dull with hopeless disenchantment. "Alien and bewildering perhaps, but abominable and loathsome?"

"Just look at them!" Her shout was shrill with her rancor, at what she discerned as an implied rebuke. "Just look at those monstrosities!"

"I have looked at them. Scores of times I have looked at them. And at hundreds more, hundreds just like them."

"And you didn't see …?"

"I saw," he said evenly, tonelessly, "but evidently not what you saw."

"Quite evidently," she mocked him. "I suppose, what you found in those obscenities was transcendental beauty and exaltation and metaphysical significance—just the way you found these qualities in those bawdy designs at …" She stopped abruptly, suddenly aware of the venom in her voice and shocked by it, realizing that she was altogether losing control of herself and with it control of her destiny—yet at the same time knowing that she was no longer capable of restoring her command of herself. His persevering contrariety had gone too far in its assault on her sensibilities.

"At Konark?" he completed her phrase stonily. "Yes, just the way I perceived the internal truth animating those lovers."

"The eternal truth!" She flung the phrase back at him. The very evenness, the placid assurance of his reply, its calm, its equilibrium, which so acutely pointed up the loss of her own, only contrived to provoke her fury even further. "The internal truth, according to Leonard Jordan. Except that this time said Leonard Jordan won't persuade me again to see things his way. This time he won't again argue away the hideousness and scurrility of those images and figurines, those creations of perverted fancy. They will haunt me in my sleep, those bizarre scarlet freaks with faces that are either altogether featureless blotches or ghostly in their childish sketchiness—that incredible bust with its inane harlequin's grin, the black effigy with the pendent crimson tongue and bared fangs, that prototype of sheer violence and destruction ... No, Leonard Jordan will not explain away that apparently endless variety of odious, viciously grotesque trash that he introduced as 'Gopalpur's godhead.' Godhead!" she exploded. "Oh, Lord!"

"Yes," the man across the table said, dispassionately sipping his tea. "Godhead. Precisely. What you call 'odious trash' are the icons of Harchandi, the Shining Mistress, and of Bhuteshvari, the Mistress of the Spirits; of Nilamma, the Black Mistress, and Tota Ma, the Mistress of the Sea, special protectress of the local fishermen—each of them another of the infinitely diverse projections of the divine, another ..."

She would not let him finish. "Projections!" she countered, grinding the word between her teeth. "No. Not projections! Caricatures of the divine, that's what they are! Travesties of the divine! Shameless, scurrilous perversions of all that is holy!" Breathless, she paused. She had spoken her piece. There was no more to say. She had told him the truth about those pagan atrocities, the truth that no sophistry of his could discredit, no argument could touch.

Only the faint tinkle of china disrupted the momentary silence, as Leonard Jordan set down his cup, carefully, thoughtfully, before he spoke again. "Has it never occurred to you that people of a different persuasion might perceive the objects of Christian worship in much the same way as you are perceiving the objects of their reverence? That, perhaps, to them, the lacerated, bleeding Jesus on the cross might seem as repulsive, as odious, as that black face with fangs and crimson tongue appeared to you; or the fat insipidity of the simpering infant in the portrayals of the nativity quite as inane and ludicrous as that bust with the grinning harlequin's face?"

She stared at him. "You must be insane!" she murmured, her lips pallid and trembling.

"Just objective." His smile was tranquil, even serene. "Just granting the possibility of different perspectives. Recognizing the equivalence of diverse premises and viewpoints."

"You are not serious!" For all its strangled faintness, it was an outcry of despair, of agony. "No. I will not believe that you are serious!"

The impressiveness of his silence was eloquent.

"But you are a Christian, aren't you?"

"A Methodist minister's grandson," he reminded her. "Does this oblige me to a pursuit of ignorance?"

His equanimity enraged her as vehemently as his argument. "I think it obliges you to the pursuit of truth!"

"Quite so." That placid smile deepened. "I've been trying to discharge this obligation."

"Then how can you talk about equivalence?" she demanded fiercely, thwarting his attempted rejoinder. "To a Christian, there is no, can be no equivalence of unChristian perspectives, premises, viewpoints. There is no equivalence of truth and untruth, of divine revelation and fallacy. The mere notion of any such equivalence as a possibility is sacrilegious."

"But scientific," he interjected, untouched by her mounting bitterness.

"Scientific!" Her scorn was tinged with frenzy. "That fraudulent alibi of the unbeliever, the heretic! Scientific, too, your comparison of these vile idols to the imageries of the crucifixion and nativity? Comparisons which are sheer blasphemy?"

"True," he said, "so indeed they are—to the Christian communicant. Precisely as your characterization of those 'vile idols' would be blasphemy to Gopalpur's faithful."

"Once again that equation of incomparables!" she countered harshly, at a loss for some more astute rebuttal.

"However," he went on pensively, disregarding her rebuke, "blasphemy is defined solely by each given community and has relevance exclusively within its own precincts. One can blaspheme only a god in whom one believes. Thus, in fact, neither of us is guilty of blasphemy."

For a long moment she sat very still, staring from unseeing eyes into a fathomless nowhere. From across the swell of the sea, the sunset was suffusing the terrace with its radiance, but she never noticed.

"Thus, in fact, neither of us …" When she spoke again, her echo of his words was a shuddering whisper which let the rest of his phrase fade into a gasp. "Then you don't believe in God?"

He perceived the extremity of her anguish, her almost paralyzing terror at the enormity of that realization. But he resisted a passionate urge to touch her hand, hold it—sensing that this gesture would not merely fail in becalming and reassuring her but would be unacceptable, indeed repugnant to her as the undue familiarity of one who had become a stranger. He would let her question pass lest his response still widen the gap of alienation.

But she would not grant him, or herself, the refuge of silence. "Then you don't believe in God?" she asked once again, more firmly for all the tremor in her voice, demanding an answer.

"Not in the way you do," he replied gently.

She would not countenance what to her seemed evasion. "What other way is there?" she persisted rigidly. "You do believe or you don't."

"No," he retorted evenly. "I don't think there is such an alternative. Everybody believes in something—something infinitely surpassing the self and its mundane existence. Admitted or not, such belief is intrinsic to the human being, all human beings. But the nature of that belief's object is subject to various definitions, various interpretations."

"Words!" The repudiation was caustic with disdain. "Big words. You're so good at them. Pretenses of profundity: 'Various definitions, various interpretations?' No. Never. The object of belief is, and can be, only God."

"Your object of belief," he amended. "That's how you define it."

"And how would you define yours?"

He did not answer immediately. Gazing past her into the dusk that had replaced the sunset's glow, he searched for the simplest formulation of an arcane complexity which would not allow a simple explanation. "I would define it as a transcendent power," he replied at last.

"Transcendent power," she repeated. "But that, precisely, is God."

He shook his head and his hand passed across his brow, as though to smooth away the wrinkles of a spreading frown. "No, Barbara," he said slowly, and his placid tone carried a touch of resignation. "Transcendent power is not God. Itself impersonal, it has merely been ascribed to the personal god—to all the personal gods."

"Of course," she returned scathingly. "Of course it has been ascribed to Him, to the Lord Creator of the Universe ..." She broke off abruptly, struck by the sudden recall of his last phrase and only now apprehending its full implication. When she spoke again, each word, each syllable was denunciation, condemnation, "What do you mean, 'all the personal gods?'"

He noted her simmering rage and responded to it impassively. "People have worshiped many different gods, haven't they?"

"Not gods!" Her unbridled rancor hurled itself at him. "Idols, creations of rank superstition! There is but one God, the God of the Scriptures. He alone is God!"

"Is?" Again that unsmiling smile was sitting on Leonard Jordan's lips. "Is? No, Barbara. You merely presume he is. The existence of God is not a matter of objective fact but of subjective belief. No ..." The quick, determined motion of his hand thwarted her objection. "Just for one moment, please, listen to me. I want you to understand. I'm not scorning, not denigrating your faith. It is too preciously part of you, and I respect it. But I, too, have a faith, one just as preciously part of myself. Might it not be due some respect also?"

"You have no faith," she murmured bleakly. The very tranquility of his riposte was exercising a strange spell, which, compelling in its captivation, blunted her acrimony.

"I can see that it may appear so to you," he said, and that unsmiling smile intensified. "That's why I wish you listened."

She shrugged listlessly. "You wish. So I'll listen—as I've been listening all along, haven't I?"

Momentarily his features hardened. "My argument may not alter your opinion of me," he returned, "but at least it may provide more solid grounds for your judgment, when, as one day you may, you'll come to the conclusion, that faith ought not to be equated with doctrinal fidelity—in fact, cannot be so equated." His speech was steady and level, but hard as he endeavored, he could not quite suppress a nuance of despondency. From the sullenness of her acquiescence, its undertone of drab irony, he realized that her verdict was already in. Yet he was not ready to concede the irreversible actuality of their estrangement. "Not that I deny or even minimize the importance, within its limited sphere, of doctrinal fidelity," he continued. "It has its proper place and function in human affairs. For many people, perhaps for most, it satisfies a profound, an urgent, a vital need. For you, it implies an unquestioning and absolute commitment to the God of the Scriptures, a commitment, which, in my young years, I also shared, indeed shared with an ardor perhaps not inferior to your own. That, after all, was the way I was brought up, taught, indoctrinated. But in time, my mind questioned the premise of this commitment. Had the Greeks not been quite as firmly committed to their Zeus, the Egyptians to their Amon, the Teutons to their Wotan? To those people, had their gods not been as true as the Lord of the Scriptures was to me? I came to realize that the world had known countless deities. Their specific characters and qualities disclosed themselves as but tribally favored and as such insignificant imputations. What distinguished them from one another was alone the diversity of parochial beliefs. And Jehovah, the God of the Scriptures, was just a creature of yet another parochial belief..."

He paused. His glance searched across the table, as though expectant of a protest a rebuttal. But engulfed by the dusk, she was a contour of frozen immobility.

"Surely I would not believe in Zeus or Wotan or Amon. But at the same time, their communicants' very belief in them implicitly invalidated my belief in Jehovah. He was no less implausible a god than all the rest. Like them, he was just another celestial overlord whose supposed will and wonders, whose very existence and eternal presence, were just a matter of subjective presumption. Yet at the same time, I passionately felt that there is some transcendent essence, ineffable and all-encompassing …"

His voice trailed off into a few instants of absorbed recollection before he continued. "The answer came to me right here, in Gopalpur, on an unplanned, accidental stop on my first trip to India, over twenty years ago. Purely by chance, I came upon the very group of shrines, the very imageries that so appalled you. I was struck by those apparently so diverse visions of the divine, visions mirrored by an endless variety of figural projections, furnished with an endless variety of identities and appellations—a diversity steadily augmented by the hundreds of similar local sanctuaries I would subsequently visit. But what struck me even more tellingly was the devotion accorded to all those various deities, equally, indiscriminately, by all the people. This was the key. It made me realize that these icons reflected just sectarian aspects, emphases, masks of the same all-embracing, all-pervasive Power, which, to all communicants alike, was the object of their reverence and worship; that these countless deities were but personifications of this Power, mere ciphers for an Essence, immeasurably beyond human grasp and inaccessible to human definition and knowledge; that they possessed no reality whatever; that, whether as the goddesses of the Indian countryside or as Zeus or Amon or Wotan or Jehovah, they just were willful, banal materializations of the essentially insubstantial and impersonal, all-energizing, all-indwelling Power; that, precisely because that Power was beyond any human grasp and definition, any human imagination, it could assume any aspect; that because it was anonymous, it could assume any name, any identity; that its intrinsic incomprehensibility and anonymity were preserved by the infinite diversity of its parochial masks, whether by such anthropomorphic projections as those of Apollo's heroic muscularity or Isis's enigmatic beauty or, and much more pertinently, by the Indian back-country's figurative abstractions, those faceless or ghostly designs, those absurdly grinning visages, those black countenances with fangs bared and pendent crimson tongues. I realized that they were masks, symbols only, into which, exactly because of their supposed unreality, each worshipper could read his own individual perception of the transcendent Power, unencumbered by any doctrinal superimposition."

"And so," she said stonily, as he paused. She had turned her head away from him, to stare out over the sea, billowing beneath the descending darkness. She could not bear facing the shadowy figure across the table, which had become the vehicle of a decaying dream. "And so, like those primitives who hatched those awful idols, you, too, read into them your own fancies, your own invention, your own delusion, your own fallacy. For, I gather, that transcendent Power you claim to have perceived was not the God who revealed himself to Moses, to the patriarchs, to the prophets; not the Lord God who sent his son, that he might show us the way to his kingdom on earth and convey his promise of eternal life in a state of eternal bliss."

"Quite true." His voice came to her, hateful in its impervious calm, and even more infuriating in its unyielding certainty and unconscious, yet implicit irony. "The imageries of those primitives contrived to reveal to me a far less primitive perception of the transcendent Power, one that envisioned it not as some imaginary supernatural person, some capricious autocrat on a throne in some mythical heaven, some fictive nowhere above and beyond. Indeed, those imageries taught me a faith, one as impassioned and uncompromising as your own, in an Essence more real than such a creature of anxious illusion and subjective belief—in an Essence, the evidence of whose actuality is present all about us, in every grain of this earth, in every star in the sky, in every drop in the oceans, in every rock and pebble, in every tree, every flower, every animal, every man, if one is open to the experience of this actuality, this presence …"

"If one is open to the experience," she cut in, echoing his phrase in accents of sardonic mimicry. "But are you open to it? For that actuality you are citing, that self-evident ever-presence is God, the very one whom you deny, whose transcendent power you mock and denigrate."

"Neither mock nor denigrate," he amended. "I would not scorn other people's faith any more than I would my own. I simply do not identify a personal god nor acknowledge him as the vehicle of the transcendent Power."

"Yet you talk of faith!"

"About my faith," Leonard Jordan countered emphatically, sonorous with sudden, churning vigor. "My faith, Barbara, in a transcendental Power, that is not above or beyond the natural universe but within each of its integral particles—an imperishable, vital energy, which engenders the world's perpetual and infinite renewal, engenders it impersonally, impartially, offering neither reward nor punishment, unconcerned with the incidents of individual destiny, occupied solely with the sustenance of eternal life."

"A life," she interrupted scathingly, "a life unorganized by any creative design, undirected by any supreme authority, subject to no moral law; an eternal life that is wilderness, chaos without meaning, without purpose!"

He let the pain and outrage of her outcry filter into the heat-cloyed evening before he answered. "The purpose is life itself, universal life. The meaning? Who may so utterly lack humility that he would dare presume to know, or even guess at, what is forever an impenetrable mystery? Why grope for a meaning of what by its very nature is inapprehensible within the human dimension? Why not be content, marveling at the workings of an all-inclusive, all-animating dynamism in whose scheme each and every particle has its role and function, its own imperatives? Why not be content with the knowledge that each serves in some however unfathomable way to integrate the universal design by fully attending to its own potential?"

She still was gazing into the yonder of a darkening horizon. "Words," she said again, throatily. "Lofty-sounding, abstruse words is all I hear. Tangled verbiage in which I get lost. But even what of it I somehow manage to unravel does not add up to any faith in God, to any concept of salvation, to any vision of afterlife."

"Salvation?" He took up her word evenly, yet incapable of altogether silencing an inflection of ironic repudiation. "Salvation from what? From the bane of human existence? From supposed sins, whose commission has been inbuilt in us? Salvation through Christ? Through a medium rather than through one's own efforts? Salvation through grace from without rather than from insight from within? No, Barbara, I'm afraid that in the world I live in there is no room for such a concept. But as to afterlife, would not the axiom of life eternal imply as much? Surely there is an afterlife."

"Indeed?" The acrimony of her scorn creaked at him. "Afterlife, how? One who denies salvation and Christ and God would hardly believe in heaven, would he?"

"Why should he?" he retorted, disregarding the assault of her hostility. "Would the proposition of a heaven be more plausible than that of Valhalla or the Elysian Fields, or the Egyptians' Western Abode of the Dead? At one point on one's road to adulthood one ought to grow away from such utopian fairy tales, grow toward a more rational perspective."

"So, the very adult Leonard Jordan has grown away." Her sarcasm was blatant with detestation. "Yet avers the said Leonard Jordan, 'surely there is an afterlife,' one, no doubt, fitting his oh so rational perspective."

"No doubt," he confirmed, and now his voice was fraught with the austere solemnity of an irrevocable creed. "Yes, the said Leonard Jordan's world knows of an afterlife. Not one extending life in some imaginary beyond, but one perpetuating it in the minds of the living. That world knows no death; life goes on in the memory of the survivors—memories that are passed on when those that carry the immediate recall surrender their physical existence; memories that are, forever proliferating, passed on *ad infinitum*. For energy is imperishable and thus that part of the energy which is briefly materialized in the individual human form cannot, will not, be lost. Every word, every touch, every action inevitably transmits that energy, to leave its imprint, which, in whatever infinitesimal way, will modify the world. Each of us is a vehicle of countless afterlives, just as countless generations are the vehicles of our own. Our names may be forgotten, our deeds, our very existence—but the energy which had been ours will live on indelibly. Could there be a more certain promise of afterlife?"

It was then that she turned to him in a sequence of small, reluctant movements whose deliberate slowness was measured in mounting degrees of aversion. And when, at last fully facing him through the thickening dimness, she spoke, her every word in its toneless sullenness and utter bleakness mirrored both her final desolation and final determination. "No," she said, "there is no promise, Leonard. No promise at all. Just a prospect of death without redemption, of a life without purpose, without hope of exaltation. Nothing you have told me holds any promise, any vision, any belief in a moral law, in the eternal truths …" And noting the motion of his head, its shaking with silent refutation, she went on, more sharply now, "You wanted me to listen to you. So I listened. I rather wish I hadn't. But then again, perhaps it was necessary that I should … Yes, I have been listening."

"To words," he muttered, "not to meanings."

"To meanings, too!" she rebutted abrasively, antagonized by his placid, somberly grieving reproach. "To enough of them, anyway, to be allowed a good long look at what you call 'your world'—a world without God, without faith; a world …" She paused and abruptly rose from her seat. "A world," she concluded in a voice, which, low and trembling, was unwavering in its resolve, "a world, in which I could not and would not live."

"I know," he said quietly. "That's what, somehow, I felt last evening. That's why that evening had to end the way it did: because we had not found our ways to each other."

"Nor ever would!" she retorted harshly. "For me, there is no way into your world."

"Not yet," he amended, "not yet."

"Never!" She almost shouted it.

His faint, forlorn smile was swallowed by the darkness. "There is your potential, still," he said gently.

"Not one for life in your world," she returned after a moment of shivering silence.

"Still!" His voice was firm now, assertive, assured. 'One day …"

"Perhaps," she cut him short, acidly, "one day, when you might come to live in my world."

"How could I?" A sudden accent of passion animated his response. "When one has found his own world, it becomes his only possible, only viable habitat. One could not return to a discarded world. One can grow away, but there's no growing back."

"Well," she said, stepping around the table, "then this seems to settle the issue."

"Does it really?" His eyes were upon her, boring into her, searching, assessing. "No, Barbara, I don't think I was mistaken. You will find your way."

"Perhaps I will. But it won't be your way."

"No," he confirmed thoughtfully, "not mine. It will be yours, once you've found it."

Only her silence answered him—a silence cold with rage at the compelling intensity of his eyes, the certainty of his words, the faint evanescence of a smile, most of all, the persevering closeness of a stranger from an alien, hateful world—a silence at long last broken by Leonard Jordan's gentle, melancholy voice. "This evening we missed the sunset," the voice spoke, and it turned her rage into pain, unbearable pain.

"Was there ever a sunset?" she had muttered. And then, moving past him into the nocturnal mist shrouding the terrace, she had walked toward the glitter of lights from the hotel to join her tour companions, now gathering for the farewell party.

*

The final freight cars were rumbling away, thirty, forty of them, heading south. Unhurriedly, one by one, the attendant was opening the barriers, freeing the rail crossing. Apparently not too pleased at what to him seemed a premature interruption of an engrossing conversation with the truckers, Kamesh returned. "We go," he announced redundantly and started the motor. "Go Gopalpur now. Hotel."

"I know," she told him curtly, a bit too irritably, she thought. He was just trying to be sociable; still, his voice had torn her from a review of a squandered past. Perhaps, she considered, she ought to be grateful rather than annoyed that he had rescued her from the memory of that last evening when they had missed the sunset; when she had left Leonard Jordan for the forced, nonsensical jollity of the farewell party, for too much drink to deaden the pain and the short hours of liquor-numbed, nightmare-racked sleep. Yet instead of relieving her, somehow the man's casual reference to Gopalpur and the hotel only contrived to focus her recall of those interminable moments that had witnessed her departure four years ago.

*

Much as she would have preferred to be spared the leave-taking, she had known all along that her anxious hope would be in vain. She spotted him at once, standing at some distance, motionless, while she proceeded to the bus and boarded it. When she had seated herself, he slowly walked over to her window. His countenance seemed somewhat gaunt, she thought, but this might be due to the shadows painted by the morning sun's slant. His step was firm, his bearing poised. Impressing itself on her, his unruffled deportment sharpened her resentment.

"Have a pleasant, safe trip home, Barbara," he said, calmly, impassively.

She had anticipated just such a deliberate aloofness from him and had prepared her reply. "Yes, thank you, back home to a world in which I fit."

He nodded, and there again was that unsmiling smile she had come to know so well. "Perhaps some day there may be a different world to fit in," he remarked with an odd touch of solemnity.

She had expected some such comment as well. "Never!" she averred, and even its calculated coldness could not conceal that single word's animosity. But as she tried to turn away, to escape the searching intensity of his eyes, she could not—his glance held her as in a vise.

"There's always another sunset for those ready to experience it," he said, and then, never letting that gaze swerve from her, he said softly but with utmost, irrefutable conviction, "Yes, one day ..." And then he stood there, motionless, watching the bus pull away.

The trip back had proved to be safe enough, though hardly as pleasant as he had wished for her. Throughout the twenty hours of flight, she never shut her eyes for the merest spell of slumber. Afraid of the dreams she could not control, she kept herself awake with a countless succession of black coffees and continuously engaged in hectic, chatty conversations to blot out the image of a lonely figure receding into the sundrenched distance, diminishing, fading away. She was aware that she was increasingly becoming a nuisance to her fellow tourists but could not help herself. She dreaded even one moment's leisure which might leave her to her thoughts and memories and contemplations, to a recurrence of that spell of total desolation she had experienced when the bus had rolled out of the hotel's gate, out of Gopalpur.

It was only when, exhausted to a point of near collapse, she espied Jenny, that she had been able to take hold of herself.

Far ahead of her mother, with whom she had come to meet her aunt at the airport, glowing with excitement and affection, the child was rushing toward her, open-armed. "Oh, Aunt Barbie, Aunt Barbie!" she cried, abandoning herself to the embrace. Then, suddenly looking up with frightened eyes, she asked, "Has anything happened, Auntie, anything bad?"

She buried the child's head in another tight hug to elude those eyes' troubled intuition. "No, darling, nothing bad at all." Her labored smile tried to appease her niece. "The trip was wonderful. It's only that the flight's so long; I'm just tired."

"I'm so happy to have you back, Aunt Barbie!" Jenny muttered slowly, falteringly, unconvinced by the assurance. She had not missed the tremor in her aunt's voice.

"Of course, your aunt's tired," Gloria said. It was not from her that Jenny had inherited her sensitivity.

And then they were on their way home.

But that home in Philadelphia, she almost immediately discovered, somehow no longer provided the world in which she would fit, that world secure in its conforming traditions and unquestioned preconceptions to which she had referred with such scornful certitude on that last evening—the very same home she had left but a few weeks earlier, yet oddly, indefinably, she found herself no longer truly part of it. From the first day of her return, she was inexplicably yet irrefutably beset by a vague, nagging sense of alienation. A shadow had interposed itself, dividing her, distancing her from the world she had known, the world in which she had lived. Prey to an awareness that was as rancorous as it was inescapable, she recognized the identity of that shadow. Try as she might to undo, efface, obliterate it, rage as she would at it and at herself for allowing herself to be its victim, she could not banish that unsubstantial presence nor escape from it—a presence which, on the contrary, only kept expanding its persistence and forcefulness in proportion to her instinctive inability and her deliberate refusal to share the experience that had engendered it. However she might at length describe her visits to Agra and Delhi, Jaipur and Varanasi; however, more casually and as perfunctorily as possible she might convey her impressions of Khajuraho and Bhubaneshwar, even of Konark, not with one single word would she ever touch upon Gopalpur, the Sorada road, Nirmal Jhar. Those four days remained excised from her accounts—in their exultation and pain, their ephemeral promise and perpetual debacle, they were hers alone, must remain hers alone.

For she realized only too clearly that, had she ever essayed to share those four days' experience, there would be no one to comprehend it. While imposed by her own determined choice, her silence was dictated as well by the condition of the world to which she had returned. Perhaps, had her niece been closer to adulthood, that condition might have proved more promising. Their intimate mutuality and the girl's strange, intuitive acuteness of grasp and empathy might well have encouraged such a communication. But however mature for her eleven years, Jenny was still a child; her prepubescent mind must not be burdened with emotional perplexities to which it could not possibly relate—even though it sometimes seemed she might cope rather better than her elders. Her mother, for one, was certain to make any such sharing an exercise in futility. In her frigid staidness, so unlike her own offspring, Gloria would meet such a disclosure in terms of her own inculcated suspicion of and aversion to any emotional exuberance. Her lifelong retreat into the safety of strictly controlled feelings would ensure incredulous incomprehension and mortified rejection of her sister's passionate involvement. In its own, more subdued way, her response would have proved hardly any less hurtful than her husband's, whose obtuse, adamant dogmatism must implicitly prohibit any such confidence. A true-believing fundamentalist and inveterate moralist, Ted Lansing would, with the intrinsic malice of the righteous, gloat over the debacle of his sister-in-law's infatuation, judging it to be the just punishment for her sinful, carnal inclination. Even if a tropical evening's flaring desire had never been translated into consummation, what mattered was the mental offense, the spiritual delinquency, and to that effect he would quote the Scriptures, which was his favorite as well as habitual means of documenting his virtuous self-importance.

Instantaneous and unqualified in its instinctive assertion, the realization that her life's most profound—paramount—experience was condemned to remain her lonely secret, that it was utterly impossible to impart it to the world to which she had returned bewildered, even frightened her. For this, after all, was the very world in which she had fitted, of which she had unquestioningly and comfortably been part—a world of shared beliefs and attitudes, interests and concerns, routines and activities; a world which was an extension of the one in which she had been raised and which, only slightly modified, had been her habitat throughout her married days; a world whose climate had shaped every facet of her being, whose way of life had determined her own; a world which had never admitted any awareness of loneliness, as, resting on commonly held presumptions, there had been implicit understanding and acceptance—yet now a world which, for all its welcoming familiarity, seemed, at first vaguely, then with every passing day more palpably troublingly changed.

Only after several harassing weeks of struggle had she come to recognize that it was not solely Leonard Jordan's shadow that imposed on that world a sharpening aspect of alienation, nor was it the burdening secret of that shadow's presence that invested it with a deadening sense of loneliness—that it was not the world of Philadelphia that had changed, not the environment of the Lansing home, but her own self. This change revealed itself to her through her own responses to that environment. Whereas in the past she might have on occasion silently deplored her sister's all-too-pronounced intellectual sloth and what would seem to her somewhat excessive churchliness, now she could not repress a growing critical resentment. Whereas her brother-in-law's holier-than-thou homilies might have irked her, now his missionary zeal and biblical exhortations aroused in her a just-barely-suppressed chafing impatience which progressively turned into antagonism and clandestine opposition when she observed his unflagging efforts to inculcate Jenny with the narrowness and intolerance of his convictions. Only too well and bitterly did she recall that same endeavor on the part of her own father and its effect of stringently delimited horizons and as stringently stinted emotions, of—how had Leonard Jordan called it?—of an unrealized potential. She determined that her beloved niece must be awarded a more favorable chance for a sunset encounter's denouement, different from her own disastrous one. Her attempts at providing the child with some measure of counteracting influence did not long go unnoticed, and politely but firmly she was apprized that they were undesirable and unacceptable.

Resolved not to hurt Jenny by subjecting her to the subtle but mounting friction and placing her in a dilemma of divided loyalties, she thought it best to quit the family circle and move to a nearby apartment hotel, restricting herself to twice-weekly, noncontroversial visits. This decision had been welcomed by the Lansings, who, although puzzling over the cause, had gradually come to appreciate the deterioration of the harmonious closeness which for so long had prevailed. With tacit but apprehensive disapproval, they had discerned her small but pointed deviations from the established patterns of conduct and pursuits, adherence to which had heretofore been taken for granted—deviations in which the escalating estrangement found their external manifestation most disturbingly in her marked preference for secular over religion-oriented literature and her desultory and often edgily impatient attendance at church services.

Yes, contrary to the Lansings' predictable interpretation, these displays of self-assertive independence from the customary and expected standards of Christian rectitude did by no means betoken any slightest break in her creedal fidelity or even the most insignificant weakening of her faith, the most trivial faltering of her devotion, or the most minute modification of her beliefs. In fact, her confrontation with Leonard Jordan's appalling vision of a universe bereft of God and heaven and afterlife had deepened her religious commitment and fortified the certainty of her own convictions. It had crystallized in her mind the shape of the world in which she belonged, the only one she wanted to live in or could ever live in. Yet at the same time that confrontation had raised her awareness of coexisting worlds— divergent from and in opposition to her own, discrepant not only in their external manifestations but also in their internal motivations, framed by disparate presumptions, persuasions and beliefs which called for exploration, not for their own merit's sake but for the purpose of vindicating, by their inadequacy and fallacy, the incomparably superior merit of her own world.

Now, withdrawn to the solitude of her new chosen environment, unencumbered by the demands of a sociability marred by the tensions incident to her progressive estrangement, she dedicated herself to those explorations, untiringly intent on making up for what she felt she had failed to make the focus of her endeavors. She was intent on reaching at last for the stimulation of expanding knowledge which, she now resentfully realized, the preclusive dogmatism of her upbringing and her own indolent acquiescence in the censorious rejection of any and all speculations about non-Christian worlds had denied her.

True, her youthful interest in foreign lands, peoples, and cultures, evoked by a brilliant and enthusiastic teacher, had always remained an undercurrent, even throughout a marriage, which, by its emphasis on financial and social advancement, had stymied its pursuit. Only during her years of widowhood had it found at last some, if but desultory and inadequate, expression. Even on her travels she had apprehended foreign lands in terms only of their sceneries and their inhabitants only in terms of their artistic and technological accomplishments, in terms of edifices and monuments, paintings and products of native handicrafts. She had been thrilled by the grandeur of Greece's ancient temples, the symmetrical loftiness of the pyramids, the majesty of Japan's colossal Buddha effigies, but she had never inquired into the motivating inspiration of their architects and artists, into the ideational and emotional contents of the displayed forms. It was this failure, she now perceived, that had perpetuated a sense of personal insufficiency, of lacking vitality, even emptiness. She had observed but not experienced—for it was the underlying inspiration which alone conferred the experience. Dimly and with barely subdued dismay, she now realized that it had been her encounter with Leonard Jordan that had made her perceive that such inspiration might, in its own alien way, perhaps prove comparable to the devotional zeal prompting the builders of Europe's cathedrals, those glorious creations of Christian dedication. Within her, there lingered the forlorn echo of a melancholy phrase: "You heard the words, not their meanings." Indeed, she had surveyed the forms without contemplating the meanings, which were the key to any experience. If that key were used, perhaps even the imageries of the Indian backwoods might come to seem less outrageous?

When this notion made its first forays into her awareness, she rejected it with vexed determination: she would not be involved with those hideous idols. India and things Indian must be off limits to her explorations. India and Leonard Jordan were one in her recall of an unforgiven debacle, were intrinsically fatally interlinked, inseparable, hatefully identified with each other—hatefully, for it was there that she had been compelled to behold a world which was inimical to her own; a world in which his mind had found a home but from which she had had no option but to exile herself. It was India where a missed sunset had canceled the promise of three preceding ones; where a hope had been born and an illusion lay buried. No, India must be exempt from her mind's journeys toward broader horizons, for that journey would but invigorate the pain, the regrets, the rancor that was trying to abate but could not; would only fuel the passionate fascination that she was seeking to shed and could not. If she was unable to banish that ever-present shadow, at least she would refrain from a venture which was bound to sustain it. One day perhaps, when that shadow had relinquished its possessive hold on her, when the experience of India had receded into a safely remote distance and Gopalpur had become just another point along a long-ago trip's itinerary, she might be ready to inquire into the ideas that had shaped the lovers of Konark, the implausible image of Nirmal Jhar, the bizarre icons of Gopalpur, and Leonard Jordan's unholy vision of the world—one day. But would there ever be such a day?

For the present, there were untold cultures to be examined, waiting for the effort—ancient and contemporary perspectives of human existence, a plethora of actuating notions, diverse beliefs, hypotheses, doctrines—an all but inexhaustible variety of presumptions and theories concerning the creation of the universe and the evolution of man, about the purpose and destiny of human existence, about the nature of the supernal Essence governing the boundlessness of creation and the Essence's countless embodiments as specific personal deities, male and female, benign and destructive, adorable and monstrous. There was the unceasing thrill of each new discovery from the bewildering vastness of myths and esoteric speculations, of occult conjectures and theological certainties; of creeds and cults, of religious fancies and metaphysical schemes, sometimes profound, often abstruse, a few of them somehow rationally tenable, but most of them irrationally bizarre, implausible, absurd. Yet the most exhilarating, engrossing, and thought-provoking discovery of all was the gradually deepening realization that everywhere, regardless of their preposterous extravagance and manifest nonsensicalness, regardless of the margin of validity granted to the ideational and ethical substance, these divinities all had been or were the vehicles of some community's uncompromising faith and fervent worship.

It was a troubling, at times agonizing, discovery, for it was fraught with the echoes of a voice, reaching for her through the darkness descending over a surf-flooded beach, of words she had mocked, denounced, rejected—echoes which invested the ever-present, unyielding shadow with aggravating immediacy and forcefulness, fraught as well with a steadily expanding and steadily more anxious recognition, that, were those words not just an echo now, were that ever-presence not just a shadow now, her repudiation might not be so caustic, so unconditional, so absolute. Surely she would never concede any validity to the wayward contention that affirmed those pagan beliefs' equivalence with the transcendent verities of the Christian Gospel. There could be no equivalence of fallacy and Truth. Yet there were moments when a phrase—had she read it somewhere or had Leonard Jordan coined it?—would obtrude on her memory: "There are no true religions, only true believers."

In such moments, she found herself unable to quite dismiss a speculation that, however erroneous the premises, however delusive the resultant conclusions of their diverse creeds, those pagans seemed as committed to their visions of the divine, their images of godhead, their tenets, their rituals, as she was to her own; that though pursuing bewilderingly alien, totally unacceptable ways, in their unqualified devotion, their spiritual submission to a higher and sacred authority, in their doctrinal fidelity and scrupulous observance of their respective sacraments, they appeared to be the equals of any Christian fundamentalists.

She sensed the danger looming in such speculation, in a cognitive process which was inherently self-extending. She tried to shy from the gathering momentum of her new perceptions, to stem the deepening peril, but she could not escape its eventual materialization. There was no way of disciplining her mind to ignore that shadow, to refuse its demand for her intellectual integrity, deny its insistence that she peruse each cognition's cogent ramifications and acknowledge her explorations' implicit message. She must own up to the conclusion—which taught that no vision of the universal design was delusive to its devotees, no perception of the divine ever erroneous to its adorers, no god ever false to his communicants; that Truth was defined by—and possessed validity only within—its given religious fellowship; that there were countless coexisting truths in countless coexisting parochial worlds, governed by countless coexisting deities, each of them distinguished from, and uniquely exalted above, all the rest alone by the sectarians' subjective presumption.

Stupefied by the implicit heresy and terrified by the threatened consequence, she flinched from those conclusions, yet she could not extricate her mind from its captivity to their cogency. There was that shadow, ever more ineluctable, and the cadence of a voice ever more sonorous, ever more persistent. "The existence of God is not a matter of objective fact but of subjective belief," it said again and again, haunting her mercilessly with its excruciating, utterly unthinkable, yet utterly irrefutable suggestion that subjective belief, which had engendered the innumerable worlds of diverse deities and the wondrous world of her own God, might equally engender a world without a god. Might, within its own conceptual orbit, such a world not be rightfully coexistent with all the others—and with her own? As such, might it not claim an equal measure of acceptance? Might Leonard Jordan's subjective creed then not have been entitled to as much consideration and respect as her own? Again and again she shrank from such contemplations. Yet each successive flight seemed to end by intensifying her preoccupation with that encounter in the sunset, with its aborted promise, with a denouement that might have been...

The denouement that ought to have been—her mind's compulsive revisiting of the Gopalpur experience abetted arguments in support of that forlorn realization. After all, had Christianity not always coexisted with worlds of diverse visions and persuasions? Was it not even now, two millennia after Jesus had conveyed God's message, existing in a world in which two-thirds of humanity had remained untouched by, and adamantly unconcerned with, that message—a world, two-thirds of whose denizens hearkened to different revelations, entertained different perspectives of life, worshipped different deities, or recognized no deity at all? Yet were not those two-thirds of the human race men and women as noble and as vile, as cruel and as charitable, as honorable and as corrupt, as ethical and as unscrupulous, as wise and as inane as their Christian counterparts? Why, then, could there have been no such coexistence between two human beings, a coexistence founded on their mutual, vital need for intimate fellowship? Why had the paramountcy and imperative of that need not overruled the petty divisiveness of subjective beliefs? Why?

But she knew the answer, which, against all her attempts to deny it, progressively forced itself upon her: it was her rigid dogmatism, the vicious hostility bred by her uncompromising intolerance of divergent beliefs, that had slain the one promise of fulfillment her life had ever known, would ever know. Yet though this awareness of her own failure had gradually taken hold of her mind, it was only after many months' increasingly festering, grieving regret that the full dimension of her loss had been starkly, inexorably brought home to her. It happened on one of her regular visits to the Lansing home when, with Ted on one of his periodic business trips and Gloria by some unexpected but unavoidable social obligation prevented from exercising the neutralizing influence of her usual, carefully arranged presence, she found herself alone with her niece for the first time in nearly three years. Framed by the still chilly dusk of an early spring evening, the unexpected boon of this exceptional occasion found them at a loss for words. Long minutes of a strangely heavy silence ticked away, as, sitting by the window, she kept watching Jenny, who, now nearly fourteen, had grown into adolescence. All the while thinking what a lovely young woman this child was going to be, she wondered at what appeared to be an oddly troubled expression on Jenny's quiet, beautiful face. Perhaps it was only the shadows of the descending dimness, she told herself, but she could not quell a mounting uneasiness that defied her efforts of formulation, when, abruptly, the girl's subdued, slightly tremulous voice broke into her perplexity.

"I've been missing you, Aunt Barbie."

She knew instantly what was meant but, not prepared to admit that meaning, she replied, feigning surprise and chafing at the falseness of her evasion, "But, darling, I've been coming to see you all the time, haven't I?"

"Oh yes ..." The faint accent of repudiation could not be missed. "You've been over to our place all right. But you haven't been here for me."

The meaning was out in the open. Still she flinched from it. "You know this is not true, Jenny," she muttered uncertainly.

"Isn't it, Aunt Barbie?"

"I've been always there for you, always!" she answered, perhaps a bit too harshly, unstrung by the unwavering demand of the challenge.

"Not the way you used to be there—not talking and listening, really talking and really listening to each other, the way we had been all those years, before you went to India; that's how I've been missing you."

Staring at the young, earnest face, she was swept into momentary muteness by a tide of searing pain and undefined anxiety. "I've been missing you this way, too, Jenny darling," she countered helplessly. "But there's never been a chance ..."

"I know." There was sudden bitterness in the gentle voice and an inflection of scorn. "I know. Dad and Mom. They wouldn't leave us to each other, would they? But even if they had given us our chance ..."

Achingly, she perceived the nuance of sorrowing doubt in that unfinished, fading phrase and felt Jenny's deep eyes reaching for her, searching.

"India!" she heard Jenny say. "There was a man there, Aunt Barbie, wasn't there?"

It struck here with shattering force. This had not been a question but a definitive assertion. This child, then, had fathomed what her elders had never even suspected; had known all along; had for those past three years been sharing her aunt's secret, troubling over it yet keeping it inviolate as a treasured burden. Never had she been as proud of Jenny, as gratefully moved by her concern, her intuitive understanding. Never had she felt so close to her niece, had she loved her as deeply as just then. Never now could she consider prevaricating. To this rare child one must not lie; there could be no subterfuge, no skirting of the truth.

She drew the girl's head to herself, kissed each of those comprehending, knowing eyes. "Yes," she said softly, "there was a man there."

"You cared for him." Again not a question but a declaration. And it was vibrant with tenderness, not an adolescent's but a young woman's tenderness.

"Yes, I cared for him."

There once more was that glance reaching for her, searching: "But, he did not care for you?"

She could not quite suppress a tear in her slow, hurting reply. "No, darling. I think he cared for me, too."

"But not strongly, not completely enough?"

There were some long, struggling moments, before she found her answer. It was no longer a matter of lying to Jenny but of lying to herself, and she was determined that this time, for once, she would own up to the truth she had for so long tried to discredit. "No, Jenny," she said, "he did care quite deeply, quite completely enough." And responding to the chilling touch of the girl's doubtful glance, she reaffirmed, with a conviction that was certain, unequivocal. "He did. I'm quite sure of that."

An instant of forlorn, bewildered silence passed, before the question groped for her through the dimness. "Yet you did not stay with each other?"

Staring past her niece into a black nowhere, throbbing with agony, she said tonelessly, "No, we did not stay with each other. There were differences that could not be reconciled."

"Differences …" The echo carried an accent of utter incredulity. "But there was love. Your love and that man's. Strong enough, complete enough, you said so yourself."

"There are considerations that outweigh love," she retorted tightly, appalled at the throaty note of uncertainty, that had crept into her speech to mock its rigid averment.

"Outweigh?" Jenny repeated, stressing the word, framing it with disbelief. "Outweigh, how, Aunt Barbie? What is there, what could be there more precious than a man's love?"

"And what about God's love?" she countered, shivering with a grinding sense of her rebuttal's irrelevance.

"God's love." In the now almost complete darkness, the girl's voice seemed overwhelming, spellbinding in its fervent conviction, "How could one experience God's love more wondrously than through a man's love?"

And from a nowhere that seemed to close in on her, there was another voice speaking, "An Essence, whose actuality is present in every grain of this earth and every star in the skies, in every flower, every animal, every man." Leonard Jordan's voice, now speaking, "that Essence you call God, how could it manifest itself more surpassingly than through a man's love?" It was then, through Jenny, her beloved Jenny, that the full dimension of her loss had revealed itself to her.

And it was through the dismal sequence of incessant self-confrontations that haunted the restless days and sleepless nights that followed that at first tentatively and dimly, then with ever-brightening clarity, a realization came to dawn. Perhaps that loss might, after all, not be irretrievable. Conceivably, her inquiries and speculations during those past three years, her new insights and responses had carried her far enough toward Leonard Jordan's world, perhaps to a halfway point where they might be able to meet and reconcile their different perspectives? *How could one experience God's love more wondrously than through a man's love?* Jenny's challenging question reverberated endlessly through her mind. There was the key. A man's love was God's love expressing itself in the human dimension—a man's love. Leonard Jordan's love.

Ever more forcefully, insistently, compellingly, the thought took hold of her. Reaching beyond the bounds of her own beliefs, she might harmonize with his. Traversing the straitjacketing narrows of her own world, she might come to accept the one he had found as equally valid, equally livable, might impart verity to that parting phrase of his:

"There's always another sunset for those ready to experience it," and to the utter conviction of his final words: "Yes, one day." One day.

"One day there might be a different world to fit in," he had asserted, a different world for her to live in one day. Had that day arrived? Might there be another sunset still? Had the one they had missed that last evening at Gopalpur not foreclosed fulfillment but only achingly postponed it until she would achieve the potential he had perceived to be hers? Another sunset?

The suggestion of its possibility grew in persistence, the more possessing as it was fraught with deepening anxiety. Only another confrontation with Leonard Jordan could test actuality against hopeful dreams, yet the viability of such an encounter was shrouded by uncertainties. Three years had elapsed without one single word of communication. She was honest enough to concede that, given the circumstances of their parting, it would have been for her to undertake an approach. Yet three winters had gone by when a letter could have reached him in Gopalpur. She had been incapable of coping with the hurt of a shattered illusion, incapable of rising above the restraints imposed by her guilty awareness of her own part in the debacle. And now that Jenny's passionate plea had opened a new vista, a new promise, spring had already succeeded that last squandered winter, and Leonard Jordan had once more moved beyond any chance of contact. Now that the day he had so confidently predicted might have arrived, she must wait for another of his Indian sojourns, wait another six months or more to face the verdict.

But while impatiently decrying it, she was grateful for this forcibly protracted delay. It afforded another reprieve to her nagging quandary. The explorations, discoveries, insights gained in those past three years had indeed moved her a long way toward Leonard Jordan's perspective—but would this be sufficient to make her fit to pass the test? Intellectually she had come to acknowledge the conceivability of a world without God, but emotionally it remained as inconceivable as ever. What seemed theoretically admissible—would it prove practically acceptable? However, now that at last she might be prepared to concede their possible coexistence, could the contrary visions of universal existence and creation's transcendental purpose hope to be merged? The proposition of a life without the security accruing from one's trust in a governing divine will and guidance, devoid of the solace promised by a heavenly afterlife, had lost none of its terror. Then, if that last winter she had written that letter, how could she have truly asserted her readiness for the experience of another sunset, for that total communion which alone could vindicate another encounter? If she had exposed herself to the test, would she have been capable of meeting its challenge?

Even in her most euphoric moments, she could not shed her lurking doubt. Yet more agonizing, she was beset by a nagging sense of permanent futility. Even after the six months' reprieve, she might not be ready. Spring might die, summer pass, autumn fade into winter. Leonard Jordan would once more be back at Gopalpur, but this letter might not be written; not then, indeed not ever ...

Spring did die, summer passed, fall spread its chills to turn into winter, and this letter had not been written. It never would be written. For there had been that cataclysmic day in November when her world collapsed, disintegrated, vanished. When, stunned beyond comprehension, shattered beyond recovery, maddened beyond the restraints of sanity, she had sat among the mourners returned from the cemetery—sat there and heard, as from afar, the dreary voice of the Reverend Fletcher drone on into the grieving silence, repeating the stereotyped pieties he had offered at the graveside; sat there, still unable to grasp how Jenny could be gone: the sweet, beloved Jenny, whom two days ago they had found in a deserted lot, raped, mutilated, stabbed to death. She had sat there, gripped by an overpowering sense of preposterous, outrageous absurdity, as she beheld the assembled friends and neighbors, beheld Gloria and Ted, Jenny's own parents—beheld them all vacuously nodding their vapid assent as the Reverend Fletcher intoned, "The Lord giveth, the Lord taketh; unquestioning of His wisdom and His design, we must bow to His will and accept His decree; for God …"

She had leapt to her feet, shouted the minister into petrified muteness, screamed at him, "What God? Stop that gibber, that farce, that obscenity! And you there, Gloria and Ted, will you keep seconding his lie? Has the image of your own Jenny's ravaged body been wiped from your minds? That image, was it not ghastly enough to disown this scurrilous travesty? That image of abuse, of atrocity, of wanton cruelty! God's design, God's will you say? Lies, preacher, lies! What God could ever design, could ever will such abomination? What God could ever allow it? What God could create a world in which it could come to pass? No God would, no God could and still be God! Damn you, preacher! Damn your lies! There can be no such God! This very world, in which such horror can exist, bears witness that there is no God, no God at all!"

For one more instant she had stood there, surrounded by a shocked silence that was broken at last by the Reverend Fletcher's tremulous gasp, "Oh, my dear sister, we must pray for you, that you be forgiven."

She had answered him with a burst of cold fury. "Oh, be still now, you fraud! And save your breath praying for me! There is no one to pray to, no one to forgive!" She had then stormed from the room, slamming shut the door behind her.

And had slammed shut the door to the world which had been her home to walk through wastes of defunct beliefs and ruined faith, broken certainties and wrecked promises, into a world that knew no

God, no son of God, no postmortal bliss, but only fallacious fictions of human fancy, temporal ciphers of the eternally unfathomable, transient testimonials to man's ignorance and inanity—a world in which the image of the deity stood exposed as but the figment of parochial invention, a banal materialization, a personalized mask of a transcendent Essence that permeates the universe of human reality and alone could offer to pain and grief a prospect of healing restoration. Greeting a world, which, bereft now of its God but no longer looming as a terrifying void, a boundlessness of abysmal darkness and unredeemed hopelessness, now spread before her as an infinite horizon, luminous with as yet amorphous but slowly crystallizing assurance; greeting a wondrously mysterious world reverberating with the swelling echoes of unforgotten phrases. "There is your potential ... You will find your way ... There always is another sunset for those ready to experience it ... One day, yes, one day." Beholding a world which knew of yearning, of love, of total communion—the only fulfillment and ultimate security this life could grant. Abandoning herself to a world of compelling actuality which brooked no hesitancy, no delay, which scorned the intermediate irrelevance of letters ...

Ten hectic days later, she had been on her way to India. To Gopalpur. To Leonard Jordan's world. To another encounter in the sunset.

*

Her pulse was quickening in inverse proportion to the slowing car. Already they had left behind them the characteristic green arch, which, formed by the intertwining branches of opposite trees, domed the road like a portal to the village. Steadily, the increasing flow of laggard bullock carts and leisurely pedaled bicycles combined with the swelling medley of pedestrians to retard their passage past sights whose vivid familiarity defied the flight of time and struck her with immediacy, as though it had been only yesterday that a morning's walk had revealed them to her—the outline of a church at some distance off the road; half hidden in the overgrowing greenery, the cluster of ramshackle structures housing Gopalpur's deities; the well and the women with their water urns; skirting a corner of shoddy hovels, the tiny market with its colorful piles of fruit and vegetables; the post office and, across the thoroughfare, the tea stall, fronted, as before, by two rickety benches; the barber shop and further along, the small mosque; the rows of paltry but clean dwellings, some with exquisite, often complex ornamental designs, decorating the grounds in front of their thresholds, chalked there by the households' women so that the gods might take pleasure in visiting these abodes and favor them.

Kamesh seemed to sense her escalating impatience. "Much traffic," he grumbled apologetically, "much people ... like on Jagganath puja, when come to bathe in sea."

"A festival today?" she asked idly, trying to tone down her mounting irritation, as once again the car was forced to a halt.

He shrugged. "No Lord Krishna festival. Maybe Tota Ma puja—who knows?"

"Tota Ma," she muttered, recalling.

"Adivasi goddess." His reply creaked with the orthodox Hindu's condescending disdain of deviate worship, as again he inched the vehicle past an obstacle toward the crumbling building that harbored the generator and the hole-in-the-wall branch of the Bank of India, where the road forked off to run through the arid stretch of wind-blown dunes extending to the hotel.

The hotel, Leonard Jordan. The awareness that only a few moments now separated her from her journey's goal brought on a hot surge of anxious exultation—and with it a flashing recapitulation of the fantasies that had preoccupied her throughout the long flight—envisioning the imminent meeting's possible scenarios, scenarios feverishly pursued and endlessly revisited so they might keep the image of Jenny from her mind, scenarios of hope and redemption, scenarios…

Leonard Jordan might, by some fluke of chance, be lingering near the hotel's entrance. It would be a welcome setting, for the likely presence of others, strangers, would blunt the impassioned tension of that initial confrontation. She might find him sitting in front of his room, at the table, working on his notes, though she thought it more probable, that, given the early afternoon heat, he would have sought his refuge in the fan-cooled comfort of his quarters. His irritable, "Who is it?" might respond to her knock on his door; or perhaps he would come to open it—stand there, framed by the door, amid incredulous, staring silence. Or, again, having espied her arrival through the window, he might rush to meet her halfway across the terrace—would he find words or just take her into his arms? And she, would she be able to command a last modicum of poise or just let herself go and cry?

But then, he might not be at the hotel at all; the odds were rather better than even that he was off on one of his research-bent visits to the interior. All along, she had considered this contingency, had anticipated and prepared herself for it. She would wait for his return, wait out whatever days or weeks of restless impatience his absence might impose. No matter, she would be there to greet him—not at the entrance, exposed to the neutralizing presence of haphazard strangers, exposed to the incursions of curious scrutiny. No, not in the glare of the day's sunlight. She would conquer her impulse; it would be another sunset that would witness their reunion …

The uniformed guard unfastened the chain to throw open the gate to their passage, then stood back to watch the car drive to a halt in front of the two men who stepped out to receive the guest. The smaller, slighter one, dark-skinned and bright-eyed, conjured up a searing recall as he approached, smiling and bowing. He had been there, too, four years ago, on that morning of the bitter parting. And now, as thought to give the proper cachet to a completing cycle, he was there again to observe an ardent return: the assistant manager, Leonard Jordan's friend.

"Welcome back, Mrs. ..." he said, pausing in search of his memory, "Mrs. Easterly."

"Thank you." Her rejoinder betrayed her surprise. "You still remember, Mr. ..."

"Ghose," he completed, his perfunctory tone stressing his own unimportance. "Indeed I remember. And this is Mr. Virang, new manager."

"Happy to serve you, Madam." The taller man bowed with impeccable dignity. His speech suggested schooling in England. "We appreciate the honor you are doing us by returning to our establishment. We shall endeavor to make your stay most pleasant."

"I'm sure."

Mr. Ghose ignored the impatience of her reply. "Mrs. Easterly enjoyed our hospitality three ... no, four years ago," He elaborated unhurriedly. "With American tour, I believe, sharing room sixteen with another lady."

She turned to him. "What an extraordinary memory!"

"Some guests one would not forget, would one?" Somehow, Mr. Ghose's phrase seemed to carry a faintly melancholy accent. But, too fleeting to allow definition, it was canceled by the sober courtesy of the inquiry, "If Madam prefer old room? Number sixteen happens to be unoccupied."

"Yes, by all means." Her assent painted her growing restiveness.

"We shall take care of your driver, Madam, and the baggage," Mr. Virang announced, beckoning to the waiting servant. "When would Madam wish her tea to be served?"

"Any time," she muttered fretfully, "any time at all."

And, swiftly moving past the manager, she proceeded through the passageway between dining room and parlor, onto the arcade and a few steps beyond, to let her glance sweep across the terrace, searching, hoping … The window of the corner room was tightly shuttered. Pushed toward the edge of the raised arcade, the table in front of room twenty-one was empty, the two chairs vacant, encompassed by a heat-scorched stillness, which spelled the message—the one in whose world she had come to live was not around to receive her, take her in his arms, reassure her. This day's sunset would remain unshared.

Still gazing, she stood there motionless. Only a slight droop of her shoulders signaled her disappointment. For all her rational anticipation, all her reasoned calculation of the odds favoring Leonard Jordan's absence, she had nonetheless nurtured an irrepressible expectation. Now, confronted with its frustration, she could not escape the inevitable letdown or quite suppress a gust of vexation—somehow, absurdly, she felt that he ought to have intuited her crisis, her need, her readiness, he ought to have forgone yet another venture in exploration to be here for her.

Dimly, she became aware that she was not alone, that the two men had followed her at a discreet distance and were watching. Squaring her shoulders, she turned to them, blinking, as a blinding ray of the afternoon sun struck her eyes. Addressing the taller of the two, her voice was steady, almost casual, "Mr. Jordan, when is he expected back?"

"Mr. Jordan …?" the manager repeated quizzically.

"Mr. Virang took over here only last summer," Mr. Ghose interrupted. "He has never met Mr. Jordan."

"But!" The sudden agitation that reverberated through her incipient rebuttal abruptly faltered then expired, overwhelmed by the petrifying realization that among all the scenarios her mind had projected, there was one that had remained unenvisioned—that his research might have been completed, his sojourns at Gopalpur ended, a realization that struck her as with a frosty, numbing fist. "You mean …" she finally said, each word dragging with a crushing burden of desperate apprehension, "You mean, Mr. Jordan has not come to Gopalpur this year?"

It was only after an interminable instant of silence that Mr. Ghose spoke softly, "Mrs. Easterly, Mr. Jordan died."

"Died," she muttered after him uncomprehendingly, as though the word were foreign to her dictionary. Then, shrilly, "died!?"

"I am sorry, Mrs. Easterly." The quiver in the assistant manager's quiet voice left no doubt about the sincerity of his sorrow and compassion. "Truly sorry. It happened almost two years ago. Collapsed unconscious right in front of his room. His heart failed." He seemed to divine her mute, forlorn question, shook his head. "No, not here. A servant saw him drop. He was immediately rushed to Berhampur, the University Medical Center. They said there was still hope, but two days later …"

"Two days later," she echoed stonily, staring into an opaque infinity which began to spin about her, dizzily accelerating.

"Madam!" Mr. Virang took two quick steps toward her. He had caught her momentary sway, was primed to lend her succor. "Perhaps Madam may wish to rest. May we help? Some brandy perhaps? A cool drink?"

His words floated past her ears, but their accent of troubled concern somehow registered on her mind. "No, thank you," she murmured, "I'll be all right."

"Are you sure?"

But she didn't hear Mr. Ghose's anxious query. She was already walking across the terrace, past the hedges of blooming flowers and whispering palms, past the lounge chairs beneath the checkered parasols, past the corner room with the shuttered window, to sit on the steps leading down to the beach—sit there, her dry eyes sightlessly resting upon the billowing blue of the sea, sit there, searching an immensity of loss beyond grasp for understanding, for an answer, searching, yet conscious of the futility of the search, the futility spelled out by a placid yet intense voice that last, desperate evening four years ago, "Why grope for meanings?" it had said, "meanings that would be entirely incomprehensible within the human dimension." Yet she searched on compulsively, hopelessly, driving her mind through the dooming wastes of the unfathomable.

She had not heard the approaching steps, but she perceived a presence behind her even before the words reached her. "Lady not stay here. Sun too strong, make lady sick."

She knew this voice, inextricably part of the Gopalpur experience— its warm timbre, its oddly becharming lilt had not been forgotten. "Ramlu," she muttered, turning to face him.

"Yes. Ramlu. Lady remember." There was pride in his assent and an innuendo of gratitude. He seemed unchanged except for a few more furrows crossing his gaunt, bronzed features. He helped her to her feet, then, leading the way, he guided her into the shade of the arcade. "Come quick as can. Korapalli. Car pass by. See lady. Mr. Jordan's lady."

"Mr. Jordan's lady," she repeated, and suddenly there were tears welling up unstoppably, cascading torrentially, soaking the man's shirt, as she buried her head against his chest.

Ramlu stood very still. Only once, ever so faintly, his hand passed over her hair. "Yes," he said deeply, "me cry, too, when Mr. Jordan die. Wife also cry. Mr. Jordan good man. Friend. Best friend. He tell me, watch out for lady, when she come."

She raised her head, looked up at him, baffled.

The somber ghost of a smile crept across his face, framing his quiet nod. "Achcha. Mr. Jordan wise man. Know lady come. He always tell, lady back one day."

"One day …" A sob shivered in her voice. Those words had been the last she had heard him speak, words lost in the squeal of turning tires as the bus was starting toward the gate and beyond it.

"Yes," Ramlu said softly, "He tell again just before … before he go."

Her lips trembled with the question, "You were with him, when …?"

"Me there all time, in hospital." His deep-set eyes had a glint of surprise, as though they were asking, 'but how could it have been otherwise?'

"All time. Mr. Jordan he wake up. He speak with me. Doctor say he better, he live." Slowly spreading somberness seemed to accentuate the gauntness of his bronzed face. "He not believe doctor. He know. Mr. Jordan. He always know. So, next evening come …"

"A second heart attack?" she asked as his words faded into a weary shrug.

A nod, lips pressed tight, not allowing themselves the relief of a sigh. "Me hold his hand. Close eyes." There was a lilt of profound tenderness in his quiet voice. "Go with him to burning grounds. Bury ashes, like he tell."

She searched his grave countenance for an answer she never doubted. "Sorada Road?"

"Sorada Road," Ramlu confirmed. "Take lady tomorrow morning."

"Yes, will you, please," she said. "Thank you so much."

"Thank me?" He shook his head, slowly, emphatically. "No thank me. You Mr. Jordan's lady."

Her shoulders contracted with a chill. "I might have been," she whispered, aching, turning away quickly, as, slanting, a reddish gleam touched her face. The sky was readying itself for another sunset; she could not endure it.

Then they stood there, lost in timeless, disconsolate silence, until at last the man spoke again. "Lady no stay here. No be alone this night. Lady come to my house. Wife make welcome. Rohini honored to serve lady. Me honored also."

She followed him without even attempting a protest. She knew this was how Leonard Jordan would have wished it. She followed him along the arcade, through the passageway which led to the exit, past Mr. Ghose, whose slight nod to them confirmed his explicit understanding. Then she sat in Ramlu's car on her way to Korapalli—to an interminable evening of affectionate warmth, of unobtrusive intimacy, of grieving kinship; of protracted silences, only occasionally broken by brief, terse exchanges, which avoided any reference to the subject of their shared, mournful memories. She hardly touched the ample, carefully prepared meal, just forcing down a few token bites lest she offend her hosts, though certain that their poignant empathy and their own sorrow alike would preclude any notion of offense. Then there were many cups of tea, punctuating the stillness of a wakeful togetherness which stretched deep into the night, until at last, weariness demanded its toll, and she dropped onto the silken pillows Rohini had prepared for her for a few short hours of leaden slumber.

Shortly after sunrise and a perfunctory breakfast, Rohini shyly embraced her, and Ramlu helped her into the car. As though by tacit but compelling agreement, not a single shred of conversation interrupted the long drive. They seemed bound by an internal accord to preserve their shared captivity to the remembrance of another day, four years earlier—a remembrance fraught with a keenly aware poignancy of that other day's contrasting climate—as they progressed past the villages and hamlets along the branch road, the railway crossing, the narrow streets of Berhampur, the tree-lined highway to Aska, the Krishna temple with its glaring depictions of garishly tinted lover couples, the quiescent, jungly woods along the Sorada Road.

"Here." Almost brutally abrupt, Ramlu's voice tore her from the grip of crowding, desolate déjà vu. She had not noticed that they had stopped. "Here," he repeated more softly. Already he was holding the door open for her. He strode ahead of her along the brambly foot path, carefully bending away the overhanging twigs lest they whip against her face or entangle her hair, keeping them solicitously out of reach, as once Leonard Jordan had cleared the way for her.

And, like once before, as spellbinding in its otherworldly quietude, the pond lay before her, its blueness glittering with the reflections of the morning sun between the countless lotuses riding on its gentle, breeze-blown ripples, its solitude alive with an ineffable breath of solace. For a timeless instant, she stood overwhelmed by the sensation of a presence as immediate, as possessive of her as four forlorn years ago—Leonard Jordan's presence, speaking, *this is the way I felt when I first discovered this spot the year after Miriam died. But I was not alone; here, never alone. This is not a place to visit alone ...* And she knew with a certainty beyond rational grasp, mystically comprehending that not ever would she be alone, that always he would be with her, as Miriam had been with him always—Miriam, who had taught him the meaning of life and shown him the way to his world. *That world knows no death,* the solitude was whispering with words once spoken. *Life goes on in the memories of the survivors.* No, never would she be alone. Slowly, at last, she turned her glance, searching. Only now she discovered clearly what, passing that ancient tree, had touched her mind but vaguely before: beneath the gnarled roots, a simple, stone-fashioned structure, carefully covered with a coat of chalk but already slightly fissured by the incursions of the weather was a square pedestal, scarcely four feet high, with a triangular top roofing a shelf within a niche.

Beside it, Ramlu was standing, motionless but for a faint nod now answering her glance. "Samadhi," he said, his eyes pointing. "No cross, like Mr. Jordan wish. No lie, he say."

"No lie," she repeated. "Yes, I understand. This memorial, your work," she added. Not a question, a certainty. "It is here, isn't it ...?"

Another nod, grave and placid. "Me take urn with ashes. Dig. Cover hole. Make Samadhi. Place for mind to be with Mr. Jordan."

"You've come here before," she said, her eyes upon the withered lotus blossoms in the Samadhi niche.

"Come often." Again his rejoinder was faint with an inflection of surprise, as if to ask, but how could it be otherwise?

"Thank you," she muttered under her breath.

But he heard it and merely shook his head. Wordlessly, he reached out to remove the dead flowers, strewing their brittle remains on the ground. Then, rolling up his pants, he stepped past her to wade into the knee-deep water and pluck a fresh supply of lotuses. Returning as silently as he had gone, he deposited them on the shelf to replace the discarded offering of another day. For some moments he stood, hands folded before his bowed head, engrossed in meditation, his mind communing with the one who had been his friend. Then, stepping back, he straightened, his face creased with the ghost of a tender smile as he fingered a pocket to extract from it a tiny wooden box, which he held out to her.

"Lady take," he said. "Mr. Jordan tell, give to lady."

Gingerly she accepted the box and lifted its lid. Trembling, her lips tightening to cage a wrenching sob, she stood motionless for endless moments, staring from eyes slowly clouding with hot moisture, staring down at the golden chain with the six-pointed star and the pressed lotus blossom mounted on a square of white cardboard. "Miriam," she whispered. Shaking, her hand groped toward the Samadhi, set down the box on the ledge. "It's hers."

Quietly Ramlu took it from the niche, handed it back to her. "No leave here," he gently repudiated her. "Somebody come, steal … Mr. Jordan, he tell, lady keep."

"Lady keep," she echoed, wrapping her fingers around the box, incapable of any thought but that the gift, Leonard Jordan's final gift, had been meant to be hers. And again, "lady keep," drowning in a tide of happiness which was pain beyond bearing; only now perceiving the full extent of the truth when she had replied, "He did care quite strongly, quite completely enough" to Jenny, who somehow had known it all along—Jenny, who should have been her own child and Leonard Jordan's, offspring of total communion; Jenny, who was no more, yet whose passing had shown her the way to a world of fulfillment, and to a Samadhi, a place for the mind to be with the one who had offered her that world …

She shivered. Clutching her treasure to herself, she sat down on the moss next to Ramlu, seeking security in the closeness of his presence, his surrogate presence—and finding her refuge in his comprehending silence. For a long time they shared the solitude, side by side, absorbed in the evocations, watching the rays of the climbing sun play in glitters like soundless giggles on the pond's flowered surface until, oddly responding to an unspoken consensus, they rose simultaneously in continued complete silence to retrace their path to the car and drive back the way they had come.

As they passed through Aska, their mute concordance was broken by her plea that they pause at the Krishna temple. When they did, this time she did not, after but the most cursory inspection of the figurations, turn away, repelled and dismayed. Unprovoked by their erotic extravagance, not offended by their carnal flagrance, she could let her eyes linger upon those crudely disingenuous, artistically impoverished, and almost self-parodying imitations of the Konark models. Sometimes dimly smiling at their coarse, unbridled directness, she recognized their identical message and abandoned herself to the spell of their motivating inspiration: the concept—how had Leonard Jordan defined it?—of universal life's eternal perpetuation through total communion, that very experience which might have been, but now would never be, hers, but which she had come to perceive as the goal of all human search, the hub of all human fulfillment.

Prompted by an obscurely relevant compulsion, she clasped the six-pointed pendant about her neck before she returned to the car. If Ramlu had noted the gesture, not a single comment betrayed his observation. But the furrows across his brow seemed to smooth with a sheen of quiet contentment as they continued on their homeward ride, wrapped again in their tacitly agreed mutuality of silence. When, slowing the pace, they entered Korapalli, he turned to her and asked, "Would she honor his house once more by accepting its hospitality?"

Expressing her grateful appreciation of his invitation, she declined. For the remainder of the day she would prefer to stay by herself.

"Then tomorrow, perhaps?" he suggested.

She demurred. Tomorrow she would leave. No, not to go home—she would travel on, to Thailand, to Japan perhaps, or to Indonesia, wherever opportunity might seem most favorable. New sights, new impressions, new insights might give her mind pause from its memories.

Home? She thought, keenly captive to the verity of Leonard Jordan's phrase, *home is where we love.* Home? Not in Philadelphia, not in Gopalpur. Jenny, her little Jenny, was no more, nor he, to whom she had come to find her home.

Ramlu seemed unsurprised, as though he had rather expected her decision. "Achcha," he replied placidly. "Tomorrow, after breakfast, me drive lady to Bubaneshwar. To airport, flight to Calcutta." And then he turned to his wheel, accelerating for their final lap to Gopalpur.

Mr. Ghose was standing near the entrance when they pulled up at the hotel. Helping her from the car, he informed her that lunch was waiting for her. There was an intimation of fretted solicitude about his manner, a hint of protectiveness that touched her.

"I will be all right," she told him. "In fact, I feel quite all right."

"Yes," Ramlu confirmed earnestly, "lady well now." Still, this swift exchange of meaningful glances between the two men did not escape her—glances bespeaking a complicity of concern. But before she could manage another vapid phrase, Ramlu turned to her. "Me back tomorrow, after breakfast," he reminded her with finality, and started the engine.

"Mrs. Easterly leaving," Mr. Ghose remarked, watching the car move out. It was not a question, merely the assertion of a definite anticipation.

She just nodded, stepping past him to proceed to the dining room.

She was late for the serving. The few other guests were already busy with their desserts—a Bihari couple from Patna who scanned her with rather unrestrained curiosity, not altogether hiding their reproof of a female, whose unseemliness of traveling unaccompanied and thus unguarded disconcerted their orthodox sensibilities; a younger couple from Calcutta, preoccupied with their three children; a middle-aged missionary, undeniably British and proudly advertising the fact, who seemed eagerly primed to get acquainted, but, frustrated and intimidated by her self-absorbed mien, thought better of it. Still, partaking of her meal but sparingly and rapidly, she caught up to finish almost simultaneously with the rest of them and immediately repaired to her quarters. Drained by the morning's experience, it had not been for food she craved, but for a cool, calming shower and a languid respite on her bed.

That respite, however, proved not quite as extended as she might have wished. She had hoped for a stretch of restorative sleep, but a vague, unfocused consciousness of some important yet unaccomplished errand kept preying on her mind. The sun was still high in the sky when rather suddenly this restless demand defined itself to her and imposed its dictate.

Mr. Ghose must have been keeping an eye out for her. When she emerged from her room, he intercepted her at the exit. "Anything we may do for Madam?" he inquired, apology in his self-effacing smile.

"No, thank you." There was an edge to her reply, sharper than intended. "I just want to visit … to look around the village."

"Ah yes, I understand." His bright eyes were acute in their scrutiny, belying his rueful tone, which asked her to excuse his obtrusion. "Guests from abroad always like a taste of local flavor. Some of the sights, the native ways, no doubt they must seem quaint, intriguing, I suppose. But perhaps Madam may prefer to go out later, nearer to sundown? This is not a good time. Too early, too hot. Might affect Madam, cause considerable discomfort."

"I will be fine." This time the edge in her rejoinder was not altogether inadvertent.

"Perhaps. We should hope so." The assistant manager's deference harbored an accent of unyielding insistence. "At any rate, Madam ought not go out alone, just in case." He deftly anticipated her protest, thwarted it. "Also some of the folk here may be quite bothersome. See foreign lady, try to make her buy all sorts of things. And of course, some will come begging. Madam does not speak local language, may not find right way to deal with them. Perhaps some may not be pleasant. Backward people, you know. Fear outsiders, fear evil eye. So," he added determinedly, "Madam, please not walk about by herself."

"I'm not afraid, Mr. Ghose." Her impatience was quite overt now as she made ready to step past him. "As I've said, I'll be fine."

"Mrs. Easterly, please!" Ignoring her irritation, he held up a hand. "We do feel responsible. Allow someone to come with you."

The urgency of his plea made her pause. She appreciated the genuine concern prompting his insistence. "Well …" she muttered noncommittally, struggling with her misgivings at the prospect of some alien presence interfering with her errand's completion. But the man's anxious persistence, she realized, was in response to Ramlu's behest;

she could hardly refuse him. "Perhaps then, someone may come along some of the way. Are you offering me your company, Mr. Ghose?"

"Much as I would be honored, Madam. I'm afraid, not." His denial was rueful. "Mr. Virang being off today, I am in charge. I could not leave my post. But if it please Madam, my daughter would be most proud and happy to be permitted. Deepti, she is a quiet child. She will be no burden to Madam; just make sure of being there, if need be."

"Deepti," she repeated. "Deepti. Yes, seems someone mentioned her to me, most favorably."

"Did someone?" Mr. Ghose replied discreetly, beckoning to the graceful, dark-complexioned girl, who evidently had been waiting for her father's call and now emerged from the parlor to stand before her, hands folded in greeting. "I hope Madam will find her worthy of that, that someone's judgment."

"I'm sure," she said warmly, acute with an instant sense of affinity. "I shall be glad to have her along. Thank you, Mr. Ghose."

"Thank you, Madam." There was relief in the assistant manager's response. Then he stood watching them make their way across the dunes, with his daughter trailing one step behind the taller woman.

Engrossed in a jumbled flight of memories, she did not become aware of her companion's deferential demeanor, until, already halfway along the main thoroughfare, the girl in the blue, gold-fringed sari quietly moved ahead of her to shield her from a mendicant, then once more fell back to keep her distance as soon as the unwelcome approach had been averted. Embarrassed, and irritated at herself for so long having tolerated such obeisant restraint, she motioned Deepti to her side. "You ought not to stay back like this." The repudiation was edgy with a note of dismay.

"This is my place." The large, deep eyes were looking up at her shyly. "I am lady's servant."

"Not a servant. A friend. That's what I like you to be, if you care to be, my friend."

"Yes." The softness of the reply carried an accent of subdued tenderness. "A friend, happy to serve lady."

"Friends do not serve friends; they just help each other."

A faint smile framed the gentle refutation. "It is honor to serve lady, American lady. American people good people, kind people."

And suddenly, as though apprized by an inner voice, she understood the girl's warmth and tenderness—and her praise, accruing to her now, because there had been another American. And as she spoke, she was certain of the answer to her faltering question, "You knew Mr. Jordan, didn't you?" And reading the anticipated affirmation from the cloud of sadness painting those quiet, darkly beautiful features, "You knew him well—liked him. He was a friend."

"Mr. Jordan …" The reply was a shiver. "I visit in the hospital. He not speak with me then, just smile at me, just smile."

A hand reached out, quivered over the silk, that covered the girl's fine, smooth hair, "You, too, miss him …"

"Mr. Jordan." A cadence of grief and dreamy passion alike deepened the youthful voice. "Everybody miss him. Good man, kind man. Often he sit with me, speak with me, help me with English study. Tell about America, about other countries also, about men and gods. Mr. Jordan, he knew so many things, he teach me …"

"Yes, he taught me, too." The words, aching, faded into a forlorn silence.

It was only when, walking side by side, they had left the post office behind them and the government rest house, and had passed beyond the row of beggarly dwellings that spread outward from the fruit market, that their self-absorbed reticence was fractured.

"Lady wish to go on? Gopalpur finished. No more houses. No more people. No more to see, just road."

For all its timidity, Deepti's comment jolted her from the grip of her contemplations. Bewildered, it took her a few moments to focus her thoughts for a reaction to the implied suggestion. "I know. Just a bit further along, there's something I'd like to look at."

"Something?" But the perplexity of the echoed word almost instantly yielded to a vivid expression of sudden understanding. A slender, fine-fingered hand was pointing to the swell of ground some distance off the road and to the stately edifice silhouetted against the cloudless sky. "Oh? Lady wish to visit church, pray to Christian God."

"No!" The rebuttal was grating with unbridled rancor. The proposition had struck her with a sense of utter absurdity as well as uncontrollable loathing. Its evocation of Jenny's lifeless body, of a wake, of the Reverend Fletcher's fraudulent litany, had taken possession of her beyond any margin for rational consideration for an overpowering, frenzied moment; then Deepti's anguished stare, large with fright at the furious harshness of the rebuff slowly restored her to sanity. Ignorant of those cataclysmic days in Philadelphia, the girl's assumption had been so innocently logical. "No," she repeated quietly, regret and apology gentling her tone. "It's not the church I wish to visit. It's a place Mr. Jordan once showed me, a place …" Wandering, her glance found the target of the search, "right over there."

She felt her companion for one instant stop short, heard her startled whisper, "Mandir? Devi mandir?" And responding to her questioning look, the faltering explanation: "House of goddess?"

"Yes, house of goddess," she affirmed, touched by the aptness of the accent of incredulous wonderment at a decision which to Deepti must seem paradoxical, and which once would have seemed utterly incongruous to herself. "Will you come with me?" And then they were traversing the expanse of rock- and refuse-littered underbrush toward the tumbledown cubicles that held the objects of Gopalpur's devotion. Inside their domiciles, amid random arrays of ritual paraphernalia and floral offerings, some long withered, others still fresh, the idols appeared precisely as her haunted memories had retained their images: there again were those scarlet figures with featureless blotches for faces; those counterparts of theirs, with countenances so weirdly spectral in their unskilled sketchiness; that grotesque bust with its unsettlingly fatuous grin—there, all of them staring at her, yet oddly not striking her as hideous monstrosities now or as odiously scurrilous creations of perverted fancy, but conveying an aura of inconceivable otherworldliness, of transcendent mystery. *Masks of the all-embracing, all-pervasive Power,* a quiet, firm voice echoed through her mind, a man's solemn voice. *Ciphers of an Essence immeasurably beyond human grasp, inaccessible to human definition and knowledge.*

Slowly she proceeded from cubicle to cubicle, from altar to altar, from idol to idol, with every new sight increasingly captive to wonder, unaccountably fraught with awe—proceeded, absorbed in a cognition that defied formulation, in an expanding consciousness of a reality, the very suggestion of which she had rejected four years earlier, a reality which, however enigmatically intangible, was an irrefutable presence now. "One day," Leonard Jordan had averred, "one day."

Totally engrossed in her experience, she had been oblivious of the girl in the blue, gold-fringed sari, who, trailing her from sanctuary to sanctuary, had been unswerving in her demure and silent companionship. Now suddenly, alerted by an extrasensory perception, she took cognizance of that still figure with hands folded, of that young countenance with an inward smile, endowed with uncommon, stunning loveliness—a smile whose strangely luminous enchantment was addressed to the idol within the shrine, that black effigy with pendant crimson tongue and bared fangs and eyes balefully aglow to complete its grimace of sheer destructive violence. That effigy, the very starkness of whose terror ... yet reinforced by the rays of the afternoon sun slanting directly upon it, the terror seemed oddly subverted, indeed voided, by the garlanding necklace of fresh, still fragrant red and yellow blossoms.

A sudden spark of intuition invested her question with foregone certainty, "That wreath, those flowers, it's you who brought them here?"

A nod, still transfigured by that radiant smile. "This morning I bring ... Often come, make puja to goddess, my goddess."

The timbre of devotion was too intense for disregard. "Your goddess?"

Another affirming motion of that finely contoured head. "Harchandi—name same as my own, Deepti, meaning ..." a pause, searching for the English term. "Shining? Yes, shining one. Harchandi, meaning shining one also—shining mistress."

"Shining?" she repeated, turning once more to scrutinize that black embodiment of ferocious fury and lethal destruction. The girl's glance followed hers. Slowly broadening with understanding, that radiant smile countered her perplexity. "Oh, Harchandi seem terrible to lady? Lady not know true goddess. Harchandi, she now angry; she hate bad spirits. Make them be afraid, make them go away, so they not hurt good people. Hate bad men also. Punish them when do wrong." The dark, glowing eyes were resting on the idol, and the smile was deepening. "American lady not fear. American lady good, kind. Harchandi good, kind also. Harchandi love good people. Always she help, always she protect. Always she give hope." Dropping low, the gentle voice was vibrant with a fervent lilt, "Harchandi, she so beautiful, so lovely, so happy, so much light, Harchandi, she Shining Mistress, lady see?"

"Yes," she said slowly, "yes, I see," wondering why comprehension had been so tardy in bestowing itself. Had there not all along been that placid, knowing phrase nestling in her mind, "The gods, all of them, are masks only, into which, because of their unreality, each worshipper may read her own perception of the Transcendent Power."

"Yes," she repeated once more, firmly, "I do see."

The girl's gaze was still riveted on the goddess's effigy. There was a ring of profound gladness and contentment to her reply. "Lady see now. Mr. Jordan, he see also."

"Yes," she muttered, turning aside, vainly struggling to deny expression to the onslaught of pain, "he saw, he taught me to see."

She felt eyes seeking her, searching her, penetrating her; heard, as from afar, words reaching her. "Lady, she love Mr. Jordan," words that were not a question but an assertion; words that were fueled not by an adolescent's but a young woman's empathy; words that left her breathless, petrified by the cadence of an echo, which, scorning the inroads of time and space, summoned up the image of a dusking early spring afternoon, of a beloved presence, of a voice intense with the certainty of inward knowledge and eloquent with the verity of intuition—a verity that would allow no more prevarication. Jenny, Jenny! The pain within her was screaming, rending her, overwhelming her with tears she was incapable of repressing.

Ever so lightly, ever so shyly, ever so tenderly a hand touched hers. "I also cry, when Mr. Jordan die."

Slowly, each movement irresistibly compelled, she turned to Deepti. Through the misting film of burning moisture she beheld the little figure in the blue, gold-fringed sari, those dark-hued features, which in their very contour, their every trait, were so unlike Jenny's and yet, incongruously but irrefutably, seemed so much like Jenny's, as though by some mysterious grace of fate a life lost had been resurrected in a new body. It was Jenny, her Jenny, to whom she bent, whose brow her lips grazed with a kiss.

The touch of that hand was firmer now. "I cry also," Deepti repeated, her eyes fixed upon Harchandi's effigy. "But cry no more. Goddess kind, help me, take sorrow from me. Tell me, Mr. Jordan, he not die. In mind, he be with me always."

In its affectionate assurance, that quiet voice encompassed her with infinite consolation. Obeying the dictate of an ineluctable impulse, her glance followed the girl's to come to pause, linger upon the black icon with its pendant tongue and bared fangs, that mask of beauty and kindness and hope.

For time unmeasured, they stood, hand in hand, in consonant silence amid the radiance of a sun descending toward the horizon—a silence that persevered when at last they retraced their way along the main road, oblivious of their shared, heat-encumbered weariness; persevered, when, instinctively responding to the American lady's unvoiced plea, Deepti hung back at the arcaded rim of the terrace to watch her cross the flower-framed green toward the two steps dividing it from the sandy stretch that marked the fringe of the beach and watch her stand there motionless in her willed solitude, then, as though wakened by the touch of the sunset's first glow, slowly half-turn to let her eyes rest upon the quiescent corner room with its shuttered window and the empty table and chairs in front of it, let them rest there for timeless moments before lowering herself onto those steps, to sit there, her sight lost in the blue boundlessness, which was reddening, then gradually purpling with another day's fulgent departure.

Still watching her, Deepti felt that somehow she was part of what, with the certainty of intuitive comprehension, she recognized as a memorial service for one she had admired and revered, for one she would never forget. Fleetingly, an echo churned her mind, a poem he once had quoted and of which she recalled only the last line "… are sisters under the skin …" An echo whose recapture was fraught at once with profound sadness and intense happiness. *Sisters,* she thought; *be Harchandi kind to my sister, as she has been kind to me. May she take her grief from her also and give her peace and hope.*

She for whom the prayer pleaded was still sitting on those steps, her feet covered with fine grains of sand blown by the gently rising breeze. Her still figure was suffused by the magical gift of a horizon aflame with ruby radiance, her lips alive with soundless words, reaching for him who was not sharing this sunset and yet was so inseparably part of it. *I've come to you,* they said, *come to you all the way. Yes, Leonard, all the way, but too late.*

You came, as soon as you were ready, the susurrant surf, foaming across the rim of the beach, answered back.

Not soon enough. Destiny would not let you wait for me.

Perhaps I was not meant to wait. The transcendent design may allow no room for another Miriam. Perhaps perfect communion can know no duplication. Still, it was good that you found your way.

Found my way to you.

To yourself, Barbara, as I knew you would. There was your potential. There was a world of a novel, brighter vista, of more profound meanings, latent within you. You would discover it.

It is your world I discovered.

Not mine, Barbara. Your own, once you found it.

Yet the one to which you showed me the way, guided me. And now that I have come, ready to live in it, it offers me no home. For, did you not yourself so aver, home is, where we love? But the one I loved has left me to live alone in that newfound world.

Has he, truly? Has he left you, Barbara?

His ashes are resting under a tree by the lotus pond.

Have you forgotten? In the world I lived in, and which you came to share, death knows no finality. The infinitude of afterlife mocks the transience of temporal life. Were you alone when you stood under the tree by the lotus pond, in front of Ramlu's Samadhi? And now, in this sunset, are you alone?

There is but the memory.

The afterlife, the afterlife.

It is not enough, Leonard. No, it is not enough. It was not afterlife you promised, but life—life together, total oneness, one day, when I had found my way. There was to be another sunset ... What happened to your promise?

For long, distressed moments the surf seemed hushed, as though muted by the caustic bitterness of her reproach. At last, with a new wave rolling in, it was murmuring again, sadly, ruefully, I did not anticipate ...

Forgive me! Appalled by the obtuse injustice of her indictment, the soundless words were burning on her lips. *It's just that I so hoped, so longed for that sunset.*

And now its promise has failed you ... but has it?

And suddenly, for all her desolation, a strange, incongruous tranquility spread within her, as the soft whisper came to her once more.

But has it failed you? Is there not your hope, still, and your longing? Do they not hold the promise?

Do they?

There will be another sunset, always, for those open to its experience.

I came here, open to it, oh so unreservedly, so unqualifiedly open! But you are not here to bestow it on me.

Yet the experience is waiting to bestow itself. The person, Barbara, the person is but its incidental medium, its chance embodiment. Don't you see? Only the fortuitous object of your yearning was lost; its intrinsic impulse remains. And as long as it does, it will find another medium, another vehicle, another embodiment of the yearned-for experience.

Another embodiment? There never will be one like you.

Not until you meet him.

From down the beach a splash of spraying froth was coming to her like a gentle giggle. Oddly charmed, she let its mockery pass unchallenged, wonderingly aware that repudiation would be mere pretense.

Not until you meet him …

The echo of the subtle suggestion lingered on, enigmatic in its assuagement and consolation, yet resonant with assurance that filled her with a sense of tranquility, of internal security and undefined expectation.

Not until you meet him ...

She repeated the phrase, slow with dawning comprehension. She was still young enough, with enough life left ahead, to grant her another encounter in the sunset. And wherever, the one with whom she might come to share that experience, he would indeed be another Leonard Jordan. For like the one, with whom to fulfill her potential she had journeyed to Gopalpur, he would be but what her yearning would create. Her passion would bestow on him, as it had bestowed on the one now resting by the lotus pond, such fascination as would make him fit her dream's aspiration.

With one last fulminant display of iridescent splendor, the sunset had turned into the bluish vagueness of dusk. She rose from the steps but did not move away from them; she stood there, her eyes lost in the darkening swell of the billows. Somehow, somewhere, she felt with deepening certainty, there would be another sunset, and the one encountered in its glow would, like Leonard Jordan, become a vehicle for her longing's projection, become the guide to her fulfillment. Wearing another mask, donned by the image she had fashioned, he would define her new reality—a mask, she repeated, suddenly shivering, a mask.

But what other reality was there? Her mind strayed to a dilapidated cubicle and a girl in a blue, gold-fringed sari in front of it, to the icon of Harchandi the Shining One, whose crimson-tongued, fangs-baring mask harbored an image of beauty and kindness and grace, which was reality to them who so endowed it; like, too, the terrifyingly hideous goddess of Nirmal Jhar, whose essential sublimity and benignity Leonard Jordan had apprehended because his vision of the world had defined her image for him.

It is the images, she thought, the images we fashion for ourselves, that formulate all the reality we may perceive—our images of the universe and its mysterious design; of the transcendent Power that energizes its perpetuity; of nature and our environment; of the human substance, of ourselves, and of those around us; of the private world in which we exist; our images, each a mind-fashioned model, a mirror of individual hope and longing. It is their aggregate that determines the reality in which all of us must find their destiny, the reality that begets the only world, in which life can be lived, in which fulfillment may be attained …

Within her was a vast stillness, infinite peace. In another sunset she would be ready to achieve this world. Obeying a sudden impulse, only peripherally aware of its cogency, she started toward the arcade, toward the quadrangle of columns guarding the shuttered corner room, seated herself at the table and incongruously searched the fading twilight for the fumes from incense sticks. For a fraction of an instant, she was captive to the irrationality of a doomed expectancy. Then this spell of absurd self-deception broke and was gone, and quietly, with mournfulness free of self-pity, she accepted her loneliness, oddly confident of its impermanence.

One day, she repeated to herself, her lips stirring with the words' muttered articulation, words echoing with an ascendant sense of profound gratitude: Yes, some day, some day she would find that world, that reality, that fulfillment. She would find it because Leonard Jordan had shown her the way, had charted new horizons, had revealed new meanings, had evoked a new perception of human existence, had, however then incomprehensible by her, however rebuffed and scorned, had given her what was his to give, given her what he had been given, given by Miriam …

Impelled by a purpose beyond her conscious cognizance, her hand ran to her neck, felt for the pendant, let her fingers explore the six points, let her fingers linger with a delicate, shy caress before unfastening the clasp and setting the golden keepsake down on the table by the side of the cardboard square with the pressed lotus which she had extracted from her pocket with the slow tenderness of almost reverent care.

From somewhere along the arcade, one of the servants emerged, paused momentarily, puzzling at her motionless presence, then proceeded past her on tiptoes, inconspicuous and unnoticed.

Absorbed, she was staring down at Leonard Jordan's legacy. It had been Miriam through whom he had found his world; Miriam, whose devotion, abetting her intuitive grasp of his latent proclivities, had opened him to new perceptions and insights; who, bestowing on him the experience of a total communion, had taught him an incomparably meaningful, infinitely fulfilling vision of human existence; Miriam had given him that which would be his to give, that which he would pass on to one whose latent disposition he had fathomed beneath the overlays of hidebound beliefs and constraining presumptions, to one who herself could pass it on to him she might meet one day. Yes, Miriam would live on in her bequest.

Suddenly, from some unwitting depth, a vision sprang to her mind—the image of a lithe, lovely girl in a blue, gold-fringed sari, of a kiss touching a dark-complexioned brow for a brief instant of passionate intensity. And she knew that in that compulsive gesture of an incongruous yet internally cogent affinity, it was the tenderness that Jenny had evoked in her that she had passed on; she knew that Jenny was living on, deathlessly, living on not in some preposterously imaginary Beyond, but in the here and now of human remembrance: the survivors would carry the imprints of all she had been, all she had given, pass them on as an infinitesimal but inalienable ingredient of mankind's inheritance.

"The energy," the dimness about her was vibrant with a soundless whisper that seemed to reach for her from the shuttered corner room, "the energy that has been ours will live on; could there be a more certain promise of afterlife?"

"No, Leonard, none," she answered under her breath, her eyes pinned to that golden star and the white blossom, abandoning herself to the ever-expanding, wondrous tranquility within and nature's quiescence without; abandoning herself, secure in the knowledge that Leonard Jordan's faith would be vindicated. Were there not Ramlu and Mr. Ghose and Deepti, to whom he had given of himself, were there not all the others his presence had touched? And was there not she herself, who had found the world he had made her discover; and would there not be the one, to whom one day she would pass on this legacy, the one in whom she would resurrect the presence of him she had encountered in a Gopalpur sunset, the presence that had defined her reality?

Through the lowering dusk that seemed strangely luminous, she beheld the tokens bequeathed to her by an encounter in the sunset: In the survivors, endlessly, Leonard Jordan would find his afterlife.

Mission to a Foreign Place

Near the bank of elevators, the nurse, Linda, stepped in his way. Her glance was an apology for breaking him from his contemplative absorption.

"On your way out, Rabbi?"

"Not quite yet." Pausing, he smiled at her, as always pleased to behold her still youngish, a bit impishly pert, face, which, it seemed to him, just now was wearing a quite uncharacteristic, oddly puzzled expression. "There are a couple more I thought I might look in on briefly."

"As usual," she replied, discarding any effort to keep an inflection of warmth from her tone. "With you, there are always a couple more and then still another couple more, aren't there?"

"Unfortunately." The cadence of his reply was responding in kind to the sincerity of her implied praise. "Unfortunately, there always are too many sick people. Too many who need some encouragement."

"Yes," she replied softly. "I know. That's the way you look at things… your vocation," she added, letting her eyes for an instant rest on him. "That's why I thought, perhaps, you could spare a few minutes to look in on eight twenty-five?"

"Eight twenty-five," he repeated, trying to match number and patient—and failing. "A new arrival?"

She shook her head. "He's been here for a while. He … I don't think he's got too much time left."

"Oh!" he uttered. His shoulders narrowed with the faint shudder, which, for all these years as the hospital's chaplain, for all the deaths witnessed, still remained his irrepressible reaction. And then once more, frowning. "Eight twenty-five, and here for some time? I can't recall having visited …"

"You haven't," Linda confirmed.

"But should have?"

"No, Rabbi," she said, ever so slightly accenting the title. "There would've been no reason for your visit. But now Mr. O'Rourke has asked for you."

"O'Rourke?"

"Francis Xavier O'Rourke."

"And he asked for me?"

Rather gravely, her head moved with a nod. "No, Rabbi. There's no mistake," she assured him, and suddenly he understood the puzzled look on her face: it fully accorded with his own perplexity.

"Of course," he answered the unspoken question reaching for him. "Thank you for telling me. I'll go see Mr. O'Rourke right now."

"I knew you would." The blue of Linda Donlevy's eyes deepened with a spark of gratitude and fondness, and fleetingly her hand touched his as she brushed past him.

Of course he would, Saul Marcus reaffirmed to himself, listening to the rhythmic echo of her steps fading away in the quiet of the deserted corridor. Of course he would visit Mr. O'Rourke; as Nurse Linda, always sensitively alert, had remarked. This was how he perceived his vocation—not as a religious ministration but a humanitarian one. Or perhaps as both, he corrected himself; in their essence, were these two endeavors not, quite beyond merely coinciding, actually identical? To him it seemed so. Had always seemed so, he thought, as he made his way toward room eight twenty-five. No, not merely seemed so—it was his truth, the very creed on which he had founded, indeed which had made possible, his function as the rabbi of the neighborhood congregation. The proposition that serving his creatures was not merely the best but the only real way of serving the eternal God of Israel had been the primary guide to, and the paramount principle of, his ministry. It was a proposition which, he reminded himself with a pang of aching regret, had inevitably caused his never formal but profoundly internal alienation from a father he had loved but could not understand; a proposition that Isaac Marcus, though eventually compelled to tolerate, could never share nor even accept.

Not that Isaac Marcus was a sterile fanatic. He was a strong, decent, even kindly man, lacking neither in emotional depth nor in intellectual acumen. Bred in Judaism's best tradition, he was fully living up to its ethical demands—he was utterly devoted to his family, conducted his business with the most scrupulous honesty, and was actively engaged in many charities, not simply from a sense of duty but obeying the imperative of his own conviction. And, dedicated to the strictest orthodoxy, his commitment to his God always retained its unequaled and unrivaled priority. It was a commitment whose fulfillment he perceived and sought in the most punctilious observance of the Biblical laws and the relevant rituals. Inevitably, it had been his foregone conclusion that his firstborn son was, like his own oldest brother, destined to study the Torah and the Talmud toward the achievement of the rabbinical office. For generations this had been the

Marcus family's tradition, and any alternative pursuit seemed beyond consideration.

But Isaac Marcus's implicit presumption had been increasingly disappointed. In spite of the unequivocal example set in his home; in spite of the orthodox teachings expounded in his parochial school; in spite of all expressed parental disapproval and constant censure, from early on Saul had displayed proclivities pointing toward a progressively more liberal interpretation of religion, toward a selective critique of its doctrines and institutions, toward a concept of faith which, rather than pursuing ritual observances and prayerful litanies, would apply Judaism's ideational substance to people's everyday needs and concerns. Stubbornly, the growing boy had made it clear that the rabbinical vocation would not satisfy his vision of the world and of life itself. But incapable of bringing himself to altogether defy his father's wish, he had studied at the yeshiva while at the same time taking up social science and psychology at Columbia University.

It was a compromise that Isaac Marcus could not help conceding and which rankled the more fiercely when this firstborn son of his, after graduating from both institutions with top marks and highest honors, was chosen to preside over the small reform congregation whose digressive viewpoints and practices appalled and repelled him as heretical—if not outright blasphemous.

Isaac Marcus felt deceived: the heir to his family's tradition might be a rabbi to all the world, but God knew he was no true teacher of his law. Formally following the venerable ancestral pattern, he substantially betrayed and disfigured it. Bitterly but silently, Isaac Marcus had lived with his disgrace. He could not suffer to set foot in the tiny synagogue where his son officiated—in that place of iniquity where men and women attended services side by side, as equals before the Sacred; where ritual was at best a perfunctory adjunct to the secular endeavors of furthering the consciousness of Jewry's cultural heritage, pride in its achievements, and a sense of community; where his son, his own son, would rather serve the ephemeral cares of men than the eternal glory of his Lord God.

Serve the cares of men, Saul Marcus mused, as, for an instant he uncertainly stopped in front of the closed door to eight twenty-five—that was what he had all along been trying, what the nurse, Linda, understood he was trying to do, what had prompted her suggestion that he try here, now. Mr. O'Rourke had asked for him, she had asserted. Mr. Francis Xavier O'Rourke. Surely she must be mistaken—whatever the man's cares might be, Francis Xavier O'Rourke asking for him? Even just inquiring whether Linda's plea had any basis whatever might prove a presumptuous imposition and an embarrassment that could easily end up with him making a fool of himself. But then, better a fool in the commission than a failure in the omission of one's human duty. He knocked at the door.

"I'm Rabbi Marcus," he announced himself, rather less resolutely than he had hoped.

"Yes." The response came to him through the ray of afternoon sun that was slanting through the window and across the bed. The man occupying the bed was lying on his back, his head slightly turned toward the door, his face carved with merciless poignancy by the day's brightness. Grayish and paper-thin, his skin stretched taut, almost pellucid over its frame; his eyes were embedded in deep, dark-rimmed hollows, half shuttered now by the partially lowered, pallid lids, reinforcing the impression of utter weariness pervading the quiet figure. But the voice was clear and surprising by the contrast of its sonorous timbre. "Yes. Thank you so much for coming to see me, Rabbi."

"Nurse Linda mentioned ..." Saul Marcus faltered, still lingering on the threshold.

"Yes." The wan ghost of a smile answered him. "Nurse Linda. She's a dear. Got her Irish eyes open. She, too, had you pegged right. Won't you come in, sit down for a trice?"

"If I'm not disturbing just now, Mr. O'Rourke."

"Disturbing me?" The half-drawn lids were lifting themselves to reveal a quizzical glance. "I was expecting you. Perhaps not quite so soon ... But it's good of you to get here so promptly, so there'll be still time ... No, no!" the man on the bed forestalled the attempted objection, raising a feeble hand in protest. "No need for that, Rabbi. No need. I know the score, even if the doctors hedge about the truth. We just know when we're getting there, don't we? Inside, somehow, we hear the bell toll. I listened. I know. It doesn't scare me. No way. After Saipan and Guadalcanal you don't scare easy ... Not about the fact of having to go, anyway. Besides, they're doing all they can here, to make the trip easy for me, and that's all I care about: not to be in pain, not to go moaning and groaning, making a spectacle of myself. To go with some dignity—you understand that, Rabbi, don't you?"

"Yes." The assent was grating hoarsely, aching with the memory of that wrenching hour, when his grandfather had passed on, kicking and screaming, fiercely fighting against that last breath. "Yes, I understand."

"I thought you would." There again was that ghost of a smile. "I had you pegged right. But then ..." The oddly resonant voice interrupted itself, pausing while another quizzical glance sought the visitor. "You're looking at me as though I seem familiar to you?"

"Familiar?" Saul Marcus repeated, only now fully aware of his vaguely troubling sense of déjà vu. "Yes, in fact, somehow ..."

"From the television commercials, no doubt." The explanation carried a ring of almost bored casualness. "I've been in dozens of them.

Cars, jewels, lawn mowers, electronic software, you name it. For the past ten years, ever since I quit acting … Oh!" There was a hint of irony in that voice now. "Nothing spectacular. Rather over-reckoned my talent, I did. Never made the big time. Just stock, provincial stages … After nearly twenty years of that, you've had enough. Besides, you're not getting any younger, and the commercials pay better, too. So …" The feeble hand moved on the hand moved on the cover, restively as though to determine that this subject warranted no further conversation. It was a few moments before the man on the bed spoke again. "I suppose you were wondering, Rabbi, when Linda told you. But you see, several times, through the open door, I've watched you pass by. You looked like someone one could talk to. Even when one's name is O'Rourke."

"That makes no difference," Saul Marcus muttered.

"What's in a name?" O'Rourke said softly. "But no, there's a difference, all right. Only, on a certain level, it becomes irrelevant. People either understand or they don't. I got the idea that you're one of those who do; there aren't too many. That's why …" His eyes, quite open now, fastened upon his visitor. "Again, thank you for coming, Rabbi."

Saul Marcus shook his head. "No call for any thanks, Mr. O'Rourke. I'll be only too happy if I can help."

"I thought you could." The faintness of a smile was no more; his lips were pressed in a hard, thin line, which invested the sick pallor of sunken features with even more appalling starkness. "Yes. Talking may help. Talking out one's burden, things that one ought to have done, yet has failed to do. Things one regrets but can no longer change nor atone for … Yes. Talking out thoughts that have been on your mind all along, but which you conveniently managed to run away from. Until a time comes when you've got to stop running … until a time comes," he repeated stonily, "like now. Then you call for help. For someone to whom you can talk out what you should've talked out with yourself long ago. For someone who understands." That ghost of a smile was back but oddly warped with whimsical ruefulness. "Going on such a far trip, you don't even want to take along too much excess baggage; you'd take care to travel light, would try to unload, wouldn't you?"

"I suppose so," Saul Marcus conceded slowly, weighing every word with contemplative care. "Would seem only natural, Mr. O'Rourke. And certainly I'd be glad trying to help you in this very way. But willingness may not be quite sufficient. I may offer understanding, but I may not be equipped to provide the sort of comfort and consolation you may be looking for."

On the pillow, a weary head was moving sideways and back in a gesture of refutation. "I'm looking for neither, Rabbi," O'Rourke replied, and there was an accent of harshness, almost of shrillness, roughening his even voice. "Comfort? There can be none, as long as one can't reverse one's failure. Consolation? In death, there is but one: the knowledge that you've lived your life fully, have taken the best advantage of what experience had granted you, and, in turn, have given the most of yourself that was granted to you to give … But have I? That's the point, Rabbi. That's the point."

"I'm sure you've been trying …"

"Have I? As I've read someplace, 'That which you gave will never equal what you've been given.' So with me, too. That's the point, Rabbi."

"I see." The comment dragged with an accent of doubt. "I think I can discern your burden. But is discerning it, comprehending it, all it would take to help you? The fact still remains—I may not be the proper person to assist you in its unloading."

The Glitter and Other Stories

"Because my name's O'Rourke?" The harshness was escalating. "Because I'm Francis Xavier O'Rourke?"

"Yes," Saul Marcus returned quietly, "because. My viewpoint may prove too different, my perception of your burden, my approach to the question of relief. My response may not be congenial."

"Or it may." The Irishman's tired voice gained a spark of unexpected, strangely inapposite brightness. "Seems to me, when people remind themselves of their humanity, they turn out to be congenial. That bit of humanity is our last recourse, isn't it? That's what I've been hoping for." The fitful motion of a languid hand forestalled an uneasy rebuttal. "But I don't blame you, Rabbi Marcus. I, too, understand: you want to be considerate, fair, judicious. As the representative of another faith, you feel you're on a mission to a foreign place and must take care not to trespass the natives' preserve. You think a priest would be better suited, would be more—what was your word?—more congenial. Naturally. A priest …" The spark in his dark eyes died away. "Oh yes, Father Richmond's been here, all right. Came just an hour or so ago. He didn't stay long when I didn't care about that other world but about this one right here and now, figuring that, while still alive, this would be the time for being concerned with life down here. There will be plenty of time to concern myself with the one in the Beyond, when I'm getting there. Father Richmond didn't see it that way," O'Rourke went on, his brittle lips quivering with a breath of somber amusement. "He thought such an attitude was most unworthy of a dying man. Especially of a Christian. He became quite impatient with me. A bit riled up. After all, he had come to prepare me for eternity. But precisely when you're facing that prospect, you'd want to speak to someone who would listen to you as a man, not someone who pretends you're speaking to God. Besides, there was no need for any preparation. The part I was about to play didn't require any auditioning. My performance was going to be automatic, and, at worst I could always ad lib. After forty years at it, you get to be good at it." A drab little chuckle filled a momentary pause. "When I so told Father Richmond, he didn't stay too long. Though he was reluctant to leave before he'd done his thing: confession; review of your supposed sins; contrition; repentance—the whole menu. I would have none of it. Would've been as indigestible as the one dished to me half a century ago when I discovered that I had too sensitive a stomach."

Abruptly, prompted by some serious dismay, Saul Marcus bent toward the sick man, his usually smooth brow furrowed. "You've … you've broken away from your faith?" he asked, unable to quite suppress a tremor in his voice.

"Not from my faith, Rabbi," O'Rourke said, blinking as a slight movement of his head brought the ray of afternoon sun to bear directly on his eyes. "I never quit believing in God and Christ and the promise of redemption and life eternal—but the Church, that's another matter altogether."

"Another matter altogether …" Slowly, Saul Marcus let himself lean back again in his chair to listen, every fiber of his body tensed, to the echo of the phrase he had repeated—an echo lingering on, unwilling to fade, pervading the moment's silence and transforming the room into a place not so foreign any longer, a place to which he had traveled before. He, as well, had never quit believing in a divine presence; but his father's intransigent, hidebound dogmatism, that had been another matter altogether.

"It goes all the way back," O'Rourke's voice reached for him, a voice even and quiet, yet by its so unexpected resonance riveting his attention. "All the way back to the summer after high school graduation. To those singular, incomparable days of a first love, a first kiss, a first embrace." There was a hiatus, ever so brief, before the voice went on, its sonority now gently vibrant. "Deirdre. My own age. Not really pretty, but so beautiful—the person, Rabbi, you understand? The inner glow. The honesty, the purity of feelings ... From a jealously church-bound family like myself. So, somehow, it happened: two young people, being young, finding their moment of true mutuality ..." O'Rourke paused again. On the bed cover, the bony fingers of one hand fleetingly clenched into a fist, then relented again. "Of course, at confession I told the priest, as always—automatically, the way I'd been brought up, the only way I knew. Well, not all our priests may be like Father Conlan, though most of those I've met didn't differ too much from him. Anyway, he was another Irishman whose heart didn't beat in his chest but in the Vatican; whose inspiration didn't come from Jesus but from the Congregation for the Doctrine of the Faith ... He came down on me with all the thunder of his perverted godliness. Canted at me about depravity and sin and the need for penance. That's when something in me snapped. Sure enough, a thousand times I had, thoughtlessly, mechanically, recited all that litany about temptation and mortal transgression, about contrition and repentance by which alone one might redeem one's soul; but that had been just words, witlessly parroted. Now those dead doctrines had become living actuality, immediate and palpable, in all their hideousness naked to my apprehension. Abstractions had become grinning monsters, roused to frighten me. Yet somehow they didn't, for the reality of my own experience discredited them. There they were, their proclaimed holy truths, belied by the most wonderful event God's grace had bestowed on me—oh, so utterly belied! 'Sin!' Father Conlan might shout, but how could loving be sin ever? 'The evil of carnal lust,' he might scream at me, but how could be evil what was part of one's God-given nature? When God created us to be human, He must've willed us to be human. Father Conlan might bellow about damnation, but how damnation, when I felt blessed? He might belch forth his piece about penance, but penance for what? For giving and being given happiness? Penance, when its very exercise would be treason, betrayal of Deirdre as well as of myself, denying as it would be the marvel and exaltation of our oneness? Penance—that would not only debase the wonder of passionate mutuality as a shabby, dirty, worthless aberration but denigrate the truth of Deirdre's love, and of my own as well?"

The voice from the sickbed lost itself in another brief spell of silence. Prey to exhaustion or perhaps merely captive to images of the past, O'Rourke had closed his eyes. Having moved his head out of the sunbeam's reach and now touched by the shade, his features gradually shed the rage that had flooded them, seemed softer again. But his lips still were pressed tight in that thin, hard line, which so forcefully conjured up the form of a skeletal mask.

Then, in tones more brittle and slightly creaking, O'Rourke spoke again. "That very instant, like lightning striking its target, something snapped. In the midst of Father Conlan's tirade I walked out, straight out of the confessional, and I never walked back. When I insisted that I wouldn't, ever, my father forbade me his house, and my mother got herself blisters on her knees, praying for my salvation, running to church every day. But I wouldn't set foot in any, haven't done so since that day of confession. And I kept right on with what Rome's offal had called 'sinning.' Not with Deirdre, though. On Father Conlan's advice, her people sent her away. Much as I searched, I couldn't find her again. Which may have, though I hope it didn't, put a stop to her 'sinning;' it sure didn't to mine. After a while, life went on, and there were others. Several of them. But mind you, Rabbi, no cheap, sleazy stuff. No fly-by-night dalliances. They would have degraded my first experience. None of those affairs did, even if they wouldn't last for a lifetime. Perhaps they couldn't. The kind of life that seemed to me the only viable one, that of an actor, made me move from place to place, which was hardly conducive to settling down. Or maybe that's just a subterfuge. Maybe I simply couldn't commit myself, couldn't overcome a sense of guilt, as though a commitment would be a betrayal of Deirdre? I don't know, Rabbi, I've never managed to quite figure it out."

The sick man's eyes had opened again. Saul Marcus felt them reaching out for him, asking him for a comment, waiting for it. Not for long. Saul Marcus did not require any lengthy cogitation to respond to the pleading glance. "There's no need for figuring out why you're human."

A smile was softening the thin, hard lips. "I knew you were someone one could talk to," O'Rourke said. His lids were drooping again; he was returning to his memories. "Yes. I was human, wasn't I? Sinfully human. So there were successive encounters, successive attachments. Not too many, either, because women who really can mean something to you are few and far between. And any other sort of involvement didn't apply. Each that came my way was founded on true mutual affection, on honest emotions. Each was fulfilling and happy, for whatever duration fate had designed for it. Nearly always, they'd last for quite a while. The final one, with Rose-Ann, for fourteen years, until she died three years ago. We'd lived together without the benefit of clergy—and none the worse for it. She was a beautiful person, in many ways reminding me of Deirdre. She had met her own Father Conlan and drawn her own conclusions. We kept on 'sinning,' and if we ever had given it a thought at all, we would've shared the conclusion that carnality was a wondrous, unique blessing and God's special gift to mankind—and that repentance was for those alone who, instead of gratefully accepting it, were mocking God's own intent by renouncing or disparaging this intrinsic element of their human heritage."

"Yes," Saul Marcus muttered absently, engrossed in an image suddenly evoked, the image of Arlene, whom his father had openly rejected and his mother had silently detested, suspecting that she had surrendered her virginity prior to becoming his wife and thus by her very presence at the altar was disgracing the name of the Eternal One; this fault proved equally as unforgivable as her resolute refusal to hide her lovely blue-black hair beneath the canonically prescribed wig, or to submit to the ritual baths, maintaining that a daily dip in her own tub was keeping her adequately clean.

Arlene, my Arlene, he thought. Inside him there was an echo of words spoken evenly, and now reverberating acute with irony, *you feel you're on a mission to a foreign place.* Yet there she was, his Arlene—and there was Francis Xavier O'Rourke's Rose-Ann, and his Deidre—natives of places which did not seem altogether so foreign. How had the man on the bed phrased it? "On a certain level differences become irrelevant, when people remind themselves of their humanity, they turn out to be congenial."

"Yes," Saul Marcus said once more. "Only they need repent who despise God's gift." His glance lost in the far-away of sunlight beyond the window, he thought of Arlene, who had been His gift to him; who had bestowed on him the fullness of her emotional support and, concomitantly, the strength and courage to defy parental opposition and condemnation and to pursue what he deemed his calling—had bestowed it ever since those days at Columbia, when they had begun to keep each other's company, had bestowed it throughout the unforgettable years when she had been his lover, unstinting of her passion, asking for naught but his equal devotion, ready to remain his lover without the trimmings of marriage license and wedding band. Only their shared desire for offspring had urged upon them their acquiescence to a ceremony—which added nothing to the actuality of the communion, which was their incomparable treasure, except an irrelevant certificate of public approbation. Here she was, his Arlene, and there they were, Deirdre and Rose-Ann, and those others in between, who had bestowed like fulfillment on Francis Xavier O'Rourke, and like happiness: no foreigners to each other, but sisters under the skin.

"And yet," the voice from the bed was cutting into his musings, softly yet oddly compelling in its recaptured resonance, "and yet there's cause for repentance: not for any of Father Conlan's imaginary theological 'sins,' but for a guilt more subtle, more profound, and irrefutably real, a failure not of commission but omission, and it can't be atoned."

A long moment passed, before Saul Marcus spoke carefully, "But recognizing whatever one's guilt, and assuming one's responsibility for whatever failure, and hurting in doing so, is that not of itself atonement?"

"No!" The response was creaking with bony determination. "No, Rabbi, it isn't. Not when you're honest with yourself. Because you cannot revisit your past and revise it."

Struck by the aching bitterness of the phrase, Saul Marcus abandoned himself to a pang of compassion. "And there is your burden of it?" he asked at last gently. "Your past unrevised?"

"A load on my mind." The reply was a shudder of sound. "It's been there for a long time now. And getting heavier all the while. Ever since Rose-Ann's passing. These last days here, it's just grown too heavy to carry along. That's why …"

"Yes," Saul Marcus spoke, unconscious of a curious inflection of tenderness. "That's why I am here."

O'Rourke seemed not to hear. "A load on my mind," he said again, and a breath of awe was shivering through every weary word. "The failure of your past. Of not having paid your debt to life fully; of having taken from it without returning its gift. The failure of not having given of yourself all you had been granted, had been meant to give. To those, most conspicuously, most unforgivably, by whom you had been given …" His lips pressed tight against the hurt of words, which were forcing their passage. "Been given so much, so unselfishly, so unreservedly, so generously … Deirdre. Rose-Ann. Thelma. Vicky. One or two others … From each of them I reaped happiness, yet denied them their full share of the harvest. How do you atone for that? How do you square the accounts? No way, now, is there? And worse yet, not even being sure, if you were allowed to revisit the past, that you would, or could, square them. Being aware of the probability that you might fail again. Fail in the same goddamned, miserable way, all over again!"

"The probability? Hardly," Saul Marcus interposed, trying to dam the burst of escalating desolation. "Hardly, given the kind of man you are."

"The kind of man I am." For all the low-pitched drabness, the echoed phrase was simmering with self-baiting scorn. "That's just it, Rabbi. That's just the point: the kind of man I am, the kind of man I've been, have come to be. For you may cut loose from your church: all you need is a Father Conlan to open your eyes. You may cut loose from your family: all you need are parents who won't tolerate a renegade in their sanctified house. But from your self's debility there's no cutting loose."

"Sometimes," Saul Marcus faltered, frowning, searching his mind for a valid contradiction, "sometimes …"

"No, Rabbi," O'Rourke scissored the attempted objection, "not sometimes, not ever, not from your self's debility. Not from the pattern of conduct it has shaped. If you think you can do it, you're just fooling yourself. There are your childhood experiences, your youthful perceptions, your early incalculableness. That's what sets the pattern. No way of cutting loose from that. Cling to you like a hunchback, and there's no surgery to remove it, Nor, if there were, would you be likely to be looking for any. That hunchback is so much part of you, most of the time you wouldn't be aware of it. Until …."

The word faded, a barely repressed sigh, into another hiatus of silence, which, Saul Marcus felt keenly, brooked no interruption, no alien intrusion into the privacy of self-confrontation.

Seconds passed like hours before O'Rourke spoke again, in a low, laboring voice. "The hunchback. You're stuck with it for life. And it defines the kind of man you are ... The parental example. No matter how far you seem to have grown away from it, no matter how effectively you think you've rejected it, rebelled against it, it keeps controlling you—it's kept controlling me, all right," he added, and the acid of the remembrance further accentuated the skeletal cast of his features. The parental model. Furnished to me by a solid Irish couple, united in their dedication to God and country, to hard work and piety and discipline. No disagreements there, no controversies, no quarrels—at least, none I witnessed. Each accepting and scrupulously attending to their respective shares of domestic duty. Clearly it was the circumstance of their identical backgrounds and identical mentalities that had been both the motivation and the foundation of their marital bond. Exclusively? I don't know. There may well have been some emotional affinity too; they didn't seem to be unemotional people, nor sensually impoverished ones, either. The Irish rarely are, so why not give them the benefit of the doubt? There may even have been real love between them, but at that I can only guess. Or, whatever feelings there might've been, they were never permitted any expression, whether by some slightest revealing gesture or even just verbally, by any most trivial term of endearment. Least of all when such expression might've carried any hint of erotic intimacy. There was an implicit, incontrovertible taboo, one never broken, nor even once transgressed. The parental model, Rabbi, becomes an inalienable bequest, a hunchback ..."

An inflection as of a virulent chuckle momentarily curled those bloodless lips with a breath of spectral irony. Progressively the sick man's speech had been coming more slowly, laboriously, sustained only by some indomitable impulsion.

"The hunchback, for the longest time—in fact most of my life—I didn't realize I was wearing it; or, perhaps, somehow knowing I couldn't shed it in any case, didn't want to acknowledge my disfigurement. Only when I was standing in front of Rose-Ann's casket, with the awareness of how much I had loved her and wishing I could tell her, it suddenly came to me that I had never told her. Not once in fourteen long, beautiful years—not once! It struck me hard. A bolt of realization, more shattering perhaps even than the finality of her demise, that I had let her go like this, without one word, the one assurance that would've made all the difference to the moment of departure. Can you imagine, Rabbi, in fourteen years of giving me her all, not hearing it once? How it must've hurt her, how she must've missed it in that last hour of the farewell! And then, gradually, memory was taking me back to those before, to Deidre and Becky and Vicky, to all those I had loved—and, looking back, I began to understand those silences that sometimes seemed so sad, so hungering—silences that seemed to be asking for that one word, waiting for it, waiting for what there was in me all the time, a passionate truth—yet I withheld it from them. But people, Rabbi, people need to be told, need reassurance, reaffirmation. Words are not just sound. Some words can be uniquely precious gifts. And they were mine to give, yet I wouldn't give them, ever—not to Deirdre, not to any of the others, not even to Rose-Ann, when …"

"When …"

The echo whispered through the abrupt, utter stillness, reverberating on and on, more awesome than a scream from the abyss, reverberating in the visitor's mind, a final jarring note of a desperate song, whose descant was transforming the foreign place that Francis Xavier O'Rourke inhabited into the so dismally familiar one in which he, Saul Marcus, had dwelled: a solid Jewish home, firmly maintained by parents united in their dedication to the punctilious observance of their Eternal One's law, to hard work and duty and discipline, to a life revolving around synagogue and hearth and the proper rearing of the son who was their pride and hope; parents united by identical backgrounds and identical goals, predetermined by identical mentalities, which spawned the years and years of ordinary days lived quietly side by side, untroubled by any flagrant controversies, free of any open disputes—and bare of any intimation of mutual affection. Their so conspicuous shared dedication to the family unit was inbuilt dictate of tradition, a facet only of their zeal to accomplish the Eternal One's commands, with no reference to their own natures' demands. Possibly, in the privacy of their bed chamber, Saul Marcus thought, there might have been some measure of more sensitive interaction, though he doubted it. Isaac Marcus and Esther Loeb had been brought together by their respective fathers' longstanding arrangement and joined into marriage by the willful insistence of those old friends and members of the same orthodox congregation, At any rate, whatever more personal communication might have existed between them, it never had found any expression.

Perhaps, it occurred to him, it had been his adolescent perception of this emotional barrenness and his intensifying abhorrence of what seemed to him an unendurable impoverishment of the human potential—yes, perhaps it had been this perception that had triggered his rebellion and launched his search for a vocation which promised richer human rewards, this very vocation, which, by its worldly rather than theological inclination, had completed his alienation from the parental pattern. But had it, really? Words came back to him, like ghosts raised to haunt him, words spoken by that man O'Rourke, "You may cut loose from your church, from your family, but you can never from your pattern of conduct … there is the parental model …"

The hunchback, Saul Marcus repeated to himself, staring at the man on the sickbed. *Was he, too, affected with it? Had he, too, been withholding that precious word, that needed affirmation, that gift of reassurance? Had he expressed himself to Arlene, had he told her how much, how very much he loved her? He must have, of course, he must have. But then, he was not sure. How come he could not recall any precise instance, any actual phrasing? There must have been occasions in all these years together, those incomparable, fulfilled years … and yet, had there been such silences, too, silences sad and hungeringthat were asking for that one word, when she had been waiting for him to speak it, and he had failed to respond?* He tried to remember. Yes, there had been silences between them, often and prolonged—but not that kind, no, their silences had been profound with contentment, vibrant with joy in each others closeness, or placid with a pervasive fondness, with an intangible mutuality, with a certainty, unquestioned and absolute, that was hers as well as his and had fueled the enchantment of those silences. Perhaps sometimes he had interrupted such spells of mute communion with a whispered disclosure of feelings too powerful to be kept inside, perhaps …? He hoped he had. Yet, even if he had never found his way to such verbal expression, had not his Arlene's contentment and joy and impassioned fondness of themselves testified to her awareness of his love?

Arlene knew, he told himself, swept by a wondrous sense of unburdening relief. Oh yes, she knew! There might have been no words, but there had been a thousand small gestures, a thousand subtle glances, a thousand pregnant smiles; there had been the never missed celebrations of their private anniversaries, the countless endearments, the ever-present eloquence of that special lilt enriching their most sober everyday conversations with a touch of intimacy; there had been those countless signals, each sending its message … no, Arlene had not been left asking, waiting, hungering.

"This calamity of death, Rabbi," the voice from the bed broke into his ruminations, a voice drained and flat, now uncannily bereft of its erstwhile resonance. O'Rourke lay motionless with his eyes open. "The true calamity of death does not reside in the prospect of having to leave the bounties of this world but in having to depart with one's debt to life unredeemed and now forever unredeemable. And I owe so much, Rabbi, so much!"

"Owe so much!"

There was the susurrant echo again, forlorn and desolate, but, as though stilled by the quiet confidence of the other man's smile, not lingering on.

"Do you, Mr. O'Rourke?" Saul Marcus asked placidly. "Do you really?"

"I told you, didn't I?" the sick man retorted fretfully. On the bed covers, his hands were moving restlessly, and his chest was heaving with fitful spasms of breath.

"Yes." On Saul Marcus's lips the smile was deepening. "You told me. About Rose-Ann and Deirdre and those others you loved … You did love them, didn't you?"

"Every one of them." O'Rourke spoke it as in a solemn vow. "Deirdre especially, perhaps because she was the first? But Rose-Ann most of all. And yet …"

Saul Marcus would not let him finish. "And you showed them you cared?"

"Showed them?" A shiver, as of pain, flitted across that haggard face. "Showed them, I don't know."

"But you tried to show them?"

"When one loves …" For an instant, the voice trailed off; those dark eyes were returning from that clouded infinity to seek the questioner with a glint of repudiation. "Of course I tried. As best as I knew how."

"Yes," Saul Marcus assented, every word a slow emphasis. "Of course you tried, and no question, you did show them. That's the way it goes when one loves: one does reveal one's self."

"But …"

"One does!" Saul Marcus repeated, firmly, decisively. "One cannot help revealing one's self, one way or another. Hasn't it ever occurred to you that Deirdre and Rose-Ann—that every one of those women in your life understood that words weren't your way? That in those silences they shared with you they were not sad or hungering, but by their own silence respecting your way? Had they accepted your inhibition, that 'hunchback' of yours, never asking, never waiting for what, they realized, was not yours to give, contented by the happiness and fulfillment you were giving, knowing full well the truth of your feelings? Yes. Mr. O'Rourke, knowing—for didn't their response, didn't their own love prove that they knew? Oh, they did know, Mr. O'Rourke, every one of them … Deirdre, in those short, unforgettable days of summer; Rose-Ann, when you held her hand in that final farewell. They knew what was in you, as all of them had known. And that knowledge canceled all debts."

The man on the bed lay very still, listening to the reverberating cadence of a passionate conviction, drinking in to the last every reluctantly fading whit of sound. Slowly the lids drooped back over his eyes, reinforcing a hint of serenity, which, expanding, endowed that skeletal mask with a touch of transcendent beauty.

"Thank you, Rabbi," he spoke up at last, terminating the passage of what seemed interminable moments. "Thank you for coming, for listening, for talking … had you pegged right. Guessed you would be no foreigner …" With every word, his voice grew more brittle and softer, gradually dropping to a mumble, dragging with every fragment of a forced effort.

"I have tired you," Saul Marcus said gently.

"Yes," O'Rourke muttered, "I'm a bit tired."

"You ought to rest."

"Yes, rest, rest …" The words fell into the quietude of the chamber, mere sonant breath but suffused by the glow of an inward smile.

Saul Marcus bent closer, "If you'd like me to stay with you …?"

On the pillow the frail movement of a weary head conveyed the negation. "Someone else may need you …"

"Perhaps so," Saul Marcus agreed, rising. He understood. Francis Xavier O'Rourke wished to be with Deirdre, with Thelma and Becky and Vicky, alone and undisturbed, so he might tell them at last … and with Rose-Ann—it would be she who was going to hold his hand when …

"God be with you, Mr. O'Rourke. I shall be looking in on you again later."

"Later …" A whisper, trailing, losing itself into the golden beam of the afternoon sun.

As noiselessly as he could manage, Saul Marcus moved toward the door. Almost on the threshold he was stopped. For all its softness, the voice coming to him from the sickbed was clearer now, stronger.

"Rabbi Marcus?"

"Yes, Mr. O'Rourke?"

"Your people have a greeting of their own … shalom, isn't it?"

"Yes. Shalom," Saul Marcus said. "Meaning 'peace.'"

"Peace …" O'Rourke repeated. "Yes, peace … Shalom, Rabbi, shalom …"

He was lying on his back, motionless. On the covers his hands were resting, still. Beneath the covers, his chest was swelling and ebbing with the rhythm of a feeble, but placidly even, breath.

Mister Flannery

A few steps along the pebbled pedestrian walk past the gate, he paused. Momentarily, a glint of the still-frosty early spring sun had flitted across the man in the gardener's overalls, revealing a touch of familiarity about the wizened profile, of old acquaintance remembered but eluding an immediate identification. Puzzled, he stood still for another look.

The man by the flower bed beyond the wide driveway appeared to sense the visitor's gaze. He turned, for a brief instant and leaned on his spade, then dropped it to start moving along the narrow path between the square parcels of turned-up soil. "Paul!" he exclaimed. "Paul Devlin!"

"Father Flannery?" The response was half question, half statement, mirroring the perplexity which attended the moment of uncertain recognition. "Father Flannery, is it?"

"Mister Flannery," the man in the overalls said softly.

But Paul Devlin's mind did not register the correction. He was too engrossed in his surprise and dismay—surprise at the so totally unexpected and, within the given environment, so paradoxical encounter; dismay at facing a countenance, which, refuting all reasonable expectations of passing time's impact, in the space of barely seven years seemed to have aged thirty years. Once fresh and healthy, even a bit florid, it was now sallow, bony—haggard and deeply lined; its once smooth brow was crisscrossed by furrows; its eyes, once bright with energy and cheer, were now lusterless within dark-rimmed hollows. Although still tall and broad-shouldered as ever, the figure had an air of frailty about it, and while keeping itself erect, it somehow conveyed the impression of a stoop.

"Indeed, Paul Devlin!" the man in the overalls repeated, cutting into the other's appalled observations. "Back at last. Been a long time, Paul. It's good to see you." Yet a faint hitch of hesitancy curiously qualified the warmth of the welcome.

"Good to see you, too." The answering phrase conveyed courtesy without conviction. But it was not just the discomfiture attending one's confrontation with a man's evident deterioration that added to its reserve a hint of strained coolness, even of animosity. "It's always been a privilege meeting you, Father Flannery."

"Mister Flannery."

This time Paul Devlin did not miss the quietly emending emphasis. It made him realize what initially had confounded him and blocked him from instantaneous recognition. For only now his awareness was fully alerted to the appearance of the one who called himself 'Mister' Flannery, to the appreciation not only of that somewhat bedraggled gardener's outfit, but, far more baffling, the absence of the Roman collar and the detail of the now thinned out, almost white hair, which had dispensed with the tonsure. "Mister Flannery?" he repeated, staring. "You … you left your faith?" The question was faltering with a lump of incredulity. John Flannery had seemed so singularly devout, so extraordinarily committed to his ministry, maybe excessively so …

"Not my faith." A brittle smile fleetingly touched the pale lips. "Only my service to the Church." A small gesture thwarted an uncomprehending comment. "Life exacts its price, Paul. Men's needs change. The perception of duty changes. Sometimes one comes to discern different priorities." Another motion of his large, but now so languid hand dismissed any further discussion of that subject, as he went on quietly, "You're looking well, Paul. Very well, indeed. Seems success becomes you. Made quite a name for yourself, haven't you? Not so long ago I read that fine piece in the National Geographic. About those excavations, a Hittite site in Anatolia."

"Oh, that." A shrug, a distant nod. "Just an excerpt taken from my dissertation. The full book's due for publication this fall."

"Congratulations. I'll make sure to get a copy. Yes, you do look well," John Flannery said once more, quickly, ignoring the hint of impatience in the young man's response. "A little heavier, perhaps, than I remember you, and this deep tan—an incidental bonus of your work, of course, the constant exposure to the weathers … But altogether you haven't paid your toll to time at all. It's quite a while you've been away, seven years? Eight? Whatever; it seems much longer than the calendar tells, anyway, longer than you had originally expected."

Paul Devlin would not evade the question lurking behind the apparently casual remark. "Not really. In fact, my estimate of that dig's duration proved rather too generous.

The dig was completed ahead of the twenty months allowed. The conditions had turned out rather more favorable than anticipated. Actually, I could've returned a couple of months earlier than projected."

"But you did not return," John Flannery spoke at last, tentatively trying to bridge the gap of silence that had suddenly sprung up between them.

"No, I did not return." The inflection of impatience was more pronounced now, its accent of bitterness not altogether intent on hiding a nuance of resentment. "Just then, another promising site further to the southeast had been discovered. They inquired whether I would care to take part in its exploration. So I joined that team. After all, there was nothing to come back for at the time, was there?"

"At the time …" John Flannery listened to the echo of the phrase fade into a new gap of silence bleakly extending between them. "At the time," he repeated to himself. That time had been just after Winnie Brennan had been married to George Mulvey. No doubt, Paul Devlin had learned that she was no longer there for him to come back for—if ever she had really been there for him. But then, even the precarious possibility had been quashed and whatever stubborn hope might have lingered …

"There were your parents," John Flannery muttered vapidly, dismally aware of the suggestion's lame incompetence.

"My parents, yes, they were there." A breath of drab irony tainted the response. "Of course, I'd want to see my parents, wouldn't I? But there wasn't enough time available to make a trip home feasible. So I had them come over to visit with me. Spent a few pleasant days with them in Ankara … Damn it!" Paul Devlin interrupted himself; suddenly anger was roughening his voice. "What for, this shabby, stupid subterfuge? I just didn't want to go back, that's all!"

"I understand." John Flannery's mumble dropped into another abyss of stillness, which seemed vibrant with an indictment, to which he could offer no defense.

*

Indeed, he understood. Just then his home town was the last place on earth Paul Devlin would have wanted to visit. The news of Winnie Brennan's wedding must have proved too shattering, too devastating a blow. He could not have faced those streets, those houses, those trees, each screaming at him with memories of days past and mocking him with the actuality of days present and future. For even to those who had opposed the eventuality of their lasting association, there had been no question whatever of his love for the shy, graceful girl—a love as deep and honest, as total and abiding as hers for him; a love as passionate as it was elementary, yet which, John Flannery knew, had never, except for one single, wondrous, self-forgetting kiss, been allowed any physical expression.

Not that Winnie Brennan would have rebuffed the attempt, John Flannery knew—she had been too completely possessed by her emotion—but no attempt had ever tested her innocence. Young though he was and himself entirely unencumbered by any belief in his Church's imprecations against carnal sin, Paul Devlin had sensitively appreciated her profound religious commitment and the torment of guilt to which such an experience would have subjected her. From the very outset of their friendship, he had determined that any further intimacy would have to wait until their bond could be legalized; had so determined, notwithstanding the self-evident circumstance that it might be a matter of years before he would be sufficiently established in his field to found and sustain a family.

Paul Devlin had always been a dreamer, the man in the gardener's overalls remembered, a beautiful, gifted dreamer of noble dreams, even though those dreams were sadly devoid of any debt to Christian spirituality—which was why his dreams of Winnie Brennan had been doomed. And he, John Flannery, erstwhile priest at St. Catherine's, had had a hand in its dooming. His involvement had not been prompted by any personal antagonism or by excessive zeal, he told himself, wearily repeating what he had been telling himself over the years of self-searching scruples; told himself in rebuttal to the acrid accusing silence, amid which he stood there, blindly gazing past the visitor into the chilly brightness of the spring day. No, whatever carefully considered supplemental intervention he had allowed himself had been urged upon him by a conscientious conviction that, for all the indubitable sincerity of their love, these two young people were fundamentally too ill-matched for their relationship to succeed. He had known them both since their childhood, although by no means equally well. Initially, his acquaintance with Paul had been sporadic and casual, confined to mere superficial observations. Fostered by a free-thinking parental home, the boy's manifest religious indifference and willful, almost demonstrative avoidance of church attendance would neither afford nor encourage a priest's opportunity for closer contact. Only much later, a progressively clearer and increasingly more favorable picture of Paul Devlin's personality had emerged, a picture no less valid for being conditioned by Winnie Brennan's fascinated references to her beloved one.

No less valid also, John Flannery had perceived, were her references in their incidental revelation of that personality's disturbingly detracting aspects, and consequently, his second-hand appreciation of the young man had fortified his hardening conviction concerning the eventual calamitous conflict, which, given Winnie Brennan's mental frame, seemed inevitable—a conviction that, he felt, imposed on him the human as well as clerical duty to exert his efforts toward guarding the girl against a certain seriously, perhaps irreparably, detrimental experience. For, unlike his perfunctory acquaintance with the Devlin boy, his apprehension of Winnie Brennan's character had been thorough, due not alone to his close social association with her family but, even more decisively, to his function as her confessor. Steeped in her absolute faith, she would withhold nothing from God's and Christ's representative, not one single thought or dream or fantasy would remain her secret. Thus John Flannery had learned of her infatuation well before her parents' first inkling; had been privy to every phase of the sprouting emotional mutuality, from its very incipience on the day of her explosive, fateful encounter with Paul Devlin.

That encounter had owed strictly to accident. It had been occasioned by the centennial celebration of the town's original charter, which, as all such affairs, had brought together the medley of the locality's composing elements, uniting for a few hours of trivial cheer—communal segments, which, of diverse social status, interests, and viewpoints, would ordinarily not be prone to mingle. Born into different sets and reared toward the different goals and expectations envisioned by the divergent presumptions of, respectively, a professor of history at the university and a thriving real-estate and insurance broker, Paul Devlin and Winnie Brennan were most unlikely to meet and, in fact, had had no previous acquaintance whatever. Fleetingly, here and there, they might have caught a glimpse of each other, passing in the street. If so, such a glimpse would have beheld merely some irrelevant presence without any awareness of the other's person.

Too many factors would militate against any interested association. Six years Winnie's senior, Paul had been educated in public school by his own choice, sharing his father's distinct aversion to private academies, particularly parochial ones such as St. Catherine's, which she had attended. His persistent shunning of church services would not only alienate but implicitly exclude him from the circle in which she had been groomed to move. While, just having graduated from Catholic high school, she was vaguely pondering how she might best serve God and mankind at the same time, he had been engrossed in his final postgraduate year, determined to supplement his father's accomplishments as a historian by his own efforts in archaeology, a pursuit which, he maintained, would expand the scope of people's appreciation of their antecedents by not only verifying the supposed events of the still unexplored remote past but by pushing further back its frontiers.

And yet, improbable, indeed implausible as any accommodation of such so sharply contrasting backgrounds and conflicting proclivities would seem, the simple fortuity of finding themselves standing side by side at that centennial, of a conversation engaged in at first casually but soon with deepening ardor, had evoked a response of overwhelming immediacy, an enrapturing sense of internal concordance, an experience of emotional mutuality infinitely beyond any either had ever known or even dared imagine—an experience all-encompassing and totally compelling whose continuity neither could have foreseen.

When John Flannery, through the agency of the confessional, had first been apprized of the incipient and rapidly intensifying attachment, he had been touched by the utter honesty of its innocent fervor, yet he was not without a nagging sense of troubled concern. Impressed though he was with Paul Devlin's high intelligence and equally singular concept of ethics, his sensitive decency and mature sense of responsibility, the fledgling archaeologist's not just secular but unabashedly irreligious bent was as reprehensible as it was alarming for its potential of future controversy and the even more perilous eventuality of jeopardizing a Christian soul's salvation by diverting the love-struck girl from her path of faith and devotion. He had indicated his priestly apprehension, but, anxious lest he frighten his confessant with stronger, more threatening exhortations and perceiving that his gently cautioning words were drowned by the tide of dreamy passion, he had decided to mute his own fruitless admonitions and rely on the certain and hopefully more effective intervention of her parents.

This intervention had not been tardy in asserting its correcting influence. True, although hardly cheered by their Winnie's choice of company, James and Margaret Brennan had at first been grudgingly tolerant of what they insensitively judged to be a child's passing fancy, a mere puppy love. This stolid appraisal allowed them to be spared their confrontation with the uncomfortable truth: that their daughter was a puppy no longer—not a child but an emotionally as well as physically fully developed young woman. This initial inertness had been abetted by the conveniently becalming observation that the pair's meetings were occurring exclusively in public—in the park, in the local ice cream parlor, at ball games. Nonetheless, when soon enough these trysts became more frequent and prolonged and the escalating extent of their Winnie's involvement increasingly evident, when the indications of a serious and possibly lasting relationship could no longer be ignored, the parental counterattack had started in full force. Disparagement and spite, scornful criticism and carping censure building in rancor and vehemence unfolded into a steady and preoccupying routine. Ever suspicious of intellectuals and contemptuous of academicians, whose net worth was confined to the limitations of their always measly salaries, James Brennan, as a staunch churchman and president of the Catholic club, would be vitriolic in his gibing rejection of one whose father was known to discuss Jesus as a historical personage rather than as a divine savior and to oppose many of the church-sponsored causes. On her part, his spouse, whom he would, even if half-jokingly but with excellent reason, call more papal than the Pope, interminably vented her righteous detestation of that unbeliever, who planned a life dedicated to expanding the knowledge about pagan worlds, which, untouched by Christ's message and thus steeped in godlessness and immorality, were implicitly unworthy of decent people's consideration.

But to their mortifying surprise and mounting exasperation, the Brennans had found their campaign of vituperative denunciations and dire warnings floundering on the rocks of a quiet—but for that no less definite—resistance. So unexpectedly displayed by a heretofore unquestioningly obedient, unexceptionally cooperative, and implicitly trusting daughter, this recalcitrance, signaling ramifications far weightier than at first supposed or even imagined, was bound to sharpen their anxious awareness of a looming and totally unacceptable prospect. Yet however ineffectual, that strategy of verbal assaults remained their sole option. The girl's refusal to argue, to refute, or even dispute the merits of the heated contentions; her quiet endurance of parental wrath as well as the occasional calmly presented appeals to her common sense, filial duty, and religious obligation; her progressive withdrawal into seclusion, which allowed her refuge in her new world of new horizons—all suggested that any attempted interdiction of her further association with Paul Devlin would more likely be answered by open defiance, an eventuality they were not prepared to test. Thus the bitter harvests of domestic discord continued throughout that fall and winter and early spring as inevitably as the young pair's progression toward a future together.

Still, while those incessant harangues did not put a stop to their ever more frequent contacts, they had not failed to exert their subtly corrosive impact. Gradually, a note of creeping despondency frayed the ardor of Winnie's fascination. Keenly apprehended and tenderly respected, it imposed an accent of cautious restraint on Paul Devlin's responses. Tenuous and undefined yet achingly insistent doubts clouded her once unequivocal trust in the verity of her own emotions and his, subverted her once categorical certainty of their commitment's mutuality—doubts that gained in blighting distinction as, with the days of late spring, the always implicitly accepted prospect of a lengthy separation was rapidly approaching its actualization.

She had always understood that, once Paul had passed his final tests, field work abroad would be the key to, indeed the premise of, his dissertation, his doctor's degree, his career. Now those tests were behind him, and the excellence of his performance had earned him a most prestigious offer to participate in the excavation of a newly discovered Anatolian site. It was a unique opportunity, a chance he could not refuse. She did comprehend and yet did not. Intelligence and emotions were at loggerheads: true, the pursuit of his vocation demanded his sojourn abroad, but why would his love, unlike her own, not override any other consideration? Were his feelings not quite as unqualified, as all-encompassing, as all-absorbing as hers? Was a separation, which to her seemed unbearable, quite endurable to him? Both despondency and doubt consolidated their hold on her, when, with his departure just a few short weeks away, he rejected her readiness to assent, in heedless defiance of parental opposition as well as religious presumptions, to an immediate civil wedding so she might accompany him on his assignment. However moved by this passionate, self-oblivious proposal, he remained firm in his decision not to expose her to the rugged conditions of weather and accommodations and the inherent privations of such an enterprise nor to the inevitable pangs of guilt over living in a union unsanctified by the blessings of her Church. Neither would he prematurely assume a responsibility which, in good conscience, he could live up to only after he could establish himself professionally as well as financially. The Hittite exploration was the stepping stone to their future together. It would occupy him for some thirty months. He would hurry back to her the very day the dig was terminated, happily certain to have laid the foundation on which to build that future. Thirty months, to be sure, were awesomely long for him no less than for her; but they were young, with a long life lying ahead for them to share—but it must be a settled, externally as well as internally secure life he was going to offer to her. He had explained and re-explained himself. She had listened and listened again. Her mind had followed him, but her feelings had not.

It seemed only logical that the Brennans, observing their daughter's aggravating agitation, should have appealed to him, the then Father Flannery, for assistance. Dimly aware that their callous antagonism had forfeited their child's confidence and realizing their own resultant futility, they were bound to consider that recourse to their priest would be the only way to prevent the denouement they dreaded most, the precipitous civil wedding their Winnie had contemplated and, unknown to them, Paul Devlin had already repudiated as a viable solution.

The Brennans had banked on the girl's ingrained trust in her confessor's counsel and on the latter's deftness of persuasion; he had not disappointed them. Speaking to her, not in tones of religious authority but of concerned friendship, never censorious or doctrinaire in his comments, never reviling the character or belittling the sincerity of the man she loved, he let genial reasoning gently widen the breach that her own doubt had begun to open. Had her response to the first man in her life not perhaps been too impulsive, her total involvement not perhaps too rash, too premature? Could it not be that Paul Devlin's rejection of their relationship's immediate legalization indicated, on his part also, second thoughts along similar lines? Might more thoughtful consideration not raise some justified questions regarding their actual suitability, their fine attunement, their enduring compatibility—questions whose final clarification, her Paul had come to recognize, would require a possibly substantial period of self-searching, unencumbered by the pressures of close and continual contact? And might she herself not be best served by such a hiatus of tranquil reflection and undisturbed, uninfluenced reexamination of her own mind?

The subtle cogency of such a rational argument had not failed its purpose. The quietly insistent advice, all the more potent as it was coming from a source she had inherently credited with special, God-given inspiration, had convinced Winnie Brennan. On the very last day before his departure, she had informed Paul Devlin of her wish and decision to dispense with any and all communication between them during the term of his absence. Any exchange of correspondence, she contended, would only render the pain of separation more acute and thus compromise their future relationship. Stunned and bewildered, for the first time at a loss to fathom her thoughts and motivations but anxious to avoid a last-minute dispute whose memory might linger on to deepen her desolation, he had agreed to honor her resolve. Although he would not affirm the validity of her proposition, his assent was not as grudging as she had feared. Somehow he managed to persuade himself that, given the incontrovertible certainty of his own unswerving commitment and her presumed equally unfaltering one, a period of silent submersion in their passionate dreams would assure a union of even more profound mutuality of even more intense happiness.

Throughout the interminable string of work-filled Anatolian days and lonely Anatolian nights, this certainty had endured undiminished in its glow, until that evening near the conclusion of his sojourn when a letter from an old classmate casually mentioned Winnie Brennan's recent marriage to George Mulvey. After reading that one brief sentence over and over again, Paul Devlin had known he would not go back home. Not for a long while. A long, long while.

*

"I understand," John Flannery repeated, a shiver in his voice answering the indictment of that yawning silence. "But it's been a long while since …"

"Yes," Paul Devlin said woodenly, "a long while."

"And so, finally, you have come back."

"Back?" The younger man shook his head. A thin, cheerless smile warped his lips. "Not to stay, anyway. Just for a visit. A brief one—a few days, a week, maybe. Just figured this might be the best use of an overdue vacation. Thought it was about time, after a whole year of married life, to introduce my wife to my parents."

"Oh!" The spell of a mute pause allowed for adjustment to the surprise. "I see. I'm glad for you, Paul. Very glad."

"Thank you." A perfunctory nod and that cheerless smile again. "You'd find an even better cause for felicitations if you knew Sidney. Like my parents … Marvelous how they've taken to her. Particularly my mother, on first sight. It's her intuition; knows a real woman when she sees one. And that's Sidney. As fine as they come. Met her at the second dig; she was a member of the team, a most valuable one, too. Everyone there thought the world of her, everyone adored her. And not just because of her looks, either. Though in her own way she's quite stunning, really. Chinese and Scottish decent. Makes a fine mixture, at least with Sidney it does. Highly intelligent and knowledgeable and efficient. And reliable. And all woman. Straight, and decent, and warm, and devoted—not just a wholesome person, but a whole person."

The phrase faded without leaving an echo, lingering through another silence that was gaping up between the two men. For all its rather breathless fervor, oddly devoid of any resonance, the accolade struck John Flannery with a sense of internal irrelevance, like a lesson well learned, often rehearsed, and recited by rote, now eerily enlivened by an inflection, which, ever so subtly, yet ever so inescapably, was conveying the counterpoint of an unspoken, qualifying 'but,' of a comparison which would not be stifled, of an image willfully repressed yet never defunct; of a memory alive after all those years and surviving into the new bond's actuality.

John Flannery shuddered with the chill of his perception, of an awareness fraught with the rending revelation of pain endured and desolation never shed—and with the crushing burden of self-indictment. Although, he told himself, it should have come to him the very instant he had first beheld the visitor. Was Paul Devlin's presence, the very fact of his coming here, not evidence most eloquent of the past's unyielding aliveness? The past, to whose pain and desolation he, John Flannery, goaded by his own presumptions and convictions, his concept of sacred duty, had contributed so substantial and decisive a share. But he had acted in good faith, he answered the accusing silence, had only meant to help the best way he knew. Could he be justly faulted for his well intended counsel which had come to determine two lives' courses—a counsel which even now, in the distant retrospect, seemed reasonable and prudent? And yet a counsel whose damning echo now reverberated in Paul Devlin's unvoiced 'but;' in this counterpoint of comparison. Only too well had he apprehended this aching counterpoint, and, abetted by the frozen stare facing him, he knew that Paul Devlin was aware that he had apprehended it and comprehended it. There, between them, raised from the past, was the image of Winnie Brennan, haunting their silence.

"Paul," John Flannery said softly, "Paul, it wouldn't have worked."

"Wouldn't it?" An accent of acid repudiation insinuated itself into the flat reply. "Who can tell? What the grounds, on which to tell?"

"The constellation …"

"It was denied the test!" Paul Devlin cut in harshly. "The constellation was the fundamental one of two people loving each other."

"I never doubted that," John Flannery said evenly. "No one did, not even her parents, I think. But love reigns the short run; in the long run, it's compatibility that will pass the test."

"Compatibility." A strain of unchecked animosity framed the rejoinder. "The question of religious harmony, you mean."

"That's part of it, yes."

"But the paramount one, wasn't it?" Sarcasm honed the edge of hostility. "The one that overruled—in fact canceled—all other considerations."

John Flannery winced with the thrust of the implied denunciation. But when he countered it, his tone was calm: "No, Paul. Other considerations were given their proper weight. It's the total picture we ought to look at. There were other incompatibilities, too—of backgrounds, of personalities, of life goals. As I said, the religious issue was only part of the problem. But wouldn't it quite naturally prove an important one? Surely, it was the most obvious, the most flagrant one. The constellation of Winnie Brennan ..." He sharply drew in his breath, faltering for a split instant. "Winnie Brennan, the uncompromisingly faith-bound Catholic, and Paul Devlin, the intransigent atheist."

"Agnostic."

A small wave of a weary hand and a brittle smile crumbling on parched lips quashed the amending interjection. "Agnostic, ah yes! To your mind there is a fine point of elegant intellectual differentiation. But to the true religionist there is none, Paul. None at all, between denying outright the existence of God and, because of the supposed 'lack of incontrovertible evidence,' proclaiming as 'unfeasible' any knowledge of His existence. For to them who believe the actuality of His existence is absolute and ultimate Truth. But ...," another quiet gesture stymied an incipient objection, "but you haven't come to pursue any theological arguments, have you? So, have it your way and call yourself an agnostic. It does not alter the problem of that incongruous constellation. There you were, the dyed-in-the-wool agnostic, and she, unassailably absorbed in the Truth."

Paul Devlin said, coldly, "One might not share another's belief, yet respect it."

"One might." The response was tardy, winding its way through a long moment of reflection. "But would one? Could one? More to the point, could you?"

"When there is affection and good will …"

"There was no doubt of either, Paul. Surely not in your case." The assurance was heavy with a cadence of undefined sadness. "But affection and good will may not always prove sufficient. Not in a confrontation of equally strong convictions: when your own commitment to unbiased detachment and scientific objectivity collides with …" Again that faltering, pained hiatus, "… with your mate's immersion in the mysteries of her creed, mysteries accessible and acceptable alone to those of faith. Remember Pascal's dictum, *'Credo quia absurdum,'* I believe, because it's absurd?' That was a fervently committed believer's conclusion: that the absolute, unquestioning faith in the given creed's propositions and doctrines is the religionist's only alternative to sharing the outsider's perspective—the outsider to whose critical logic these same propositions and doctrines would be bound to present themselves as utter absurdities. Yours is the outsider's perspective, Paul. For a while you might have tolerated, but for how long could you have maintained respect for a commitment to 'absurdity?' Don't you see, Paul?" Though firmer now, yet John Flannery's voice was still grating with the touch of despondency. "It wouldn't have, it couldn't have worked."

Paul Devlin's stare was a burning stake driven into the man in the gardener's overalls, his voice a blast of sardonic stridor. "And George Mulvey? He had all the proper religious credentials. Yet it didn't work all that well, either, did it, Father Flannery?"

The older man stood motionless; in a fraction of a second he seemed to have aged a hundred years. Shrunken and withered, a ghastly shadow of his tall, broad-shouldered self, he was wasting through an interminable moment of mute agony. "Mister Flannery," he muttered at last mechanically. And then, more loudly, in a voice, whose creak mirrored the gnarled ashen appearance of his features, "No, it didn't work, it didn't."

*

It had not worked; nor, John Flannery knew, could it have. He had known even then, five years ago.

Hoping and praying that Winnie Brennan's marriage would yet turn out well, in his more soberly thoughtful moments he had recognized that he was hoping against hope, praying for a most unlikely dispensation of divine grace to a union, which, he at last perceived, had been foredoomed. Early on, it had been such flashes of harrowing but irrefutable insight that had restrained him from acceding to the two families' pleas to exert his influence in support of their plans for their children's matrimonial connection. The same profoundly conscientious conviction that had prompted his discouragement of Winnie Brennan's involvement with Paul Devlin, then had kept him from actively abetting her fitfully unwilling, yet progressively inextricable approach toward George Mulvey. Neither had he counseled against that prospective match. As incessantly he had told himself over the intervening years, told himself with a searing sense of culpability, this abstention from open objection had proved tantamount to tacit condoning, when his priestly advice might have made the difference, might have backed the girl in her opposition to the families' concerted and unrelenting pressure, might have halted her resistance's gradual erosion and made her stay out of George Mulvey's way.

Winnie Brennan had known George Mulvey practically all her life. Given their families' prominence in the same circle of prosperous, zealously church-bound Irish Catholics, membership in the same prestigious country club, and frequent partnerships in mutually profitable business deals, social contact between the youngsters had been inevitably constant, though never reaching beyond marginal courtesy. Never had there been the slightest inclination, much less initiative, toward closer companionship. This was not due to George's being several years Winnie's senior—in fact, this age difference should have been just right for enhancing their compatibility. Nor was it merely a lack of mutual attraction or common interests that prevented a more personal association. Rather it was an instinctive, almost organic antipathy which fostered an unexceptional routine of keeping their distance from one another—an antipathy, which, on his part, took the form of haughtily demonstrative and abusively pointed indifference to the retiring, shyly introspective girl; and on hers, of a deliberate, determined reserve which did not overly strive to disguise how thoroughly, in her quiet way, she detested his boisterous self-promotion, his macho swagger, his self-important strut; how she despised the flippancy of his conversation, the irrelevance of his concern, the crafty spuriousness of his well-rehearsed charm which rarely failed to earn him the flirtatious connivance of less discriminating females. But she would have been even more irreconcilably repelled had she known about his womanizing and gambling, his taste for easy money, and his aversion to the exertions of steady work—and most particularly his cynical disdain of religion, which, to stay in his parents' good graces and so to assure their continued funding of his escapades, he deftly masked by his displays of conventional piety and his regular, if perfunctory observances of the prescribed rituals.

George Mulvey was not evi, nor was he altogether lacking in redeeming qualities. He was fitted with a quick wit and an appreciable talent for industrial design. Whenever he might choose to apply himself, he would execute his assignments with considerable efficiency. Had his natural endowments been allowed unfolding in a healthier environment, they would have made him a more decent, more worthwhile person. As it happened, he was simply the product, the beneficiary as well as the victim, of too much conspicuous opulence, too unremittingly competitive social ambition, too much convenient indulgence, and too little unpleasant discipline. By the time his parents noted the result, the drift proved irreversible. No matter how they tried to minimize their George's defects in their own minds, at length circumstances had forced upon them the awareness of his heedless, extravagant, not rarely wayward conduct. More than once, they had had to extricate him from some tight situations; while these incidents could be kept from public knowledge, they could not escape their increasingly troubled observation—the more troubled as their belated attempts to make him change his ways would, by their futility, only point up their own past failure and present impotence.

It was their deepening anxiety that had bred the Mulveys' notion that a quiet, devout, domestically trained and oriented girl like Winnie Brennan might, as wife, succeed, where they had failed; her calming influence and constant availability, supplemented by the comforts of a home of his own and the pride in his eventual offspring, might turn their George toward a more responsible lifestyle. And once this notion had taken shape, it had been pursued with urgent persistence.

Although at first not unexpectedly meeting with their son's roundly scornful rejection, gradually this proposition had evoked an increasingly acquiescing and at length grudgingly affirmative response. After all, Winnie Brennan was pretty enough, and if her ingrained modesty and subdued reserve did not rouse any purple dreams, such deficiency always could, and would, be compensated for by some more liberated and uninhibited company. Besides, her open disdain of his person's would-be glamour and her pointed refusal to even acknowledge it had long irked and provoked him. There might be a nice dividend of vengeful thrill in bending her to his will. Above all, though, the prospect of a sumptuous house, bought and furnished by his father, and of a monthly allowance, substantial enough to ensure the continued indulgence of his expensive proclivities, presented inducements too seductive to forgo. They seemed well worth a try and would sweeten the efforts of a tedious and precarious courtship.

Predictably, these efforts had been eagerly welcomed by the Brennans; they had intensely and hopefully encouraged them, trusting that time and constant pressure would eventually break down their daughter's resistance—an opposition too manifest to go unnoticed or be willfully overlooked. Her reaction to the young man's sudden, unsolicited, and, on the face of it, so incongruous demonstrations of amorous interest were too clearly a display of not only puzzled resentment but firm and no more than marginally polite rebuff. Yet though her evasions of his ostentatiously attentive company were too consistent to be misinterpreted, to her parents' relief George Mulvey seemed deaf to the eloquence of her display. Once he made up his mind to pursue what he had come to view as a profitable deal, he was determined to achieve its successful transaction. Never having been denied what he wanted, he was not going to let Winnie Brennan deny him now. She might be unresponsive to his flirtatious flatteries, which only embarrassed her; she might be impervious to his long-practiced charm, the hollowness of whose routines she perceived only too well; she might be bored by his conversation, unamused by his flippant witticisms, and unimpressed by his glowing projections of a carefree and luxurious future, but he never doubted that sooner or later she would come around and do his bidding.

George Mulvey never realized that he was endeavoring to overcome a far more potent obstacle to his advances than just her own portion of their own mutual antipathy—her unyielding dream of Paul Devlin, her captivity to an at once wondrous and painful, inescapable memory. He had no inkling whatever of that dream; he was the last person with whom she would have shared it. But, although she neither would share it with her parents, they were by no means oblivious of its obsessive presence. This very awareness made the budding courtship seem even more attractive to them, its success even more desirable, and their own efforts to that end even more compelling. For with every passing day, their anxiety escalated. Every day moved Paul Devlin's return yet another step closer, an event which, they entertained no doubt, would bring with it the denouement they feared most. This time their Winnie would not again be accessible to persuasions, not even to those attempted by her revered Father Flannery. This time she would have her way, unless prior to her dream's chance of materialization she were securely restrained by the sacramental vows of matrimony. A speedy effectuation of those vows, then, was essential and in fact imperative. Now the opportunity did exist, bearing the identity of George Mulvey, and it offered all the credentials of social acceptability.

And this was the one and only real opportunity. For although Winnie was not wanting for admirers, her withdrawn manner had kept most of them at a friendly distance. There were no satisfactory candidates for marriage. One of the only two who seemed seriously interested was, as a Protestant of Scandinavian extraction, implicitly ineligible; the other, although solidly Irish and churchgoing, came from the other side of the tracks, with nothing but personal decency and a kind disposition to compensate for his evident and apparently permanent lack of tangible prospects. Thus uncontested, the field was left to George Mulvey, who was both eligible and obviously aspiring to provide the solution for the Brennans' dilemma—perhaps not the perfect one, they might tacitly admit to themselves, but certainly the sole readily available one. They were not altogether insensible to their daughter's averse attitude, but they utterly failed to appreciate the very compass of her repugnance. Adolescent dislike, they persuaded themselves, was amenable to change, particularly when assuaged by a wedding band and the pleasures of a sumptuous lifestyle. Nor were they altogether ignorant of the prospective groom's failings, but again, they did not appreciate the extent of his malfeasance. And, like his own parents, they consoled themselves with the convenient belief that the influence of a proper and devoted spouse would alter the pattern of youthful dissipation.

Ironically, neither her suitor's increasingly impatient persistence nor her parents' relentlessly grinding exhortations prevailed. Winnie Brennan's weary acquiescence to George Mulvey's efforts had owed to the very tenacity of her passionate dream. It was her very captivity to it that had prompted her assent to this marriage. The dramatic suddenness of her announcement had startled all the parties involved, baffled them with a sense of implausibility, almost irrationality, coming so abruptly as a total reversal of the defiant opposition that had adamantly persevered for some eighteen stressful months and for whose reversal at that juncture no tangible cause, no fathomable reason appeared to exist. Yet a more perceptive observer might well have discovered a clue in the insistent demand of the bride-to-be that the wedding be arranged as fast as the religious regulations would permit—a stipulation which, though greeted with even more perplexed surprise, had naturally elicited prompt and eager cooperation. Without delay, the banns had been published at St. Catherine and the preparations perfected. On the earliest feasible date, the ceremony had been performed, the vows had been taken, the matrimony been solemnized—precisely three months before Paul Devlin's scheduled return.

As more keenly sensitive minds might have discerned, it was the very imminence of that return that had dictated Winnie Brennan's apparently incongruous decision and the oddly precipitous effectuation of the ensuing proceedings. It was the steadily approaching specter of a reunion which must turn into a confrontation she had come to dread—a confrontation from whose ineluctable, desperate and insufferable denouement she could see no escape but flight into the refuge of a prior bond whose protective walls of sanctified legality Paul Devlin would never attempt or even wish to breach. George Mulvey alone was there to offer this refuge. Eventually, to be sure, she might have found a vastly preferable one. But there was no time, there was no alternative, not given the prevailing emotional climate. For although all efforts had failed to change her opinion of, or mitigate her aversion to, her family's favorite suitor, gradually the incessant badgering had taken its toll, inducing in her a state of despondent apathy which rendered her sufficiently pliant to tolerate his company. Even so, this slow process of internal debilitation would never have reached the point of crisis, nor, however powerful, would the ever-deepening desolation of loneliness and alienation or the increasingly less repressible yearning for an affectionate and tender male presence have pressured her into consent to that marriage. It was the ultimate, shattering demise of her dream that had enabled—compelled—her acceptance of a once so implausible connection.

That demise was the inevitable culmination of the long lingering, self-inflicted malady that had had its creeping, corrosive inception even before Paul Devlin's departure. Once entered into her consciousness, the cancer of doubt had spread its lethal infection. Even though she herself demanded and, death to his objections, insisted on their abstention from any communication during the term of their separation, her beloved one's adherence to their agreement baffled, then disappointed, and at last alarmed her. Somehow, paradoxically, his respect for her decision came to be perceived as a betrayal. However unacknowledged, there had been her expectation that his love might overrule his promise, that the imperative of his commitment would never permit any protracted silence. Thus, with every passing month, with every additional aching week without any word from him, her expectation mounted. And with each day of futile waiting, her initial doubt about their eventual compatibility transformed into doubt about the actuality and truthfulness of his love to burgeon into certainty that his emotion, which had seemed so profound, had been devoid of real substance—a mere infatuation engendered by desire and fancy and possessiveness. Wrenchingly extended by her own not merely undiminished, but heightened passion, this certainty turned into the obsessing conviction that the depth and verity of their feelings were totally and irreconcilably unequal, thus creating a relationship she could never accept, much less endure. At the same time her awareness of her own unyieldingly persevering passion terrified her, as it compelled the devastating realization that a personal confrontation with Paul Devlin was bound to end up making her captive to the old fascination, the old magic of their apparent mutuality, to the illusion of a communion—thus condemning her to a life of one-sided, subservient love. Every day that moved the day of his return closer advanced her another step into the wilderness of escalating panic, with no one but George Mulvey to rescue her from it.

He was willing and ready, if she was. She persuaded herself that she was. After all, physically he was by no means unattractive, he was intelligent enough, and no man could be altogether worthless. There might be more subtle traits she had not yet discovered, perhaps even tender and lovable ones. At any rate, the wall erected by the legal bond would ensure her safety from a dooming encounter. The constant company of a husband, the preoccupation with a new household, her matrimonial responsibilities, all would combine to assuage the internal turmoil and in time let her settle down to a life, if not of happiness and fulfillment, at least of soberly come days.

*

"It didn't work, it didn't ..." For a long, shuddering instant, the echo of John Flannery's bald admission was filling the void between them—a cadence of utter wretchedness, that, even when it at last faded, kept reverberating through Paul Devlin's mind, waking it to an awareness of pain and anguish, which made him regret the caustic thrust of his implied denunciation.

"I didn't mean …"

The perfunctory motion of a withered hand halted the rueful phase. "It's all right, Paul." The other's speech had regained its bony evenness "You have a right to mean it the way it was meant. You have a right to your bitterness, your sarcasm, your recrimination. Your indictment of me could never be as complete, as severe as my own. No," John Flannery went on, thwarting an assuaging rejoinder, "not for my belief that a union between Winnie Brennan and yourself might not succeed and acting on his belief. Even today I'm inclined to subscribe to that assessment. My indictment is for recognizing that her marriage to George Mulvey could never work, yet failing to act upon this insight. It could never work," he repeated softly, "and it didn't. That's why I'm here. That's why Winnie is here." For all the attempted repression, the pain and anguish were back in his voice. "That's why you are here, isn't it?"

"Of course!" A note of perplexity crept into Paul Devlin's reply. "Wouldn't you expect as much?"

"Certainly." A nod, hardly perceptible; a voice, stony in its flatness. "You'd come to see her."

"As soon as I heard …"

"To see Winnie Brennan …?"

The question in the muttered phrase was not lost on the younger man. It found its response in a fleeting ghost of a smile. "My wife? She knew, where I went and why. There are no secrets between us. Sidney knows about … about Winnie to the last particular of involvement and feelings. She understands. While my parents seemed rather uneasy about this visit, she actually encouraged it." There was a pause, as though in expectation of a comment, before Paul Devlin spoke again. "It wasn't my folks who told me. Wouldn't want to upset me, I suppose. It was a guest who casually mentioned that … that calamity. Just the bare facts. No one could or would offer any explanation, any detail."

"Neither, really, can I," John Flannery answered the implied inquiry, every word dragging with an aching memory. "I only know what everybody knows, no more

than what, I assume, you've already been told, how, one May evening three years ago, Winnie Brennan …"

"Winnie Mulvey," Paul Devlin cut in. The correction was tight with an inflection of animosity. "There was no more Winnie Brennan then, was there?"

"Winnie Mulvey, then," John Flannery assented emptily, his voice faltering as with a choke. "Yes, that evening she went for a drive into the countryside. Seems the car went off the road. Smashed against a tree. A stroke of good fortune would have it that a patrol car happened by only a few minutes later. That's how the ambulance got there in time to take her to the hospital … In shock, of course, unconscious, apparently from the severe blow on her head, when it crashed into the windshield. Almost miraculously, though, the physical damage proved not to be too serious. A broken leg, a couple of cracked ribs, cuts, bruises. They healed fast and completely. That's all I can tell you about… about the accident."

"The … accident?" However brief, the hesitation had not escaped his attention.

"Yes," John Flannery insisted rigidly, "an accident."

"Was it?" The accent of the question was acid.

A long instant crept away before the older man spoke. "Surely, what else but an accident?" The shiver in his voice faded into another silence. But the gaze that was boring into him, mercilessly, ineluctably, demanded an answer. Slowly he shook his head. "No, Paul. Not Winnie. Not with her kind of faith. She never would have burdened her soul with a mortal sin. No, it must've been an accident."

"I'll accept your judgment," Paul Devlin said coldly. "As far as it goes. An accident, then. But there are accidents which are willed. Unconsciously, but willed nonetheless."

"I wouldn't know about that."

"Wouldn't you?" The retort was flung with a sharp edge of punishing repudiation. "What happened, Father Flannery?"

"Mister Flannery," the man in the gardener's garb muttered automatically. "I told you." And then, compelled by the gaze that kept boring, boring relentlessly, "What happened before, you mean?"

"Before," Paul Devlin affirmed. "What led up to it?"

The reply was tardy. "About that, there's truly nothing I can tell you."

"Truly?" The rebuff was unyielding in its scorn. "How, truly? You must know about it, about them, about that marriage."

John Flannery shook his head. "I'm afraid I don't, Paul."

"You married them, didn't you?"

"Yes, I married them." Momentarily an onslaught of agony distorted the haggard countenance into a frighteningly cadaverous mask. But then the creaking voice went on, grinding on, word for laggard word. "But my involvement ended right there. Their new residence was in another parish. They attended services at St. James. It was Father Hollings who was hearing their confessions. There was no more contact, not even with Winnie, though I had hoped, that after all these years of close friendship and confidence, she, at least …" Another shiver ran through the frail figure. "But then. I had married them. Had I not forfeited her confidence?" The fitful motion of a trembling hand anticipated an acrid comment and stifled it. "So you see, Paul? There's nothing I can tell you from personal knowledge. Just bits of hearsay, of people's flighty observations, precarious impressions, half-baked deductions, fanciful assumptions, idle guesswork."

"I understand," Paul Devlin interposed, brusquely dismissing the explanation. He would not grant the evasion. "Scraps of unreliable information. Still, cumulatively they would be adding up to something, wouldn't they? There would be a core consensus, enough to let you form an opinion?" There was that cutting edge in his speech again. "An opinion, perhaps, that this matrimonial venture wasn't going all that well." It was not a question, but an assertion, blunt and irrefutable, constraining John Flannery to respond.

"Yes," he said, his voice brittle with weariness, "I couldn't help concluding that there was trouble afoot."

*

Indeed, it had been apparent that there was trouble afoot from the very beginning. Word was abroad about the account of a neighbor, who, chancing to attend a conference in Bermuda, where the newlyweds were spending their brief honeymoon, had noticed the groom, only three days after the nuptials, in the hotel's bar past midnight, by himself, drinking—hard stuff it appeared, and rather too much of it. And on the following afternoon had observed the bride, by herself also, wandering along the beach, aimlessly, as though in a daze. Soon after, another parishioner, a friend of the family, had remarked on George Mulvey's constant exhibitions of ill temper and the curious circumstance of his hardly ever being seen in his wife's company. In time there had been too many reports to be laid to mere gossip—about his spending long evenings at gambling parties and painting the town red with ladies known to have been, not altogether innocently, associated with him in the past. There, too, were the cumulating references to his spouse's so conspicuously pallid, harrowed looks whenever she was encountered on one of her frequent, eventually almost daily, visits to the church, where she would spend ever-longer hours in prayerful prostration—looks, which some talebearers would describe as strangely 'haunted,' 'hysterical,' even 'frenzied.'

No, there could have been no escaping the conclusion that this marriage was in trouble and apparently getting ever deeper into it. There had been no way for John Flannery, then still the priest at St. Catherine, to hide from his mounting anxiety about his own role in what rapidly tended to assume the marks of a looming disaster. It was not, though, his steadily aggravating sense of guilt alone that fostered a passionate wish that he could help the young pair, could at least somehow ameliorate the condition which he had no choice but at last to diagnose as unsalvageable, as an incurable malady of a human relationship. He indulged no illusion that he could reach George Mulvey. Long ago he had found him impervious to any moral or even just plainly commonsense argument. With Winnie Brennan, however, he could look back on a long-existing bond, forged not only by their shared religious devotion but by their mutual affection. If only he could revive her former trust and confidence, perhaps he might be able to mitigate her obvious distress. Searching for a way, he had turned to her parents, but they proved incapable of offering any assistance. They attributed their daughter's anguished unhappiness to the detrimental impact of her husband's reprobate and humiliating conduct, without exhibiting the slightest notion concerning some perhaps more fundamental cause of what, dimly and uncomprehendingly, they, too, had come to recognize as a progressive deterioration of her personality as well as a full-fledged, apparently irreversible estrangement. Their Winnie's contact with them had become more and more sporadic, entirely formal, and totally uncommunicative. Appalled and helpless, they had eagerly seized upon their priest's suggestion and were only too glad to convey his message—that he would much welcome his former confessant, whenever she might drop in to see him.

Winnie had not responded, had in no way even acknowledged his offer of supportive intervention, depriving him of whatever small measure of self-redemption it might have afforded him. Her persistent silence, which he could only interpret as a deliberate, pointed rebuff, had left him brooding and given to ever more harassing self-incrimination. He wished he could believe that her new confessor might extend to her the succor that he himself was being so definitely precluded from providing, but he could not deceive himself entertaining this hope—too well did he know Father Hollings as a hidebound zealot and stern disciplinarian, dedicated to the letter rather than the spirit of the Gospel, gifted with the fervor of evangelical eloquence but with scant human understanding and even less compassion. Concerned only with the glories of eternal life in the hereafter and disdainfully indifferent to the tribulations of earthly existence, he would be long on strictures and exhortations but short on sympathy. There would be no consolation coming to her from that source, no alleviation of her distress, which, as the consensus of worried acquaintances suggested, seemed to be intensifying with each passing month.

Nor had these reported observations proved to be mere gossip or fanciful exaggerations. He himself had had occasion to appreciate their truth, when, once or twice along main street, his and the young woman's paths had happened to cross. On each occasion, he had been profoundly shaken when he was forced to realize that those observations of her expression and demeanor as haunted, hysterical, or frenzied had, if anything, been understated. He himself would have thought 'maddened' a more fitting description. At each of these rare, accidental encounters he had sought to approach her, speak to her, however briefly—a few words might help, words he had long prepared in his mind for just such an opportunity: a priestly reminder that the Church, while forbidding divorce, did condone a couple's separation. But not even once would she afford him this meager satisfaction. Deaf to his greeting, blind to his waving hand, gazing straight ahead without any sign of recognition, she would hurriedly brush past and deftly elude his attempt at even one instant's communication. Until at last he had managed to step in her way swiftly enough to foil another stratagem of evasion—and he had come to wish that he had failed in his endeavor that time as well.

Finding her escape blocked by his tall figure, she had stopped abruptly. From hollows, which the taut pallor of her mask-like features made seem yet deeper and darker, a stare had reached for him, enveloped him—a stare not sparked by hostility, which, guiltily understanding, indeed half expecting, he could have dealt with, but one lit by an anguish beyond endurance, a terror so awesomely blatant that it stymied all speech, thwarted the advice he had readied. And then, as though she were reading his thoughts and divining his intent, her voice, for all its soft flatness shrill, had come to him, "Until death do you part." And once more, in the same cadence of piercing tonelessness, she repeated, "Until death do you part." Then she had walked past him, left him standing there amid the bustle of main street, listening to the echo of damnation that would not be stilled.

That had been the last time their paths had crossed, some two months before the accident.

*

"And now she is here." A rasp of muffled stridor, Paul Devlin's voice broke the spell of mute remembrance. Cursorily, as though loath to linger, his glance was straying to the stately building at the far end of the garden. "Has been in this," his lips tightened with a momentary choke at the word, "this sanatorium ever since."

"Yes," John Flannery said after him, "ever since."

"Taken here directly after her discharge from the hospital, they told me." The stridor was gaining in acuteness. "For what they called convalescence, until 'her mind would clear up;' some sort of 'disturbance,' my parents explained, but that was all they knew or would let on about her condition. A disturbance!" Paul Devlin repeated harshly. "It's been some three years; a disturbance?"

A slow nod answered him. "Yes. That's the official description the Brennans preferred, the one they insist on even to this day."

"With her in this … sanatorium?" There was sudden anger in the younger man's voice. "It's just a shamming euphemism for a private asylum, isn't it?"

"I'm afraid so." The reply was a shudder of sound. "But euphemisms are precious, even shamming ones, when you want to hide the truth—above all from yourself. Euphemisms serve to sustain the fiction of hope."

"The fiction of hope?"

"Can one blame the Brennans for clinging to it? After all, it's their daughter in there. But of course, somewhere deep down they know better. They've got to know better."

"The fiction of hope?" Paul demanded once more, every word an accent of horror.

The man in the gardener's outfit stared past him. A shudder dropped his reply to a near whisper, "I wish I didn't know better."

"But you do." The rejoinder was compulsion that left no chance for evasion. "You might as well tell me the real story, the truth about Winnie."

"The truth about Winnie," John Flannery repeated after him, his voice breaking again with every spasmodic scrap of speech. "Amnesia, total amnesia. It is as though the past never existed. No recognition whatever, not even of her own folks."

"Yes?" Paul Devlin prompted. There had been an inflection of trepidation, an instant of hesitation; he had not missed it and was waiting.

"It's not just her complete lack of the past. There is as complete a dissociation from the present as well. There's no apprehension whatever of the world about her—of people, events, things, excepting only the crucifix on the wall by her bed and the painting of the Virgin. For time on end, she'll kneel before it mumbling prayers inaudibly and sometimes crying, but otherwise—no concern in anything happening around her or even to her."

"Total withdrawal then?"

"Yes, and it seems irreversible. Withdrawal into a world of her own. She's shut herself in, remains imprisoned in it—not a world of pretty dreams, either, Paul, a frightful world somehow, tormenting her with some obsession the doctors have not yet been able to find out about—a world of anguish and terror all her own, terror of which she will not tell, though sometimes it makes her cry out, scream! Oh God, Paul, just scream and scream, until the nurse gives her a needle, a sedative, which puts her to sleep."

Paul Devlin stood motionless, his fists clenched, his lips a bloodless line; he stood there, captive to the image that John Flannery's whisper of despair had conjured up in his mind: the image of Winnie Brennan screaming, screaming. Interminable moments faded into the chill of the spring day, before he spoke again, "Three years and no improvement?"

"Nor do they anticipate any." Every word came framed by agony. "Not in any foreseeable future."

"Incurable then?"

"Only God knows."

"I wish the doctors knew. That might be of some help," Paul Devlin retorted acidly. Then, more quietly, "It was that windshield's impact on her head, wasn't it?"

It was some long moments before John Flannery had regained sufficient equilibrium to respond. "The final verdict is not in yet. Seems that blow may have caused some injury to some blood vessels in the brain. But they think that trauma is only partly responsible. They consider her condition less a neurological than a psychological problem. Some even opined that the onset of the amnesia may have preceded her accident, may, in fact, have caused it."

"A most convenient opinion, isn't it?" Paul Devlin's comment was frigid. "Well calculated to exculpate her from the mortal sin of suicide."

The man in the gardener's garb just shook his head; he seemed untouched by the sting of sarcasm. "No, Paul, he said firmly, rigidly, "Winnie Brennan needs no exculpation. As I suggested before, she would never commit a mortal sin, or, indeed, any lesser one. She's always been too close to her Lord."

"And her Lord has taken good care of her; that's why she is here." The motion of a furious hand cut down an incipient rebuttal. "So much for the Lord's care. Through its dispensation she'll spend the rest of her days in this ... this sanatorium, with nothing left in her life but a crucifix and a picture of the Virgin."

"And her faith," John Flannery added quietly. "To them that have come to know its verity, it holds the sublime grace. In front of those symbols, she seems to gain some sense of peace, some reprieve from anguish, even a measure of short-lived serenity. Although you may not share that faith, you wouldn't want to deprive her of this refuge?"

A spell of silence was laced with regret and apology. "No," the reply came at last softly, "if those tokens of faith would help her, I'd bring her another cross, another picture, myself—anything at all that would offer her some relief. I just wish there were some medical means to help her.

"So do I wish, Paul." In the stillness of the garden, the words resounded with the fervor of a prayer. "Have been wishing it every day, every hour, every moment—wishing for some way, any way whatever, to improve her condition."

Paul Devlin gave a sudden start. "Every day, every moment ..." he repeated slowly. That cadence had carried a plea, a cry for understanding; it had not missed its mark. "That's why you are here, have been here all along."

"All along." A perfunctory nod. "Yes. Ever since they brought her here. Just felt that this was the place for me to be."

"And to become Mister Flannery?" Comprehension was vibrant with an overtone of awe. "Even though this meant relinquishing your identity as Father Flannigan, meant quitting your Church, your ministry?"

"There are many ways of ministry, Paul. I saw this as my way," the older man said quietly, but a new vigor enlivened his speech. "What would ministry mean, if not helping those in need of help? There was Winnie. I perceived no alternative to being near her. True, she was assured of the Lord's loving attention and of all possible medical attention, but wouldn't she need some personal attention, too? Perhaps I could give her what pitifully little of it might be in my powers. However minutely, perhaps the presence of Mister Flannery might be of more benefit to her than that of Father Flannery had been." A slight motion of his hand warded off an assuaging response to the bite of self-irony that had frayed those last words. "On occasion, I indulge the thought, or maybe just the illusion, that my presence may be of some benefit: just the fact of providing her with some human company. Every moment off my job as the gardener's helper, just being there for her. On warm summer evenings, taking her on brief walks in this garden, but mostly just sitting by her bed, speaking softly to her, reading to her, legends of the Saints, children's tales—anything, it doesn't matter. There's no reaction, no sign of comprehension, but the even flow of a human voice somehow seems to soothe the frightfulness of whatever images that world of hers imposes. And so I permit myself to fancy that I help her. It also seems the fresh flowers I take up to her every day are soothing, and the trifling presents, the little music box especially—she'll listen to that old Christmas carol over and over, for hours sometimes."

"I'm grateful to you," Paul Devlin spoke into the momentary pause. Every last trace of sarcasm had yielded to warmth and humble respect. "So very grateful for what you are doing for her, have been doing."

"Just trying," John Flannery muttered, "just trying, trying … for three years, always trying."

Paul Devlin spoke, word for shivering word, as a dawning realization compelled its expression, "How hard it must be on you, day after day, being around her, with her, seeing her like this!"

A flicker of pain across those haggard features belied the stony evenness of the reply, "One does what one must. With her, that's where I belong." Another motion of that frail hand, more decisive now, thwarted an attempted comment. "But that's my concern. Let it be that, Paul. It's not me you've come to see, have you? Seems I've taken too much time away from your purpose already."

But Paul Devlin did not stir. A frown had spread across his brow, clouding it with troubled contemplation. "My purpose … I'm not so sure now, I should go through with it," he said at last. "I didn't know … didn't expect … what you told me about her condition. Might my visit not upset her?"

"No, Paul." The refutation was deep with unmitigated sadness. "That thought occurred to me, too, the very instant I laid eyes upon you. And in fact, I found myself wishing for her confrontation with you, indeed to upset her and perhaps spark some return to reality. But it won't. As I've told you, the past is no more. You'll just be another stranger, like her parents, like her best friend, Marge, who occasionally visits, like myself. Thank God for that: not letting her remember me. How, otherwise, could she suffer my presence?" John Flannery added, grating with the echo of his caustic awareness. Then quietly again, "We all are strangers, Paul, eternal exiles from that world of hers. There will be no recognition, no response, no spark of reality. I shall take you to her."

Only when they were crossing the exquisitely tiled floor of the elegant, rather gaudily sumptuous lobby, Paul Devlin broke the oppressive silence that had persisted throughout their walk along the pebbled garden path. "This place ... George Mulvey paying for her keep here?"

"Hardly," John Flannery answered the inquiry's inflection of disbelief. "He couldn't afford this sort of accommodations; not much of any sort, really. No, her parents and his are defraying the charges."

"The Mulveys?"

"The Mulveys, yes." The astonishment and doubt framing the younger man's response demanded an explanation. "Actually it's they who carry the lion's share of Winnie's maintenance here. They're quite a bit wealthier than the Brennans, and they selected this sanatorium. They wanted the best, and this is one of the best ... No, not for reasons of prestige, Paul. They have their limitations, all right, but they're decent people, responsible people, in their own way, even caring people."

"If you say so." Paul Devlin shrugged. "Not their son, though. The way I recall George, he might not have chosen this place even had he been able to afford it."

"Then again, he might have," John Flannery returned thoughtfully, while they were proceeding toward the elevator. "Why not give him the benefit of the doubt? He did seem quite affected by that tragedy, quite shattered, they tell me, when he came to her bedside at the hospital. And as I myself could observe, he did look really distressed, distraught, the one time he visited her here."

"The one time!" The repeated phrase was emphatic with an acid indictment.

John Flannery said tonelessly, "It isn't easy confronting one's guilt, Paul. And George Mulvey has always been weak—weak rather than evil, frivolous, not vicious—spoiled, as much a victim as a perpetrator of wrongs. Perhaps, facing Winnie's disaster, his conscience got to him? Maybe that was why he started to go from bad to worse, heedlessly indulging his old, wayward pattern? Until, after a few months, he left town suddenly. Some nasty predicaments, drugs, gambling, debts, embezzlement ... There were all kinds of rumors. No one knew where he went, where he lost himself. For well over two years now, there's been no word from him, not even to his parents ... As much a victim as a perpetrator," he muttered again, grinding the words between his teeth, "a victim of ..." He broke off abruptly. "Room six ten," he at last remarked, stepping from the elevator and pointing down the long corridor.

She was lying on her bed, motionless amid the brightness of the spring day, the light pouring through the large barred window. The blue of her ankle-length robe blending with the blue of the spread's delicate design, her slender form, in its rigid flatness, seemed as though part of the broad bed whose immaculate whiteness contrasted with the dark simplicity of her hairdo. The pillow was framing the wan tautness of her face, whose fixed ceiling-ward gaze seemed absorbed in a mute dialogue with the profound quietude of the chamber—a gaze, unaware of the now opened door, insensitive to the presence of the two men pausing on the threshold.

Winnie ... Paul Devlin stood frozen into immobility, struck by the perception that his reaction to the still figure on the bed was one not of immediate, unqualified recognition but of searching, questioning strangeness; the perception hurt cruelly.

Winnie. The sight of the young woman atop the blue spread could not be reconciled with the image he had preserved in his mind, had nurtured with such bitter, yet undiminished fondness—the image, which even his unqualified and tender, happy and fulfilling union with Sidney had never effaced. To be sure, except for the deep lines about the corners of the mouth and the violet shadows ringing the eyes, the cast of her features remained in that image's likeness. But its haunted haggardness, its bony harshness etched with accents of desperate fierceness, had turned that once so infinitely familiar countenance into an utterly alien mask. Once so wondrously aglow, so passionately alive, her eyes were vacant glares, the ghastliness of their deadness rendered yet more acute by their fevering captivity to some weirdly obsessing inward vision. Once so serene in its tempered vivaciousness, so suffused by the peace of faith-bound contentment, her recumbent form somehow seemed fraught with relentless restlessness, with a suggestion that the apparent quiescence presently encompassing it was but a precarious lie, beneath which turmoil was churning, ever primed for eruption.

Winnie. Still Paul Devlin did not budge from the threshold. The short three steps' distance from the bedside yawned at him, an abysmal, unbridgeable vastness. He had been prepared for the desolation and anguish inevitably attending an encounter with emotional illness and mental debilitation, but not for this confrontation with total dissociation, for the impact of treasured memory and shocking reality in such shattering and irreversible collision. His visit to a beloved, ever unforgotten past had turned into the experience of an implausible and wholly futile present—an experience, which, he now knew, the man at his side had correctly anticipated. There would be no scope whatsoever for the gentle words he had intended, for the consoling assurance that her person, her love, the beauty of their days together would always retain their verity. There would be no recognition, as John Flannery had warned him; he would be another stranger among strangers, whose speech would be sound without meaning, whose presence would be apprehended as an unwelcome or at best obliviously tolerated intrusion into her world—a world which, he keenly and achingly perceived, had divorced itself from reality and barred itself against the terrors of its access.

He still stood chained to the threshold. He would not be an intruder. A slight touch, a quiet glance conveyed to the man at his side his decision to withdraw, to leave the woman on the bed, the woman that was Winnie and yet was not, undisturbed in her engrossment, which would allow no sharing—a decision whose insightful aptness earned the mute affirmation of an understanding, somberly compassionate nod.

It might have been a flutter of movement caught in the corner of an eye, or the scraping of a retreating foot ruffling the stillness—whatever, it pried that stricken countenance from its absorption. The fixed gaze peeled itself from the ceiling and slowly strayed toward the source of the distraction, at last finding the two men still framed by the doorway, coming to rest on them for some moments of utterly vacuous perusal. And then, with savage suddenness, the woman jerked, heaved, as though struck by a high-voltage charge, and the mask-like blankness of her face contorted with a scream that seemed interminable in its inhuman shrillness. Submitting to some irresistible compulsion, her legs, half opening, were pulled up against her body: for one shrieking instant only, before, with what seemed a supreme effort of will, they were pressed tight again. Then she was shrinking, shrinking back against the headboard. Stopped by it in her maddened flight, she crouched, her arms thrust out in front of her twitching form, as though to ward off some ghoulish assault. Words dripped from lips racked by convulsive gasps, words eerie with unearthly dread.

"Not enough ... The nights, not enough, not enough? Now coming to me in the day, too? No, no, not again ... Incubus ... No, not again!" And then, more ghastly even than her screams, a moan, "Oh God, I'm so full of sin. All these years. So full of sin!" Inch by horror-driven inch she slid off the bed, onto the floor, until she was kneeling before the cross on the wall and the image of the Madonna, sobbing, whimpering, crying out, "Oh Jesus, help me. So full of sin … Oh Holy Virgin , pray for me … pray for me!"

At last John Flannery roused himself from the grip of petrified terror. Advancing into the chamber on legs that threatened to buckle with every staggering step, he pressed the call button. Needlessly—alerted by the piercing wails, the nurse was on her way, syringe at the ready. Then he kneeled by the side of the weeping woman's swaying figure, a calming, soothing arm lightly around her shoulder, his ashen lips silently trembling with his own prayer, until the nurse, after an instant of expert appraisal, proceeded to administer the hypodermic and, with his rather feeble help, to lift the listless, spasmodically shaking body onto the bed.

"I'll be staying with her for a while. She'll be all right." The nurse's glance asked the men to leave.

Only when they had traversed the lobby and emerged into the garden, the persistence of their shared, horror-born muteness was broken.

"I didn't know!" Uncannily reverberating in its very faintness, John Flannery's mumbled groan was an outcry of stark anguish. "My God, I didn't know!"

Paul Devlin did not respond. He rigidly stared straight ahead, avoiding, as he had been all along their joint way from the sickroom, even a glance at the man at his side. He could not endure the sight of those tormented features, their cadaverous chalkiness. Nor did he wish to endure it. Vaguely but irrefutably, animosity had again been building in him. Still unstrung, still groping for some way of coming to terms with the shock of his own experience, why should he be called upon to deal with another's internal chaos? Upstairs there was that demented, disintegrating shell of humanity that was she who had been his Winnie once; his was the prime, the paramount claim to pain and grief—his, no one else's. Yet, somehow, he felt and grudgingly knew, that there might be an agony even more overwhelming, more excruciating than his own, a wretchedness that indeed called for some kindness, some compassion, some consolation.

"I didn't know!" At his side, John Flannery was gasping it over and over, compulsively, helpless before the swelling tide of desperate insight which forced its expression in distraught fragments of panic. "I never imagined … It's always been you … all these years, always you … Adultery of the mind … sinfulness … and I, and I … Oh my God, I didn't see … ah!" The muffled outcry was drowned in an onslaught of inaudible sobs that were rocking his whole body as he stood there, his hands clasped to his face, clawing at it—stood there amid the golden brilliance of the spring day, which poured over him as though in mocking refutation of his desolation.

"Father Flannery," Paul Devlin said gently, "you must not let yourself be destroyed by imagined guilt."

"Imagined?" a trembling voice muttered after him, "imagined?"

"Imagined!" Paul Devlin repeated firmly. "Some of your endeavors may have turned out badly, even disastrously. But could those endeavors have been different? Weren't they determined, in fact dictated, by your faith, your vocation, your ministry?"

"Were they?" Relaxing their frenzied clasp, the blue-veined, shaking hands were dropping, as the ravaged face turned toward him with a bleak stare. And once more, "Were they?"

"Yes!" The assertion was even more emphatic, even more urgent. "You acted as you must. Whatever the consequences …" Paul Devlin drew in his breath sharply. There was the image of a woman writhing on her bed, kneeling in forever unanswered prayer, obsessed with her sinfulness, irretrievably captive to her hell … But there was that man by his side, a man just as hell bound, a man who perhaps might yet be stopped from his final descent into the abyss. "Whatever the consequences, Father Flannery," he quickly went on, "they were beyond your control. However you may have erred, however you may have failed in the end, you believed what you were doing was right, and you had every right to so believe."

"Did I?" John Flannery returned, his voice creaking, but oddly sober, almost even now, as though the other's quietly insistent argument had at last broken him from the spell of delirious distress. "Did I have a right to so believe?" A sudden glance, no longer bleak, but lit with consuming rage, barred any argument. "No, Paul. There was no such right. I merely presumed there was—yes, presumed! And that's why Winnie Brennan is here now … why you are here now, visiting her who never should have been and never, except in name, was Winnie Mulvey. That's why …"

"Why you are here." For all its softness, the completing phrase pierced the abrupt, shivering pause.

"Yes." A flicker of self-baiting acrimony across the haggard features belied the stony equanimity of the reply, "That's why I am here."

Paul Devlin did not want to lend voice to it, but his thought would not allow itself to be suppressed. "Penance, Father Flannery?"

"Mister Flannery," the man in the gardener's garb amended automatically. His gaze was running into a boundless distance, as though in search of some hidden truth, some recondite insight, some final answer. "Penance?" he repeated slowly, shaking his head. "No, Paul. I'm afraid, no penance. Even the attempt would be futile. There is no penance that could redeem one's ultimate betrayal of God. There is no way of balancing one's sacrilege."

"Sacrilege?"

"Sacrilege!" John Flannery affirmed in a voice, which, in its bony flatness, seemed devoid of human sound. "As an unbeliever, Paul, you may be lacking the concept: you cannot commit sacrilege against a God whose reality you do not recognize. But when you know God, and yet …" He broke off abruptly. Again his countenance became a rigid, forbidding mask. His gaze still lost in the blue, sunlit boundlessness, he nodded faintly, as though acknowledging the answer he had found, the insight, the truth. "It's not the unbeliever who is damned. In His infinite wisdom and understanding and everlasting goodness, the Lord will smile at men's ignorance and condone their folly; He will take pity on the blind and show mercy to them that know not what they do. Damnation is for them that perceive His glory, His transcendence, His purpose, and yet betray His Truth and defile it … No, Paul, there is no penance to square this kind of sin, none, Paul, none!"

Returned from that mysterious infinitude, from their exploration which had rewarded his quest for definitive cognition, his eyes now had come to rest on the younger man, intense with an irrefutable demand for an uninterrupted hearing. "You are a decent man, Paul, a magnanimous man. Great hurt was done to you; yet worse to one unforgettably dear to you—yes, irreparable hurt, and you're well aware of my own part in its infliction. Yet, surmounting your own pain and just bitterness, you find it in yourself to argue for my exculpation. There you are, Paul, teaching me what I should always have known: that kindness and compassion, the generosity of the spirit are the believer's potential privilege, not his inherent monopoly. Though, paradoxically it is this very decency and magnanimity of yours, this very demonstration of ethical fiber, which renders my exculpation even less viable, for it even further underscores and more acutely defines the error of my prejudice, the biased thoughtlessness of my judgment … my misjudgment, if you will, that concordance of religious belief was the indispensable, all-overruling premise of harmony."

The eyes still reached for Paul Devlin, adamant in their severity, strangely compelling, foreclosing any moderating objection, any mitigating comment. And as John Flannery went on, word by gradual word, his voice, drawing on some untapped residue of strength, recovered some of its resonance of days long past. "Exculpation, Paul? Because, as you maintain, I believed what I was doing was right? Oh, possibly some case of the sort might be made for my initial sin: the sin of commission. Somehow one might, precariously, justify it on the grounds that I may have been too ignorantly steeped in the doctrines of my creed, too zealously committed to its injunctions to respect the design of Providence which had let two human beings find each other; that, perhaps, my vocation may not have left me with any option but to pervert that design by my preprogrammed advice in the solemn exercise of my implicitly presumed authority—a sin of priestly arrogance, a sin of commission, yet still one that might allow for some marginal excuse. But what of the sin of omission? Wasn't I aware of George Mulvey's character and of Winnie Brennan's? As not merely an old friend of their families but as both young people's confessor, could I have been ignorant of the intrinsic and irreconcilable disparities of their temperaments and aspirations, their instinctive mutual aversion, their fundamental incompatibility? Where then, where was the basis for my advice and my priestly counsel, my authoritative intervention? To be sure, assuaging my conveniently disowned, yet not altogether stilled apprehension, I would take refuge in the pretense of humbly, piously trusting Divine Providence to rectify the apparent misalliance. There was the sin of omission, Paul. One so much more damning and beyond any claim to exculpation—because all the time, deep down, I did not believe I was doing the right thing, keeping silent, keeping aloof ..."

"Yet all the time hoping for the best," Paul Devlin said quietly, seizing the opportunity of a briefly faltering pause to try and stem what he sensed was another rising tide of self-scourging acrimony, "hoping for the best, as we all would, knowing such hope to be the only recourse of our failures."

"There are failures which admit no recourse." The retort was bony, unyielding in its repudiation.

"You know better!" Paul Devlin had not missed the eloquence of the glance straying to the building, to the window six flights up, or the anguish that twisted the pallid countenance—an anguish that swept through him, too, quite as mercilessly, quite as violently, but to which he must not allow himself to succumb—not now, when his support was so desperately needed. "Failure is part of the human destiny, even … even calamitous failure. Why not accept for yourself what surely you would concede to others?"

"Why not accept?" John Flannery said after him, his voice curiously vibrant with astonishment, with sudden wonderment that it took Paul Devlin to ask a question that should have been raised long ago. "Why not …?" For an extended moment, he seemed engrossed in a contemplative dialogue with himself in search for the answer he ought to have found long ago. And the boon of its belated discovery was mirrored by a subtle but perceptible stiffening of his sagging shoulders and a straightening of his pain-etched countenance with a touch of tranquility.

"True, why not accept?" he said once more, and, however faint, an odd inflection of somber irony trailed his speech. "You're right, Paul. Why have I not accepted my failures? Because I have not found the humility to forsake the arrogant prepossessions of my erstwhile ministry, of a priesthood that claims for itself different and supposedly superior standards: a superior order of humanness, a superior dispensation and superior authority. Because I insisted on indulging this fallacy, I could not countenance the inadequacies incident to simply being human.

Yet, perhaps ..." He paused, ever so briefly, for another dialogue with himself. "Yes, perhaps to them that recognize this fallacy and discard it, to them may be offered a modicum of reprieve from their sinfulness. For only as we admit being mere ordinary men, equal to the average of mankind in the endowments of our minds and the frailties of our nature, we may earn the right to accept our failures as part of our very humanness—accept them, neither frivolously exculpating ourselves for our errors nor glossing over them with cheap repentance, but ready to pay the price. Yes, Paul, once we've shed the preposterous presumption of our God-given special status and authority, some manner of penance may, by the Lord's grace, lighten the load of our guilt ... even my own. Yes, there may be a measure of penance, sufficient to redeem our sins of commission and omission."

Abruptly he fell silent, and as abruptly, the touch of tranquility yielded to a new assault of haunting torment which hardened into a mask of bony rigidity. "Redeem my sins of commission and omission," he amended tonelessly, "but not ..."

"Haven't you accomplished this measure of atonement?" Paul Devlin interrupted swiftly, acutely apprehending the other's sudden change of temper and determined to forestall a relapse into the depth of his self-engendered hell. "Haven't you accomplished it many times over, right here; haven't you performed more than your due share of penance already? Is there no end to guilt, no 'enough'?"

His burst of protest was stopped by a stare that burned into him from eyes aglow, in a face that once more was cadaverous haggardness and pallid agony. "Enough? No, there is no enough, there cannot be," John Flannery insisted. "I told you, Paul, there's no penance, none whatever, which could expiate sacrilege ... yes, sacrilege!" he repeated, savage with a clamor of vengeful loathing that seemed to twist every fiber of his body. "To those of faith, there is no more consummate damnation. To those of faith … You can't comprehend this, do you, Paul? Sometimes, in moments of weakness, I envy the likes of you, who don't comprehend, who are bound by no belief in the Word—envy them, wishing, just wishing for escape. But there is none, not for those of faith. I would not dare compound my betrayal of God by taking the life He gave me—compound my damnation …"

John Flannery's lips lay silent for a long moment, allowing those last words to die away, mere shuddering ghosts of sounds, drowning in a tide of dread that seemed to engulf his whole being. Glistening in the sunny brilliance of the spring day, tiny beads of sweat spread across his brow, coating its gnarled furrows. But he was oblivious to the sticky trickle of moisture, oblivious to the chill trembling through his body, oblivious to the world about him—impervious to all but the vision of a young woman writhing on her bed, kneeling in maddened prayer, screaming out the secret of her sinful passion and the terror of her soul's perdition.

Then, at last returning from his own inferno, he spoke again, word for slow, creaking word, "Damnation, to you that has no meaning, does it? Be it granted to you never to learn it. But no matter how you may reject the notions of purgatory and hell, there is the reality of damnation … There is, don't you see, Paul? Don't you understand? There they were, before the altar, George Mulvey and Winnie Brennan, who should never have come there, yet brought there by my sins of commission and omission. There they were, victims of my failures, and I joined them, pronounced them man and wife, knowing that I was sanctioning a bondage, not sanctifying a bond. Yes, knowing. Yet I blessed their marriage in the name of God. You hear, Paul? Blessed them in His holy name! But would He, who is infinite wisdom and goodness, who is love and mercy unbounded, would He have blessed this union? Would He have blessed what was doomed by its intrinsic discord? No, Paul, never He! It was I who did, I, John Flannery, taking the name of the Lord in vain, pretending that I was carrying out His will and acting by His authority, when I was as ignorant of His will as any man alive and usurped an authority never conferred on me. Yes, there they were, standing before his altar, and I spoke to them, 'What God hath joined together ...' That was betrayal, blasphemy, desecration, sacrilege!"

The forbidding waving of a determined hand stifled whatever appeasing demur Paul Devlin might have essayed. Now finding its voice after years of silent turmoil, the cognition of ultimate guilt was too obsessing, too compelling, to suffer any interruption of the self-condemning testimony. The trial must go on, unhampered by any spurious claim of mitigating circumstances. The full burden of the indictment must be satisfied, the guilty verdict be rendered, and there would be no appeal for clemency.

"Oh, to be sure," John Flannery continued, "deep down within, carefully smothered by thick layers of self-serving sanctimony, there were stirrings of conscience, harried by the truth that wouldn't be altogether denied. However willfully subdued, however artfully evaded, they were always there, those stirrings—even while I was standing at the altar, sealing that misbegotten wedlock, they wouldn't rest. Nor would they through all the days thereafter. In those desultory moments of more honest confrontation with myself, they would persist in haunting me with self-doubting quandaries. But of course ..." Fleetingly, an inaudible chuckle of utter scorn painted his features with a spectral grimace, "of course I would find an expedient and most gratifying escape. There's always pious sophistry, isn't there, to take recourse to? Was not everything throughout the universe happening in accordance with the Creator's design? Who was I to question the unfathomable wisdom and ultimate beneficence of His decrees?

Whatever the ostensible contrarieties and detrimental frictions governing its fundamental constellation, the matrimonial venture of George Mulvey and Winnie Brennan must have been part of that design, must have been willed by God; so, consequently, also my own instrumentality in its consummation. There was the Lord's eternal master plan, and I was but its chosen tool. Then must my endeavors, my actions not have been as He had ordained them? How could I have imparted His blessing to that couple, except He willed me to impart it … impart it by His authority and in His name? Ah, it was such a comforting, such an exonerating, even elevating argument! It not only appeased my occasional pangs but allowed me to view myself as the humble and faithful medium of God's design. For nearly three years, it would serve to sustain me, dissipate my apprehensions, smooth those stirrings within—even when some disturbing rumors would reach me, even when those haphazard encounters with Winnie would leave me appalled with her distraught, ravaged appearance … even when …" The memory choked off the rest of the phrase, replaced it with another deadly chuckle of self-scourging contempt and the virulence of another spectral grimace.

Then, in a voice that was grating flatness, John Flannery spoke again, "For nearly three years," he repeated, "I indulged this sanctimonious subterfuge. And then it happened. That evening in May. The smash-up against a tree. The disaster. No, Paul," he forestalled the attempted contradiction, "not suicide. I told you, it couldn't have been that, not with Winnie, not with her kind of faith. But I suspected that it had not been a simple, tragic accident, either, but the denouement of a foredoomed, ever-escalating calamity. And I knew this as a certainty, when I came to see her in the hospital …"

There was another spell of aching silence, coerced by the recall of that sickbed visit, of a young woman staring from eyes maddened by a shattered mind, of a cataclysmic terror painting her countenance.

"That very moment I knew: not the precise cause of her anguish, her desperate flight from reality, her flight from the sin she could not help committing—not until today did I learned it ..." Alive with a consuming horror, his gaze seared Paul Devlin; for but a brief instant, then the glare died as abruptly as it had flared. "Not until today ... though I should've guessed it. But I didn't muster the courage to probe. One makes sure not to question when one dreads the answer; when truth is terror, one tries to run. But that scream at the bedside, there was a truth I could not run from: the truth about myself, about my life, my blasphemy, my sacrilege. There, on that bed, was the evidence. God never had willed that marriage, God had never blessed it. On His altar I had perverted His design, had taken His name in vain. Pretending an authority He had never granted, the servant had betrayed his master, had defiled the sacrament He had entrusted to him. After that, there could be no Father Flannery. After that, there could be no more priestly presumption, no more attendance at services celebrated by my accomplices in sacrilege, by frauds, impostors, usurpers, charlatans like myself, who would hear confessions as though, in His omniscience, the Lord needed any intermediaries; mountebanks, who by their trickery compel their trusting victims to share the secrets destined for Him alone, thus to enhance their own power over them; who would pronounce blessings and condemnations, convey grace and absolution, though forever ignorant of His own judgment; who would offer prayer on behalf of their dupes, as though their intercession could alter the Creator's plans for His creatures."

John Flannery paused. Straying from the younger man, his eyes groped for new inward horizons of insight. When he spoke again, his countenance was rigid, his voice adamant with implacable severity, "That time, by that bedside, I saw the truth ... About myself, my failure, my ultimate immorality. And about God, who will not be trifled with—a truth that spelled the end of Father Flannery, the cleric. But not of John Flannery, the believer; for only through faith, unqualified in its certainty and absolute in its humility, could further life be endurable, could existence still retain some meaning. And it is because there is this faith, there could be no more Church. Whatever the issue, it is between Him and His creature alone. You listen to His voice within yourself, and He will show you the way. He showed me mine. That's why I am here, Paul; here, not to perform an act of penance, for none would fit the enormity of my failure, but simply in pursuance of what I know I must do, am called upon to do for all the days of my damnation …"

He broke off suddenly, as though struck by regret over having said too much. Flickers of despair, his eyes reached out from the dark-rimmed hollows of a cadaverous mask, reached out into a horrid infinity of immeasurable guilt. "This is just another day," he then said tonelessly, turning away, "I'd better get back to my work." And once more, as he slowly made his way toward the plot of ground alongside the pebbled walk, "just another day."

"Damnation?" Paul Devlin ached with compassion, watching him stand there by the half-dug-up flower bed and pick up his spade, each movement automatic like a robot's. "Not damnation, surely. Not for a man of faith. For is not the God, in whom you believe, infinite wisdom and goodness, love and mercy unbounded? Whatever your failure, whatever your sin, could that God do other than extend His forgiveness?"

John Flannery never turned around. It was a long while before his answer came, strangely vibrant. "You may be right, Paul. We must never lose sight of the Lord's wondrous ways … Yes, you may be right: forgiveness is the essence of the divine; and it is the prerogative of the divine. But I am human: how can I forgive myself?"

"Father Flannery!"

"Mister Flannery," the man in the gardener's outfit said stridently, and, heaving his spade, he thrust it into the black soil with a violence whose force seemed utterly beyond the limits of his haggard frailty—thrust it, driving the blade clear through the neck of his shadow on the ground.

The Glitter

Rippling with the brilliance of the noon sun, boastful in its near-Olympic dimensions, the pool shimmered across the broad, mosaic-tiled terrace. The pseudo-gothic glass-paneled door, firmly shut to preserve the air-cooled comfort in the vast parlor, allowed the slanting rays to point up the silver and crystal sparkles of the assorted antique vases and goblets, jewel boxes, and exotic curios displayed on mahogany shelves.

How much more imposing, yet how much more splendid must all this seem in the evenings, when, exposed to the scores of lights from the chandelier, Emily considered, when, billowing gently with the reflection of the moon, the pool would be touched with the gleam of fairy-tale romance.

She was still standing, notebook tucked under her arm, near the center of the silent room. She had ignored the curt invitation to be seated: it would be a little while; Miss Trent was somewhat behind her schedule, the sharp-featured, efficient-looking female had advised her in a flat voice. It had been more than a little while since. But some obscure, vexing inhibition had kept her shying away from the brocade-upholstered chair that the secretary's perfunctory gesture had singled out—shying away from it as though its occupancy by the likes of her were somehow inappropriate, even presumptuous.

The likes of us, Emily repeated to herself; irrepressibly, a twinge of resentment accompanied her deepening awareness of the incongruity attending her presence amid such an environment. Her resentment was not of wealth and luxury generally nor even of its ostentation. Her small-town American upbringing had too completely inculcated her with admiration for the socially successful and had encouraged her vicarious enjoyment of their glamorous exploits, of a lifestyle so endlessly conveyed and persistently idealized by periodicals and advertisements—a lifestyle by which some day, perhaps, she yet might achieve.

No, her resentment was directed at this particular wealth and luxury, focused specifically on the glamour confronting her here and now, on the world and the lifestyle of Trixie Trent, which was so mercilessly reactivating her forever lurking sense of perennial deprivation. Here, all around her was a world in which, she was achingly reminded, she did not belong—yet precisely the one to which she so passionately craved to belong: a lifestyle of which she so fervently wished to be part, but from which she found herself permanently exiled. Still, it was not the surrounding accouterments of material abundance that goaded her acutely nagging jealousy. Those were merely most desirable accidentals, gratifying accessories, highly appreciated frills of the one quintessential thrill: the limelight, the glitter of a neon-flashed name, the roars of applause, the splash of headlines, the accolades of public acclaim, the bouquets of obsequious adoration, the many-splendored tributes to celebrity, the very stardom that which would rescue its achievers from the damnation of anonymity, to bestow upon them an identity that, once and for all, set them apart from the gray mass of amorphous humanity—the dazzle of the center stage, which this Trixie Trent, torch singer and dancer, leading lady of musical shows, had so gloriously realized, and which for her, Emily Robinson, had remained an obsessing dream beyond any prospect or even realistic hope of attainment.

Her life had known no floodlights, no curtain calls, no baskets of flowers, no VIP receptions and triumphal farewells, no glossy smiles on magazine covers and titillating tidbits in the gossip columns, no mansion with Olympic-size pool, no antique silvers and exotic crystals, no whirls of champagne parties and sultry courtships—none of the glitter of success and distinction, none of the tokens of fame and instant recognition that might have rescued her from anonymity. For Emily Robinson there had been no chance of multi-chrome neon lights blazing forth her name from boisterous marquees. Taunting in its unattainability, her dream had obsessed her with eternally lurking acrimony at having been stymied not only due to her parents' staid and uncompromising opposition to a career exposing her to the frivolities and abuses of the music-hall and café-society sets, an interdiction that precluded any of the indispensable early training toward that so explicitly unacceptable goal—but even more decisively, due to her own, pitilessly dream-wrecking endowment with a keen, incorruptibly self-critical mind, which, in front of a mirror, would compel her to perceive the actuality proclaimed by her reflected image: an unremarkably pretty face, an ordinarily proportioned body, whose soft fullness might please but would hardly provoke, hips a trifle too broad and legs just slightly too short and plump to excite desirous male and envious female fantasies. She had looked into the mirror far too often to not, at long last, acknowledge its discouraging message.

Yet, while acknowledging it, she had never resigned herself to it. The dream would not die, nor would hope: if nature and circumstances had conspired to foil her direct access to center stage, she might by a roundabout way still claim a measure, at least, of recognition and prominence, of secondhand stardom through the reflected glory of an affiliate's attainment. Even if, as she had gradually come to suspect and had at length secretly admitted to herself, her endowments were inadequate for prevailing over her parents' antagonism and the imperfections of her physique, they would prove adequate enough for rousing the romantic interest and connubial urge of Bertram Robinson, a biologist of reputed near-genius, the consensus of whose teachers and peers predicted a future of extraordinary achievement and highest distinction. Her revised dream projected her as the spouse of a Nobel laureate, a world-famous celebrity, a guest in the governor's mansion and even at White House receptions.

But this expectation, too, had been thwarted. From the outset of their marital venture, the prospective instrument of her burning ambition offered incontrovertible evidence that there would be no basking in vicarious fame, no exultant escape from the bane of humdrum anonymity. A quiet, serious man utterly dedicated to his science, Bertram Robinson showed himself singularly indifferent to public honors, stubbornly unconcerned with prominence and prestige, societal rank, and personal recognition. To him, the pursuit of such baubles was a sheer waste of precious time and energy which might be devoted to further study and research. After three miserable years of constant altercations, her incessantly nagging complaints, indefatigably vociferous promptings, and unremitting, if fruitless, intrigues designed to push him toward a climb up the social ladder, the mismatch had reached its inevitable denouement. The resulting divorce had shattered her dreams. The fantasy of a heady limelight life had to yield to the actuality of an obscure civil-service job. Though conscientiously and punctually transmitted, her ex-mate's support for their infant daughter still left her no alternative to the unglamorous task of augmenting this alimony by some income of her own.

But if her dream had been shattered, it would not be laid to its final rest. On the contrary, the very dreariness of everyday work among everyday people, the treadmill of vulgar routine, only sharpened her urge to escape the deadening sense of personal insignificance that was her situation's inevitable concomitant. A long life ahead still beckoned, and she was determined not to let it cheat her of her due. Debacle existed for those alone who could accept it: the debris of future promise, with which her marital misadventure had left her, must not—would not—be permanent. She fully subscribed to the poet's dictum that, even from ruins, new life would sprout ... eventually. Oh yes, eventually. Bertram Robinson did not present the only avenue to a spot in the sun. Where there was a will, there would be a way.

"Mrs. Robinson?"

The voice startled her. Eyes pinned to the sparkles of the pool beyond the tiled terrace, mind lost in its chafing ruminations, she had been oblivious of the movement of a door opening in back of her. Even so, it was not the jarring suddenness of an unnoticed presence or the woman now stepping across the threshold that compelled a long moment's struggle to collect herself: the surfeit of familiarity engendered by the countless likenesses on posters, in periodicals, and in newspapers ensured instant recognition. Rather it was the quality of the voice, the character of the presence, the hoarse, throatily clouded pitch of the brief cadence, disturbingly discrepant from the metallic timbre that blared out her songs from the stage and from scores of records and tapes; even more incongruously, the commonplace, unimpressive, indeed inconspicuous image of Trixie Trent, superstar— an appearance that seemed implausible as she stood there, the careless, almost sloppy wrap of a housecoat dissembling the famed, so glowingly cited suppleness of her dancer's body and all but concealing its celebrated erotic suggestion. The surprisingly sparse and rather slipshod application of makeup divested her features of the seductively provocative charm with which the magic of the floodlights and the artifices of fawning photographers had endowed them, revealing lines of morose harshness and the lusterless depths of weary eyes.

"You asked for an appointment?" that hoarse, throaty voice rent the instant's silence. "Yes, Miss Trent." Emily managed to mask her bewilderment. "And thank you so much for finding time to see me."

A languid shrug. "Finding time, why not? A bit of cooperation makes for good public relations, doesn't it?" There was a nuance of mockery about the husky voice and a breath of acrid self-irony. "Besides, the mornings are my time-off from playing prima donna, affording me the leisure to cater to my foul moods and thus be truly myself. Why not make yourself comfortable, Mrs. Robinson?" A perfunctory gesture pointed to one of those brocade-covered chairs. "What may I offer you? Care for a drink?"

"I appreciate your courtesy, but …"

"Some coffee, perhaps, tea?"

"Thank you again." The response was edged with uneasy regret. "But really, I can't, mustn't … It's against regulations on my job."

"How inconsiderate!" Trixie Trent remarked vapidly, seating herself directly opposite her guest, across the round, glass-plated table. "Your job, of course … the Department of Social Justice, is it?"

The inflection of disdain fleetingly crisping the guttural voice was not lost. "Yes … you may be wondering."

"Wondering?" A brittle smile warped the woman's full lips, then died. "Amid the glut of the bizarre and the absurd, which is the routine of the habitat, one stops wondering about anything at all. Though, of course, this sort of an encounter does represent kind of a novelty. In this setting," casually a long-fingered, bony hand swept around the parlor, "in this rarefied sphere of society's darlings, one does not likely have much truck with your particular outfit … with any government agency, really. Except, naturally, Internal Revenue …" Her smile, unsmiling in its drab derision, passed across her lips again. "So then, what was it you asked to see me about?"

Emily's answer was tardy, and, faltering with dismay at the sudden rankling of impatience which had so unexpectedly unveiled as sham the fragile air of affability, lacked the tact and sensitivity demanded by the delicate nature of her mission, "about a problem New York has requested us to discuss with you."

"New York?" Abruptly the other woman's languor seemed exiled by an accent of antagonistic wariness and the lusterless apathy of her glance was acute with a glint of belligerent alertness. "What about New York?"

Stiffening, Emily sat up straight. Perturbed though she was by the drastic change in her hostess's demeanor, she would meet the challenge, would see through this distasteful assignment, would not be intimidated or distracted from her purpose by the ominous stridor of the voice leaping at her across the table. "They requested the local agency's assistance," she returned quietly, tightly.

"Who's they?"

"The New York Department of Social Services. Asked us to establish contact, following up on their two letters, which were never answered."

"Letters? What letters? … Oh, I see!" Trixie Trent rasped, the initial puzzlement of her stare yielding to an angry grimace. Fitfully, her long-fingered hand reached, pressed the buzzer. Her lips were furled with a muttered imprecation. "That goddamned, no-good loafer again …!"

"Yes, Miss Trent?" The sharp-featured, efficient-looking female was standing in the door, pursuing her inquiry in the same flat, crisp voice that had responded to Emily's advent.

A guttural snarl, "Annette, call Fred. He's to send my correspondence over here, at once. All of it, now!"

"Right." That Annette person seemed to be used to her employer's commandeering unpleasantness, inured to it.

"And let me have it as soon as it gets here!"

"Right." The secretary pulled the door shut behind her departing figure.

"Fred Cochrane." Trixie Trent's comment was acid with invective. "He's supposed to handle my correspondence while I'm abroad … Just got back from Australia day before yesterday."

Emily nodded. The newspapers had been expansive in their coverage of the star's return, of her long tour's spectacular success.

"He's a goddamn loafer, Fred is," Trixie Trent added, in the way of a soliloquy rather than a communication, "a no good leech like all the rest of them. Par for the course. If he were just half as lazy as he's arrogant and greedy, maybe he might be of some use. Bet he didn't even open those letters. Ah, not Fred Cochrane … Wouldn't bother with anything that didn't look likely to promise a fat commission. Maybe it's time to kick him hard, where it hurts … Oh, what's the use!" she murmured, staring out through the pseudo-gothic arch of the glass door, across the terrace, across the pool, staring into the sunglutted distance.

Emily sat back, disquieted, waiting for the geyser of anger to cool. But it was not the strident vulgarity of erupting acrimony that was sending a shiver down her spine—a shiver born of an irrefutable intuition that this man Fred Cochrane was but the present instant's conveniently palpable victim of Trixie Trent's venom—but the sense that, lurking beyond this eruption there was a rage far more profound, far more encompassing, a rage, which, for a frightening moment, transformed the countenance across the table into a mask of age-ravaged, almost cadaverous decrepitude. For a split second only. Then Trixie Trent awakened to the sting of her visitor's appalled silence. Shattering the spell of vacant contemplation with a wooden laugh, she said, "Oh, what the hell! Ol' Fred, he's really no worse than the rest of them. I had to blow off some steam, I guess. Never mind. It's my regular morning routine, being in a foul mood. This morning especially. Had a rotten night. Barely managed to get myself out of bed, when you arrived … No, no," she added, waving a perfunctory hand, "that's quite all right. You kept your appointment on time. Only I'm still in a bit of funk. Will be a while yet until that pill works. You're surprised?" A long sullen gaze reached for Emily. "Amphetamines." The ghost of a morose tremor belied the casualness of the commentary. "Without them, no way for the likes of me. No way to get through their days, and especially their evenings. Depression doesn't play too well on the stage, does it?" There again came that brittle, toneless laugh. "Pills. Stardom's diet. You get high, you forget, you perform. You keep up your diet, for otherwise …"

Otherwise … Emily felt another shudder rippling down her spine. Escalating into throaty shrillness, the word reverberated in her ears, piercing her mind with its acrimony. Otherwise … She needed no filling in of the abruptly muted, unfinished phrase. There had been too many accounts of her hostess's unbridled temper, of her lapses into trespassing the threshold of due constraint. Over the years, the society pages had had their field days keeping track of Trixie Trent's riotous escapades, exploiting her recurrent explosive episodes—not a few of which had graduated from verbal abuse to physical confrontation. Like that face-slapping incident, when a playful tycoon's hand, impervious to her unresponsive mood, had proved too persistent in its amorous explorations; or the famous scuffle with a producer who would not accept her interpretation of contractual duties; or, not so long ago, the rather more drastic encounter that had landed her in court after she had, passionately provoked by disparaging insinuations in a gossip column, clamped those long-fingered bony hands around the neck of its authoress and only some outsiders' fast intervention had prevented the likelihood of actual strangulation and saved her from more serious criminal charges.

Otherwise, Emily repeated to herself. Perhaps those had been occasions, when the star had neglected her diet?

"Anyway," Trixie Trent's voice, more even, more quiet now, broke into her contemplations, "all this is neither here nor there. It's not what you came to see me about, is it? Let's have it, then. It'll be some time before Fred's messenger can get here. But no doubt, you're familiar with the contents of those letters from …" there was a momentary break in her speech. "From New York. So, suppose you tell me why the Department of Social Services should be concerned with me."

Emily nodded rather stiffly. Its motion ever so slightly stilted, her hand reached, flipped open her notebook. She could well have cited the substance of those communications almost word for word, but, taken aback by the other woman's unmistakably sharpened accent of animosity, she determined to respond with a demonstrative display of professionalism. "The New York agency's concern is in reference to one Mrs. Troyanczik …"

Only a wall of silence greeted her waiting pause.

"Mildred Troyanczik," she elaborated.

Only the gaze of icy eyes answered the pointed emphasis on the full name.

"Mildred Troyanczik," Emily repeated slowly. That shudder revived, pricking up and down her spine. Staring at the immobile figure across the table, she muttered, "You do know her, don't you?"

"I did know her," Trixie Trent replied stonily.

"But …?"

"I did know her," Trixie Trent said again, with a finality that would allow no argument, no contradiction. "Did know her once. Haven't seen her or had any contact whatever with her in nearly twenty-five years."

Hasty with an undefined imperative, Emily bent over her notebook, hoping to hide the shock to her emotional frame of reference, which for long moments rendered her incapable of speech. "Mrs. Troyanczik," she said at length, never looking up from the scribbled entries, which seemed oddly blurred. "She is now a ward of the Department of Social Services."

"I see." The reply was creakingly level. "What you're saying is, she is on welfare."

"Receiving public assistance." The amendment stressed the official terminology, as though some loftier nomenclature could enhance the dignity of the condition.

"No difference." The refutation was drab with scorn. "A handout is a handout by any name. That is what Mrs. Troyanczik's getting; that's what she's asked for."

"Not exactly," Emily disagreed uncertainly, faltering, thrown off balance. That frozen voice gripped her with an obscure sense of anxiety. Distraught, she kept her eyes glued to the notebook, pretending to quote from its page. "It wasn't her doing, applying for help. In fact, it seems, at first she even objected to receiving any. False pride, I suppose. Or just plain ignorance of the opportunity. Whatever, the Department couldn't allow her to go on picking scraps from garbage cans, much less to be evicted and thrown into the street by her landlord. Alerted by some neighbors, it intervened; actually, it seems against her will, they arranged for an emergency grant, thus forestalling homelessness and providing cash for some subsistence-level food."

Emily interrupted her recital, hoping that the purposeful hiatus might encourage a reaction. There was none. Struggling against an indefinable yet deepening spell of oppressive distress, but left no alternative, she went on, trying to suppress a note of recriminatory harshness. "As further investigation revealed, Mrs. Troyanczik had, due to a long history of alcoholism, never held any job for a period sufficient to establish her eligibility for any alternative form of governmental aid and remained without any means of self-support. The agency decided to extend assistance to her on a permanent basis. That was some four months ago."

Again she paused, waiting for some response which might ease the burden of her task, a response whose further denial now seemed inconceivable, unimaginable to her. After waiting through an eternity of rigid, frigid muteness, she continued at last, investing word for word with the escalating stress of repressed animosity, "Ever since, this has been Mrs. Troyanczik's status and condition."

"So?" Trixie Trent said.

Emily gave a start. The anger, the antagonism, the loathing, which, like creeping poison, had been building in her, was drowned by a tide of pity, stirred by the blatancy of desolation that counterpointed the wooden flatness of that monosyllable and evoked a sudden awareness of a torment that pleaded for understanding and indulgence and sympathy, for words sensitively chosen and explanations inoffensively presented.

"The law," she said carefully, "the law stipulates the mutual responsibility of parents and children to provide needed support. This responsibility is deemed compulsory; wherever adequate means are available, it must be discharged, before the community's responsibility may be called upon. This is what those letters intended to convey to you—your required cooperation in assuming your legal obligation."

"My legal obligation." Brief in its grating acerbity, a chuckle trailed the repeated phrase.

Only after some futile instants of perplexed wait for some further comment, Emily went on, speaking softly, almost imploringly. "Yes, Miss Trent. You may not have seen Mrs. Troyanczik, may not have maintained any contact with her for nearly a quarter-century, but this legal obligation still persists. After all, she is your mother, isn't she?"

"That's what she told them?" The rejoinder did not attempt to hide its rancor.

"No!" Emily's reply was raw with a flash of rekindled antipathy. "She did not tell them. She wouldn't; she actually did all she could to keep it her secret. It was some neighbor who informed them of the connection. Even then she balked at admitting it, until forced to own up, when investigation secured proof positive that, incredibly, she was in fact the mother of the celebrated Trixie Trent."

"Incredibly," the other woman took up the word, and there, once more, was that acrimonious chuckle, "Yes. Incredibly, indeed."

"But undeniably!" Emily stared at her hostess, stunned by the caustic blatancy coarsening her husky voice. "There's documentary evidence."

"Of what?" The refutation was a whiplash of scorn. "Of Mildred Troyanczik's having given birth to an infant Theresa, fathered upon her by Stepan Troyanczik, who died in the war. Battle of the Bulge."

"But, that child Theresa Troyanczik …"

"There's no child Theresa Troyanczik!" The interruption was scathing vehemence. "There has not been, ever since she got to be four years old. That child disappeared when Trixie Trent was born, and there's been only Trixie Trent since."

"But …"

"Trixie Trent. That's what my passport says. That's the name the signatures on my contracts show, my driver's license, my credit cards, my tax reports." Those full lips curled with bleak sarcasm. "Documentary evidence, Mrs. Robinson. Documentary evidence, there it is. Trixie Trent, it says. And Trixie Trent has no mother—never had one!"

For what seemed a crushing infinity, Emily sat silent, trying to cope with the confounding ambivalence of the response. All her emotions, all her notions of ethics, all her personal beliefs and presumptions of human values were rebelling against the cold-blooded, cold-hearted intransigence of that despicable creature across the table. And yet, despicable? There, once more, had been the cadence of utter desolation, trembling in that last phrase, an accent of unrelieved pain, as of a mortally wounded animal, crying out for compassion—a compassion she could not bring herself to deny.

"Still," she persisted at long last, in a voice that was seeking to have her quandary take refuge in the professional's trained aloofness, "still, there remains the legal connection."

"The legal connection." Trixie Trent was gazing past her into some boundless, clouded distance. "Yes, I suppose, that remains. No doubt, those communications meant to remind me of it. As well as, I assume, of the fact that failure to comply with the attendant legal requirement might eventuate its enforcement by the court. Right, Mrs. Robinson?"

"I suppose there would be such a clarifying reference to the letter of the law, which would leave no alternative." The hesitant phrase was pointed in its stilted precision. "This is why, when the lack of any response appeared to suggest your refusal to comply, the local agency was asked to intervene. Surely they'd wish to exhaust every option before taking a step so embarrassing to a person of your position and prominence."

"How very considerate!" Trixie Trent said, and the dreary mockery of her chuckle carried an echo as of a distant dirge. Then her weary shrug ended an aching pause. "However, if I had received those communications, my response would have precluded any embarrassment. I know my liability to the community. I have always paid my debts. Even if I could, I would not allow Mrs. Troyanczik's maintenance to become the taxpayer's burden. I would've indicated as much to the New York agency. My willingness to indemnify them for whatever grants were disbursed to Mrs. Troyanczik in the past as well as for such as might have continued to be granted to her in the future, as long as my contributions would be forwarded directly to the agency, thus obviating any contact with the recipient."

"I see." Emily muttered falteringly, beset by another assault of a nagging despondency.

"That's it, then," Trixie Trent added in the same dully impersonal tone. "I shall settle my debt as soon as the relevant bill is submitted to me. And thereafter, every month, a check will cover the full amount of the legally prescribed public assistance grant. Your report of this interview may so advise your New York colleagues—not forgetting to stress the proviso, if you please, that this arrangement must be kept strictly confidential."

"I see," Emily said again. But even while she was uttering it, she was aware of the mechanical comment's untruth. She did not see, she did not comprehend at all, did not even begin to fathom the personality of the one confronting her, her impulses, her motives, her contradictions, her bewildering impact on her own sentiments—an impact causing her reactions to alternate erratically between sympathy and repugnance, vague pity and flagrant detestation.

"Which," the throaty voice ripped into the tumult of her complexity, "should satisfactorily complete the purpose of your visit."

"Yes, in a way." The rejoinder was fraught with an irrepressible nuance of hostility. Stung by that voice's unfeeling indifference and icy determination, Emily was prey to another of the pendulum's vehemently abrupt swings toward repugnance and detestation.

"In a way?"

"Well," a split second's pause gained time for an accent of deliberate poignancy. "It seems I should mention a passage in one of those letters, a speculative hint, as it were, a hopeful suggestion that perhaps …"

"Yes?" A prompting, acute with irritation.

Emily sat up stiffly. The pendulum had reached its extreme latitude of repulsion. "There was a reminder that life on public assistance is no bed of roses, that the allowances are calculated to provide for barest necessities only, the baldest minimum of subsistence, and, indeed hardly even that. It makes for a rather cruel condition in which to spend one's old age, a frightful hardship that should be spared anyone and whenever possible."

"I agree," Trixie Trent interrupted, but her level tone was laced with venom. "However, your lecture is neither here nor there. Mrs. Troyanczik will receive what the government has determined to be an adequately maintaining grant. It's what the system will offer. I might quarrel with its present arrangements, but I'm not about to change or improve them."

"Our concern is not with the system and the arrangements right now!" The rebuke was delivered more impetuously than intended. "It is with your mother's lot ..."

"Mrs. Troyanczik's!" The correction was flat with unyielding emphasis.

"Mrs. Troyanczik's, then."

"I'm not about to change or improve her lot, either."

"Not about ..." Emily repeated, staring at the woman across the table for long moments of petrified incredulity. "But ... but you can't mean that, Miss Trent!"

"Can't I?"

"Could you?" The words trembled from lips suddenly dry and salty. "No. You couldn't. Not you, not the person you are, a person known for her charity, her contributions to scores of causes— considerable contributions, even lavish ones—orphanages, hospitals, drug rehabilitation centers, medical research, libraries, you name it. Yet you wouldn't try to improve ...?"

A bony hand's abrupt flick guillotined her speech. Then, oddly contrasting the explosiveness of her gesture, Trixie Trent's repudiation came calmly, fraught with inflexible finality, "I'm afraid you'll have to be satisfied with my decision, Mrs. Robinson. Your agency may oblige me to meet my legal responsibility; it cannot oblige me to explain myself. I've stated what I'm prepared to do, what I will do. That, and no more. Which, it seems, should clarify the extent of your mission's success."

Through a spell of abysmal silence Emily sat rigid, struck into helpless immobility by an ambush of overwhelming anguish, as though she were witnessing the exposure, unbearable in its appalling nakedness, of some inconceivable monstrosity, some awesome abomination.

"Yes," she conceded at last, laboriously struggling up from her seat, as though against some intangible burden. "Indeed it does clarify the issue. I shall make out my report to that effect and leave it to the people in New York to proceed accordingly." Still unable to quite shake herself free of that obsessive anguish, she gathered up her notebook. "And thank you for letting me take up your time. I wish it could've been spent on some more pleasant subject."

"That's quite all right." A noncommittal shrug. "You were just doing your job. It isn't one conducive to pleasantness, is it?" Trixie Trent paused, before adding, in a voice suddenly almost affable, with half-smiling softness, "A lovely child …"

A perplexed stare answered her. Only then Emily realized that the remark referred to the snapshot that had slipped from between the covers of the notebook.

"Your daughter, I take it? May I?" Already Trixie Trent was picking the color print from the table.

"Of course." The assent was eager with a flush of pride. "The most recent photo. My little Roberta. Just turned eight last month."

"Just turned eight," Trixie Trent muttered absently, her eyes engrossed in the likeness. "Really, a beautiful girl."

"So people say." The assent's pretense at modesty amplified rather than diminished the flow of boastful elation. "Yes, I suppose she's pretty enough. And bright, too. That's not merely in my own prejudiced judgment, but …"

"Bright." From across the table a slow nod. Those eyes were still engrossed, oddly fascinated. "Bright, yes, that's how she looks, even in this picture."

"Even in this picture?" Emily said after her, uncertainly, slow with a vague sense of bewilderment. A not so subtle inflection of ambiguity had not escaped her; nor had the passing frown.

"Never mind," her hostess said, still staring at the likeness in her hand. "It's just that I'd like a more casual, more natural mode of presentation. I don't favor too careful, too conscious posing." She paused ever so briefly, before adding, with a sudden accent of acerbity, "particularly on the part of children."

"I understand." Emily's assent was vacant sound, filtered by the awareness that she did not understand at all. Not this kind of comment, coming from one who all her life had so deliberately been a party to the gloss of public display; from one whose every appearance, every costume, every gesture, every smile was the product of cunningly calculated staging. "Still, there are occasions, aren't there, when this type of presentation may seem called for, like this one, which commemorates Roberta's latest success, when she came out on top in the contest …"

"On top," Trixie Trent repeated woodenly.

"She often does." The elaboration was vibrant. "Most of the time, in fact. She's quite talented."

"Is she?" The guttural bleakness of the response was a sonant replica of the harsh, almost cadaverous mask, into which the other woman's countenance once more had transmuted itself.

"Oh indeed!" Captive to the impulse of her exultation, Emily was deaf to the barely constrained fierceness of that grating cadence, blind to that mien's bizarre contortion. "It's everybody's opinion. Consensus has it that she's just too gifted to miss making it big. Wherever she appears, wherever she competes, they rave about her personality, her attractiveness, her vitality and charm, about that supple body, those graceful movements of hers, and about her unerring flair for using her assets, her unfailing sense of rhythm controlling her every step, about her voice, too, not a grand one really, not an operatic one, but that's hardly essential for a popular performer. Besides, her music teacher has no doubt, that, with proper work and application, it's going to be better than adequate … Ah yes, my little one. Everybody's predicting a great future for her, a brilliant career. Not quite as brilliant, perhaps, as your own, Miss Trent, not many are as blessed with the stuff that makes a superstar. But again, who can tell? When there is the drive, the stamina, the will to keep striving for the top … In fact, it's you who are my Roberta's prime paragon, the shining example that's sustaining her incentive and ambition. After all, she's got the tools that may let her realize what … what others may only dream about. Yes, she's got the tools, the talent. And the awards to prove it … Oh, you should see the array of prizes she's won and …"

Dazzlingly, a diamond flashed from a long, slender finger as another whiplash motion of the bony hand decreed the midsentence demise of the fervent gush. "I'm sure I would be duly impressed," Trixie Trent said in a voice whose creaking scorn made no attempt to mask its strain of unmitigated savagery. "But I've seen plenty of those medals and plaques and gilt tinsel crowns—first prizes, second prizes, third prizes, special awards, the whole lineup. No need to see your little Roberta's. I've got my own exhibit. Right here, two flights up—a whole attic full of them. The spoils of endless grinding competitions. Trophies from an unremitting chase of contests: Miss Kindergarten, America's Little Darling, Junior Miss Bathing Beauty, Little Queen of the Harvest Festival, Children's Wear Foster Girl, what have you … There they are, up in the attic, each marking another merciless step of a youngster's progress toward the limelight glitter; marking it from the day an ordinary four-year-old named Theresa Troyanczik passed into oblivion and the prospective Trixie Trent was born …"

Momentarily, a fleeting shudder stopped the flow of words.

Then the voice creaked on again. "That room upstairs is called Mildred Troyanczik's Memorial Chapel. But there hasn't been any worshipping in there; it's kept locked all year round. One needs no mementos of what one can't forget … Not ever, Mrs. Robinson. Not those interminable hours, day after day, of instructions, of practices, of rehearsals, dancing, singing, bows and curtsies, cheesecake poses. Not those incessant sessions of dress fittings, the gamut of flounces and ribbons and laces, of hairdos and manicures. Not those trips all over the country, New York, San Francisco, Dayton, Minneapolis … never seeing, always being seen, and acclaimed, above all, acclaimed. No city too big, no town too small, no place too insignificant, if it would but offer another chance for yet one more triumph, one more prize earned by the well-taught, coyly insinuating, self-exhibiting gyrations of a pre-adolescent body exposed to the greedy appraisals of occasional talent scouts and the sly, fevered, lip-licking ogling of would-be child-molesters …"

Again the relentless voice faded, plunging Emily into a silent void vibrant with acrimony, leaving her standing there, rooted to the spot, as though by some maledictory spell; standing there, incapable of any response, not daring to stir, watching the tips of long slender fingers whiten and grip the rim of the table's glass top as though intent on crushing it. Then, ending an eternity of unaccountable fright, unchanged in its creaking stoniness, it came to her again.

"Yet another triumph to celebrate. Another triumph, certified by yet one more spangled trinket, upstairs, behind that locked door. There are scores of them, Mrs. Robinson, each a testimonial to still another successful display of Trixie Trent, child prodigy. Except there was no prodigy, just a mediocre talent persistently staged. And there was no child, none whatsoever, only a fledgling star. And every one of those trinkets, too, standing as a testimonial, each in its own way, to the bloated praises and jubilant boasts which would follow each first-prize performance; to the sullen airs of disappointment attending a second prize; to the bitter reproaches and nagging exhortations brought on by the ignominy of a mere third prize; to the alternations of vicious berating and devastating silence that would punish the occasional failure to make the winner's circle. But then, after all, these routines worked out for the best, didn't they? They ensured one's solid preparation for life in a world peopled by strangers only, a world knowing only three classes of inhabitants: adoring audiences, jealous rivals for the top billings, and the gray, negligible mass of uninvolved outsiders—apart, of course, from the subhuman species of potentially critical reviewers—a world peopled by admirers, fawners, professional contacts, drinking companions, occasional bedfellows. But friends? Never. The grind of competition would foreclose one's learning how to gain any and, even more surely, how to hold them."

Transiently, a toneless chuckle filled the vacuum of another hiatus with an accent of uncanny menace. Those long slender fingers were still digging into the tabletop, venting on it a rage that was allowed no reflection by the stony bleakness of their owner's voice. "One's got to be prepared for that sort of world, doesn't one? To be sure, Trixie Trent was being prepared all right. Those trophies upstairs attest to how well. But then, one might expect no less, given the advantages of goal-directed guidance and unflagging support from a singularly dedicated coterie of attendants such as the budding prima donna enjoyed. Unfailingly, Trixie Trent could rely on the devoted efforts of an indefatigable coach, an unsparing drill mistress, a skillful couturier, a clever makeup artist, a supremely effective publicity agent, an ever-ready producer, director, stage manager, an ever-present chaperon. Each of them embodied in the person of Mildred Troyanczik, who, bloated with self-importance, insisted on promoting the claim of being Trixie Trent's mother."

There was that toneless, uncanny chuckle again, still more acute now in its accent of savagery, a chuckle pregnant with violence, leaping at Emily, engulfing her with a sensation of intangible menace, haunting her still spellbound mind with images of a tycoon's slapped cheeks, a producer's scratched face and torn necktie, a gossip-columnist's half-throttled throat—images reinforced in their ominous suggestion by the raucous voice from across the table. "Mother? For the meaning of that word Trixie Trent would have to look it up in a dictionary … No!" Abruptly the stridor yielded to a cadence of almost tender mellowness, "No, that isn't fair. Not altogether true, either …"

There had been an inkling once, briefly, of that word's meaning: that morning in school, when, after another of those routines of crushing silence and virulent denunciation in the wake of an unsuccessful performance, she had succumbed to the despair of the sleepless night just past, had broken down in tears; when Irene Walter, the unassuming spinster who taught sixth grade, had called for a substitute to take over the class, had led her by the hand down to a bench in the courtyard, had let her sob-racked face find the soft warmth of a calming shoulder, and had listened to whispered pain pouring out irresistibly—just listened—and had spoken at last quietly, affectionately, telling her that failure was but a passing incident, an inevitable ingredient of human existence; that success had a thousand facets; that life offered untold possibilities to someone like her, someone blessed not only with a beautiful physique but with a fine brain, an imaginative, fertile mind that would assure excellence of achievement in a large variety of fields; that stardom as an entertainer was not the only worthwhile goal; that there were so many alternative avenues open to one like her, who had so much to offer.

There had been an inkling, that once, of that word's meaning; she had never forgotten that discovery. Never forgotten, either, whenever an engagement or itinerary would entail a sojourn in the east, to visit with Irene Walter or to send her a monthly check to supplement the meager pension of a retired teacher.

Still, even throughout that uniquely precious morning on the bench in the schoolyard she had known that, in its sanguine innocence, dear Irene Walter's encouragement was doomed to irrelevance. Trixie Trent's reality would embrace no untold possibilities, no alternative avenues; there never would be, never could be, any choice. From the day the child Theresa Troyanczik was reborn in her new identity, her road had been blueprinted—a road leading, irreversibly, from contest to contest, prize to prize, trophy to trophy, toward the crucial eventuality, when her placing as a runner-up in the Miss New Jersey beauty pageant would prove sufficient to rouse the active interest of a small-time talent scout with a keen eye for the big chance, sufficient to make her, in return for some discreet favors, the beneficiary of his enterprising acumen and extraordinary prowess as an impresario and ensure her rapid progress from an obscure nightclub in Memphis to a more prestigious one in Dallas and, via casino shows in Las Vegas, on to Broadway and Hollywood, to superstar tours abroad and television specials; progress along a road that had been carefully mapped and irrevocably dictated by one Mildred Troyanczik, who, glorying in the ever-brightening splendor of her own frustration's creature, would keep promoting her claim of being the new public idol's mother.

"But comes a time," Trixie Trent continued, emerging from the aching moment of silent remembrance, her voice regaining its full, grating acrimony, as, magnetically fastened to the color print in her hand, her eyes were burning upon the blond-curled, lovely yet oddly frozen, brightly yet vacantly smiling countenance, "comes a time when you grow up, when your mind will strip itself of its dependency, will seek its own perspective. Comes a time when you suddenly look back on a childhood that never was, on a past despoiled of the essential experiences—the very foundation on which, alone, an adulthood of fulfillment and happiness, indeed of proper human function may be built. Comes a time when you at last glimpse the truth and discern the vanity, the selfishness, the fraudulence of your past's despoiler; when you no longer suffer the exploiter, the parasite of your success, the maggot feasting on your internal decay. Comes a time … Yes, comes a time—but too late to escape the bondage of applause and adulation, of liquor and pills and sleazy affairs."

Abruptly, as though propelled by a long-accumulated explosive force, she rose from her seat. But curiously, indeed quite implausibly contrasting the startling vehemence which had compelled her body's motion, her speech was level in its throaty huskiness, "There, Mrs. Robinson," she said, every word jarring in its finality, as, with her fingers crooked like claws, she flung the photo back across the table. "That's yours. As I've advised you, I shall meet my legal obligations in regard to Mildred Troyanczik. There's nothing more to add, nothing more to be accomplished by your visit. So I suggest that we terminate it now! As I've mentioned, my morning moods are rather unpleasant. Today's version is no exception, and the amphetamine has started working. It seems best, that you be on your way, before it reaches its full effect. I might get to be high enough to do your daughter a favor and choke you."

She turned away sharply and stepped to the pseudo-gothic door; stood there, staring out through its sunsparkled glass, never watching her visitor gather up snapshot, notebook, and purse, never watching her leave as noiselessly, as inconspicuously as the trembling haste of her tiptoes would permit; stood there, staring out across the mosaic-tiled terrace at the pool's rippled surface, at the shifting glitter, which was but a tinseled sham of brightness, a broken reflection of the midday light's splendor; stand there, wanting to cry. But the tears would not come.

Flowers

Bustling with her usual determined efficiency, Robby threw open the door and held it ajar for the burly man to pass.

"Flowers for you, Miriam," she announced, pointing at the sizable gaily pink and green wrapping, which hid the bouquet he was carrying in.

"For me?" The slight sideward motion of the head on the pillow stressed the disclaiming inflection of the feeble voice.

"That's right." Roberta Carlson, the nurse whom everybody on this hospital ward knew only as 'Robby,' turned to the orderly. "Just put them down here, on the table. We'll find a vase for them somewhere."

"No, no," the woman on the bed said. "These couldn't be for me. Must be a mistake."

"No mistake, dearie." Already responding to the buxom gray-haired nurse's glance—which was a command—the orderly had deposited his burden and, followed by her watchful eyes, was leaving. "No mistake at all. Look for yourself." She held up the wrapper to exhibit a black marker's large, bold lettering. "Mrs. Miriam Weisman, ward three, room four-seventeen," she read off. "Couldn't be plainer, could it?"

"Still …"

The quick wave of a fleshy hand smothered the protest. "Flowers are sent to people here every day. Today it's your turn, and about time, too!"

"My turn …?" The murmured echo of the phrase came, a cadence of bewilderment, of puzzled incredulity.

Nurse Robby let it fade into a long moment of uneasy silence. She was at a loss for a believable comment, afraid she might not quite manage to keep its tone from betraying her own disbelieving astonishment. Until she had double-checked that unequivocal direction on the wrapper, she had been equally certain that this delivery had entered room four-seventeen in error. For better than three weeks now, this patient had been lingering away her days, and there had not been one single visitor, not one single letter, not even a single phone call inquiring about her condition. All along, she had been wondering, uncomprehending how such a lovely person, one so quiet and unassuming, so undemanding and uncomplaining, so attractive and pleasant, should be so utterly alone, so totally abandoned.

The more incomprehensible, Robby reflected, as, with her eyes glued to the floral gift, she was busying herself with unwrapping it, the more perplexing, considering that Miriam Weisman was a widow, only thirty-seven years old, who, before her disease had wasted her features and chemotherapy, administered too late to save her, had thinned out her wavy dark hair to a state of near baldness, must have been a handsome, indeed a most desirable woman. Palpably possessed of rather more than adequate intelligence as well as of subtle charm, which, even in her present, failing condition still remained distinct, she surely could not have been lacking her share of admirers. Making her loneliness seem even stranger, Jewish people always had a flock of concerned family attending them, didn't they? Besides, with a winning personality like hers she could not have failed to make lots of friends or at least close enough acquaintances among her fellow employees at the bookstore, where, as she had mentioned, she had continued on her sales job until just two months ago, when her deteriorating health had finally foreclosed that option. There should have been visitors and letters and phone calls; and yet ...

"My turn?" the voice from the bed repeated, its placid evenness tinted with a trace of wonderment," but there's no one ..."

"Obviously there is." Nurse Robby had just succeeded in exposing the heads of the flowers. "See? Aren't they gorgeous? Gladiolas and lilies and carnations—and even three roses. You see? There's someone all right, someone to whom you must be very dear."

"My husband's been dead for ten years." A nuance of tremulous desolation accented the brittleness of the murmur.

"I know." Nurse Robby could not quite keep a creak of harshness from her comment. She felt like crying, swept by an instant's recall of her own callous, forever drunk scoundrel of a husband, whom she should have thrown out long before she had finally mustered the courage to face unencumbered loneliness; crying, at once, from empathy with her patient's unredeemed grief and from envy of a passionate remembrance that her own wedded days had denied her. "Still, there's someone, isn't there? Someone who sent these flowers?"

"Someone? I wouldn't know."

"We shall find out who—just as soon as I get this paper off this bunch. There's bound to be a get-well card, telling you ... Hey, Luella-May!" she called out to the nurse's aide who was passing by the open door. "Will you please find a vase for these?"

"Sure." The thin, smallish figure in the hallway stopped just long enough to cast a perfunctory glance at the half unraveled bouquet.

"I think there's one in four-twenty, where the old lady moved out yesterday."

Moved out ...

Nurse Robby listened to the even rhythm of the fading steps along the corridor, listened with a dim sense of wondering appreciation. *That Luella-May, she was all right; where she came from, they did not get a lot of education, did they, but this did not seem to make her any less sensitive, any less thoughtful in choosing her words.* "Moved out ..." Yes, old Mrs. O'Toole had moved out of four-twenty. Straight to the funeral parlor, just as two days ago Joan Woodling had moved out of four-seventeen here, to leave Miriam Weisman as temporarily the sole occupant of the semiprivate room.

Temporarily, Robby repeated to herself. All the long years of service had not taught her how to keep from shuddering at the thought: very temporarily. It would be but a day or two, perhaps just hours, before this occupant, too, would be 'moving out.' Her voice had an odd touch of hoarseness, as, pausing in her search, she said, "Seems there is no note."

"No note?"

"From the sender. But let me look some more." Then a head full of gray hair under the white bonnet was shaking with baffled dismay. "Nope. Can find none. Must've detached itself, lost on the way up here somehow." A shrug. "Well, anyway. I guess you'll figure out who was remembering you."

"Will I?" The bloodless lips were barely stirring. From lusterless eyes, sunken in a pallid face, the woman on the bed was staring at the polychromy of blossoms, rendered still more resplendent by a ray of morning sun slanting through the window.

"Sure enough you will," Robby averred with somewhat forced conviction, just as an urgent buzzer went off outside. "Oh, darn it! Bet it's the guy in four-eleven again! Keeping me on the go all the time, he is, nagging me with a thousand silly complaints. They aren't all like you, dearie; most of them ... Ah, there you are!" she interrupted herself to turn to the girl in the door. "Good! Got us that vase all right. It's a nice one, too, just right for these flowers. You'll take care of them, will you now, Luella-May? So Mrs. Weisman can really enjoy them. Myself, got to look what four-eleven is about this time," she added hurriedly, already on her way out, as the buzzer was snarling again. "See you in a little while, Miriam."

Then the room was silent while the nurse's aide was deftly placing the flowers into the vase, arranging stem by stem with a curiously artistic flair for harmonies and contrasts.

"Would you like them nearer your bed, Mrs. Weisman?" she asked softly when she had finished.

"Thank you, Luella-May." The figure between the white sheets did not stir. "They're just fine where they are. They look so lovely in the sunlight."

"Don't they? I gave them plenty of water. They should last quite a while." A faint hitch slowed her last words, and, for a long instant, the brown eyes in the deep black face lost their usual luminous shimmer. Yes, the flowers would last ...

Faltering with rueful concern, Luella-May stepped to the bedside. "Maybe I straighten out your pillows a bit? Prop them up, so you may get a better view?"

The ghost of a wan smile met the suggestion. "You are so kind, Luella-May."

"Kind?" The repeated word lingered in the stillness of the room. "It's no kindness, doing what one likes to do."

As though recaptured by the impulsive phrase, the luminous shimmer had returned to the intense brown eyes as the slender girl bent to her task. It was true, she realized with a touch of astonishment, she did like to put out for this patient, do those small extra things for her that might enhance her comfort—did like it, even though the recipient of her little favors was white.

Luella-May was not too fond of white folks. Those back home in Meridian, Mississippi had not provided much cause nor incentive for affection. And when, shortly after her graduation from high school, she had come up north and started on this job, she found that discrimination just wore a different face: the variance was one of form, not attitude. The façades of routine courtesy and, occasionally, perfunctory camaraderie were too transparent to conceal the ingrained conviction of intrinsic superiority, no matter how the so-deliberately-careful displays of affability would endeavor to keep her from being hurt by any undue reminders of her natural, inherently underprivileged, status. But, however unreminded, she knew the score: Meridian, Mississippi, or New York, New York, white folks were the same all over; one could not, one did not trust them. One did get along with them, said hello in the morning and good-night in the evening, and in between performed one's day's work as best one knew, and that was as far as it went.

Except for this one here, this white woman Miriam Weisman, Luella-May admitted to herself, perplexed, aware of the painstaking tenderness that framed her effort as she was settling the patient's frail head against the propped-up pillows; except for this one here. But why? She had never paused to ponder the reason for her steadily deepening fondness, had accepted it as an improbable but undeniable fact, had somehow unquestioningly taken it for granted and acted upon it. Perhaps it was just an instinctive response to her day-by-day witness to patiently, humbly endured distress. Perhaps her unconscious appreciation that, for once, she had not been exposed to the insult of condescending compassion with her misfortune of having been born an inevitable underdog but treated with the inconspicuous regard accorded to an equal; perhaps simply an internal process of identifying her own friendless loneliness, her own unnoted and unremembered existence with that of this patient? Whatever the reason, it kept guiding the delicate gentleness of her helping hands.

It was the arrival of Dr. Klein that interrupted her self-searching reflections. After a brief pause of silent observation from the threshold, he advanced into the room.

"How are you feeling, Miriam?" His smile remained fixed as he carefully seated himself on the bed's edge and grasped a limp hand to take its pulse. The gesture was as automatic as his inquiry. Further examinations and her usual cheerfully reassuring replies had become equally pointless. The only concern left was to reduce suffering as far as pharmacology would allow. "Any pain?"

"None, doctor. None whatever. The stuff you prescribed for me yesterday …"

"Yes, it's rather potent. So you've been comfortable?"

"Just tired, Doctor. Very tired."

He nodded, staring past her. "Of course. That's to be expected, Miriam."

His voice was low and his eyes remained pinned to the empty wall in back of the sickbed. Even after a long life of medical practice that had seen its ample share of untimely and tragic demises, some leave-takings still struck him with a keenly wrenching, traumatic impact.

Miriam Weisman's particularly. He had known her, had treated her, for many years, all the way back, when her husband was still alive. All along, she had been one of his favorite patients, quietly admired for the strength of her character, the depth of her emotions, the courage of her convictions. Yet it had not been until the moment when, for a fleeting spell of weakness, she had leaned against his shoulder after she had demanded the truth from him, unadorned and unqualified, and, hurting with every word more desolately than he could remember, hurting ever since he had buried his own wife, he had told her the truth, unadorned and unqualified: it would be but a few months, perhaps only weeks.

She had not lingered on his shoulder, had taken a short step back, and faced him. "Thank you for telling me," she had said evenly.

His murmur had been aching. "You demanded it."

"The truth," she had replied. "The truth, and you gave it to me."

"Yes." Her composure let him regain his own. "I respect you too much to have done otherwise, Mrs. Weisman."

"Miriam," she had corrected him softly.

"Miriam," he had repeated, gratefully accepting the intimate bond that the shared

burden of truth had forged between them.

"I have to go now." Herbert Klein was rising. "Make my rounds. Quite a few more yet to look after. Though, when I'm through, I'll stop by again."

"As always."

"Of course. As always," he affirmed. "Wouldn't want to miss our daily little chat, would I? Ah, flowers!" he exclaimed momentarily stopping on his way out. Somehow only now he had consciously apprehended the vase on the table. "Quite a beautiful arrangement," he added slowly, trying to keep the inflection of surprise out of his comment.

"Luella-May arranged them." The voice from the bed was faint.

"Really!" His glance swept to the nurse's aide before returning to the floral display. "Truly a labor of love."

"I was just trying …" the girl muttered timidly.

"This tells more than just exquisite taste," Herbert Klein refuted her. And then, still struggling against that accent of astonishment, "And who is the admirer, Miriam? Or is it a secret?"

"To me it is, Doctor." Her labored smile mirrored the weariness of the puzzled reply. "I have no idea, who."

"No idea?"

"There was no note," Luella-May remarked.

"Well …" Herbert Klein paused at the door, faltering with a pang of regret that it had not occurred to him to bestow the cheer of such a gift on that lonely woman between the white sheets. "I'm sure you'll solve this riddle, Miriam, long before I get back to you."

"I wonder …"

"Anyway," he observed. "Who—it doesn't matter so much, does it? The real point is to be remembered. Until later then."

Luella-May's glance followed him as he stepped into the hallway. There, she thought, there went another white person she could learn to like. "I've got to get going myself now," she said. "I'll be seeing you again in a little while. Right now I've got to tidy up in four-twenty-four, before Mrs. Simonetti's folks come to visit. Every day they come …" She broke off abruptly, swallowing hard at the phrase. It took her a long moment to add, a bit breathlessly, "Of course, that's different. Her people, they're locals, just from across town. It's easy for them. Not everybody has folks living so close-by. Yours, they are … Wyoming, I think, you mentioned?"

"Yes, Wyoming." The confirmation was listless.

"Wyoming, that's far away, isn't it?"

"Yes," Miriam muttered, "very far away." Very far away, she repeated to herself, watching the girl moving toward the door and beyond it— much farther away than it showed on the map, much farther away than Luella-May could imagine, worlds away.

Even had her folks been locals from just across town, they would not be at her bedside. To them, she had been an outcast, alienated and shunned, as though a carrier of some leprous contagion, ever since the day she had scandalized one and all by renouncing her betrothal to Jerome, son of the Reverend Jonah Baker, the repentance-or-hell-thundering evangelist and head of the rabidly fundamentalist congregation that counted her father as one of its most uncompromisingly devout elders. To them she had died the day she had packed up to go east and spite her people's sacred commitment, by not merely associating with the unbelievers, heretics, and recalcitrant sinners who profaned the Lord in the den of iniquity that was New York, but by not marrying one of their kind. And to them she had been buried, finally and irretrievably, the day she had converted to her husband's Jewish faith. Thus she had not only brought down irredeemable shame and ridicule upon the family of Jason Tyler III but had forever forfeited every last chance of salvation and become prey to the devil and the fires of eternal perdition.

For fifteen years now she had been buried—and, unmarked and willfully untended in potter's field of bigotry, her grave had never been visited by any kin from the country town near Lander, Wyoming. No one from Jason Tyler III's household dared offend the Lord by remembering one damned by His just wrath. Most assuredly, none would mock Him by sending flowers, even if somehow they had learned of her present condition.

Except, of course, Uncle Joshua—but then he was not, never could have been, part of that household. Yes, Uncle Joshua would have come to see her, to cheer her with his concern and his warmth, his wealth of stories and anecdotes—and yes, with flowers, too. He had loved flowers and animals and people, anything that was alive. He had always maintained that God's real presence was not in a church but in all living things; in his creatures, not above them in some improbable heaven.

Her eyes rested on the flowers, sadly and gratefully. Yes, such might have been Uncle Joshua's kind of gift, but long years ago he had perished somewhere in Malaya.

It had been he who had guided her initial, if at first imperceptible, progress toward what the sectarians of her hometown would come to regard as her descent to hell. The oldest brother of her mother, he had been the black sheep of a blamelessly devout and impeccably respectable clan. As such, on his occasional visits he had been met with the minimum of grimly cordial hospitality that Jason Tyler III felt compelled to extend to a close relative, no matter how he loathed the renegade who had run away from home to work his way through college and become a world-traveling reporter for one of the wire services; who, spending most of his time among foreigners, quite frankly admitted his dedication to the exploration of their unChristian and therefore implicitly unsavory and often altogether savage ways rather than to the worship of the God of the Holy Scriptures.

Even as a youngster, she had intuitively perceived, that, except for her own presence, Uncle Joshua might never have paid his sparse visits to the house of Jason Tyler III and a sister who submissively did her husband's bidding. But lonesome after a failed, childless marriage, he had been too fond of his little niece, to eager to be buoyed by her fascinated response to his tales about the beauties and wonders, the diversity of human possibilities throughout the world outside—tales which had fostered her first inkling that there might be some viable and perhaps more attractive alternatives to her own folks' ways. Amid an environment of stony rectitude and restrictive sternness, she had increasingly basked in her uncle's undemonstrative but quietly eloquent affection, had never ceased to adore him, even after a final showdown with the Reverend Jonah Baker had foreclosed the unwelcome iconoclast's further visits to her parents' home. She would always remember that flash of controversy, which at the time had frightened and yet in some strange, obscure way exhilarated her: when at last Uncle Joshua had lost his patience with the pastor, who, partaking of the family's dinner, never stopped declaiming about the evil of humanism, the ungodly belief in evolution, and the Bible's sole and incontrovertible Truth regarding Divine Creation. "God may indeed have created this world," the mentor of her early years had remarked, "but the preachers surely haven't improved it any." After which he had abruptly left the company around the dinner table, only to mail to the reverend the photo of an orangutan and a pocket mirror, together with the penned advice. "Compare and repent!"

Never did she forget Uncle Joshua. Nor had his affection for her ever waned. How he had glowed with contentment, when, visiting her and Ben shortly after their wedding, he had sensed the happiness pervading their union. That had been their last encounter, before fever claimed him in some Asian jungle village. It was on that final occasion that he had, as though prompted by an unconscious premonition, presented her with a small album of snapshots from his journeys that, across the years, had remained her special treasure; presented it, accompanied by a bunch of flowers ... flowers much like those on the table in front of her now, yes, much like these, if perhaps somewhat less elaborate.

Still more precious than album and flowers, his truest gift to her had been his sparkling tales and vivid descriptions, his amusing anecdotes and whimsical observations, his humble appreciation of every new experience and his dreamy reach for ever new horizons—the magic of distant and wondrous worlds shared with her in the years of her youthful growth. Those were the gifts that had become the architects of her life, stirring her to an ever-deepening awareness of the mental prison that held her captive, prompting her ever-escalating yearnings for her own slice of the richer, more meaningful, more vital world outside—yearnings that were intrinsically incompatible with, and proved inevitably antipathetic to, the prospect of a married future with Jerome Baker. Yearnings which were inescapably bound to seek their fulfillment and eventually find it with someone who was part of that world and made her part of it; yearnings which at last, irresistibly and irrevocably, compelled her to disavow her engagement to the minister's son even well prior to her encounter with the one who would answer them; yearnings which would produce her first giant step toward damnation and that unmarked grave in the potter's field of bigotry, which knew no flowers ...

Only sixteen years old and raised on the uncompromising presumption of religious and parental authority, she had obediently agreed to the signal honor of affiance to the Reverend's own son. Three years hence she was going to be Jerome Baker's bride, when, after graduation from divinity school, he would join his father in presiding over the church and its congregation and shepherding the faithful toward God's waiting paradise. But three years was too long a span not to allow for Uncle Joshua's yarns to be recalled and compared to the dreariness of prayerful homilies; too long a span for lingering longings not to be revived in all their contrasts to the life her prospective groom was ready to offer: interminable evenings of shared contemplations on some verse of the Scriptures began to seem to her less and less the ultimate romance. Ever more persistently and vexingly, young Jerome's pompously bragging declamations of how he would extend his church's specific doctrines to rescue the reprobates from the devil's clutches and lead them to a glorious hereafter not only bored but repelled her. Eventually the zealotry and intellectual poverty of his one-track mind had become unendurable. No matter how many souls he might save from hell's fires, her own prospect was for a life in limbo.

"Less concern with God, who in His omnipotence does not need it, and more concern for man who in his frailty does, would make the world a happier and more livable place," Uncle Joshua had once observed. Remembering the phrase and quoting it had rung down the curtain on her engagement to Jerome Baker and raised it on her role as an outcast from the company of the righteous and blessed.

"How are you doing, dear?" Nurse Robby was sticking her face through the door, trying hard to dissemble the compassionate worry that clouded her routine inquiry. She did not wait for the meaningless euphemism of a reply, the ever-uncomplaining reassurance which they both knew as a lie. "Just came by to tell you. About these flowers. Called the florist, maybe they forgot to attach whatever note there was?" She sighed. "No go. They couldn't remember the customer, and they swore there had been no note at all. Strange, isn't it? But, after all, what's the difference, as long as you enjoy them? Whoever from, sooner or later it'll come to you."

"But there is no one," Miriam Weiss said softly. "No one."

Not since Ben, her Ben, had been taken from her, so young, so brilliant, so full of life …

It had been after some two years of emotional exile and social ostracism among her people in the wake of her break with Jerome Baker that she had met Ben on a trip to New York, the trip she had won as her prize in an essay contest conducted by a national organization of travel agencies. On a tour to the public library she had, overwhelmed with awed wonder at the apparently inexhaustible multitude of books, hung back and lost contact with her sightseeing group. A young man at one of the long desks observed her bewilderment when at last she emerged from the grip of her fascination—a young man whose quiet, unobtrusive smile encouraged her to accept his offer to show her around the premises, which, he told her, his work had made his second home; a young man whose soft-spoken, unassuming, respectful friendliness rendered her totally oblivious to his alien presence. He introduced himself as Ben Weisman, an instructor in history at the university, currently laboring on a book on myth and historical reality. A book which, he hoped, would earn him a professorship and the security of tenure.

As he was guiding her through the library's various sections, her response to his brief explanations and concise comments was immediate, fostered by a delight never experienced before: there was knowledge and imagination, skepticism and humor, qualities of the mind never encountered within her hometown environment; there was freedom of exploring thought and uncensored expression that answered a suppressed need within herself. All at once, a new universe was unfolding before her, the very universe of which Uncle Joshua had always spoken and which now seemed suddenly within her reach—and which, she somehow knew, this chance-blown stranger, who was so unlike the people back home, could make her grasp, claim as her own, live in …

She let the stranger, who, as though transfigured by some arcane miracle, seemed a stranger no longer, take her to dinner, and to lunch and dinner the following day—and every one of the remaining four days of her New York sojourn. Every hour, every minute of those dreamlike days was spent together, on walks around town, in the cloistered silence of museums, at a concert in Central Park, on a boat ride up the Hudson. And when he saw her off at the airport, they both knew that their parting would be but temporary. No plans had been mentioned, no promises made: internal certainty was in no need of words. Their kiss at the instant of final leave-taking, their first kiss ever, contained all the plans, all the promises. They would get together as soon as the work on his book was completed and their common future assured. Until then there would be their longing and their letters.

Letters there had been—twice a week, three times a week for four months: sweet, tender, passionate, intimate letters. For four months, and then, abruptly, Ben's letters stopped coming. Puzzled, distraught, frantic, she kept writing: Was he ill, had some disaster befallen him? Why, just why did he not let her know? If he needed help, or care, support of any kind, she would be on the next New York-bound flight to be with him.

But there was no reply. Through sleepless, haunted nights she kept searching her mind for whatever mistake, whatever offense she might have committed. But even her most extravagant imaginings failed to suggest a guilty cause, leaving her with the unendurable but increasingly irrefutable conclusion that the man of her dream had ceased sharing her dream; that, perhaps, some other woman …?

However fiercely she struggled against it, that specter kept besieging her with escalating vengeance. No use telling herself that betrayal did not fit the Ben Weisman she knew, yet, after all, how far did, could knowledge of a person reach after a mere five days' acquaintance?

Crushed by what at length seemed the only plausible explanation, she carried on, mechanically attending to the routines of life back home, working in her father's real estate office, while increasingly withdrawing into herself to rummage through the debris of her illusion. But on no account, not even for the sake of a love which she knew could never again find its equal, would she debase herself by attempting any contact with the object of that love, by intruding where she was not wanted, not needed. There would be no more one-sided correspondence that could not but display her as bare of pride and unabashed by humiliation, chasing after a man who had rejected her.

Thus weeks crept by, desperate, tormented weeks of futile quest for a reason, an answer, an intuition, which somehow might restore her self-confidence; endless, maddening weeks, until the day when, by a most unlikely fluke, she found out that Ben's letters had been intercepted, as had been her own, as well as several phone calls from New York some months ago. Raging with a hatred she had never suspected herself of being capable of, she had not even troubled to confront her father or her brother, who, aspiring to proving himself a worthy Jason Tyler IV, had been the instigator of the scheme. She had taken herself to the post office, where she was safe from any further interference, and placed her call. Two or three terse sentences, and then the man at the far end of the line had said simply. "Please, come!" The next morning she had been on the bus to Cheyenne and on the plane to New York.

"Time for your pill, Mrs. Weisman." Luella-May was bending over her, the words floated toward her as though from a far, foggy distance. "The pill ... The kind the doctor ordered for you yesterday." The slender hand was extending the paper cup to her half-open lips.

"Yes, the pill ..." A languid sip of water smoothed the intake of the tablet.

"Is there anything you'd like me to do for you?"

Only a slight sideward movement of a head on the pillow answered and the merest wraith of a smile, a smile directed not at the troubled figure of the nurse's aide, but at the sun-gilded flowers on the table and at an image, as yet untouched by the edges of a slowly expanding darkness ... the image of flowers waiting for her, a small vase full of them, on the dresser in the hotel room Ben had secured for her: violets and pansies around a single rose—reaffirmation to her with unequivocal certainty of what she had known that very instant in the airport, when she saw the glow in his eyes as he spied her emerging from the door: reaffirmation that she had come home, for home was wherever she would be with him; home was where one loved and was loved.

The accommodations Ben had selected were modest but comfortable enough even for occupancy proving more extended than originally anticipated. He had intended them to be her domicile for a matter of only a short few days before their civil wedding, which would obviate the complications attending an interfaith marriage. But she would not have it so, insisting on the delay incident to her receiving the rabbinical instruction preliminary to her conversion to Judaism. He had never demanded, never suggested nor even contemplated such a step, considering it a superfluous and altogether meaningless formality: whether a priest or a rabbi, a minister or a city clerk resided over the exchange of their vows, the truth and validity of their bond would be confirmed alone by the quality of their union. Yet, though agreeing in principle. she remained firm. She loved a Jewish man, she wanted to be part of his world; above all, she must bear him Jewish children. Moreover, she reminded him, a proper religious ceremony conducted by a rabbi would please his parents, indeed ensure her welcome into the family.

But, however reasonable, this expectation had proved a disastrous miscalculation. Unlike her husband, Morris, a quiet, warm-hearted, but indecisive man who all his life had labored to provide the best he could for his family, Malka Weisman would not be reconciled to her son's choice of a mate. Frigid and frustrated, intellectually unendowed and temperamentally volatile, she could find emotional security only in her unalterable captivity to, and total dependence on, the premise and presumptions, injunctions and disciplines of the hidebound parochialism in which she had been raised. Conversion or not, to her the gentile from Wyoming would not only forever remain an alien but a noxious and despised intruder, a slyly seductive usurper of her boy's natural and God-willed attachment to his mother. In spite of the willfully and conveniently ignored fact that this attachment had already long before been severely frayed as the prejudices and ritualism she had managed to impose on her all-too-pliable husband had utterly failed to take hold on her increasingly independent-minded son, her endlessly contentious complaints and censures had at length succeeded in driving him from the family's household. She had by tortuous subterfuges and self-deceptions managed to somehow discount the reality of this evolving breach; but now this bride-to-be was offering final, irrefutable evidence of her son's defiance and unforgivable defection. She would not tolerate this evidence; she would make its source the focus of her long-churning wrath.

From Malka Weisman there would be no flowers, ever.

When Ben proposed to introduce the abominated stranger from Wyoming, Malka would not receive her. Instead, behind his back she would call on the one who was worming her way into becoming her daughter-in-law. Unloading all the venom of her fury, she would tell Miriam to leave her boy alone and go back to where she belonged; here, with Ben, she would never belong; she, Malka, would not suffer her son to be weaned from his faith by one who, for all the sham charade of conversion, could never share that faith, never be part of its traditions; she, Malka, had not brought up her son to waste his prospects, which included a wife worthy of his present attainment and his even brighter future, someone of his own kind. She would not permit her Ben to be ruined by some scheming female who, by beguiling pretensions, was entrapping an innocent; a gold-digger, a concubine hardly better than a harlot … There were some more choice epithets, before, certain that her invective would be effective in putting an end to any wedding plans, Malka Weisman had slammed the door of the hotel room.

Malka's expectation, though, proved unjustified and the effect of her intervention rather counterproductive: as soon as Ben, sensitive to a nuance of depression that had resisted her effort at dissimulation, had pried from his Miriam the truth she had wished to hide from him, he reached for the phone. The conversation was entirely one-sided and brief, each of his sentences snapping with the honed finality of a guillotine: any further slightest insult to his wife-to-be, even as much as a deprecating gesture or offensive glance, and Malka Weisman was going to have seen the last of her son, forever.

There had been flowers in the vase on the dresser that evening, too: the usual rose circled by pansies and violets, mutely eloquent heralds of his love and commitment and now equally poignant symbols of the calamitous rift his mother had caused.

"But she is your mother," she had protested, distraught. "The woman who has given you life."

His refutation was calm decisiveness. "And you are the woman who is giving meaning to that life and who will be the mother of my children. Unless a man knows his priorities, he has no right to have a wife." She thought she had never loved him quite as ardently as just then.

Even so, she dreaded the guilt of precipitating an irreconcilable estrangement. "Look," she had reasoned with him, pointing to the announcement of their impending wedding, which, routinely sent, had been returned with the word 'wedding' crossed out and replaced, in brother Jason Tyler IV's angular hand, by the words 'final damnation,' "look, your mother's attitude is no worse than my own folks."

"True," he replied grimly, unrelenting. "She just proved that backwardness and zealotry are not exclusive to any one group. But offered by a Jew, this proof is just one more shade reprehensible. Having suffered through two thousand years of persecution, Jews should know better than to indulge the same bigotry." Then he had kissed her tenderly, holding her in a long, passionate embrace.

Two weeks later they were joined by the rabbi who had dispensed the religious instruction that would enable her one day to bear Jewish children for her Ben. Tense and intense, the ceremony was as brief as ritual form allowed. It was witnessed only by Herbert Klein, Ben's physician; Alec McLeod, his closest friend and member of his faculty; and Morris Weisman, who for once, the first time in a decade or more, had abandoned the quest for domestic peace and defied his spouse when she adamantly refused to attend the event and be part of what she would never recognize as a valid union.

True to his warning, Ben would never see, never speak to Malka Weisman again. Ever so often he would meet his father at the latter's place of employment to share a brief lunch hour with him. Occasionally Morris Weisman would, on the sly, drop by his son's place for a hasty cup of coffee and a timidly fond chat with his daughter-in-law.

Dear old Morris Weisman, yes he might have sent her that puzzling anonymous gift of flowers over there on the table … Yes, he might have been the one, if he had lived. He had called her from his hospital bed, when his heart told him that he would not have many more opportunities; he had asked her to come, as soon as he was assured that his spouse would be safely otherwise preoccupied. He had greeted her with a grateful smile. "Such a short life my Ben had," he said softly, "but what time was granted to him together with you, you made him very, very happy. I want to tell you, thank you, and …" he paused to laboriously raise himself from his pillow. "Well, I'm just an old Jew, and not a very devout one at that, either. But I would like to bless you." And as she gently bent her head close to his, he kissed her on her forehead and mumbled the ancient blessing of a father for his child. "Miriam," he then muttered, letting himself sink back, waving a faint hand at her, "good-bye, daughter Miriam. I just wished you to know that you have given my Ben the best one human being can give to another."

"Daughter," the old man had called her; and as a daughter she had mourned his passing, as a daughter grieved the loss of a father. Morris Weisman's parting words had been a most precious bequest; they had at last endowed her with the certainty, which, prey to her constant self-doubt, had been eluding her. Surely, she had tried to give her best to her Ben, give him all that was hers to give, yet she had always wondered whether that 'all' was enough, whether his fulfillment was truly equal to her own. She could only hope it was, and in moments of profound happiness, his response had made her believe it might be. But when he was gone, and with him the tender reassurance of his response, the doubt had returned with ever more nagging persistence—until that hour at the hospital bedside when Morris Weisman's blessing and final affirmation had allayed them; yet not quite allayed them, for even that singular, treasured bequest had fallen short of altogether stifling her sense of failure, her sense of having deprived her Ben of the ultimate, crowning token of their otherwise perfect bond of emotional and physical communion. She had not borne to him the offspring they both had so ardently desired and so dreamily projected as the living evidence of their love.

The memory of that failure had never been stilled, no matter how she might realize that the blame was not entirely deserved. In full agreement with each other they had decided that they were young enough to afford a few years of intimate mutuality unburdened by the responsibilities and restraints imposed by parenthood, a few years of joyful anticipation, during which period he would finish his book. Both of them had unreservedly concurred in this decision and had, living in their own enchanted world for each other, experienced three incomparably beautiful years which witnessed the completion of his book, its publication, its critical acclaim, and his impending advancement—three years, almost to the day, until that night, when Lieutenant Lombardi from the local precinct had rung their door bell. "Would Mrs. Weisman come along?"

A patrol car was waiting out front to speed her to the hospital. On his way home from his evening class, her husband had been stabbed by some muggers. Not even taking time to throw a coat over her flimsy dressing gown, she had rushed into the chill of the autumn night. But her desperate haste was rewarded only with the grant of a few brief, endless minutes of holding Ben's hand while his life was ebbing away in a coma from which he never awakened.

In the cemetery, Dr. Klein and Alec McLeod were at her side as well as Rabbi Kurland, who had married them. In a flash of desolate intuition, she perceived that Morris Weisman was wishing to join her, share his own bereavement with her—but felt compelled to stay by his hands-wringing, hysterically sobbing wife's side at the opposite end of the open ground. He stared ahead into some infinite void, deliberately avoiding looking at her. She understood. He was still incapable of coping with his burning shame over Malka's conduct at the funeral parlor, when she had demonstratively turned her back as her son's widow approached her to find reconciliation in their common grief.

Precluded by Jewish custom, there had been no flowers to accompany Ben's last journey. But ever since, twice every year, on his birthday and their wedding anniversary, she had placed a small bouquet on the grave: a single rose amid pansies and violets, the private cipher that had always spelled the message of their love ...

Momentarily, the contours of the blossoms in the vase on the table blurred, only to re-emerge with intensified clarity when the film of moisture that clouded her sight had dissipated. Those gladiolas and lilies and carnations and the three roses, so much more sumptuous, so much more luxuriant they were than Ben's subtly modest cipher of devotion, and yet, they, too, spelled a coded message of affectionate remembrance. But whose …?

Perhaps the answer no longer mattered now, she told herself. There would be no more opportunity to respond, to thank the anonymous donor of that floral gift. Yet somehow, incongruously, it still did matter to her, still seemed important to know. Straining to hold off the creeping, relentless advance of weariness, she was searching for a clue, groping for it through a gently but inexorably deepening dimness. Being thought of fondly always mattered; being remembered always mattered … being remembered?

But her ever more stressfully wandering mind was engaging only in another review of implausibilities: neither her distant past nor her more recent one would yield an image, a name, an identity.

In her days with Ben, their intimate world of mutual exploration and discovery, of shared experiences and shared dreams, had been too self-sufficient to readily lend itself to frequent intrusions by even the few selected outsiders it would on occasion admit. Ben's inclination had never been toward an active social life; his temperament and his interests alike had not favored the pursuit of what he dismissed as unessential contacts; her own circumstances as a stranger to her new environment and an exile from her old one had perforce precluded her own contribution to the spare circle of acquaintances, mostly fellow academicians, among whom he had been moving rather peripherally. To be sure, Ben had lost no time making her part of that circle, and she had been unreservedly and cordially accepted into it. Still, her link to its members had remained too casual to persevere for any extended period after his demise, too shallow to permit any reasonable expectation of remembrance after a decade's slow passage, much less to evoke the tender gesture of a floral tribute—even if anyone had been aware of her condition and confinement in this hospital.

In the initial phase of her widowhood, perhaps, it might have been different. Then there had been Helen Bernstein, an associate professor of contemporary American literature, who had established a more personal relationship with her. Yes, Helen might well have been one capable of such warmhearted attention, but soon her own marriage had transplanted her to one of the more distant suburbs, and her own emotional involvement had kept her from following up on what had never amounted to more than a loose affinity. There had been Ed Finley, a social-sciences scholar, who once or twice invited her to dinner with his family, but it was not long before that connection had gently faded. There had been Arne Evenson, a professor of psychology whose own psychological insight was neither acute enough to keep him from considering her sudden, traumatic loneliness as a vantage for his own essay in courtship nor subtle enough to comprehendingly accept her determined rebuff; and who, after withdrawing in a display of acrimonious pique would have hardly been one to gladden her with a token of care. There, too had been loyal Alec McLeod, whose genuine human concern and always respectful friendship had offered her the only support she found throughout those first three years of lonely grief—always available to her, yet always keeping his distance. Every so often, he would take her out for a dinner or some off-Broadway show until his appointment at the University of Oregon reduced their association to an intermittent and gradually diminishing correspondence; then, after his own attempt at matrimonial happiness, to no more than an exchange of Christmas greetings.

Still, even so, Alec McLeod would have been the kind of person to order flowers for her all the way across the country, if he had been aware. But of course he was not, could not be: she had never let him know of her progressively failing health and the dooming prognosis. But yes, otherwise those lovely flowers might indeed be his way of telling her that there was someone to fondly remember her.

Someone, but if not he, who else?

Hardly any of her fellow employees at the bookstore. There were only few of them, and, all the while she had been tending that sales job, none of them had evinced such qualities of character or mind as might have made their company sufficiently appealing to her. They belonged to a world essentially alien to the one to which Ben had introduced her, in which she had lived with him and in which she continued to live with his memory. To none of them had she confided the cause of her request for a leave of absence. Even Frances Wills, the one with whom she had from time to time shared an irrelevant lunch hour, had absorbed her shrugged response of 'private reasons.' Moreover, Frances was permanently short of funds and rather stingy to boot; even had she somehow learned of her coworker's plight, she might possibly have invested her dollar's worth of bus fare in a dutiful visit, but never would she have contemplated the outlay for so lavish a bouquet—gladiolas and lilies and carnations, and even three long-stemmed roses.

Three long-stemmed red roses!

How in heaven could she not have known at once, the very instant Robby had stripped the wrapping off this gift? How could she have been in doubt of their sender's identity, when that floral trinity spelled out the name clearly, as definitely as any lettered signature? That, of course, was why there was no attached note: No need for explaining the self-evident. Were not these roses Adrian's own signature, his personal cipher, hearkening back to that evening of five years ago, the evening of her birthday—hearkening back, to bespeak his persevering remembrance, and, most likely, his impending visit?

Yes, surely, this would be Adrian's way of announcing himself. Shy, considerate, subtle as always, he would not want to startle her with his sudden appearance at her bedside, uninvited, and so totally unexpected after more than a year's silent interval. Now truly this was his way, having these flowers precede his call, prepare her for it …

Adrian, of course! Dear Adrian, who would not forget.

She had met him on her summer vacation six years ago. As an art historian specializing in Renaissance culture, Adrian Kern had been in charge of guiding the tour group to Europe she had joined. From the very moment of their formal introduction at the airport, their rapport was instantaneous and mutual, even that first night, in flight across the Atlantic. They engaged in animated conversation over cups of coffee after every evening's dinner throughout the two weeks of that trip. And their exchanges would grow more spirited, more rewarding—yet remain restrained and free from any suggestion of intimacy.

As much as she enjoyed this unexpected sociability, at times it would stir pangs of uneasiness. She had undertaken this tour in memory of Ben, selecting it because it would allow her to visit some of the sites he had traveled, some of the sights he had so often glowingly told her about, yet which destiny had barred him from showing to her, as he had so fervently planned; sites and sights which, as she urgently felt, he would have wished her to experience with him, yet which now she was experiencing in another man's company. But while this realization disturbed her with a sense of incongruity, of inappropriateness, even of guilt, hers was also an awareness of an internal cogency that prompted the continuation of this association. There were elements in their acquaintance that were bound to cement and escalate that initial, purely instinctive affinity. On Adrian Kern's part it was the happenstance that he had attended a series of Ben Weisman's lectures and come to admire the scholarship, insight, and intellectual integrity of their presentation. His ensuing idealization of the man had transferred itself to the widow, the more inescapably so since her views reflected so much of her husband's. On her part, it was the impetus of an irresistible fascination as she discovered her new companion's maturity of mind and character, qualities, so many of which constantly remained her of Ben. Again and again, Adrian Kern's breeding within a staunchly German-Protestant environment struck her as an oddly capricious paradox. His was an ideational and ideological kinship with Ben that transcended the diversity of their backgrounds as well as the gap of almost ten years between herself and her young friend.

Thus, inevitably, the evenings shared in the hotel lobbies, bistros, and cafés of Spain and France and Italy would, upon their return, find their counterparts in New York: meetings at a quiet coffee shop in her neighborhood after his weekly lectures, to which he invited her and which she would never miss; dinners together in some inexpensive restaurant; and, complementing that summer's surveys of the Louvre and the Prado and the galleries of Rome and Florence, visits to the local museums would buttress their pursuit of a relationship, which for all its affinity and deepening fondness remained reserved and remote. Though both of them were conscious of a profound mutuality, they were equally aware that their constellation would not endure any venture into a precariously testing reality; that if their precious affinity was to be preserved, the intangible barrier constructed by their insights must not be breached.

For months it had held fast, for nearly half a year—until the night of her birthday. That night there had been three roses waiting for her on the table of the French restaurant, which Adrian had selected for their celebration, three long-stemmed red roses and the gift of a high-priced art book she had long coveted but hesitated to acquire, and a bottle of champagne. There had been felicitations and banter, and happy little jokes; and, hazily expanding, yet ever more palpable, an air of sensuous closeness. And there, quickening and demanding, had been the impulse of four years' celibate loneliness and pent-up yearning. That night she had not, as all the times past, parted with him in the lobby of her dwelling. For one long instant he had paused at her suggestion that he come upstairs, had hesitated before accepting.

Then there had been the eloquence of silent tenderness and the passionate response; the orgiastic unrestraint of consummation and then an interminable stillness of lying side by side, each mourning the demise of unreality and grieving at the birth of a reality which they shared but could not share. It was only when the dawn shimmered through the blinds that her nagging sense of guilt at last shaped itself into whispering words. "I disappointed you."

His response took its time coming to her. "It was not my name you called out … then," he said softly.

"Oh!" she murmured forlornly. She had hoped that her brief gasp had passed unheard, that the truth had remained hidden from him. Trembling, her hand sought his, touched it. "I'm sorry, Adrian, so sorry!"

He did not stir. His reply was even, almost aloof. "No, Miriam. There's no cause for regret. You were just true to yourself, to your commitment. I should have known better than aspire to what did not belong to me, and never would." And then, after what seemed an eternity of shrouded stillness, he added, his voice churning with emotion, "But when one cares so much!" She winced, knowing it was a lover's funeral dirge. Lingering on, its bleakly impassioned echo was drowning all efforts at further communication.

Some time later, when the morning sun was already touching the blinds, they had terminated their side-by-side solitude, had left the bed, had showered, dressed, and gone to the coffee shop—a desolately sad intuition had warned her that he might prefer not to have her prepare breakfast for him. Then a sparse remark wearily passed across their table advising her that he was going to accept the position the University of Pittsburgh had offered him. There was no need for explaining that, but for the night just past, his decision would have been different. She just nodded, and silence had taken over once more.

Only when they stepped into the street he spoke again, tersely. "You understand, don't you?"

"Yes," she had said. "Yes, I do." And then, even more softly, "You deserved better."

For the fraction of an instant, a smile painted his face with a glow of gratitude. "But not everyone can be as lucky as Ben Weisman," he said, staring past her into some distant, forbidden void. And then, quickly, he drew her hand to his lips and pressed his kiss to it, briefly, before turning abruptly, incapable of enduring the quavering pain of her good-bye and the sight of the wetness in her eyes.

Three days later he had phoned her. Knowing him for the man he was, she had expected to hear from him, though perhaps not quite so soon. She reciprocated the warmth of his inquiry, assuring him that she was doing well enough; his response conveyed a similarly encouraging white lie. For all its tender undertone, their quiet exchange carefully skirted any reference to their recent experience. They both fully comprehended that any such reminder would only needlessly aggravate their shared distress, keep alive the trauma of an involvement, which had forfeited its viability. Irrefutable, this realization framed their mutual agreement, when he informed her of his impending move to Pittsburgh, that they would desist from any further communication. Words would prove too precarious; letters would be haunted by the ghost of their debacle; no matter how scrupulously impersonal their phrasing, their very composition would be bound to stir repressed yearnings into aching consciousness.

Yet, the day after his departure had brought three long-stemmed red roses, and his note: "Thank you for giving me everything that was yours to give me. I shall never forget." And neither would he: on each of the four occasions since, when an engagement as guest lecturer took him to New York, he had, recalling her pleasure at his discourses, phoned to advise her of his arrangement for her attendance. Certain of unfailing acceptance, his glance would search the audience for her; their eyes would meet, and their fond smiles; but there would be no shared dinners to follow, like once. Still, on each subsequent day that trinity of roses had greeted her, his message of nonforgetting. The last time, fourteen, fifteen months ago; and now again ...

Adrian, dear Adrian. He must be in town and coming to see her. But how had he learned of her whereabouts? She had told no one where she would be spending what she knew would be her last sojourn, except, naturally, Dr. Klein. Yes, that must be the explanation: probably she had casually mentioned her physician's name to Adrian, way back, when; he would remember, always would, whatever concerned her. He must have, worrying, turned to this one available source of information, when, attempting to invite her to yet another of his lectures, his phone calls had remained unanswered. But then, why had the doctor not let on, that she might expect a visitor?

Never mind, though, it did not matter; only those flowers mattered, their message, their promise that Adrian was coming to see her. Soon, she hoped, soon, so she could tell him that she, too, had not forgotten; tell him what lately so often had crossed her mind: that perhaps, if only she had been able to wait longer for that barrier to decay and crumble away, there might have happiness for them ... there was so much of Ben in him.

But he must come soon so she still could tell him. Oh, how good it would be to see him once more, to see Adrian, whose roses told her that she would always be remembered, always …

She smiled at the flowers as she closed her eyes. She must rest a while; she must not be too tired when he arrived.

She did not hear Luella-May enter or the girl's quiet steps as she approached the bed; did not perceive the nurse's aide's petrified gaze or her dark, slender fingers pressing the button on the night table three times; did not see Nurse Robby rush through the door or her tight-lipped nod and immediate reach for the emergency switch when she had joined Luella-May's rigid figure by the bedside; did not apprehend Dr. Klein's hurried arrival or feel his examining touch or the slight tremor of his hand as it slowly drew the sheet over her still face. Nor was she aware of a long spell of silence of which she was so centrally a part, or of the physician's low, strangely hoarse voice, at last saying, "You'll notify them downstairs, will you, Robby?"

Mutely nodding, the nurse watched him walk into the hallway before getting on her way to trail him. Barely suppressed, a sigh softened the usual briskness of her speech, as, already on the threshold, she turned to the nurse's aide. "There's nothing more for us here. You might as well come along. The fellows from the morgue room will be around in a few minutes."

But Luella-May did not follow her outside. After some moments' lingering halfway to the door, she walked back to the bed on tiptoes, as though afraid of disturbing the peace of its still burden. Inch by gentle inch she folded back the sheet until it exposed the contours of an ashen neck and haggard shoulders. With motions as inanimate as a marionette's on a puppeteer's string, she pulled a chair close and sat, hands limply folded in her lap, staring at the pallid countenance, whose eyes, even through the lids that covered their sightlessness, seemed to reach for the flowers in that vase on the table, and whose rigid lips were perpetuating the brittle wraith of a happy smile; she sat, staring down at the white woman she had learned to like.

Luella-May felt the salty sting of tears that would not be denied. She could not help crying for her, who for all those moribund weeks had been lying there, alone and unremembered, until it had been almost too late; could not help crying for dead Miriam Weisman, and crying for her own living self; wondering who would be sending her flowers when it was her turn; hoping it would not have to be some nurse's aide on a hospital ward.